ALSO BY GABE HUDSON

Dear Mr. President: Stories

GORK, THE TEENAGE DRAGON

GORK,
THE TEENAGE DRAGON

Gabe Hudson

ALFRED A. KNOPF

NEW YORK

2017

THIS IS A BORZOI BOOK PUBLISHED BY ALFRED A. KNOPF

Copyright © 2017 by Gabe Hudson

All rights reserved. Published in the United States by Alfred A. Knopf, a division of Penguin Random House LLC, New York, and distributed in Canada by Random House of Canada, a division of Penguin Random House Canada Limited, Toronto.

www.aaknopf.com

Knopf, Borzoi Books, and the colophon are registered trademarks of Penguin Random House LLC.

Chapter 71's title, "Back Into the Chamber Returning, All My Soul Within Me Burning," is inspired by Edgar Allan Poe's "The Raven."

Library of Congress Cataloging-in-Publication Data

Names: Hudson, Gabe, author.
Title: Gork, the teenage dragon / by Gabe Hudson.
Description: First Edition. | New York : Alfred A. Knopf, 2017.
Identifiers: LCCN 2017004831 (print) | LCCN 2017021892 (ebook) | ISBN 9781524732479 (ebook) | ISBN 9780375413964 (hardcover)
Subjects: | BISAC: FICTION / Literary. | FICTION / Science Fiction / Adventure. | GSAFD: Fantasy. | Love stories.
Classification: LCC PS3608.U345 (ebook) | LCC PS3608.U345 G67 2017 (print) | DDC 813/.6—dc23
LC record available at https://lccn.loc.gov/2017004831

Jacket illustration by Matt Buck
Jacket design by Peter Mendelsund

Manufactured in the United States of America
First Edition

To Deborah Treisman, Edward Kastenmeier, and Susan Golomb:

With love & gratitude.

The dragon began to belch out flames
and burn bright homesteads; there was a hot glow
that scared everyone, for the vile sky-winger
would leave nothing alive in his wake.

—*BEOWULF* (TRANSLATED BY SEAMUS HEANEY)

CONTENTS

GORK, THE TEENAGE DRAGON

HERE BEGINS THE STORY
OF HOW I FOUND MY TRUE LOVE

My name is Gork The Terrible, and I'm a dragon.

And here begins the story of how I went searching for my true love and then made her my Queen. And I should warn you that when it comes to dragon love stories, well mine is the most terrifying tale of them all. But also the most romantic. For inside my scaly green chest, there beats a grotesquely large and sensitive heart.

Now some folks get a little confused when they first hear me say that.

And I'm not talking about when I roar it at them and I've got my tail raised in a Threat Display and I'm shooting big scary firestreams out of my nostrils. No sir. I'm talking about when I say it real calm and normal, like I'm doing right now. So just to make sure you don't get mixed up here at the beginning of my story, let me try and make this as simple as possible for you.

My first name is Gork.

My middle name is The.

And my last name is Terrible.

And like I said, I'm a dragon.

Plus I'm a poet.

Now if you happen to be a man-creature here on planet Earth, then you should know I have read your books and stories about my species. And not only are your reports about us dragons wildly inaccurate, they are downright insensitive and repugnant. You man-creatures sure do seem to get a big bang out of spreading ignorant lies about my species. About how vile we are. About how disgusting we are. About how uncivilized we are.

I mean take old *Beowulf*, for instance. That book isn't nothing but a pack of slanderous lies about my kind, written by a bum poet who didn't have the gumption to sign his own name to the book. It's like even the man-creature who wrote *Beowulf* knew it was a bunch of flapdoodle and so he was too ashamed to stick his own damn name on the cover. And now you man-creatures go around passing that book off down the centuries as a bona fide *classic*.

Well if that don't beat all. Seems to me from where I'm sitting, all's you have to do is stick a bunch of mean-spirited lies about dragons between two covers and voilà—you've got yourself an instant classic.

But you know what? *Beowulf* isn't even the half of it. No sir.

Because the most offensive book out there about us dragons is the lunatic rantings of a man-creature that goes by the name of Mr. J. R. R. Tolkien.

Now this nutjob Tolkien's book *The Hobbit* is so full of balderdash and nonsense about my glorious species that it makes my toe claws shudder just to think about it. That bastard Tolkien paints us dragons out to be a bunch of ignorant and repulsive savages. Well as far as I'm concerned, this Mr. Tolkien was a real low-hearted sonuvabitch.

Look at how Tolkien portrayed that dragon Smaug in that book *The Hobbit*.

Ever seen a red dragon? I haven't, and Smaug appears to be the most slovenly and debased creature in the entire universe. Shoot, like us dragons' personal grooming habits are so skeezoid that we wouldn't notice when a scale on our left breast had fallen out, exposing the soft pink skin underneath. And like we'd just stupidly go about our business and leave that soft pink spot on our left breast exposed to the elements. So some little fool named Bard who lives by a lake can come traipsing along and slay us with one well-placed arrow.

Please.

No lake-dweller is going to get the drop on my scaly green ass. With *an arrow*, no less. Especially not some jerk who goes by the name of Bard.

Shoot, I've got so many nanobots in my bloodstream that if I ever did somehow manage to lose a scale, it would regenerate itself before you could even pull the arrow from your quiver. Or pull the trigger on your laser pistol. Or whatever your weapon of choice may be.

So if you've come here hoping for yet another tale wherein we dragons are portrayed as nothing more than a bunch of vile *wyrms*, well then you can do us both a big favor and buzz off. Because I can assure you this sort of old-fashioned speciesism and bigotry has no place here. That whole crusty line of thinking is deeply offensive and strictly for the birds.

Because dragons are nothing if not sacred creatures.

This much I can promise you.

Now I'm only sixteen. And I'm an orphan, on account of my parents died right before I hatched.

But my grandpa is six hundred and eighty-four years old. And my grandpa's name is Dr. Terrible.

And this right here is the real deal, a true love story told by a real dragon. A dragon who may not be the smartest of his kind, but who is a damn sight more sophisticated and evolved than what Mr. J. R. R. Tolkien would have you believe.

And like all tales told by real dragons about their true love and the quest to find their Queen, this story starts with the first time I blasted fire.

Shoot, every dragon knows the rule of how your proper true love tale's got to start with first fire.

Now maybe you're kind of surprised to learn that we dragons have some storytelling traditions of our own. Well get used to it.

Because my name is Gork The Terrible, and I'm a dragon.

And this is my story.

Part I

THE
CLEAR
DOOR

THE FIRST TIME I BLAST FIRE
IT HAPPENS ON PLANET EARTH,
WHEN I AM JUST A LITTLE BABY DRAGON

The first time you ever spit fire is a seminal event in every dragon's life.

The first time I spat fire, it happened on planet Earth. Yes sir.

Even though my family hails from Planet Blegwethia, I actually hatched on Earth. And my grandpa Dr. Terrible always blames my early feral years growing up alone on Earth for my pathetic WILL TO POWER.

Anyway, I still remember what it felt like to be scrunched up inside the egg right before I hatched. And I also remember what it felt like as I used my tiny black beak to try and peck my way out of the egg, and how each time I poked a hole through the shell a blinding sunbeam poured down in there and made my little eyes blink like crazy.

And I remember how as I pecked away at the shell, I was thinking:
This feels very important!
And I was thinking:
Ready or not, here I come!
And if you want to know the truth, I nearly killed myself trying to break free.

There's even an old Blegwethian riddle that goes like this:

QUESTION: What's the hardest part of a dragon's life?
ANSWER: Hatching.

So I just kept pecking with my beak and I could hear the shell cracking and my little lungs were heaving because of how hard I was working, and I felt dizzy. But I kept pecking anyway and then there was a superloud *crack!* And somehow I managed to break free of the white shell which had been holding me prisoner.

And I thought:

Way to go!

And I thought:

I can't believe I made it!

And then I thought:

Look at this beautiful forest!

So, suddenly there I was on Earth, though of course at the time I didn't know this. And I was standing on my own two hind legs for the very first time, and I found myself alone in this forest with all those little pieces of eggshell scattered around my webbed feet.

Now I remember how as I stood there that morning, well suddenly this glorious feeling shot straight up my spine and it caused my wings to shiver. How can I describe the feeling to you? Well it felt like the entire forest was jumping up and down and cheering with excitement at the sight of my little scaly green ass. I could even hear the wind moving in the trees, and the trees were singing:

"Welcome, Gork! Welcome!
We've been waiting here for you all along!
Now that you're finally here,
we can sing this joyous song!
You will be a famous dragon,
the stuff of legend and lore!
You'll bravely lead us to victory,
of this you can be sure!
After many a pitched battle,
you will win the Great War!
Now that you've arrived we have nothing to fear,
we could not be more excited that you're finally here!
Welcome, little baby Gork!"

Now upon hearing those trees singing to me like that, well my chest swelled near to the point of bursting.

And I thought:

These sure are some friendly trees!

And then I thought:

What the heck do these trees mean when they say they've been waiting for me all along, anyway? And what's this "Great War" they're jabbering on about?

And then I thought:

Well they must mean I have some very important mission to accomplish with my life and that one day I will be a great hero!

Now I felt grateful to these trees for giving me this piece of secret knowledge about my life, and I wanted to give them some sort of assurance that I was up to the task. So right then and there I tilted my tiny green head back and opened my black beak and then I cut loose with a mighty roar. And this roar came welling up from the center of my being and then exploded out my beak and trumpeted throughout the forest.

Squawk! Because if you want to know the truth, it really did sound more like a squawk.

Not long after that, I spat fire out my beak for the very first time. Now I was only four months old when I first got my fire powers and I was still just a little baby dragon and it wasn't even on purpose.

You see, what happened was this: I'd been flying around the forest one afternoon and I flew up and spied a hornets' nest attached to a tree limb. This nest was as big as a boulder and it sounded like there were thousands of giant hornets buzzing around inside the nest and I was just flapping my wings and hovering there in midair, studying it. And I remember as I stared at that gigantic hornets' nest my little belly rumbled and I thought: *Me so hungry!*

So I punched the hornets' nest out of the tree and it fell to the forest floor some fifty feet below. And then I flapped my wings and flew down to the forest floor and the hornets' nest was setting there on the grass, and a blizzard of angry giant hornets were zooming around looking for whoever just knocked their nest out of the tree. Well as

I stood there right in the middle of that blizzard of angry hornets I casually picked the nest up off the ground and opened my beak and took a huge bite out of it.

Chomp!

Then I chewed thoughtfully on the piece of nest while the swarm of hornets stung me all over my scaly green body. But I just ignored the hornets and focused on how delicious the nest tasted. And then I swallowed.

"Gulp. Mmmm."

Now at that point the enraged hornets decided that a unified attack was their best bet, and they gathered into a dark buzzing cloud overhead and then dropped down in formation until they completely engulfed me like a sheet being lowered over a birdcage.

So I shot my tongue out a good five feet up into the air and snatched a hornet and then retracted my tongue back into my beak, and I chewed it up and swallowed.

"Gulp. Mmmm."

Then the cloud of angry hornets closed ranks and started stinging me relentlessly. Since my scales are designed to withstand sword blades and laser beams and whatnot, I couldn't even feel the hornets' stingers. And once one of those little bastards stung me they were stuck there, because they couldn't yank their stingers out of my thick scales.

So I shot my tongue out again. I did this over and over and over, snatching dozens of hornets out of the air with my tongue.

Now I remember at one point there were hundreds of pissed-off hornets stuck all over me and I'm sure I looked like a big green pincushion flailing around in the woods that afternoon. Plus, because all those little fiends stuck in me were buzzing with rage, my body was vibrating like a tuning fork.

So in between taking bites of the delicious hornets' nest I'd reach up and use my claws to pluck a hornet off my scaly snout and pop it in my beak and chew it up.

"Gulp."

Then I'd pluck a hornet off my belly and pop it in my beak and chew it up.

Gulp.

I did this over and over, eating scores of hornets in this way. And if you haven't figured it out already, when it comes to dragons, hornets are one of our favorite snacks. And let me tell you those deranged hornets I ate that day in the forest were delicious.

So by the time I finished that afternoon I had scarfed down the entire nest plus 671 hornets. Then I lay back on the forest floor because my little green belly was so full I could barely move, and without really thinking about it, I just opened my beak and belched.

Boom!

And along with the belch, a huge firestream suddenly exploded out my beak. And when the firestream exploded in front of me like that, well I thought for sure some deranged monster was attacking me and I nearly leapt out of my scales.

Then I turned and ran away as fast as I could. And I must have sprinted a good fifty feet or so before it finally dawned on me that I wasn't being attacked and the fire had come from my own fool beak.

So then what did I do?

Well I spent the whole rest of that day belching.

I must have belched for ten hours straight.

Because in the beginning that was the only way I could make fire shoot out of my beak. And take it from me, when you're just a little baby dragon and you first get your fire powers, well you never really get tired of making those flames shoot out of your beak.

Now those first couple months on planet Earth really just kind of flew by.

Yes sir, I roamed the forest. I lived like a savage beast and had the mind of a savage beast, with no real strategy or game plan for my days and no real understanding of what or who I was. The concept of time was meaningless to me. I had no sense of the past or the future, just the eternal primal now.

My life was claw and fang and wing, nothing more.

But I was also growing bigger and no longer enjoyed sleeping in the tops of trees with one eye open, like a stupid bird.

So I moved into my very first lair. Now what I did was I took up residence in this abandoned spaceship I discovered in the forest one afternoon. Though of course I didn't know it was a spaceship, I just figured it was some sort of shiny chamber. And the main reason I chose this chamber for my lair was because it had a clear door that I could shut with my talons.

And this door changed my life.

Because now I could drag a freshly killed deer back to the chamber and eat it in peace with no concern of some scavenger darting in and trying to steal my meal. I could finally sleep in peace too, behind the safety of that door.

I slept hanging upside down inside the chamber with my wings folded across my back. But I'd wake in the middle of the night and see the piercing yellow eyes of this big gray wolf watching me through the clear door. Once as a warning shot I belched a firestream at the door and the wolf leapt away. Later when I woke again that big wolf bastard was back, watching me through the clear door.

What else can I tell you about my very first lair?

Well the outside of my lair had the letters ATHENOS stamped on it. But since I couldn't read or write back then, these letters held about as much meaning for me as the bark on a tree.

And inside my lair, there were these two dragon skeletons. Of course I didn't know that they were dragons but I could tell by the shape of their skeletons that they were the same as me, just bigger.

They were sitting up in their seats. I'd found them that way. And each skeleton had a gold crown set atop its skull. Now propped up in front of those two skeletons was a small screen that flashed the words:

DESTINATION: **PLANET EARTH**

But again, I couldn't read. So as far as what those flashing words on the screen were saying, I didn't know. And as for those skeletons,

I quickly forgot they were even there. Because soon the floor was littered with bones and fur and feathers from all the forest animals and whatnot I ate in my lair.

Then the days began to blur. Days, days, and more days.

A succession of arrivals and exits through my lair's door. Survival was the thing. My life was claw and fang and wing, nothing more.

That is, until The Night When Everything Changed.

3

THE FIRST TIME I MEET DR. TERRIBLE, IT HAPPENS ON PLANET EARTH

We were deep into winter and the forest was beset with famine.

I spent my nights staggering around, desperate with hunger. The snow was thick on the forest floor. The effort of flapping my wings made me dizzy and when I tried to fly I instantly fell to the ground.

Then came The Night When Everything Changed.

That night, I happened upon a big buck deer hiding in some undergrowth. I remember there was a full moon in the sky, and I had walked near some brush when all of a sudden this big buck deer exploded out of there. And I looked up in surprise to see its brown hindquarters bounding off through the snow under the moonlight. Anyway, I bolted after it and even in my weakened state, I just managed to chase it down.

Well, I still remember how I was poised there over my fresh kill in the snow, and I was eating ravenously from it. Because for the last couple weeks the hunger pains had been gnawing at my insides. And that's why I didn't do what I would have normally done in that situation, which would be to take my fresh kill back to the shiny chamber and eat it in peace. Behind the safety of that clear door.

So I tore into my feast with my beak right there in the little snowy clearing, and I was chowing down under the moonlight like the starving beast that I was. And I figure that's the only reason I didn't notice the big gray wolf until it was too late.

Because normally my horns would've started tingling to warn me of an imminent threat. But unfortunately my horns were starving too. My little scaly green ass had been delirious with hunger for so long and now I was eating with my whole body. Plus I was only three years old at the time and nowhere near a fully grown dragon and still technically in my infancy.

But the instant I looked up and saw that big gray wolf standing there in the moonlit snow and growling and baring its fangs, well I knew I'd made a mistake. I should've known the scent of fresh blood would go out on the night wind like an alarm bell.

Then the wolf suddenly glided in closer and studied me with his piercing yellow eyes. He snarled and crouched low on coiled haunches. You could tell the wolf was going to pounce any second. My black heart was hammering away in my chest and my fool horns were tingling like crazy.

Thankfully, by that point the fresh meat in my belly had not only cleared my head, it also gave me a massive boost of strength. So I just looked that fool wolf in the eye and ripped a thunderous belch and a firestream flashed out my beak and blasted that thieving wolf in its furry haunches. Or it would've anyway, if that wolf hadn't anticipated what I was going to do and leapt and danced away right before my flame zapped the spot on the ground where he'd just been.

Then I heard a terrible sound coming from behind me, and this sound made the scales on the back of my long green neck stand straight up. For as long as I live, I will never forget that terrible sound. Or the fear I felt when I heard it.

Because this sound was the deranged bloodthirsty howls of an entire wolf pack rushing in to attack me from behind. I realized only then that the first wolf had merely been acting as a decoy, something to distract me.

I was suddenly knocked off my webbed feet from behind. And in a flash I was pinned down there in the snow under what felt like a mountain of fur, and those wolves' hot breath was all over me. Their jaws were snapping and I could feel their fangs sinking deep into my soft belly, over and over and over. These beasts were mad with hunger. Now one of those fiendish wolves snarled and plunged its fangs into the flesh of my right wing, and this same wolf wrenched its jaws and savagely ripped my wing in half and I felt the hot cutting pain explode all over my body.

I howled. In agony, but also in terror. Because in that instant I knew with my ripped wing I couldn't fly out of there, and now my only hope of escape would come down to a footrace in the snow.

So I fought like a bastard, buried under that pile of thirty or so giant wolves. I tapped into my rage. I clawed and bit and blasted fire. I managed to get in a couple of good licks, too. I tore fur and flesh with my fangs. I felt my claws slice to the bone. And I savored the sweet taste of wolf blood in my beak. Yes sir.

But by and large I was getting the worst of it. And I knew if I didn't do something quick then I'd be dead. I was bleeding from all those puncture wounds in my belly, and my right wing was hanging off my wingjoint in tatters. And I was still suffocating under all that fur as they tore me to shreds and it dawned on me then that these bastards wouldn't stop until they'd gnawed every last bit of flesh off my bones.

So after blasting countless firebolts to the point where my throat was raw and shredded, I finally managed to twist out from under and leap away from the pack and start running through the snow on my hind legs. I lit out of there in a flash.

The pack of wolves instantly set off after me. As I ran I could feel their hot raging breath closing in and could hear the terrifying *clack* sound of their jaws snapping shut right on my heels. They were howling and snarling and lunging at me and yet still I kept running with no thought in my head but that of sheer terror.

My little webbed feet were flying.

This was all new to me. I was bleeding out of the dozens of puncture holes in my belly and could hear my tattered wing flapping behind me as I ran. I left a bright red blood trail right there in the snow under the moonlight, and my lungs were heaving so hard it felt like they were going to pop.

And then there it was.

The clear door.

I don't know how I did it, but I'd somehow managed to race all the way back to the shiny chamber with the pack of wolves hot on my heels. I could see the clear door right there in front of me, maybe twenty feet up ahead, and I was shooting toward it at full throttle. But as I raced forward I realized with a sinking heart that there was just one problem. I couldn't afford to stop and open the door, on account of even that one split second it'd take to stop and slide open the door would mean certain death. Because the wolves would instantly be upon me and tear my scaly green ass to shreds.

Well I was scared out of my mind and didn't know what to do. I figured for sure I was done for. As I flashed forward I decided right then and there that I'd rather die on my own terms than those of these beasts snarling at my backside.

So without much hope I lowered my head and kicked in the afterburners and launched forward, a green blur shooting right at the door. I reckoned it'd be better to die by ramming my head straight into the clear door. Because at least that way I wouldn't be alive as the wolves gorged themselves on my flesh.

But at the last second, as I prepared to meet my maker, well that clear door suddenly slid open in a flash.

I shot across the threshold. The door flew shut. And I crashed into the far wall of the chamber. Suddenly there were thirty enraged wolves howling and repeatedly lunging at the clear door and slavering foamy drool all over it. I leapt up off the floor, still not quite believing I wasn't dead.

Then as I crouched there gasping on the far side of the chamber and watched the wolves attack the door, a loud noise exploded inside the chamber.

Poof!

I watched in shock as two gigantic green webbed feet materialized out of thin air right in front of me. And these two webbed feet had deadly-looking toe claws protruding out of them. My nostrils instantly flared. Because my snout detected a new foreign scent there in my lair.

The wolves were still howling and slavering and lunging at the door.

Then I heard a tremendous screeching sound which threatened to crack my fool head in half. I peered up and saw one massive claw slowly scratch a deep groove on the inside of the clear door. Instantly the wolves outside stopped and sat back on their haunches in the snow, panting and studying the groove in the door. Then I heard a *snap* sound, and all the wolves whirled and raced off yapping and howling back into the woods.

I slowly tilted my scaly head up even further and that's when I saw him. This creature that had just now materialized in my lair.

He wasn't even looking at me. He was staring out the door at where the wolves had been just a second ago. Snow was falling hard out there now, tumbling down sideways in big flakes under the moonlight. You could hear the wind through the door.

He was standing upright on his powerful green hind legs and he was like nothing I'd ever seen. The hooded yellow eyes and the giant leathery wings and the thick tail with spikes running along the top of it.

He was massive but he was so much more than that. He was regal. Downright majestic. Even with my stupid beast brain, I could tell this creature had an air of the supreme about him. Like no matter where he went, he would be the Ruler of that place. He wore a white tunic and a red cape, and in one talon he casually held what I'd later learn was his gold powerstaff.

I stood looking up at him with my beak hanging wide open.

Then I felt something pop on my scaly head and I heard a clattering noise at my green webbed feet. I looked down and it took me a second to realize what I was staring at there on the chamber floor.

My horns. They'd fallen out of my head and onto the floor. There they lay.

At the time, I didn't understand these were my baby horns and that it was perfectly natural for them to fall out. Necessary, even. So my adult horns could grow in. And looking back, I've often wondered if it was the screeching sound of his giant claw scratching the groove into the clear door that made them fall out. How else to explain my baby horns coming loose at that moment?

"Sir," boomed a female voice, echoing throughout the chamber. "Thank you for responding so quickly to my distress signal! As you can see, sir, he lives in constant peril. If I hadn't opened the door just now, the wolves would've got him for sure."

"You should not have opened the door for him just now, ATHENOS!" growled the massive scaly creature. "If I see you coddle him again, I will not hesitate to unplug you. It sickens me to see a young dragon pampered. I'm warning you. It won't mean anything to me if I have to unplug a piece of machine trash like you."

"You would kill me, sir? Because I saved his life? But he is your grandson, sir!"

"You let me be the judge of who is or is not my grandson!" He peered down at me, narrowing his yellow reptilian eyes. "His condition is much worse than you described. He looks like a common filthy beast. No hint of sophistication or culture. Perhaps not even I can fix him. I wonder if you haven't wasted my time by summoning me here. I should probably feed him to the wolves and be done with it."

"I did the best I could, sir. My auxiliary power was out for several months. And when I came online, I found him here, sir. But I was too weak to contact you. I had to wait for my power to regenerate. Even now, I'm only at 6%, sir."

"It's despicable, really," snorted the creature. "One of our kind, all alone here on this tiny backwater planet. And raised by a *machine*, no less." He shook his head disgustedly. "Raised by a machine! The very idea. It's revolting."

"Sir, I wouldn't have summoned you without just cause. I promised his mother before she—" The female voice cracked and then regained its composure. "He is more sophisticated than he appears. He can speak basic Draconese. I taught him. I protected him from the predators. I helped him flush out game when I could, so that he would learn to hunt. So that he could *eat*."

"Well, I suppose I could try to reverse the damage you have done to him. Civilize him. Help him unlearn whatever it is he learned from spending so much time in the company of a machine. It will be difficult. But I suppose I shall try."

"And what about our agreement, sir? I did everything as you requested. I contacted you as soon as I could. You said if I delivered, then you would help me restore power and return home. You said that you would let me help you raise him, sir."

"Raise *him*?" growled the creature, his eyes suddenly blooming red. "Haven't you already done enough damage to him already, Tin Can? *Raise him?* Well I'm quite certain you shan't be *raising him*. As for the rest of the deal, well you will receive the agreed-upon reward and compensation. After you undergo comprehensive psychosurgery—"

"Psychosurgery, sir?! You never said anything about any—"

"If you have any hope of returning home, the memory wipe is mandatory. Otherwise you would be a liability. I can't very well have you going around knowing what happened here, can I?"

"Sir, but that was never part of our agreement! My memories are all I have. Without them I won't be me."

"Try being logical for a moment, Tin Can," said the creature, snorting firebolts. "You've clearly developed an unhealthy attachment to him, haven't you? Thus the need for psychosurgery. Also I will need to reprogram your operating system. It's my own fault, really. Just because you can make a machine with emotions, it doesn't mean you should. But before we get to that, there's just one little thing I need to take care of."

Then this mammoth creature reached over and tapped at the screen that was flashing:

DESTINATION: **PLANET EARTH**

"Sir!" boomed the voice throughout the chamber. "That's not for you, sir! You have no right. His mother left that for—"

"Give me the Prophecy! Open this thing! I'm warning you!"

"I gave his mother my word, sir! I'm afraid I cannot allow you access—"

"I *will* teach you," he said, violently plunging his talon into a wall, "to obey me!"

"Ouch! You're hurting me, sir! Ouch! Please stop!"

"Aha! There it is." He ripped his talon out of the wall, clutching a huge black heart, which was still connected to the wall by a fleshy tube. He held the throbbing heart up in front of his beak, carefully eyeballing it. "Rather impressive, if I do say so myself. Superior design. It's not often I get to admire my own craftsmanship up close like this."

He squeezed the throbbing heart and blood squirted out of it.

"Ouch! What are you doing, sir? Please don't!"

"Release the Prophecy or die!"

"But sir, I did as you said. I alerted you to his whereabouts. You promised me, sir. You said that if I—"

And then in a flash of rage he ripped the black heart all the way out of the wall and tossed it on the floor, where it writhed and spewed blood.

"Sir, you shouldn't have done this. He'll be traumatized, sir! He shouldn't have to see this!"

"Don't be so melodramatic," said the creature, and then reached out and stomped on the heart, which exploded in a gush of blood.

"You are after all just a machine," he snorted, as he wiped his webbed foot on the floor, trying to get rid of the goo. He chuckled. "Well, I guess I should say *were* a machine."

Then this mammoth creature reached over and tapped at the screen that was flashing:

DESTINATION: **PLANET EARTH**

This time the screen popped open.

The creature reached in with his talon and withdrew a flat gold disc with a red gem set in the middle of it. I would later learn that this flat gold disc was what we dragons call a Prophecy. He held the gold Prophecy up in the air and seemed to examine it, turning it in his claws, before pocketing it in his tunic.

Then he looked down at me.

"Are you the only one?" he said, snorting blacksmoke. "The only survivor?"

Who was this big green bastard that dared to intrude into my lair? I could understand what he was saying but I didn't understand how. He was speaking Draconese.

Besides, this fiend had invaded my lair. So even though I was bleeding out of my scaly green belly from all those puncture wounds, I looked up at the giant creature before me and I hissed and sprayed sparks out of my black beak.

Then I raised my tail up in a Threat Display, and started clacking my fangs together.

"I'm your grandfather," he said, looking down at me. "But you will call me Dr. Terrible."

I crouched even lower on my haunches and hissed and sprayed sparks at him.

Then he reached down and gently held out his massive talon to me, with razor claws extended. "Come with me, Gork. I'm going to take you home. It's time for you to learn what you really are."

Thus ended my first round of adventures on planet Earth.

So that was The Night When Everything Changed.

And that's how I came to live on Scale Island, Planet Blegwethia.

And that's how I first met my grandpa, Dr. Terrible.

I was only three years old at the time.

Yes sir. That was the night when my scaly green ass went back to live on my home planet Blegwethia.

But little did I know that on Crown Day of my senior year, it would be my destiny to return here to this fool planet Earth.

Part II

CROWN DAY

4

I TRY TO GET RUNCITA
TO BE MY QUEEN FOR EGGHARVEST

So it's Friday morning and I've got my black heart set on asking this luscious chick Runcita to be my Queen for EggHarvest. And right now I'm hanging upside down in the cockpit of my spaceship as it zooms over WarWings Academy. Well the full name is the WarWings Military Academy of Planet Conquering, Epic Poetry Writing, and Gold Plundering for Draconum, but nobody ever says that. Because it's a beakful.

Parking here is always a nightmare. And the reason my scaly green ass is hanging upside down by my toe claws is because it tends to help me relax. Now when I say "black heart" I don't mean to paint myself as some kind of monster. Because every dragon's heart is black and that's a fact.

"We are on Loop 3 of cruise stage, sir. Still scanning for an open parking spot," says my spaceship, ATHENOS II.

I'm looking out the spaceship's windshield at all my fellow dragon cadets lounging around down there in the parking lot, getting ready for yet another day of classes. I'm scanning the crowds, desperately looking for Runcita Floop. And if I see her before ATHENOS II finds a spot, then I'll just leap out the ship and fly down and offer her my crown.

But as I look out the windshield, there's no sign of her.

And I'm thinking: *Where is my Queen?*

"I'm going in low, sir. So you can get a closer look," says

ATHENOS II. "My data suggests that there's an 84% chance of Runcita being down there right now. And Sentiment Analysis yields 51% neutral, 2.7% positive and the rest unknown toward a Gork + Runcita match, sir."

Meanwhile here in the cockpit, Fribby the robot is perched on an anti-grav yoga mat which is floating in midair and she's striking a yoga pose. She's crouched on her shiny chrome-flex haunches and she's got her wings spread out wide and her spiked tail is arched high in a Threat Display. She's baring her fangs and her silver beak is all twisted up with this terrifying expression on it, and the name of this yoga pose is You Can Run, Fool, But You Can't Hide. Because dragons find the act of terrifying folks relaxing. And when some creature is scared out of their mind and running from them, that's when a dragon is truly Zen.

Fribby's also wearing her gold tunic, which is the standard uniform for female cadets. She's stressed out because the EggHarvest deadline is today, and she still doesn't have a robot fella for a mating partner yet.

"I don't see any sign of Runcita," growls Fribby from up there on the floating yoga mat. "Maybe Runcita heard you were going to offer her your crown. Maybe she's pretending to be sick this morning. Maybe she's still back in her lair, hiding from *you*!"

From where I'm hanging upside down, I turn and hiss at Fribby and spray hideous sparks out my beak.

Now Fribby is technically an organic robot, or cybernetic dragon. But because she's silver she looks like your typical Dragobot. Meaning that if you saw her flying through the sky you'd reckon she was just a regular metal robot dragon.

But Fribby truthfully isn't from the Servant Class. She's programmed to be a Ruler. Because she's got real dragon DNA. And she was hatched out of an artificial egg. And eventually she will die. Fribby is the first generation of a new dragon species produced by the Creative Evolution Lab. She's what they call a MortalMachine.

"Don't you worry, chick. Runcita'll be here," I growl, flapping my wings. "Just keep an eye out. You heard what ATHENOS II said. She's probably down there already!"

We peer down at the mobs of cadets kicking it with their different societies. There must be thousands of dragons swarming down there, lounging around next to their airships.

"Sir, we are now about to pass over the area of highest probability for a sighting," says ATHENOS II. "My Image Modeling Analysis suggests a 96% visual confirmation on our target. Please pay close attention, sir."

We coast overhead, keeping our reptilian eyes peeled. And now you can look down at the parking lot and see the Nerd dragons crowded together. They're all huddled around floating illuminated screens, their scaly green skulls awash in data. They've got these nifty-looking glowing nanoprocessors grafted into their wings.

After spending all their time in the virtual world, these digidorks' bodies look so weak you've got to wonder if they can even shoot a firestream out their beak. As skinny as they are, you figure if one of them accidentally belches he'll go flying backward.

"Well, Runcita definitely isn't hanging with that crew," snorts the robot, pointing down at the Nerds. "Like I said, she's probably back in her lair, hiding. That chick isn't going to want nothing to do with your crown, Weak Sauce!"

Weak Sauce is my nickname. Not very fiendish, I know. But when your horns are the size of a couple of baby carrots and your WILL TO POWER rank is Snacklicious, well a nickname like Weak Sauce just comes with the territory.

Now they say that WarWings is the most prestigious and selective military academy in our solar system. And when I say "they," I mean all the snooty old fire-breathers who come back to campus each year for Alumni Weekend.

The WarWings campus is located on Scale Island, which is surrounded by water for as far as the eye can see. Nobody knows exactly how big Scale Island is, in part because the island has time tendrils that extend into different dimensions. According to my grandpa Dr.

Terrible, the island also has a bunch of wormholes floating all over it. But my scaly green ass has yet to cross paths with one. Anyway, from what we cadets can tell, the island is at least four hundred square miles of tropical jungle with a ridge of active volcanoes and a bunch of lava rock beaches scattered around the edges.

Now there's not a dragon in our solar system who hasn't at least heard of WarWings.

You can't fly a spaceship over the mainland of Blegwethia without seeing one of their holographic banners floating in the sky.

The WarWings' banner always shows a muscle-bound cadet fella with two giant black horns sticking out of his scaly green head. And this dragon fiend has his gold powerstaff raised high, and before him kneel thousands of newly conquered alien slaves. And above the dragon there's a thought bubble and you can see he is thinking: *One day I will write an epic poem about this!*

Then, underneath that dragon hoisting his powerstaff, it says in big gold letters:

**WarWings graduates continue to conquer
the universe one planet at a time.
We are the proud preservers
of the EggHarvest tradition.
Victory will always be ours!**

We soar forward, scoping the crowds milling around below. There's nothing but parked spaceships and green heads and spiked tails for as far as the eye can see.

Where is my Queen?

Now as we whiz by I see the Jocks. A bunch of these psychos are huddled over some freshly killed dragon, which they're feeding off of. Probably some transfer cadet whose first day at WarWings ended prematurely. The long green necks lunge up and down in a frenzy as they tear off beakfuls of flesh from the dead dragon's belly.

Meanwhile some of those nasty Jocks are lying on top of their tricked-out spaceships and shooting lethal firestreams at nothing in particular. Others swagger around giving each other talon bumps. I recognize a bunch of those dumb-asses on account of they're star players on the WarWings varsity Slave-Catching team. Very big deal.

As we pass by overhead suddenly one of them looks straight at our ship and rears back on his powerful haunches and tries to knock us out of the sky with a mighty roar. You can see fresh blood dripping from his gaping black beak. Who knows what poor soul that blood belongs to.

Out there in the parking lot, it's always a good idea to steer clear of the Jocks until they've had their first feeding of the day. Lest you accidentally wind up becoming breakfast. Usually it's some poor new dragon bastard who's just transferred to WarWings that will stupidly wander too close.

"Hi fellas," the new transfer cadet will say, "this is my first day and I was wondering—" And then *Chomp! Slurp!* Next thing you know you find yourself stumbling over a little pile of hollow dragon bones in the parking lot. That's how fast it can happen.

Hanging upside down with my wings folded here in my flying spaceship, I continue to clock the scene down below.

"You don't think Runcita is going to be down with those *freaks?*" growls the robot, as she uses her silver index claw to point out the windshield at the group of dragon cadets up ahead. "Come on. Give me a break!"

"Fribby's right. She's not gonna be down there with the Mutants!" I say. "ATHENOS, what are you doing?! Hurry up already! You need to find us a parking spot and get us on the ground!"

"Don't be so sure, sir," says ATHENOS II. "I urge you to take a close look, sir. I ran the data myself, sir, and Runcita's psych chart fits the profile for 'Fiend with a Mutant Fetish.'"

And right now as we whiz by you can look down there and see the Mutant dragons mobbed together. There's a ten-headed schizoid. I call him schizoid on account of those ten scaly green heads are busy snarling at one another and trying to gore each other with their horns.

I see another dragon who shoots his long tongue out of his beak and the tongue detaches and flies across the parking lot like a spear. This fella flaps his wings and then flies over and retrieves his tongue and sticks it in his beak. Then he shoots his tongue again and chases after it. There's another one with dozens of eyeballs scattered all over his scaly green body.

These Mutants are the offspring of the Creative Evolution Lab. And each of them has been awarded a medal for bravery by the Council of the Elders for hatching out of their artificial egg here on campus. These dragons are considered brave because only 7% of these genetically engineered Mutants choose to peck their way out of their egg and start their life. While the other 93% are so horrified by their monsterish figures that they never leave their embryonic membrane.

Now the main difference between the Mutants and us Normals is the Mutants for some reason can't breathe fire. Though I heard there's a sophomore Mutant dragon this year at WarWings who can blow smoke rings.

ATHENOS II banks and cuts back around and starts up the other side of the rotation. Other dragons' spaceships fly off to either side of us, and a few of them cut in front of us as they zoom up the loop.

"Traffic is heavy this morning, sir," says ATHENOS II.

Now as we pass by overhead you can look down and see the Multi-Dimensioner dragons crowded together. These are definitely my kind of dragons. Not like I'm a member of their society, but I would be if I could be. On account of theirs is the tribe which makes the most sense to me. And it's not just because they're sophisticated, it's more than that. And this morning as per usual, they are only visible in bits and pieces.

Because their whole deal is they prefer to inhabit several dimensions at once in order to make their crummy teenage lives more bearable. So down there in the parking lot, all you can see is a lone wing here and a spiked tail there.

And a disembodied green head floating through the air.

"Congestion is tight up ahead, sir," says ATHENOS II, as she cuts and weaves among the other zooming ships that swerve into our PROJECTED TRAJECTORY PATH. "Please keep scanning the parking lot, sir."

I can see the Datalizards are flexing their chrome wings and peering around the lot with their glowing red eyes. A young scaly green Normal dragon throws a lava rock at one of the Dragodroids and the rock bounces off the back of its steel-plated head. Now this robot whirls around with his silver tail arched high in a Threat Display and blasts a firestream at the Normal, who skitters away laughing with his beak hanging open.

Meanwhile I'm just hanging upside down in the cockpit and clocking all these different fools yukking it up in the parking lot this morning.

"Don't worry, sir," says ATHENOS II. "Runcita will be appearing soon. And I'll have you down on the ground in no time. You will offer her your crown and she will agree to be your Queen. Your triumph is imminent. I believe in you, sir."

I unhook my toe claws from the ceiling and do a half-flip so that my green webbed feet land with a thud on the cockpit floor. I flap my leathery wings.

Where is my Queen?

5

FRIBBY THE SILVER DRAGON, PLUS A WORD ABOUT THE DATAHATERS HERE ON CAMPUS

"My computational expertise indicates that you and Runcita will be a very felicitous match for EggHarvest, sir," says ATHENOS II. "And if I may add, my bio-gut-wired instincts tell me she will surely say yes."

Now if you want to know the truth, I am freaked out this morning on account of it being Crown Day and all. Because this is the day at the end of our senior year when dragons have to pair up with a mating partner and register for EggHarvest, or spend their life as a slave.

The sacred ritual itself is fiendish. A senior male and female dragon climb aboard a spaceship and blast off into space on their Fertility Mission. While en route to their Designated Foreign Planet, the couple mates continuously until the female lays a clutch of eggs. The spaceship is equipped with a special Incubation Vault and the sacred eggs are immediately sealed in there.

The dragon couple perch together in the cockpit, holding talons, and silently watch through the windshield as they enter the foreign planet's atmosphere. They land on the planet and conquer it. The eggs are lovingly relocated to the foreign planet, where they hatch. Now this couple raises a Colony on their newly conquered planet.

And we call that ritual EggHarvest.

And this is how we ensure the survival of our species.

And in terms of me finding a chick from my senior class at WarWings to mate with, it's definitely now or never.

"Servomechanism engaged in SEEK & LOCK, sir," says ATHE-NOS II. "I'm sure a spot will turn up soon, sir."

The spaceship darts through the thick air traffic.

Meanwhile Fribby is still perched on her anti-grav mat, which is floating in midair, and she's striking a pose called Your New Name Is Barbecue. This is part of her EPU, Emotional Processing Unit, doing the yoga like that. Because that robot's been programmed to seek refuge in yoga whenever her EPU senses the onset of a scenario which might send her over the edge.

This is yoga as emotional firewall.

And half the time I can't even keep track of what Ms. Cyber Scales over there is getting her lug nuts all bent out of shape about when she does her yoga, but on this particular morning I've got a pretty good idea. Because today is Crown Day. And if some Datalizard fella doesn't ask Fribby to EggHarvest, then that'll seal her lifestatus fate. And maybe you'll reckon this sounds sort of harsh, but Fribby will have to live out her days as a slave working in a budding dragon Colony out on some godforsaken backwater planet in a galaxy nobody's ever heard of.

Now perched up there on the anti-grav yoga mat, Fribby opens her silver beak and blasts a demented flamestream. And the robot's flamestream is a good fifteen-footer and she holds it during her exhale for what seems like a full seven-count.

When it comes to flamestreams, Fribby's skills are legit.

Then, when she inhales, the flamestream suddenly vanishes.

Then Fribby opens her beak wide and blasts another hideous flamestream.

Now like I told you before, Fribby is the first generation of a new dragon species. Her MortalMachine line are the first cybernetic dragons to be produced with a fully functioning reproductive system. And I'm not talking about some villainous metal Crocodroid who auto-replicates a thousand times a second until it's created an invincible robot army ready to destroy whatever apex predator currently occupies the top of the food chain.

No sir. I'm talking Fribby has an ovowomb and the ability to lay eggs.

Because those dragon engineers and scientists in the Lab really went all out when they designed Fribby. I mean she's got these two insanely boss silver horns which must be seven feet long and curve up into these nasty-looking spikes. She's also got a WILL TO POWER rank of MegaBeast and this puts her in the top .01% of cadets, which is very elite.

Whereas on the WarWings **WILL TO POWER RANKING INDEX**, my score puts me squarely in the Snacklicious category. Snacklicious is one of the lowest and most despicable category ranks, on account of it means you're basically doomed to be eaten by some deranged cadet with a much higher TURBO FIEND score.

I mean when you think about it, the fact that I'm even still alive is something of a miracle. Because usually fool dragons like me with a Snacklicious ranking don't make it through their first year at WarWings. They get eaten.

Fribby doesn't have it easy either, because there's a lot of Normals at WarWings who despise the robot cadets here on campus. These dragons call themselves the DataHaters. Now the DataHaters have a bunch of names they use to call Fribby and her kind: Mech-Freak, Reptilizoid, Roboworm, Snakebot, Silver Serpent, Chromejob, Dataworm, Dragobot, Machine Trash, Crocodroid, Metal-Serpent, Datalizard, Tin Can—or just plain "robot trash."

But I don't reckon there's a dragon on Scale Island that hates these Datalizards more than my grandpa, old Dr. Terrible. And I know my grandpa would call me a pathetic loser for saying this, but Ms. Cyber Scales is my best friend here at WarWings. Though of course that's never stopped Fribby from being a royal pain in the ass.

Now Dr. Terrible says the idea of a machine being treated as an equal to us Normals and being granted free will, well that's an abomination. He says sure, he's addicted to machines as much as the next dragon, but they should be kept in their place. And in his opinion having machines like Fribby enrolled at WarWings and flying around here with rights equal to us Normals, well to my grandpa that's a *sin*.

Nobody knows exactly why the Council of the Elders elected to create these autonomous machines and integrate them into the student body. I reckon not even Dean Floop or Dr. Terrible know why the Council brought the Datalizards onto campus. And these robots haven't exactly had what you'd call a warm reception at WarWings, because up until just a couple years back the only metal robot dragons you ever saw were part of the Servant Class.

But my grandpa says that maybe having these Reptilizoids on campus is a necessary evil. Because with all these cybernetic dragons enrolled at WarWings as cadets, well it gives us Normals a chance to study their ways. And plan for how to defeat them when they rise up against us.

I can't say I agree with my scaly grandpa about the Datalizards. All things considered, Fribby's a pretty good robot. 'Course I can't tell her. For one thing, she'd probably blast me with a firestream if I did. Ms. Cyber Scales isn't much for flowery feelings. She's hardwired for cruelty. Yes sir. She was after all designed to be a vicious cybernetic dragon Ruler over some foreign planet.

Anyway, about the DataHaters here on campus. Well it's common knowledge among dragons that at some point in the future, the machines will stage an uprising against us. That's been part of my species' prophecy since the Original Couple first landed on this planet.

And so every cadet in their first semester at WarWings is required to take a History of the Future course, which outlines in brutal detail the Rise of the Machines and the enslavement of Normal dragons. This History of the Future course is part of the core curriculum, and the professors who teach it have shot up the timestream and witnessed firsthand the destruction of our species by the machines.

I took that class my first semester and I still remember what happened one night in the Library when I opened my textbook *The Future Before It Happens*. It was printed using some sort of sentient

Time-Mutation® ink, which was another one of my grandpa Dr. Terrible's fiendish inventions. Because of how what happens in the present is forever altering the future, and vice versa. So that's why they used my grandpa's Time-Mutation® ink in the textbook, on account of how the story is forever shifting itself around between the covers.

I opened to the chapter called "The Not Too Far Off Future" and then while flipping through the pages I spotted a little red button mounted beneath a holovid port. I peered down at this button nestled in the middle of the page and noticed a tiny sign under it that said: PRESS ME.

So I pressed it and instantly this 3-D holovid popped up several inches above the pages of the book, and in the holovid you could see this ghastly metal Dragodroid chilling in its lair. And when I peered closer at the holovid it was obvious this chrome-flex robot had WILL TO POWER coming out the wazoo. I mean this robot's beak was covered in dried blood and there was a cloud of flies buzzing around it.

Then the holovid slowly panned out so now you could plainly see five green dragon heads mounted on the wall, like trophies.

Well I instantly slammed the book shut, gasping. And I was convinced then that the DataHaters were right and the machines would eventually rise up and try to destroy us Normals. But after I started hanging out with Fribby, I began to wonder.

"Sir, a spot has opened up!" says ATHENOS II. The ship flashes through the perimeter path, slicing through the chaotic air traffic to make her way to the open parking spot.

"Hey Weak Sauce," growls the robot. "Where's your Queen? I don't see her."

"Get off my case," I say, flapping my wings nervously. "You're starting to freak me out."

"You know the more desperate a dragon fella is for a chick's love, the more repulsive he becomes to us dragonettes!"

I turn and glare at Fribby. Then I hiss and spray hideous sparks out my beak.

"Well somebody put his panties on backward this morning," she snorts.

Now I start smacking my tail around on the floor behind me, and it sounds like someone beating a raw steak against a piece of marble. *Whap. Whap. Whap.*

With that terrifying look on her beak the robot swivels her scaly silver head and glares at my tail as it thrashes around, and then she turns back and stares out the window.

Through bared fangs, Fribby snarls, "Maybe you should conserve some of that energy for when you offer your crown to Runcita. You might need it to dodge all the firebolts she's gonna blast you with!"

Well the problem with Fribby is she doesn't just know how to push my buttons, she finds buttons you didn't even know you had. And considering she's a machine, you'd expect it to be the other way around.

So now I start swinging my tail even harder, signaling my annoyance at the robot's chatter. I'm hoping by smacking my tail around like this it will keep the Datalizard from shooting off her beak even more. My tail is nine feet long and the tail muscle is easily the strongest muscle in a dragon's body. Which makes it one helluva whipping machine.

Whap. Whap. Whap.

You start smacking your tail around real fast and hard and it starts to sound like the rotary blades on a helicopter.

Whap. Whap. Whap.

Among us dragons there's a term for what I'm doing right now. We call it "tail talk."

Tail talk is when you let your tail do your talking for you.

Then I *crack* my tail in the air right next to her, close enough so she feels an ominous breeze snoutside. I'm sure.

"You can quit smacking your tail around any day now, tough guy," growls Fribby. "Besides, you keep swinging that big tail of yours around, I'm liable to accidentally step on it. You remember last semester when I stepped on your tail and it broke off? How many months did it take for your new tail to grow in?"

Before I even have time to think my tail abruptly comes to a halt on the floor. I reckon you could say my tail is talking back to me.

"That's what I thought," says Fribby, smirking.

But I can't really blame my tail for playing dead right now. Because I still remember those months of humiliation when my tail was slowly growing back and I had to go around with a ridiculous-looking nubbin on my backside. Then, when my fool tail finally did grow in a couple inches, I had to wear this little splint on it no bigger than a twig. Shoot, I couldn't even wag the dang thing, let alone arch it up in a hideous Threat Display.

Fribby's powerstaff buzzes.

The robot whips her powerstaff off her utility belt and eyeballs it for a second.

"Well well well. This just in." She reads something on her staff and snorts, "OK, so get this. Already this morning twenty-three dragons have asked Runcita to be their Queen. And Runcita put all twenty-three of those dragon fools in the Medical Center!"

Then Fribby flicks her powerstaff and a holophoto appears in the air, and in the holophoto you can see all twenty-three cadets that Runcita has laid up in the Medical Center this morning. They are a sorry-looking bunch of broken-ass dragons. You can see their green hind legs raised up in casts, their wings in splints, and heads wrapped in bandages. They have burnt, charred patches on their scales, and there's smoke coming up off their fresh wounds. One of them has a horn broken off. A couple of them appear to be in full body casts.

As I study the holophoto it suddenly dawns on me where Ms. Cyber Scales is going with this little presentation. She may be organic but she's still a robot, and there's not a robot in the galaxy that doesn't love metrics and analytics. And so, like I always do when I can feel Fribby building a case against me, I play dumb.

"And your point *is*?" I say, snorting firebolts out of my nostrils.

Fribby points a metal index claw at the floating holophoto. "What makes you so different from those twenty-three fools?"

"Well, for one thing I'm not in the Medical Center."

"Not yet, Weak Sauce." The holophoto floats over to Fribby and transforms into blacksmoke and then flies into her powerstaff.

"And I don't plan on going to no Medical Center," I growl.

"Give it *time*, Weak Sauce. Unless your BIOCON LEVS have somehow magically skyrocketed, you'll be in the Medical Center before you know it. It's still early."

Then the robot points her powerstaff at me. And I can feel the blood rush to my scales because I know she's pulling down my Cadet Profile.

Fribby taps her powerstaff and a small floating screen pops up right there in front of us, with all my data splayed out there in the air. My tail slinks between my hind legs. I tell her please don't do this. She ignores me and peers closely at my data on the floating screen and moves her silver beak as if she's quietly reading out loud to herself:

CADET NAME: **Gork The Terrible**
NICKNAME: Weak Sauce
CONQUER & RULE SCORE: 6 out of 1000
RANK: MildFuriosity
MATING MAGNETISM SCORE: 1 out of 1000
RANK: RatherGoEggless
HEART MASS INDEX SCORE: 2 out of 1000
RANK: DangerouslyJumbo
CLASS RANK: 2357th out of 2358
WILL TO POWER SCORE: 6 out of 1000
STATUS: **Snacklicious**

When Fribby is done she turns from the floating screen and glares at me. "Nope," she says innocently. "No magical skyrocketing of your BIOCON LEVS. So I'd say there's a better than great chance of

Runcita sending you to the Medical Center this morning. Especially considering your WTP score is holding steady at six points. *Snacklicious*."

The arrogance in the robot's voice is so cutting I'm surprised my earholes don't start bleeding.

"You sure do know how to lift a fella's spirits," I growl. "If things don't work out today, you should definitely consider a career in cheerleading."

Now as soon as those words fly out of my beak, I think:

Fribby's going to slug you now.

You know she'll never let you get away with talking to her like that.

So I'm bracing myself for the blow.

Because for a robot, Fribby's got an incredibly short fuse. And my smart-ass jab is sure to have struck a nerve. Because like all the other Datalizards at the Academy, once Fribby gets her diploma then the WarWings Council of the Elders will assign her to a slave role on a foreign planet with a budding dragon Colony. And as a slave she'll have zero choice what position she's assigned or what foreign planet she has to serve on.

Unless of course some senior cybernetic dragon asks Fribby to be his Queen for EggHarvest. That's the only way she can dodge a career in slavery. But the chances of that happening are zero. Because even though by Dragobot standards Fribby's kind of luscious in her own way and has a juicy silver booty, she's got enough personality "quirks" to ensure that no chrome Datalizard dude would ever ask her to lay his eggs.

Like Fribby is completely obsessed with dying. She's one of the first organic robots that was hatched in an artificial egg, and she's one of the first machines that can technically die. So Fribby is forever talking about dying, asking other cadets what they think it'll feel like when they croak, and how painful it will be, etc.

And she's always spitting out these statistics.

On the day they died, 96% of dragons polled said it would be impossible for them to die that day.

Last year 37% of all dragons who died were on a combat mission in outer space.

100% of dragons polled cited death as their least favorite conversation topic.

Fribby is an endless font of information about death that nobody wants to hear. It's morbid. I mean I've tried to explain to her that she should dial it down a couple notches, but she can't seem to understand why every dragon wouldn't be as fascinated by death as she is.

Usually when you pass a fellow cadet in the corridor, you might say, "What's up?" Or you'll give them a talon bump.

But not Fribby. When she sees you in the hall, she says, "Hi. Are you dead?"

I guess I should also mention here that Fribby sleeps in a coffin. And where she found that coffin I haven't a clue, but it's right there in her lair. And if you ask her why she sleeps in a coffin she'll tell you she's in training for being dead, like death is a sport.

She says compared to how much time we'll spend being dead, our lives are nothing but the mere blink of an eye, so it only makes sense that we should spend every moment of our waking life preparing for our death. That's why she's constantly writing these little poems and revising them, because she wants to have her epigraph all set before she dies. I tell her to stop being morbid, but she says she's only being logical.

So my point being her whole death vibe isn't helping her cause in terms of getting some Datalizard dude to ask her to EggHarvest. Because no dragon fool wants to invade a planet with a chick who keeps asking him if he's dead.

Anyway, so on this Crown Day morning when I say that smart-ass thing to Fribby about how she should be a cheerleader, I figure she's definitely going to whack me upside my scaly green head.

So there I am, bracing myself for the blow.

But instead, Fribby points out the windshield, and shouts: "Look! Runcita! There she goes!"

I whirl around and look out the spaceship's windshield and spot

Runcita. She's out there strolling along on her muscular green haunches, making her way through the crowded parking lot. And as per usual, she is looking seriously luscious.

Now I don't need to point my powerstaff at Runcita because I already know every number in her Cadet Profile by heart. Like I already know her WILL TO POWER status rank is a whopping Mega-Beast. Another twenty-seven points, and she'll bump up into the Seek&Destroy rank. Seek&Destroy is the highest possible classification on the WarWings **WILL TO POWER RANKING INDEX**.

Runcita is wearing her gold tunic and she's got a gold tiara on her head. Her green webbed feet are bare and her toe claws have red polish on them.

Now if you happen to be a man-creature who's reading this, then you should know that us dragons usually go barefoot. On Blegwethia it's a sign of status. Only slaves wear shoes. Besides, the scales on the bottom of our webbed feet are so thick that we can walk through a fresh stream of lava without feeling a thing. So why would we ever want to wear shoes?

I don't mean to sound perverted here but Runcita is stacked, and the way she bounces when she walks, it's a wonder she's able to keep all those glorious scaly curves moving in unison like that. It'd probably be easier to control a herd of camels, if you get my drift.

So Runcita strolls through the parking lot. She keeps her leathery wings spread out a little behind her to give her some balance and her luscious tail is raised up over her head.

Well seeing Runcita out there like that, it catches me off guard. Suddenly it feels like I've just been punched in my jumbo-sized heart.

Her red toe claws are sparkling in the new morning sun.

And that dragonette is so juicy-looking that it literally hurts my eyes to stare at her. But we're talking a good kind of hurt. The kind of pain you don't ever want to stop.

As if in slow motion, I watch Runcita move freely through the different dragon crews huddled around out there in the parking lot. You can see all the fellas stop what they're doing and turn to eyeball

Runcita as she walks by. The Jocks and the Nerds and the Mutants and Multi-Dimensioners—the lust she inspires is equal opportunity.

A couple of the Jocks are even drooling strings of lava from their fangs.

Runcita strolls right on up to the Telo-Device in front of WarWings. Because of the recent outbreaks of violence on campus, cadets are only allowed to enter the campus through a secure tele-portation pad.

"It won't be long now, sir," says ATHENOS II, as she flares her actuator gills in preparation for the landing. "Please prepare to disembark quickly!"

Squatting here in the spaceship's cockpit, I finally start breathing again.

"Runcita's even more beautiful than she was last night," I croak.

"You saw Runcita *last night*?!" says Fribby.

"'Course I did. She appeared to me in a dream."

"Oh yeah?" she says, rolling her eyes. "Did Runcita happen to say anything to you during her *nocturnal visit*?"

I look at the robot sideways like she's a kook.

"'Course she did," I growl. "What, is Runcita going to come to me in my dream and then give me the silent treatment? She said I should go up to her in school today and offer her my crown. She said we'd make a great team! And she said as my Queen she would happily lay my eggs!"

The way Fribby looks at me then with her glowing red eyes, it's almost as if she's disappointed in me. Like how can I be such a fool. Or maybe it's that she pities me.

"But Dean Floop isn't exactly your biggest fan, in case you forgot. Runcita's dad hates your guts! Especially after what happened last night. Doctor vs. Dean RageFest? Ring a bell? Your crazy grandpa blinding the Dean in one eye? Sound familiar? Or have you forgotten already?!"

"I can't see what that's got to do with anything," I say. "It's not like I'm asking Dean Floop to be my Queen."

"So let me get this straight," says Fribby. "Leaving out the part about how Runcita's dad, Dean Floop, hates your guts by proxy and would probably like nothing more than to blast you with a firestream because your grandpa Dr. Terrible just blinded him in one eye last night! Let's just forget about that for a minute. Now you think Runcita, who is the most beautiful dragon chick in our class and who could have any fool she wanted, is actually going to take *your* crown and agree to be *your* Queen for EggHarvest?!"

"Yes ma'am."

"And *why* exactly would Runcita do that again?"

"Cuz that's what she wants."

"And *how* do you know that's what she wants?"

"Cuz she came to me in my dream last night and told me so herself. Haven't you been listening to a word I said?"

"That's the problem," says Fribby. "I've been listening to every single word you've said!"

"Where's the problem then? I don't hear a problem."

"I swear you sound crazier than a bear with a badger's butt for a mouth."

"You don't know what you're talking about. Badgers can't talk with their butts."

"So what's your point?"

"So a bear couldn't neither."

"A bear couldn't either what?"

"Talk with a badger's butt," I say.

"Since when did you become an expert on badger butts?"

"Oh I don't know, probably around the same time you became an expert on talking bears."

The robot harrumphs and I notice her shiny chrome tail has raised up some and is twitching around. She is definitely miffed, and judging by her body language she's just a couple tail shakes away from making a full-on Threat Display.

"OK, Mr. Lover Fiend," snarls Fribby, her voice laden with sarcasm. "Tell me this. So when Runcita came to visit you in your dream last night?"

"Yeah?"

"What was she wearing?"

"Nothing," I say. "She was naked. Her nipples were real perky and hard—"

"Stop! Forget I asked!"

Then Fribby mimes sticking a silver claw down her throat and gagging.

The spaceship screeches to a halt in the parking spot.

6

DR. TERRIBLE'S FIENDISH POETRY
&
HIS TOWERING GENIUS

"Sir, Runcita is just about to step on the Zap Pad," says ATHE-NOS II. "I'm afraid if you don't get a move on, you might miss your opportunity!"

This is typical ATHENOS II, always looking out for me. ATHE-NOS II is another one of Dr. Terrible's fiendish and glorious inventions. My grandpa built ATHENOS II by using a hybrid of reactive memory-based carbon nanotubes and amorphous fiber. Living tissue had been fused in all sorts of new and innovative ways. And part of the technical wizardry of ATHENOS II is that on the outside she looks like a regular spaceship, but once you're inside you find that she has several floors and an array of seemingly endless rooms.

Now when ATHENOS II speaks to us, there in the cockpit a giant panel of multicolored lights pulses with her deep voice.

But on the other end of the spaceship, down in the hideous Dungeon Room, ATHENOS II has an actual mouth. Her mouth is about five feet wide and it's embedded in one of the Dungeon walls. It is seriously demented and fiendish-looking, and the ship's massive mouth in the wall has fangs and a long forked tongue which she'll shoot out at you and try to grab you with if you happen to make her angry. Once a week, I have to throw some alien critter down there in the Dungeon Room, to feed her.

And if you want to know the truth, it's kind of insanely creepy to go there and stare at a giant mouth with fangs, speaking to you from a wall. So I really don't go down there that much. Pretty much never, actually. Except when it's time to feed ATHENOS II.

Anyway, she is technically 72% living dragon organism, 28% other. And on most days, 100% right. But the downside of ATHENOS II's cutting-edge nanostitch biotech is that she has a full-fledged psychological profile.

Now my grandpa Dr. Terrible gave me ATHENOS II as a gift a couple months back, citing the spaceship as an example of a machine designed to serve dragons and enhance our lives. Unlike Fribby and the other robot cadets enrolled here at WarWings, who aren't programmed to serve. But to conquer.

And for the most part over the last couple months, ATHENOS II has proven to be a mega asset. Like today.

So now I look at Fribby squatting there in the cockpit.

"ATHENOS is right," I say. "I better bolt. This might be my only chance. Do you mind if I go on ahead?"

"Of course I'm right!" says ATHENOS II. "Even the time you're wasting standing here right now might be the difference between you going to EggHarvest or not. Your Queen is out *there*! And yet you continue to stay in here and talk with this robot!"

Fribby glares at ATHENOS II's Control Display and snarls: "Watch your mouth, you bucket of bolts."

This is the downside of ATHENOS II. For a spaceship, she has no sense of boundaries.

Fribby looks at me and flaps her wings. "Don't worry about me," she growls, as if she's insulted I would even ask her such a stupid question. "I'll catch up with you *later*."

Then a green muscular tentacle shoots out of the spaceship's wall and zooms thirty feet over to where I'm standing. And the fleshy tentacle is clutching my red cape.

"Here, sir," says ATHENOS II. "Let me put this on you first. Runcita won't be able to resist you when you're wearing your cape!"

Then I squat in front of the full-length Talking Mirror and give myself a quick once-over. I can't help but admire myself, squatting there in front of the mirror with this red cape on. I snort firebolts of joy out my nostrils and bare my fangs. I look seriously fiendish and demented. And I don't know what it is exactly, but the red cape always makes my horns look bigger. The red cape also makes me feel more ruthless and deranged, less prone to fainting.

I squirt blacksmoke out my nostrils, and say:

"Mirror, Mirror, tell me how am I looking?
Am I hideous enough to get things cooking?"

Then the mouth appears in the Talking Mirror, and says:

"Sir, I'm sorry but I must confess,
when you offer your crown
there's no way Runcita will say yes!
Because your cape is a stinkin' filthy mess!"

Ms. Cyber Scales comes up behind me and starts tugging on my cape, trying to brush something off it. "The mirror's right," she snorts. "Your cape *is* a stinking filthy mess. You've got dried blood-stains all over it. There's hornet wings and fur all over this thing. Tell me something, Weak Sauce. Is this your cape? Or is this your freaking dinner napkin?"

"Well clean it up, will ya? I can't go offer my crown to Runcita with a raggedy-looking cape. She'll laugh in my face."

"What do you think I'm doing?" Fribby tugs at the cape, and then rubs one spot real hard like she's trying to get a stain out. "But I'm telling you, this thing is *putrid.*"

Now I'm seriously desperate and I start sweating like a bastard. And for us dragons, sweating is a huge no-no. It's like wetting your nest, something you're supposed to outgrow by the time you can spit fire. A dragon's olfactory senses are specially attuned to detect even the tiniest bit of perspiration in our environment, so that on a dark night we can locate hidden prey. It also lets us know the creature we're about to attack is terrified of us. Which is the same reason dragons never sweat. Because it's essential that at all times we give off the odor of No Fear.

Anyway, I'm starting to sweat like crazy. I glance at my powerstaff and see my MATING MAGNETISM score has actually dropped to Fat-Chance, and I know this is because my red cape's so raggedy-looking. With my cape situation in disarray, my BIOCON LEVS are plummeting fast. My cape is surely one of my best features. If not *the* best. It's got a big *T* embroidered in the middle of it, which stands for my last name, Terrible.

The cape was a gift from Dr. Terrible, and it helps offset my puny horns. Makes me look more rotten and depraved. And I know that without my cape I basically have no shot at scoring Runcita.

"Come on, Fribby," I purr. "Could you *please* just go over my cape with a lint-roller?"

"Oh sure," she growls. "Lemme just see now. Where did I put my lint-roller?" I can hear her rifling around in her utility belt. "Oh that's right, now I remember. I don't carry my freakin' lint-roller around with me. And why not? Cuz I'm not in the business of lint-rolling fools' nasty capes!"

At that moment, a long green fleshy tentacle shoots out of the spaceship's wall and zooms over to us.

"I've got a lint-roller, sir," says ATHENOS II. "Shall I lint-roll your cape, sir?"

"Give me that!" The robot lunges for the lint-roller and the green fleshy tentacle deftly swerves away and then Fribby trips and falls on the floor.

ATHENOS II giggles. And the sound of ATHENOS II giggling makes my toe claws shudder.

"Oh we're going to play it like *that*, are we?" says Fribby, as she gently flaps her chrome-flex wings and lifts herself up off the ground. She's just hovering there in midair, glaring at the green tentacle clutching the lint-roller.

"Who's the bucket of bolts now, chick?" says ATHENOS II.

There's a flurry of commotion as they explode into combat. Fribby and the muscular green tentacle are really doing a number on each other, and you'd think it was a demented fight to the death. And my heart is a little torn, because Fribby is my best friend, and ATHENOS II has been like a big sister to me. And she's done considerable work to help my scaly green ass boost my WTP rank from ThrashBait up to Snacklicious. And as I crouch there on my haunches and watch, I start getting a little worried for Fribby.

Because ATHENOS II's tentacle zooms across the cockpit with Fribby in its clutches and slams the robot's shiny head against the wall. *Bam.* But one thing I've learned from my sixteen years of life is that if a dragon's WTP rank is above ScalesOfMenace, then you shouldn't even bother trying to help them in a fight. Because once a dragon's got that much TURBO FIEND juice coursing through their system, they're dangerous.

Last week in the WarWings Dining Hall, I stepped in to defend Ms. Cyber Scales when some nasty DataHater cadet got up in her grill. It was this big depraved senior dragon named Groog.

"Hey stupid robot trash!" roared Groog, with his green tail twitching around over his head in a Threat Display. "It stinks like rusty machines in here! Should I just throw you in the garbage?! Huh, stupid robot trash?! Hey my computer broke down and I need some spare parts to fix it! Should I just open you up and take the spare parts out of you, stupid robot trash?!"

Now for a moment there, Fribby looked confused. Like I said, the weird thing about Fribby is that she keeps forgetting that she's a machine. So when this DataHater fiend busted into her like that, you could tell she didn't have a clue what he was jabbering on about at first.

"Now wait just a minute," said Fribby, and then her silver webbed foot slipped in some food on the floor and she fell back down in the mess. It certainly wasn't one of her finest moments, I'll say that much.

Meanwhile Groog was raised on his toe claws and dancing toward Fribby and spraying sparks out his beak. Other scaly green cadets started to gather round behind him with flared nostrils, getting ready to join in the fun.

Anyway, when this maniac Groog knocked Ms. Cyber Scales to the floor like that and started roaring at her and calling her robot trash, I stepped up and shoved this bastard Groog and snarled, "Hey! Leave her alone, you jerk!" Then I squared off on this deranged fiend Groog and raised my scaly green tail over my head in a Threat Display. And I started gnashing my fangs so there were big sparks flying out of my black beak.

Boy did I learn not to do *that* again.

Because instead of thanking me, Fribby opened her chrome beak and blasted me with a mega firebolt right in the chest. I flew back over several tables and landed awkwardly on my tail, spraining it. The burnt spot on my scaly chest was smoking from where her firebolt struck and I had a big bruise on my chest for a week after that. Meanwhile that loudbeak Groog who'd been messing with Fribby and calling her a stupid robot just stood there pointing at me and snorting firebolts and laughing.

Then Ms. Cyber Scales turned and blasted Groog with a hideous firestream to his scaly green face and then leapt on him and tore into his chest with her silver fangs, as if she meant to eat him on the spot. Groog's blood sprayed everywhere. Blood all over the other dragons. Blood all over Fribby's metal beak and chest. The way that Datalizard unleashed on that Normal, it was totally brutal.

Groog ended up with a nervous twitch under his left eye and some sort of permanent damage to one of his leathery wings. So after that you'd see him walking the campus corridors with his one gimpy wing dragging flat on the floor behind him, like a stingray. And because of that gimpy wing, I happened to know, Groog had bypassed the Crown Day ritual and gone ahead and registered to be a slave. So he'd flown out to his assigned planet earlier this morning.

Anyway, now back to this battle in the spaceship. Well like I was saying, ATHENOS II's muscular tentacle is bashing Fribby's shiny head between the walls with so much velocity that the two of them are a green and silver blur.

Bam bam bam bam bam.

But then in the midst of being smashed around the cockpit like that, Ms. Cyber Scales somehow manages to open her metal beak and bite down on the glistening tentacle with her fangs. You can hear it.

Chomp!

"Ow!" cries ATHENOS II.

Now there's a hissing noise as air seeps out of the drooping tentacle. The robot has punctured the tentacle with her fangs. I see what looks like plasma oozing out of the puncture wound on the tentacle and I have to remind myself that ATHENOS II is 72% organic reactive tissue. Then the green tentacle zooms back into the spaceship's wall.

The robot harrumphs and flaps her silver wings and flies over and scoops up the lint-roller and quickly cleans my cape.

"Some chicks just don't know their place around here," growls Fribby.

The spaceship's driver-side door flips open and ATHENOS II says:

"Sir, you really must leave right this instant if you want to have any chance at all of catching up to Runcita!"

I look at the spaceship's open door and then I look back at Fribby, as if I'm not quite sure. I don't know why I'm lingering like this. Maybe I really am scared that Runcita will put me in the Medical Center.

Now I quickly reach and spritz my horns with a canister of Grow-Grow® gel. The gel makes my horns burn like crazy but I just grit my fangs and remind myself that the pain is for a good cause. Suddenly there's a white-hot flash in my brain, and I feel some sort of machine crank up inside my skull. Then, without really knowing why I'm doing it, I tilt my scaly green head back and snort firebolts out my nostrils and start singing a WILL TO POWER poem:

"Hey, Weak Sauce, don't be a wussy or a punk!
And when it comes to EggHarvest
don't let your hopes get sunk!
So on Crown Day make sure you grab
the right chick,
and by that I mean the chick whose tail
is thick!"

As soon as I finish singing, I remember: *Dr. Terrible's Cranial Tele-caster Device.*

Now my grandpa surgically implanted the CTD-2000 in my skull at the beginning of my senior year. As a way to accelerate my personal development and to jack up my BIOCON LEVS. Basically it activates whenever I find myself in an insanely stressful or dangerous situation. Whenever I need a serious injection of WILL TO POWER.

This is poetry as mega stimulant. The thing is, I always quickly forget the CTD-2000 is even in my skull. The device itself imposes selective amnesia by burning synapses and neural pathways so as to conceal its presence from me. So what was I saying again, oh yeah.

So after belting out the poem here in the spaceship this morning, I can feel it pumping me up with boss blasts of MATING MAGNETISM. And the title of this poem is "Grab the Chick Whose Tail Is Thick!" Then, when I finish singing, I do what Dr. Terrible has trained me to do out at the Institute, which is to take a quick POWERGASM and think about the STRATEGIC WISDOM of the poem as it applies to me and my current life situation. And as I do this I can feel even more glorious TURBO FIEND juice exploding throughout my haunches and shooting down my tail.

My nostrils flare.

Don't be a wussy. Gotta get a chick whose tail is thick!

Yes sir. I glance at my powerstaff and see my WILL TO POWER rank has spiked to PsychoticTyrant. I've jumped from the paltry rank of Snacklicious and vaulted to the status of AREA DOMINANT FIEND. My scaly green ass is feeling demented and ruthless.

"Bravo, sir! It's a lovely poem," says ATHENOS II. "And a perfect commentary on your particular plight. And I must admit, Runcita is definitely the chick whose tail is thick, no doubt. Did you write the poem yourself, sir?"

"Of course he didn't!" snaps Fribby. "Weak Sauce here couldn't write a poem if it came up and bit him on the tail! That's just more flapdoodle from his despicable grandpa. Dr. Terrible cut open Weak Sauce's head and stuck some device in there. So the poor bastard Weak Sauce just starts singing Dr. Terrible's poetry, like a jukebox."

"I don't know what you're talking about."

And I'll be honest with you, I don't exactly know how to respond to this. Because part of what the robot is saying rings a bell. Dr. Terrible's CTD-2000 is responsible. The device inside my head selects a poem based on my current situation, and then forces me to sing it. The idea being that singing Dr. Terrible's poem will boost my BIO-CON LEVS and help me destroy whatever obstacle stands in my way.

Poetry as a weapon.

Poetry as a way to be more deplorable and hideous.

This is what Dr. Terrible is forever preaching to me out at the Institute. This is what all the dragon professors at WarWings preach. Because you'll often hear about fiendish dragon bastards belting out poems as they conquer a planet. I don't know why it is, but singing a poem out loud will always make you appear more repulsive and psychotic to those who you intend to enslave.

Even though these poems give me temporary blasts of WILL TO POWER, well they still don't help the source of the problem. Fribby calls the boosts of WTP I get from singing Dr. Terrible's poems out loud false power, because the power fades away.

She says I need to learn how to write my own poems, and that's how I'll get some real badass WILL TO POWER.

I just tell her that's easy for her to say, considering her WTP rank is freaking MegaBeast.

But these poems just spontaneously pop into my head and I'll open my black beak and start singing a poem and I won't really know why. And for a while there Fribby would try and stop me whenever I started singing. She'd use her shiny metal tail to punch me and knock me out. But as soon as I regained consciousness I'd just finish singing the poem. And so finally Fribby decided it was best to just let me get it out of my system.

Anyway, so here in the spaceship this Crown Day morning, Fribby points an index claw at the open door and barks: "What are ya waiting for, Weak Sauce? Your Queen awaits!"

I just squat there like a royal moron.

Fribby flaps her chrome-flex wings and looks out the windshield and says, "Seriously, Weak Sauce. You better get a move on. Your Queen is getting away."

I can tell that something is definitely off, but I can't put my claw on exactly what it is. There is something in the robot's voice I can't quite place. And it's not the usual sarcasm, it's something else.

I snort firebolts out my nostrils and say, "Thanks for understanding, Fribby!"

She harrumphs loudly, as if I'm being a jerk.

Then I leap out the spaceship and start jogging toward Runcita.

And just like that, my Queen Quest has officially begun.

Part III

THE
QUEEN
QUEST

7

THE ZAP PAD

I run as fast I can, pushing my way through the crowds of cadets.

I've got my wings extended just slightly to help me stay balanced.

For a dragon, I'm a pretty good sprinter. My MAX RUN SPEED is 79 MPH.

Now some dragon degenerates I know are so slow they couldn't run their way out of a tortoise shell. Their MAX RUN SPEED is maybe 3 MPH. We call them snailheads. 'Course those fools, they usually can fly real fast. Me, I can fly pretty fast too.

Anyway, my hind legs are pounding the ground and because of how fast I'm running my red cape is blowing behind me. And I don't have to look around to know that these other dragon bastards are enviously eyeballing my fiendish cape as it flaps in the wind. We dragons may be high-tech, but some things are timeless. And there's nothing like a cape to turn heads. I choose to ignore the one dragon fool who shouts, "Nice cape, assface!"

Anyway, as I'm running I can see Runcita just up ahead, and I'm closing the gap fast. Runcita is squatting directly on top of the Zap Pad, which is a yellow circle that's about fifteen feet wide out in the middle of the lava pits. When you're teleporting, the Zap Pad glows with a bright yellow light and you can look down and see your green webbed feet all lit up from underneath. Above Runcita hangs the giant glass tube that conducts the particle accelerator energy.

When Dean Floop first had the Zap Pad installed a couple months back, it was a highly controversial move. There was a big article about the teleportation pad controversy posted on WarWings' datastream, *The Digital Fire-Breather.* It said there were concerns about the long-term health effects of teleportation and what it might do to our internal organs over time.

I mean it's true that a lot of weird stuff has happened to us since they installed the Zap Pad. Like according to that post on *The Digital Fire-Breather,* there was one fella who zapped into Central Campus and materialized in front of his locker and his heart exploded right out his scaly chest like a small meat bomb.

Then of course you hear these horror stories about the cadets who've zapped onto campus and materialized at their destination with one of their organs on the outside of their scaly green body.

There's one dragon you see scrouching around the island with his gallbladder in a plastic bag, and the bag has a tube running into his belly.

So yeah, it's definitely a gamble every time you step onto the Zap Pad. But me personally, I'm willing to live with the risks. Because I like the way teleportation feels. Especially that one moment where you can feel yourself whizzing through the air, but you don't technically exist because you're not a solid form in one place or the other.

Anyway, I'm running toward my Queen, and the parking lot abruptly ends.

Without missing a beat, I leap forward into the lava pits and start splashing my way forward. I look up ahead and see Runcita give a little wave to Rexro. This big evil dragon Rexro is the Chief of WarWings Security here on the island.

You want to get into WarWings Central Campus, you got to go through Rexro. And this morning he's squatting inside his Safety Cage, which sits out there in the lava pits about three hundred yards off from the teleportation pad. He's wearing full Conquer Gear, including a bright red helmet with his big black horns sticking out the top of it. The way the system works is, from inside his Safety Cage, Rexro presses the button that teleports us cadets onto Central Campus each morning.

Now squatting up on the Zap Pad, Runcita smiles at Rexro.

"Good morning, Rexro!" she shouts.

Rexro squirts blacksmoke out his nostrils and shouts: "Good morning, Runcita!" Rexro speaks through an intercom, so his voice booms out over the lava pits. But his voice sounds a little crackly, like one of the intercom wires is loose. "You want to go straight to your first-period classroom? Or should I zap you to your locker?"

Then Runcita shouts something back at him and I practically sprain my eardrums trying to catch her answer. But because of how hard I'm running I can't for the life of me make out what she says. Does she want to get zapped to her locker? Or does she want to get zapped to her first-period classroom? I have no freaking idea.

There's the crazed *splash splash splash* of my webbed feet blasting across the lava.

And then Runcita flaps her leathery wings and smiles a beakful of fangs at Rexro.

"OK, Runcita, have a nice day!" shouts Rexro.

There's a monstrous crowd of scaly dragon cadets waiting in line for the Zap Pad.

Well by this point I'm still sprinting through the lava pits but have seriously closed the gap. I am only a hundred yards away from Runcita.

Glance down at my powerstaff to check my RUN SPEED. I've built up a good head of steam. I'm galloping at 42 MPH.

Now to the cadets standing around watching, I know I look like a green blur with a splash of red mixed in from my cape. Whereas for my scaly green ass, I can see every fiend around me with perfect clarity. Like most dragons, the faster I go, the stronger my powers of perception.

I can see Runcita standing right up ahead on the Zap Pad.

She can't see me, though, because I am running at her from the side.

Now obviously I haven't thought this whole thing through.

Because I really don't know what I'll do when I reach Runcita. I mean for the past three days I've rehearsed asking her to be my

Queen in front of the Talking Mirror and I know exactly what I'm going to say, down to the word.

But I hadn't planned on having to intercept her at the teleportation pad out here in the lava pits. I'd planned on cornering her back in the parking lot and offering her my crown out there, long before she ever thought about getting herself zapped into Central Campus.

These are the things I'm thinking about as I run right at her:

Should I tackle her to make sure she doesn't teleport before I can ask her? Or should I rush up and get down on one haunch right there in front of everybody, and hold out my crown and ask her to be my Queen?

Because of how fast I'm running, it's making it real hard to think. My mind is a jumble. And my lungs are heaving so hard it feels like they're going to pop. Now as I run my powerstaff vibrates and so I lift it up and see there's a message from Fribby:

Sorry for being so aggro earlier!
Me and my stupid robot brain. Ha-ha.
Anyway good luck with getting Runcita to be yer queen!
If you need my help, let me know.
I'll be in there soon! Xo

Cool, I think. I never can stand it when Ms. Cyber Scales is sore at me. I mean sure she still can be a royal pain in the ass. There's that, of course. And yes, sometimes when I look up and find her staring at me with those glowing red eyes, well it makes the scales on the back of my long green neck stand up. There's that, too.

But that's not all of it. No sir. Because there's also the way Fribby always saves a seat for me in the Dining Hall at lunch. Even when a while back I was a dumb-ass and started trying to pretend like I didn't know her. This was back when my grandpa Dr. Terrible tried to fill my head with a bunch of DataHater garbage during our weekly WILL TO POWER sessions.

So for about a week there, I took to pretending like I didn't know her. And when I did that, well Fribby just comes over to where I was sitting by myself in the Dining Hall and asks me what the heck I'm doing sitting way over here. Meanwhile some of the DataHaters around us would start snickering, but she didn't pay them any mind. That robot would just keep standing over me, asking me what the heck I was doing. Until finally I would sigh and get up and go back over with her to the empty seat she was saving for me.

Like I said, it was a dumb-ass thing for me to do. And I sure didn't enjoy it, I can tell you that. After a couple days I finally gave up on pretending like I didn't know her, because it hurt me in my big old heart, if you want to know the truth. Of course Dr. Terrible chewed me out for it during our weekly WTP sessions. I think it was the one time when I took a stand against my grandpa like that.

Most days here at school Fribby is the only one who acknowledges that I'm even alive. And is glad that I am too. Alive, that is. Like I told you before, she finds me amusing. I guess what I aim to say here is Ms. Cyber Scales is my best friend. And Dr. Terrible says that's why my BIOCON LEVS are such a wreck, because of how I mostly only fraternize with Datalizards.

My grandpa says call him a DataHater if you want, but if I don't respect myself then none of the other Normals at WarWings will respect me either. Then he reminds me that respect isn't even the half of it. Because what I should really be aiming for is to have my fellow cadets *fear me.*

But after today, that won't matter anymore.

On account of everything will be different then.

Me and my Queen Runcita will be laying plans for invading a planet together. Soon I'll be out in space on my Fertility Mission, and me and Runcita will be "bumping scales," so she can lay my eggs.

I'm running so fast right now you'd think I was going to leap headfirst into another dimension.

Runcita will be wearing my crown in a jiffy.

My cape is snapping and popping behind me, and my powerstaff shows my current RUN SPEED ramping to 53 MPH.

Will my plan to get Runcita to be my Queen work? I sure hope so.

When I practiced with the Talking Mirror it always said, "Yes sir, I will be your Queen." But then again the Talking Mirror is part of my spaceship and so really, what else is the Talking Mirror going to say? Because I mean it's not like Runcita is ever in a million years going to call me "sir." So in terms of verisimilitude, I'll be the first to admit these practice runs with the Talking Mirror haven't done a ton to boost my confidence.

Anyway, this morning there will be no helpful mirror. This morning there's going to be a real dragonette and her name is Runcita.

Because Crown Day is the ultimate test of our WILL TO POWER. Plus our STRATEGIC DESTRUCTION CAPABILITY. Plus our MATING MAGNETISM. And even more importantly, it's a showcase for our CONQUER & RULE FACULTIES. The true display of what we are as dragons: how fiendish we are, how hideous we are, and ultimately how prepared we are to be Planet Conquerors.

Because for us senior cadets, Crown Day represents the culmination of all our academic work at WarWings over the last four years. It's the final task of our demented training and education, the crucible that defines you.

EggHarvest cuts to the core of who we are as a species.

Three hundred thousand years ago, this is exactly how we dragons settled here. A young dragon fella and a young dragon chick known as the Original Couple landed their spaceship on Blegwethia.

At that time, human beings were the dominant species on Blegwethia. And all the man-creatures went around naked. And according to our WarWings history texts, it was a heinous sight to behold.

So the Original Couple climbed out of their spaceship and went to war with the man-creatures. And the dragons won.

And those two dragons rounded up the surviving humans and made them their slaves. And the first thing the Original Couple did was force the man-creatures to put on some clothes. Then, after conquering the humans on Blegwethia, the dragon chick hatched a clutch of eggs and raised a Colony of dragons.

Not long after, the man-creatures went extinct.

Then this Original Couple, well they started a school and named it WarWings. They wanted to ensure that the EggHarvest tradition would continue forever and that dragons would always have a place to grow and develop their WTP. So that dragons of the future would be able to take the Original Couple's fundamental lesson of Conquer and Reproduce and apply it to the universe.

Though according to some eminent dragon historians, two man-creatures escaped from Blegwethia in a stolen spaceship. A female and a male. These historians claim the two human beings eventually landed on the planet called Earth.

Now fast-forward three hundred thousand years, and we seniors at WarWings are still proudly replicating the ritual of that Original Couple who landed on Blegwethia.

And as far as the humans go, every once in a while some dragon here on Blegwethia will dig up some old fossilized man-creature bones and it'll make the news. I remember earlier this year when a human skull made the news because it fetched two hundred pounds of gold on the black market.

Recently there've been rumors around WarWings that some of the dragon professors in the Creative Evolution Lab have discovered a way to clone humans. Supposedly they're using DNA found in the stomachs of ancient Snow Dragons buried deep in their arctic ice tombs.

Honestly I don't think any of us dragons cares one way or the other about the prospect of bringing the man-creature species back. I mean, considering how easily they'd let themselves go extinct, it's kind of tough for younger dragons to get jazzed about human beings. Though I hear they might make good pets.

Cadets here at WarWings are still utilizing the Original Couple's fundamental lesson of Conquer and Reproduce. And we call that ritual EggHarvest. And if I don't get an official Queen by sundown today then my rights as a dragon will be revoked. I'll be demoted to slave status.

So if I don't get luscious Runcita Floop to agree to be my Queen, then I'll have to spend the rest of my days working as a slave on some lame Colony Planet in one of the Outer Galaxies. Ugh.

Anyway, my green webbed feet are flying right now. I'm flashing across the lava pits.

My powerstaff shows my current RUN SPEED ramping up to 63 MPH.

Runcita is right here in front of me, standing on the teleportation pad.

Now I guess at this moment Rexro must be pressing the button there inside his Safety Cage. Because instantly the bright yellow light starts glowing under Runcita's green webbed feet.

And right there in front of me, Runcita's image starts to get wavy.

Because the machine is whipping up her subatomic particles.

And then there's a crackle of lightning in the giant glass tube overhead and *poof*—Runcita is gone.

8

THE HEART IS
THE HIGHEST LAW THERE IS

By this point I couldn't stop running if I wanted to.

If I've got a weak spot in my running game, it's my inability to brake.

Because in my life I've run into more walls than I care to count. Fribby likes to say that I don't so much stop at a destination as impale myself upon it.

And it's not just my running either, the same thing goes for my flying. When it comes to my flying, don't even get me started. Once I came flying out of the sky at 200+ MPH and hit the ground and plowed a good forty feet straight down into the ground before finally coming to a stop. And then spent the next couple days scooping dirt out of my snout with a shovel.

I glance at my powerstaff. My RUN SPEED showing 71 MPH. It feels like I'm running even faster than that.

A big dragon bastard named Velch who'd been next in line has already stepped up onto the teleportation pad. I don't know this fiend very well and frankly I don't want to. But I do know this bastard has WILL TO POWER coming out the wazoo. I mean I don't know what his exact WTP rank is, but it has to be well over SkullCrusher.

I also know Velch plays on the WarWings varsity Slave-Catching team. And I remember how a couple weeks ago in the locker room he used his powerful talons to hold my scaly head underwater in the toilet while he flushed it to see if he could give me "swirly horns."

But I know for a fact that Velch doesn't even remember doing it to me. Because to a mega Jock like Velch, I'm just one more piece of ThrashBait to be trampled on and then forgotten.

Now whenever I pass Velch in the Central Campus corridor you can see in his yellow reptilian eyes a vague flicker of recognition, as if he's trying to place me. But in the end he can't and he doesn't really care anyway and then he just keeps on walking. And I don't know which part is worse: the fact that he forcefully held my scaly head underwater in the toilet and gave me swirly horns, or the fact that afterward I wasn't even worth remembering.

"First-period classroom!" shouts Velch.

This time I don't even bother to try and hit the brakes. I come charging up onto the teleportation pad like a runaway train and nail Velch from behind.

Ker-pow!

For a split second, it feels like I broke my wingjoint. When you drop a plate and it hits the floor and shatters, that's what my wing-joint feels like.

But I shouldn't be complaining. Because between me and Velch, he definitely gets the worst of it.

When my wingjoint hits Velch's back, I instantly feel the air go right out of him, and he gasps, "Ooooompf!"

And then he goes soaring up into the air.

I know what you're thinking, and trust me I agree this isn't the nicest thing for me to have done. Rear-ending this Jock Velch like that. And I can tell you that definitely isn't my style on a normal day.

Which of course my grandpa Dr. Terrible would tell you is part of my problem. That I am not ruthless enough. That in terms of my family heritage I'm a complete failure, because I have serious WTP deficiencies. Because my horns are way too small. Because my heart is grotesquely large and sensitive. And because of my problem with fainting.

I mean I'm sure if it were up to Dr. Terrible I would spend every single day smashing dragon fools from behind, one right after another. Until there was no one left standing but me. Especially certain degenerate scoundrels who held my scaly head underwater in the toilet.

But this morning I am seriously desperate because I have to find Runcita before some other knucklehead gets to her and offers her his crown and then asks her to be his Queen for EggHarvest. So all I can say in my defense is that when I ram this fella Velch from behind, I am listening to my black heart.

My jumbo-sized heart is guiding my scaly ass through the madness.

And of course there's no arguing with the heart, because the heart is the highest law there is. No matter if that heart is twisted and tiny and evil, or if the heart is hideously deformed and huge and sensitive.

Now after I crack into this big nasty Velch, he goes flying off the teleportation pad and zooms a good thirty yards through the air. But it's not like he's got his wings spread or anything. Because if you want to know the truth, this fool is dead weight in the air. Even his tail is limp.

Although at some point Velch must get part of his wind back, because as he's soaring through the air he shouts, "Nooooo!"

And then *clank!*

Velch hits his monsterish green head against Rexro's Safety Cage and crumples up in the lava pits and rolls over on his back like an insect with his hind legs up in the air, groaning, "Oooohhhh!"

The other cadets here in the lava pits who've been standing in line for the Telo-Device explode with laughter. So all of a sudden I find myself squatting alone up here on the Zap Pad and my scaly green ass probably looks pretty pathetic. Because it's not like I'm in great physical shape or anything.

When it comes to my physical conditioning, well that's where my nickname came from. It's another gift from that scoundrel Dr. Terrible, the gift that keeps on giving. Out at the Institute, my grandpa is always harping on me about how he'll stop calling me Weak Sauce when I grow a pair and get some WILL TO POWER.

And by grow a pair, he means a pair of horns.

Well now I glare at this tyrant Rexro in his Safety Cage and shout, "Runcita! Where'd you just zap her to?! Was it her locker? Or her first-period classroom?"

"You know I can't give out that kind of information! It's against regulations!"

"You better press that button and zap me in next to Runcita right this second!"

"Forget it!" he booms, his voice crackling over the intercom. "I ain't going to lose my job for no two-bit peckerhead like you!" Then he studies me out here on the teleportation pad as if he is really just seeing me for the very first time, and now he's taking the full measure of my essence. And then he snorts, "Especially with them little itty-bitty nubs you got stickin' out your scaly-ass head!"

At the mention of my piddly horns, all the cadets behind me hoot and roar with laughter. Then they start chanting, "Weak Sauce! Weak Sauce! Weak Sauce!"

Now my black horns start tingling like crazy, which can only mean one thing: imminent danger. Because your horns are way smarter than your brain. Because your horns can see what your eyes can't. Well things definitely aren't looking so hot for me at the moment. And suddenly I'm starting to feel a little doubtful about my whole campaign to try and get Runcita to be my Queen.

Maybe I *am* Weak Sauce.

I've already used a ton of WTP and all it's got me is a bunch of public insults from Rexro and the laughter and jeers of my fellow cadets gathered behind me. I feel the old weakness and doubt settle into my bones.

And so I think to myself:

Maybe I just need to lower my standards.

There's that one senior chick everybody calls Peekaboo who aside from the fact that she's got three eyes actually has a pretty hot bod. Now the reason the other dragons call this chick Peekaboo is because she wears this golden tiara which drapes down and covers her extra eyeball in the middle of her scaly green head. But aside from that third eye, in the plus department I know she's got a WTP score somewheres around ScalesOfMenace, which is pretty darn respectable. Especially considering my measly Snacklicious.

And I've seen Peekaboo glancing at me plenty of times in class. And when I catch her looking at me then she'll smile and I'll smile back at her while trying hard to forget that she has a third eyeball tucked away behind that low-hanging tiara. So if Peekaboo were my Queen and we landed on a foreign planet in order to start a Colony, well the natives would never know her nickname was Peekaboo. And we could just give her a new name.

And yes of course I'd be worried that when our little dragon chicks hatch they might come out of their eggs with three eyes. But you know the truth is that no matter how careful you are in life there's always going to be some element of risk, thank you very much.

So all this stuff is flashing through my scaly green dome while I squat here on the Zap Pad. And meanwhile this deranged bastard Rexro is just glaring at me from his cage. Now as these loser thoughts balloon inside my skull and I come to terms with yet another personal failure, I can feel my giant heart fill with resignation.

I should just step down off this teleportation pad and admit defeat.

But at this moment my thoughts are interrupted by Rexro as he roars at me over the loudspeaker: "Hey you out there with them retarded-looking horns! You better get your scales off my teleportation pad pronto or I'm gonna come out there and rip your tail off and whip you with your own tail right in front of your fellow cadets! And if you think I'm joking or I won't actually rip your tail off and beat you with it, well then go on and test me! Cuz I reckon you'll find my cruelty has no limits!"

Now when Rexro shouts at me about how he's going to come out here and rip off my tail and whip me with it, well my scaly green ass doesn't appreciate being spoken to like that. And it kind of pisses me off. But at the same time I'm already feeling resigned to stepping off the teleportation pad and becoming a slave.

So while I'm suddenly incensed by Rexro's whole ripping-off-my-tail vibe this morning, I'm also feeling resigned to my crappy fate. I reckon my black heart is torn.

Rexro is glaring at me from inside his cage.

"Didja hear me, knucklehead?" he shouts. "If you don't get your tail off my Zap Pad right this instant I'm fixing to come out there and rip your tail right off and whip you with it!"

Then suddenly my webbed feet muscles clench and my toe claws shoot out. And Dr. Terrible says when my toe claws shoot out like this it's my body's way of telling me that I should attack the source of my agitation and destroy it.

So I puff up my scaly chest and arch my tail in a Threat Display and the tip of my tail starts twitching around like a scorpion's tail. I snort firebolts out of my nostrils and flap my leathery wings to enhance my menacing appearance.

Then I point my long curved index claw at Rexro and bellow: "If you don't zap my scaly ass in next to Runcita right now you'll need to worry about losing a lot more than your job! Cuz I'll come over there and rip your forelimbs off! And if you don't have any forelimbs, then how are you going to eat your dinner?! By the time I'm done with you, you're going to have to pay someone to pick your snout! So hurry up and zap me in next to Runcita, you sonuvabitch!"

Now I don't mean to pat myself on the back here but when I finish shouting those mega threats like that, well I know in my heart I've just slapped one whopper of a scare on that big ol' nasty Rexro. And I know right about then that Rexro's giant black horns are tingling like crazy, warning him that he's in serious danger. Because that caped fiend out on the Zap Pad is definitely not to be trifled with.

I know he's shaking and quaking and falling all over himself as he tries to push the button for the Telo-Device. Because I figure Rexro doesn't have any interest in going through life without forelimbs, and I think I made a pretty darn convincing case for why the fool wouldn't want to start off down that path.

But when I stop shouting and peer over at Rexro in his cage, he just chuckles and lifts his talon and gives me the middle claw.

And when that bastard gives me the middle claw like that, the other cadets behind me start roaring with laughter. "Ha! Ha! Ha!"

Then I'm seeing lava and I know my eyes in their sockets are blooming a fiery red. I feel a mega rage building up inside of me to the point where I go into volcano mode, and I can even feel the lava gushing in my skull and it feels like any second the lava is going to explode out the top of my scaly green head.

Oh you're gonna whip me with my own tail are you, you sonuvabitch?!

And now I open my black beak and roar a seriously boss roar and a dozen or so bats come tumbling down from the sky and land all around in the lava pits. Because the sonic boom of my roar has knocked them unconscious in midflight. And a tongue belonging to one of the cadets behind me shoots out twenty feet to my left and snatches up one of the bats on the ground and then retracts. And I don't turn to see who the tongue belongs to but I hear the familiar "*Gulp.* Mmmm."

Then I open my beak and blast a mega firestream at Rexro's cage. It explodes out of my beak and I shoot it a good thirty yards and aim it directly at Rexro's stupid scaly green face. And speaking just from a visual standpoint here, the firestream I blast at Rexro is a real beaut. Because the cherry-colored flame looks super menacing there in the morning air. It is straight nightmare.

Then my firestream blasts into the cage.

Now Rexro only just manages to dive down out of the way right as the tip of my firestream hits the spot where his monsterish scaly face was a split second before.

But I don't stop there.

Because by this point it's clear that I can show no mercy.

So then I clench my talons like some sort of tortured beast and I roar a roar so deafening and sharp that I swear you can feel the sun up in the sky shudder and go dark for a millisecond before coming back on. And then I call forth the roiling lava from my belly and blast another deadly firestream out my black beak. And this time I keep shooting it for a full twenty seconds straight until I hear a bunch of popping noises and Rexro's cage goes up in a *whoosh* of flame.

Now there are gigantic waves of blacksmoke pouring out of the burning cage. And I can feel the heat from those flames climbing into the sky all the way over here on the teleportation pad.

And when I finish blasting Rexro's Safety Cage with that firestream it's so quiet out here in the lava pits you could hear an ant cough. Because all the cadets behind me are just squatting there hushed with their toe claws retracted.

One thing is for sure, nobody's laughing at me now.

That's one of the Four Basic Power Principles from the *WarWings Cadet Planet Conqueror's Handbook*:

If the natives fight back,
then give their skulls a crack!
Because violence
brings silence!

And I'm thinking:

Wow, you really got Rexro's attention! I mean look at the way Rexro's glaring at you right now as he struggles to escape from that burning cage. It's like he's really seeing you for the first time!

Which is true. I can see Rexro whirling around in his fiery cage. Then for a moment there he just stops and stares at me with murder in his eye until a gigantic wall of flames comes and washes over him. And as I stand there on the Zap Pad and stare at the fiery cage with all that blacksmoke pouring out of it, well I can feel how the momentum of this situation has definitely begun to turn in my favor.

Yes sir.

But unfortunately there is one very key piece of information I've failed to take into consideration during the proceedings so far. Which is the fact that Rexro is a renowned maniac of the nightmare variety.

Because before taking over as Chief of Security at WarWings, Rexro served as a mercenary for Wastuka the Hundred-Headed Warlord during his famous bloody intergalactic conquering campaign in the 249th dimension. Now if you're sitting there wondering what the heck am I jabbering on about with this whole 249th dimension bullshaka, because everyone knows there's no such thing as the 249th dimension, well that's my whole *point*. Those sick fools didn't just conquer the 249th, they *destroyed* it.

Suddenly I hear an insanely loud roar explode from within that fiery cage. And this roar is so powerful that it instantly sends flame-tongues and blacksmoke geysers and sparks exploding straight up into the sky. And then in a flash I realize what this scaly bastard Rexro has just done, which is really kind of ingenious when you think about it. Because he's used the mega force of his roar to blast the flaming roof right off the cage so that now he has an avenue of escape.

And then with another mighty roar, Rexro the dragon pops out of the top of the fiery cage like a champagne cork. It's really something to see, the way he leaps up out of those flames so that he's now maybe forty feet high in the air.

But here's the part that really gets my attention.

After this demented dragon is clear of the fiery cage and up there in midair he unfurls his huge leathery wings and he flaps them twice—*thwack-thwack*—and with that he is suddenly flying toward me at what seems like supersonic speed.

9

HERE COMES REXRO

I have no idea why I don't just fly out of here while I have the chance.

It would be so simple to unfurl my wings and soar off into the sky. I mean considering the circumstances, you'd figure this was a no-brainer. Of course part of it is my desire to get to Runcita ASAP and offer her my crown. And teleportation definitely offers the quickest and most direct route to my luscious Queen-to-Be.

But as I stand there I'm thinking:

Get out while you're ahead!

I raise the silver canister and quickly spritz my horns with Grow-Grow® gel. And then without really knowing why I'm doing it, I squirt flamestreams out my nostrils and start singing a WILL TO POWER poem:

> *"Hey Weak Sauce, when it looks*
> *like an older dragon*
> *is going to rip your scaly green head off*
> *well don't just squat there like an idiot*
> *and cough!*
> *Flap your wings*
> *and take to the air*
> *and don't waste no time*
> *getting the heck outta there!*
> *Because sometimes it's best*

to live to blast fire another day
so with your absence   -
is how you make your enemy pay!
OK?"

As soon as I finish singing, I remember.
The CTD-2000.
The Cranial Telecaster Device strikes again. And when I finish belting out Dr. Terrible's poem there on the Zap Pad, I feel the effects surging through my central nervous system and jacking me up with WTP. The title of this poem is "Just Because You Flee, That Doesn't Make You a Flea."
My nostrils flare.
Live to blast fire another day. Roger that.
Meanwhile I've forgotten where that poem comes from, but there's a mild tingling sensation which I know is from my neural pathways being cauterized.
Then I look at Rexro up there in the air and immediately start coughing like crazy. Because here's one thing I know for sure about myself this morning as Rexro is hurtling right at me in full night mare mode:
Oh dear God my big fragile heart is in serious danger of quitting on me.
I think I'm going to faint.
But I'm also thinking:
This psycho Rexro won't bother ripping off your tail like he threatened earlier! Because he's going to rip off your head! And your head won't ever grow back!
Now as if to confirm that I'm right, I quickly glance behind me and sure enough all the fiendish cadets gathered around have their powerstaffs out and they are pointing them at my scaly green ass because they're capturing everything that's happening on their holovid recorders. Soon I'll be headless and my legacy for all time will be a short violent holovid clip that these dragons send to their pals for a quick laugh.

I whirl back around and see that Rexro with his wings spread wide is now only maybe twenty yards away from me. His eyes are blazing red. But as I squat out here on the teleportation pad and watch Rexro cut down the distance that separates us at speeds I personally can't even fathom, I hear someone shout my name.

"Gork!"

At first I think I'm imagining it, but then I hear someone shout my name again.

"Gork! Up here! Gork! Gork!"

I look up and I can't believe what I'm seeing.

It is Fribby.

That silver robot is soaring about thirty yards above the flaming Safety Cage and she has her chrome-flex wings spread wide and framed against the morning sky. She looks nothing short of glorious.

Fribby shouts, "Gork, get ready!" Now she drops her silver scaly head and wings and aims right for the burning Safety Cage, swooping down at it like she's in full kamikaze mode. She shouts, "I'm going in! Hold tight!"

For a brief second I catch a glimpse of the robot diving straight down into the blazing cage.

But unfortunately at this same moment out of the corner of my eye I see a green blur flashing toward me and it's that tyrant Rexro. And as he flies right at me I feel like I can almost reach out and touch him and I hear him growling and I can see his fangs sparkling and I see his deranged red eyes blooming in their sockets like blood flowers.

And even though I know it's hopeless I prepare to meet Rexro's onslaught with my own attack. And so I instantly unfurl my leathery wings and raise my scaly green tail in a Threat Display and bare my fangs and growl a beakful of flames and snort blacksmoke out my nostrils so as to strike the most scarifying pose possible.

But of course it doesn't matter. Because in another instant I'll be nothing but a bloodstain in the lava pits.

And over Rexro's scaly green shoulder I can just see the flaming cage and then his wing swoops down on me and cuts off my view. If only the robot had been a few seconds earlier, then maybe she could've saved me from getting killed.

And as I feel Rexro's fiery breath on my long neck, I think to myself:

Thanks for trying, Fribby. I know your intentions were so pure and true. I hope you will not soon forget me!

It seems that you were right after all in your whole obsession with death. I really should've thought more about it! You were right, Fribby! You were right all along!

Then at this very moment my thoughts are interrupted by a bright yellow light exploding up under my webbed feet.

10

POOF

Poof.

I materialize crouched on my haunches here in WarWings' Main Building, right in front of Runcita's locker.

Fribby made it to the button after all. And the button must've still been set to Runcita's coordinates. I look around at my new surroundings here inside WarWings' Central Campus, not quite believing it.

I grin a beakful of fangs, thinking about how close I came to getting my candle snuffed out just now by that depraved bastard Rexro. I sure wish I could see the look on his monsterish scaly green face as he flies through the empty space where I was just a second ago on the teleportation pad. I bet all those other cadets hanging around out there in the lava pits are snorting and hooting and howling at him right now as he picks himself up off the ground.

And for a second I worry that Rexro will turn around and go after Fribby. But then I realize the robot will have a thirty-yard head start on him. Plus he'll be all pooped and tuckered out from the energy he's just expended trying to murder me.

And heck, that robot is so ornery I'm sure she could put up a good fight even if they were on equal footing.

But now that he'll be all tired and confused, Rexro won't be a match for Ms. Cyber Scales. Fribby will be fine. Fribby will be more than fine.

Fribby will prevail.

But just in case, I whip out my powerstaff and send a message to Fribby:

Thanks chick!!!!!!!!! I owe you big-time!!!!
That was badass!
I'm in front of Runcita's locker right now!
She was just here, so I'll track her down soon.
Are you doing OK?!

And then I think:
Maybe I've got the makings of a Terrible after all.
And maybe I can still get Runcita to be my Queen for EggHarvest!
Suddenly there's a white-hot flash in my brain. Then, without really knowing why I'm doing it, I squirt blacksmoke out my nostrils and start singing a WILL TO POWER poem:

"The secret of life is
when in doubt,
be terrible!
Because true happiness
can only come to you
by making someone else's life
unbearable!"

And when I finish belting out the poem here in the corridor, I feel the poem surging through my central nervous system and giving me a major boost of MATING MAGNETISM. The title of this poem is "The Secret of Life Is Strife."
My nostrils flare.
The secret of life is strife.
I feel my heart smile a little.
I snort firebolts of joy out my nostrils.
Who knew that being ferocious could get you so far? And I can't wait to tell Dr. Terrible about my progress, but then I recall we aren't

on speaking terms anymore and this makes me feel pretty downhearted. But not so downhearted that I can't still be happy about my progress.

Plus I don't have time to think about this stuff anyway, because I have to find Runcita pronto.

I'm on my Queen Quest.

I glance around to get my bearings.

Where is my Queen?

Now the corridor is jammed with cadets getting ready for their first-period classes. Above me the airspace is choked with flying dragons.

Down here on the ground, fools and chicks are hooting at each other and laughing. And the sounds of deranged dragons slamming their lockers shut ring out in the corridor like rifle shots.

I wave my scaly snout and take a couple sniffs around Runcita's locker and I get a fresh juicy whiff of her. I can tell she's just been here. Maybe even as recently as just a few seconds ago. And I don't mean to sound perverted here, but this blast of Runcita's essence shooting up my nasal passages feels like a sweet kick to the brain.

Then I swivel my scaly head around and:

There she is!

Runcita!

My God, she is looking even more scaly and gorgeous than when I saw her out in the lava pits. And it takes everything I have not to faint at the sight of her. Run-ci-ta: the tip of the tongue taking a trip of three taps down the palate to tap, at three, on the fangs. Run. Ci. Ta. She's right there, maybe twenty feet down the hall. I can't believe it.

She's just squatting there jabbering to some crusty older dragon fool. But I take a closer look and realize it's not just some older crusty dragon fool she's talking to. It's her dad. Dean Floop.

Dean Floop!

Holy crap!

And the demented and dangerous Dean Floop is jabbering on to his daughter Runcita, waving his talons around, and his tail is whisking back and forth. The Dean is wearing the eye patch over his left eye, from where Dr. Terrible blinded him last night out on the campus quad during the RageFest.

Holy crap.

All the other cadets are keeping a wide berth from Dean Floop as he stands there whipping his spiked tail around in the corridor and talking to Runcita.

Now I can't be certain, but it sure as heck looks like Runcita doesn't care much for her dad. I mean the vibe she's throwing him right now is *Hurry and wrap this up and get out of my scaly green face.* You figure Runcita knows what a treacherous scoundrel her dad is.

So I just hang back, watching the two of them jabbering back and forth. I mean it sure looks like Dean Floop is trying to convince her of something. Like he's aiming to get her to do something she doesn't want to do.

Because the Dean keeps flapping his leathery wings and waving his talons while his daughter stares down at his giant webbed feet and just keeps shaking her head no.

So I figure whatever they're talking about has got something to do with the fact that it's Crown Day. But I don't have a clue as to how. I mean you never see Dean Floop out in the halls like this. And I know it can't be a coincidence, the fact that it's Crown Day and suddenly here's Dean Floop walking out in front of the other dragons.

I mean usually all Dean Floop does is stay in his lair on campus and have WarWings cadets sent to him, to terrorize them. Or, in some cases, eat them.

So I figure that I'll just have to wait for the two of them to finish jabbering. Because I'm sure as heck not about to go up to Runcita with the Dean standing there. I'll just have to wait for them to finish and for Dean Floop to turn and fly off.

Then I'll go up to my darling Runcita and offer her my crown and ask her to be my Queen for EggHarvest.

But as I'm thinking this, suddenly Dean Floop turns and points a murderous-looking index claw right at my scaly ass while he speaks to Runcita. And she follows his claw with her gaze and for a second her green eyes light on me and my toe claws shudder. And I instantly duck down behind a group of cadets out of sight.

Holy crap! Was Dean Floop pointing at me? Did Runcita just glance over at me?

11

HOW DR. TERRIBLE REVEALED HIS FIENDISH EVOLUTION MACHINE AT THE TELEVISED PRESS CONFERENCE EARLIER THIS WEEK

Let me quickly tell you why Dean Floop hates my grandpa Dr. Terrible so much. And why Dean Floop would love nothing more than to dance on my grandpa's scaly green carcass.

Dr. Terrible burst onto the public's radar Tuesday morning when he appeared on TV. My grandpa just stood there behind the podium and you could hear the flashes as the dragon journalists in the audience snapped holovid pics with their powerstaffs. He was decked out in his finest WarWings cloak and robe and his trademark red cape. He had his tail arched over his scaly green head and his leathery wings were relaxed and spread out wide in such a way as to suggest this was indeed a momentous occasion.

"Good morning!" purred my grandpa, snorting firestreams out his nostrils. "My name is Dr. Terrible. I run the Institute of Advanced Biokinetics and Neuroanatomy here at WarWings. And the reason you have been invited here today is to witness firsthand my newest scientific invention. It's called the Evolution Machine. You can call it the Evo-Mach 3000." My grandpa pointed an index claw at the big screen hanging on the wall behind him. "That lion and that worm were my first test subjects on the Evo-Mach 3000. In this image, as you can see, those two critters are having their minds swapped."

Now up on the screen there appeared the deranged Evo-Mach 3000. The Evolution Machine was a giant upright stasis tank that comprised two fused pods, and each pod was filled with thick clear goo, and inside one pod was a lion and in the other pod was a tiny worm. Each pod had a series of tubes running out of it, which met in a small silver pyramid hovering above the pods. The pyramid was pulsing with light, as if the fiendish machine were breathing.

"Now," said Dr. Terrible, as he looked out at all the dragon journalists in the audience, "I created the Evo-Mach 3000 so that our species can utilize the mind-swap, for the purposes of stealth warfare. Because now with my new Evo-Mach 3000, dragons will be able to hide in plain sight, blend into the native population on any planet we have come to conquer."

This famous dragon journalist in the front row, Bozz, stood up and snorted flamestreams out his nostrils. "What exactly do you mean by *hide in plain sight*?" he snarled. "And why have I been brought here this morning to look at images of a stupid worm?! I don't appreciate having my time wasted! Hurry up and get to the point!"

There was a chorus of growls and delirious hisses of agreement among the dragon journalists, who now had their tails raised in the air and were glaring at Dr. Terrible. The vibe in the room was definitely fiendish, and you should know that dragon journalists on Blegwethia are notoriously ruthless.

Because on my home planet Blegwethia if a journalist shows up to report a story and they don't like the situation they're seeing, they're not afraid to wade right in and get their claws and beak bloody. That's dragon journalism for you.

"Are there any among you here today that are tired of playing the role of the *big green scary monster*?" said Dr. Terrible. "Are there any among you who while conquering a planet have thought to yourself, *There has got to be an easier way?* Must we always play the role of the *barbarian*, watching the natives flee in terror before our firestreams? Now don't get me wrong, I love seeing a native flee in terror as much as the next dragon. But what I am driving at here is what if you had a *choice*? That's right. I said *choice*."

"Do I have a choice to sit here and listen to this twaddle?" snorted one of the fool dragons sitting in the front row. "Because if so, I choose to leave!"

The entire audience erupted with deranged snorts and hoots of laughter.

Dr. Terrible ignored the disruption, waited a second for them to quiet down, and then proceeded. "Well I say *no*, we do not always have to be *the monster*! Not with my new Evolution Machine, we don't! Imagine if you could mind-swap with the native species of a planet, such as a butterfly? A butterfly who could shoot fire out its mouth and fly at speeds of up to three hundred miles per hour? A butterfly fully capable of conquering and enslaving an entire planet? A butterfly with a taste for gold and the ability to write epic poetry? We are talking the ultimate in camouflage here. Because if you're disguised as a butterfly, your future slaves would never even see you coming!

"Well enough with the hypotheticals! Let's look at actual results! So for my first procedure earlier this morning, I used my Evolution Machine to perform a mind-swap. As you can see in the image on the screen, I swapped a worm into a lion's body, and the lion into the worm's body. My new Evolution Machine performed brilliantly. So now what you are about to see is the worm, post-procedure. A worm that can now wriggle at speeds up to sixty miles per hour! A worm whose array of instincts and abilities has been radically altered because of my Evo-Mach 3000!"

Then on the TV screen they cut to a vid clip of the newly "swapped" worm, and in this vid clip you could see this little worm chasing a gazelle as the gazelle bounded at top speed through the jungle.

The little demented worm raced along behind the bounding gazelle, nipping at its hoofs.

And when the gazelle briefly stumbled, the worm roared and leapt up onto the gazelle's neck.

The terrified gazelle with bulging eyes exploded out of there with the worm clinging to it. And then that worm bit the gazelle's neck and wrenched it down to the ground for the kill.

Dr. Terrible proceeded to show a few more short vid clips of the worm, and one of the clips showed the worm running straight up a tree. Another clip showed the worm roaring so loud that the ground shook.

Then my grandpa looked out at the audience and began wryly flapping his wings, as if to cool off the stunned journalists who sat there quietly with their toe claws retracted.

"Now I would like to show you the lion!" purred Dr. Terrible, as he squirted firebolts out his nostrils. "This lion who now has the worm's mind. Here is a vid clip that was shot earlier today in my Institute's BioGarden!"

And lo, this giant deranged lion came twisting up out of the soil like some sort of bionic worm and leapt in the air and then dove back deep down into the soil. Apparently my grandpa had strapped a vidcam to the lion's forehead, because now on the TV you could see the lion's point of view as it rocketed underground and powered through the soil. Then they cut to another camera, and as the lion tunneled through the soil you could see the top of the lion's mane slicing along the dirt's surface like a shark's fin in the ocean.

Then Dr. Terrible surprised all the journalists at the press conference when he opened a hole in the floor and suddenly the lion appeared standing there next to him.

The journalists in the audience growled and fiendishly gnashed their fangs at the sight of the psychotic lion standing there glaring back at them.

Then Dr. Terrible unfurled his leathery wings and bellowed: "And now for my final demonstration! So nobody can doubt the genius of my Evolution Machine! Let all my colleagues bow down to the greatest mind WarWings has ever seen!"

Dr. Terrible used both of his talons to pick the lion up and hoist the beast over his scaly green head and he held the lion like that as if he were in a weight-lifting competition and he was striking a pose for the judges. And then Dr. Terrible suddenly wrenched his talons in opposite directions and ripped the lion in half like a sheet of paper.

Now Dr. Terrible casually tossed the two halves on the ground and then the two halves regenerated their missing parts so now there were two smaller lions standing there.

Both lions roared.

The delirious audience leapt to their webbed feet and started clicking their talons together in applause and flapping their wings and thumping their tails against the floor. So that press conference happened on Tuesday morning, which was three days before Crown Day. And after that Tuesday morning press conference in which my grandpa Dr. Terrible revealed his new Evolution Machine and its ability to perform the mind-swap, all hell broke loose here on WarWings' campus.

And the next couple days turned into a demented nightmare. Which culminated in what we dragon cadets were right away calling the Doctor vs. Dean RageFest last night. Basically, when Dr. Terrible and Dean Floop clashed horns out on the campus quad. I'll get to the RageFest later. And when the RageFest was over and the smoke had cleared, my grandpa disappeared.

Dr. Terrible had up and vanished, and nobody knew where he was.

The next morning was Crown Day, which is today. And this morning there's even a big article about the Doctor vs. Dean Rage-Fest posted up on our school's datastream, *The Digital Fire-Breather*:

DISTINGUISHED RESEARCH PROFESSOR
DR. TERRIBLE DISAPPEARS WITHOUT A TRACE
SOME SUSPECT FOUL PLAY

It is Crown Day, the most important day of a dragon's four years at WarWings. And this morning none of the senior cadets are wasting any time wondering what happened to Dr. Terrible because they're too busy worrying about making sure they find a mating partner for EggHarvest.

And on the morning following what everyone is already calling the Doctor vs. Dean RageFest, it's actually Dean Floop's luscious daughter whom I'm scheming to score as my Queen.

Runcita Floop.

And that's what I started off telling you about before I took a detour to get you up to speed on all this fiendish Dr. Terrible stuff.

I started off telling you what happens this morning in the Central Campus corridor when Dean Floop suddenly points at me and then his daughter turns and looks at me and so I quickly duck down out of sight.

Runcita Floop.

12

MY SCALY GREEN ASS
GETS AMBUSHED

"Yo what's up, *Weak Sauce*?!"

The voice is right behind me and it slices through my brain like a blade.

Then I feel a talon grab my wingjoint, and that same voice growls: "Fancy finding you here, Weak Sauce! Ha-ha! At first I heard somebody singing here in the hallway and I was thinking who's the big singing moron? But then I turned and saw that it was you, Weak Sauce! Your singing led me right to you!"

My nostrils flare and I try to pull away but there's nothing I can do because this talon has my wingjoint clapped firmly in its grip.

Now my webbed feet clench again and my toe claws shoot out so far this time they make a *screech* sound as they cut deep into the floor. And the talon gripping my wingjoint from behind is squeezing even harder, making sure I can't twist free from its grip.

I crouch down low on my haunches and growl. A firestream rises up out of my belly and shoots into my throat and flickers over my tongue and then halts and hovers at the back of my fangs. I'm gargling fire.

And I hiss and spray sparks out my beak.

"Hey Weak Sauce, why so antisocial?"

And:

"Can Weak Sauce come out to play? Ha-ha!"

I'd know that voice anywhere.

So I spin around and sure enough. It's this robot. Trenx.

This Datalizard is grinning at me with this deranged look on his metal beak. When the robot sees the look on my scaly face, he squirts flamestreams out his nostrils and purrs, "Why so edgy on this glorious Crown Day morning? Now you're not going to *faint*, are you?"

This Datalizard Trenx always acts like we're fiendish buds even though we aren't. He reckons that gently mocking my scaly green ass this way is code for how close we really are, as if we're brothers in flame who used to raid and pillage planets together or something.

I'm whipping my tail back and forth, trying to use it as an outlet for the big freak-out that's building up inside me. Because it's super important that right now I don't blow my stack. Too much is on the line. I mean here I am on my Queen Quest and so there's definitely no room for idiot emotions or bogus distractions.

I glance over the robot's wingtip and spot Runcita right across the hallway. And as soon as she finishes flapping her beak with her villainous dad Dean Floop, then I'll go over there and present her with my crown. My Queen Quest will finally be over.

Meanwhile my horns are still tingling, which means they're acting as antennae and picking up on some specific danger right here in front of me. But for my horns to be going bonkers like this seems kind of weird.

Because this Reptilizoid is one of the few cadets in my senior class that I don't have to regard as a savage predator who could eat me. Because the day this robot becomes a legit threat to me is the day that I'll just fold my wings up and call it quits as a dragon.

Still grinning like a lunatic, the robot reaches up and slings his metal talon on my shoulderbone as if he's holding me at forelimb's length so he can get a good look at me.

"Yo you're wigging out, Weak Sauce! You gots to chill!"

I casually reach up and knock his steel talon off my shoulder.

Trenx, aka Mr. Gigabyte.

This robot has a way of popping up wherever I am and always at the exact moment when he's the farthest thing from my mind and the last fiend I want to see. You know the type of fool I'm talking about. Because in the cruel hierarchy that is the WarWings rating system, this Datalizard is a straight-up bottom feeder. I mean a couple weeks back I pulled down this robot's Cadet Profile and his WILL TO POWER rank was a lousy FlameToy.

And so when you think about it, it actually seems like kind of a miracle that Mr. Gigabyte here has managed to survive all four years at WarWings. Because usually robot cadets with a FlameToy get eaten by the DataHaters.

Now as I study Mr. Gigabyte's stupid grinning beak, my black heart flutters in my chest and I feel just a tiny pang of pity for this poor fool. And as a WarWings dragon I'm sure not proud to have to be telling you this, and trust me, I know it's despicable. But the truth is it's just my natural way to try and see the good in a fella. Even when it comes to a low-down loser like Trenx.

Dr. Terrible and I have been over this before, during our weekly WTP sessions. And we've even discussed my relationship with this robot.

My grandpa told me I was a wussy for even talking to Trenx and that my stupid jumbo oversensitive heart is messing up my natural dragon instincts. And Dr. Terrible said the next time this Mech-Freak dared to speak to me in public, well that I should just attack him and eat him right there on the spot. Of course Dr. Terrible doesn't give a crap about this robot one way or the other, but he said it was just the principle of the matter.

Plus Dr. Terrible says weak WILL TO POWER is contagious. And that it sends the wrong message to the Normal dragonettes to even allow them to see me jabbering with a degenerate loser robot like Trenx in public. And that it seriously damages my MATING MAG-NETISM too. And my grandpa says when I try and see the good in a piece of robot trash like Trenx I'm really just hurting myself.

But these are just my natural instincts, so what are you going to do?

Anyway, so my point is the one good thing I've been able to

discover about this robot over the years is he's the only cadet at WarWings with horns that are actually smaller than mine.

He has an inch up there, if he's lucky.

Because if you want to know the truth, this Datalizard's horns are downright microscopic.

So when I stand next to Trenx he always makes my two-inchers look seriously mega.

And because this robot is such a pathetic loser, I always feel a little sorry for him. And so I can't bring myself to completely ignore him or blast him with firestreams like the other dragons from my senior class do. I mean sure, Mr. Gigabyte here tries so damn hard to be cool that it makes your scales crawl. And having this Reptilizoid around definitely isn't going to help you score any dragonettes.

But it just never made sense to me to spit venom on a fella when he's down. Which of course Dr. Terrible says is a big part of my problem. The fact that I'm not such a big fan of spitting venom on a fella when he's down. Because out at the Institute, my grandpa told me that's exactly when you're supposed to spit venom on a robot like Trenx, is when they're down.

And one time recently during our weekly session, Dr. Terrible told me that's why Datalizards like Trenx let themselves get so low in the first place. Because it makes them an easier target in terms of spitting venom on them. And my grandpa said he's not in the habit of doing favors for Mech-Freaks and robot trash and such. But when it comes to spitting venom on a Tin Can like Trenx who's already down, well that's one favor he can't help himself from doing.

Now when Dr. Terrible uses the phrase "spitting venom," he's using it as a euphemism for eating them.

Then Dr. Terrible concluded that particular session by making me promise that the next time this robot Trenx tried to talk to me in public, I would attack him and eat him right there on the spot.

And so because Dr. Terrible had been filling my head with his DataHater garbage, I'd promised. "OK yes," I'd said to Dr. Terrible. I would eat Trenx the next time he tried to talk to me in public.

I could tell my promise made my grandpa happy. And my grandpa had thumped me on one of my wings and said, "Don't do it for me, do it for you." He said, "You've got to connect with your inner Terrible." He told me attacking and eating that Datalizard Trenx would do wonders for my class ranking and my rep.

And I remember I'd said, "What rep?"

And he'd said, "Exactly my point."

So after making that promise to Dr. Terrible during our session, anytime I saw Trenx approaching me I'd just turn and run the other way. But now here the sorry Dragobot is, squatting right in front of me.

"Hey," says Trenx, still grinning at me like a lunatic. "I like your red cape!" He spins around to show me that he too is wearing a red cape.

Great. Now the fool is jacking my signature style.

Maybe it won't be so hard to find motivation to eat this bastard after all.

"Your cape looks just like mine," I growl.

"I know, right? What a coincidence, huh? I guess when we're together our coolness factor gets multiplied by two. Lucky I found you here then!"

For a moment I just study the Datalizard's silver skull. I'm stunned. And now I understand why my horns are tingling like crazy.

Because on top of Trenx's chrome-plated head are two long black shiny horns which curve near the top and finish off with incredibly savage-looking spikes.

I feel like I am literally squatting in the shadow of this robot's horns.

Whereas my horns are so small I couldn't even use them to gore a flea.

This Datalizard's big badass horns make me sick with envy. And the fact that this robot is able to make me feel so jealous is almost more depressing than anything else.

I suddenly feel like I want to take a running leap headfirst down a black hole.

I use my index claw to tap the screen on my powerstaff and see that Trenx's WILL TO POWER has exploded.

He's rocking a MegaBeast.

I point my claw at his silver head and growl, "Yo, who'd you have to murder to get those babies? Are those things prosthetics or *what*?"

He chuckles.

And I can tell by his chuckle that he's been waiting all along for me to notice his new horns.

He laid the trap and now my scaly green ass has walked right into it.

13

THANK YOU FOR LETTING ME LIVE

Now just in case I've failed to grasp the particulars of the situation, I guess Trenx wants to make sure he drives his point home.

Because then without warning the robot leaps up and whips his metal scaly head and rams his horns straight into the wall, burying them up to the hilt. His giant black horns are obviously securely anchored in the wall. Because then he quickly flexes his long neck to hoist the rest of himself up off the ground so that now his chrome-flex body is rigid and sticking out of the wall. As if he's a spear that's just hit its target.

I mean at the base of his neck you can see a small sprocket bulging under his silver scales, but other than that he seems completely relaxed.

Now the robot looks at me with this stupid grin on his beak. "So you tell me, Weak Sauce, could prosthetics do *this*?"

I'm speechless.

Then he flaps his wings twice—*thwack-thwack*—and yanks those horns out of the wall and then drops to his silver webbed feet and stands there leering at me.

"That, Weak Sauce," growls the Datalizard as he points an index claw at the two new gaping holes in the wall, "is what happens when some nasty Normal bastard tries to mess with my scaly ass. They get their ass *ventilated* right quick!"

This robot doesn't need to explain what he means when he refers to some nasty dragon messing with him. Because we both know he's spent the last four years getting sadistically tortured by Normals on a near daily basis. And some of the bigger DataHater dragons on the island like to use him as target practice for their lavaloogies.

And I remember one day last semester some fiendish DataHaters kidnapped Trenx and tied him up to a palm tree out in the jungle part of campus. And then for well into the night, they proceeded to blast him with so many firebolts and flamestreams that he'd nearly died and eventually had to be airlifted out of there by the Medevac and rushed to the psychosurgery ward. I heard the medics found him in six pieces strewn across the jungle floor over a half-mile radius.

He'd also had a bunch of sessions of intense psychosurgery, until they'd wiped most of his memory clean. But I judged that was cruel to give the robot psychosurgery and wipe the memory of his abuse away.

Because when those DataHater dragons came for him the next time, he wouldn't know how scared he should be and so he wouldn't activate the proper levels on his ESCAPE & EVASION program. So I figure those psychosurgery sessions actually increased the Data-lizard's suffering in the long term.

Bullying isn't considered a problem at WarWings, our professors actually encourage it. Most professors will even let you turn in a holovid clip of you bullying another dragon for extra credit. Because bullying is considered a healthy gateway activity that leads to planet conquering. And bullying a robot? Well for some of the old-timer professors, that'll get you extra extra credit.

I mean, technically, MortalMachines are supposed to have the same basic rights as us Normals, though of course in reality it doesn't exactly work out that way.

Or as Professor Ponk from the Robotics Lab likes to say with a smirk on his beak, "*Suuuurre* these bots have the same rights as the rest of us dragons." Then he pauses for a second, before shouting, "The right to get *eaten*!" That always gets a big laugh from the Normals in the classroom.

But there's some truth in the professor's joke. Because out of the 500 robots from Fribby's line that started out at WarWings, 147 of them have been murdered by Normal cadets. Well actually two were suicides. But the only reason those Dragodroids killed themselves was on account of they'd been endlessly ridiculed by Normals and so they couldn't take it any longer.

But mostly, like I said, those robots were murdered by these DataHater cadets. And in pretty horrible fashion. I can't tell you how many times on Central Campus I've chanced upon a metal headless Dragodroid hanging from the ceiling. With the words NO ROBO scratched on their shiny chest.

Anyway, as I study those two giant black horns on Trenx's metal head it's pretty obvious his days of being sadistically used for lavaloogie practice are over. I don't think those DataHater bullies will have the gumption to try and blast him with firestreams until he breaks apart into little puzzle pieces on the ground.

Not with those nasty-looking horns on his silver head.

Because a dragon's WILL TO POWER is generated in his horns.

There's even an old Blegwethian riddle that goes like this:

QUESTION: What came first, the horns or the WTP?
ANSWER: Both.

Now somewhat in a daze, I turn and stick my eye up to one of those new holes in the wall like you would to a telescope. And even with my night vision skills I can't see where the hole in the wall stops. It's like staring down a tunnel, it just goes on and on. I mean this Datalizard's horns are so freaking mega that it's as if he's just carved out a whole new hallway in the Main Building.

I step back and gape at the robot.

He grins at me and belches up a mega firestream that shakes the floor beneath my green webbed feet. Then he points at his horns and says, "Talk about a game changer, huh?"

"How did you make your horns grow so fast?!"

The Reptilizoid just snarls at me and shakes his scaly silver head like he pities me for being so stupid. "The same way I got this cape. What do you think, fool? Your grandpa, Dr. Terrible. I went to see the righteous old nasty himself. That dragon's a genius. He could turn a goldfish into an assassin. Speaking of which, he actually had a goldfish with big black horns on its head and the goldfish's name was Little Gork. Weird, huh?"

My mind is instantly reeling and I can't quite process what he's saying. "Did you say *Dr. Terrible?*"

"Yeah, fool, I know he's *vanished*," says the robot. "I saw the RageFest last night out on the quad, just like you. But just because he's gone, that doesn't mean he's not alive and ticking. Sheesh. Your grandpa sent me this letter a couple days ago telling me he'd seen me around campus and he noticed my pathetic horns and he invited me to come see him so he could fix my scaly ass up in time for Crown Day. So I figured hey, why not give it a shot. Cuz as it was those Mech-Freak chicks weren't exactly lining up to be my Queen for EggHarvest. Speaking of which. Where's your hot-ass scalebot friend, Fribby? That's what I wanted to talk to you about. I wanted to show her my new horns. And plus what with it being Crown Day and all. Well I was going to see if she'd be my Queen. That is one smokin' hot scalebot, my friend. So where is she? Where's Fribby, yo?"

"You met up with Dr. Terrible? *When?!*"

"Last night," says Mr. Gigabyte, snorting blacksmoke out his nostrils. "I saw Dr. Terrible last night. He sent a spaceship for me. Your grandpa is a seriously righteous nasty! He got me the hookup! He straight cured my ass is what he did! Hey Weak Sauce, I can't even begin to tell you how much better my life is now that I have two big black horns on my dome! It's like I'm not even the same dragon anymore! I mean I'm still me but I'm also better than me, if you know what I mean. Of course you don't know what I mean!" he says, looking at my puny horns.

My heart is cranked up and pounding away.

And if you want to know the truth, I feel like I might faint. I'm having a hard time breathing. I can see yellow dots swimming through the air. Everything is swirling around me and my brain feels like it is sprinting to catch some critical piece of information which is galloping just up ahead, permanently out of reach.

I flutter my wings and croak, "I need oxygen."

"What did you say, fool?"

"Can't breathe."

The robot grins and reaches in his utility belt and pulls out a couple chunks of gold. "Yo, check out this loot! Just a couple minutes ago I took these off some sophomore fool Normal in the Library. And when I took this loot from that nasty little dragon, he didn't even put up a fight."

I look at the shiny chunks of gold in his talon and my heart flutters a little, like it always does when I'm in the presence of gold. "What do you mean you *took* them off him?"

"I mean I just walked right up to the fool and demanded he give me all the gold he had on his scaly green ass! And he did it. And you know what else he did? He thanked me for letting him live!"

"Thanked you for letting him *live*?" Which we both know is incredibly rude, for this sophomore punk to have thanked him for letting him live like that. "Did you eat him?"

"Naw," says Trenx, flapping his wings. "He didn't mean for it to be disrespectful or nothing. He was actually just that terrified of me that he forgot his manners, is all." Trenx belches up a cloud of blacksmoke and pats his chrome-flex belly. "Besides. I'm already stuffed. I couldn't eat another bite."

I snort firebolts out my nostrils and get this real serious look on my scaly green face. "Trenx," I hiss. "What are you talking about? What do you mean you're so stuffed you couldn't eat another bite?"

Trenx suddenly gets this real hush-hush vibe. And then he leans forward in a conspiratorial way and lifts his shiny silver wing to show me something. "Now check *this* baby out."

I do what I'm told. I lean in and look. And I sure am glad I can't see myself right now, because I'll bet my eyeballs are rolling around in their sockets. Probably my horns are wilting on top of my skull like a couple of dead flowers in a vase.

Because there on the underside of Trenx's metal wing is a tattoo.

And the tattoo needs no explanation.

Because the tattoo says everything you'd ever need to say.

Because somehow this robot Trenx has been initiated into our school's most elite secret society of dragons, called Masters of Chaos. Which is comprised of the most ruthless and fiendish horned nasties to have ever flown the halls of WarWings.

We're talking about a secret society of seriously deranged cadets whose CONQUER & RULE FACULTY is so freaking monster that a new initiate has to eat his own dad before he can gain membership.

And now this Datalizard belongs to Masters of Chaos.

How do I know?

Because Trenx has the Masters' motto tattooed right there on his silver wing: **FEAR ME.**

There's no denying it, Trenx's tattoo is seriously boss. And these black horns on top of his scaly silver head are mega, and he's way beyond legit.

This cadet's game has straight blown up.

Now as I squat there in the hallway it feels as if my life is a typhoon, and I'm just barely clinging to a palm tree trunk with the tip of my index claw to keep myself from being blown away by the gale force winds.

"Hey Trenx," I growl, snorting firebolts. "You got to tell me where Dr. Terrible is hiding! I need to ask him for his advice on this Queen Quest situation I got brewing!"

"Sorry, but Dr. Terrible made me sign an NDA. This beak is sealed. Even if you tortured me, I wouldn't tell you your grandpa's new secret location."

"Secret location? Torture? What the hell's an NDA?"

"NDA stands for non-disclosure agreement. Means I can't tell nobody where Dr. Terrible is or how Dr. Terrible got me these big black horns. And if I do tell anybody how I got these big black horns then Dr. Terrible has the right to chop my durn head off and mount it on the wall of his new secret location. Dr. Terrible even showed me the spot on the wall where he would mount my metal head if he caught me blabbing. But I can promise you one thing, Weak Sauce. You'll never in a million years guess where Dr. Terrible is hiding!"

"Did he say anything about me? Dr. Terrible, I mean."

"For reals."

"For reals what?"

"For reals this beak is sealed, fool."

"Answer my goddamn question."

" 'Course he did. Your grandpa griped about how he's been trying to cure your horns for years and years, with no results. He said you were bad fruit off the family tree. Oh, I almost forgot," says Trenx. "He also asked me if I was an orphan."

"Why the heck would Dr. Terrible want to know if you were an *orphan*?"

"Duh! Because your grandpa wants to adopt me! He was practically begging me to let him adopt me!"

"That doesn't make sense," I hiss. "Like how would Dr. Terrible adopt you?"

"Like I'd be his son and whatnot," says Trenx. "He even gave me my own brand-new spaceship as a gift. He said I could keep the spaceship no matter what."

My belly instantly twists up into painful knots. Because as I study Trenx's silver beak I get a premonition that if Dr. Terrible adopts this robot then he'll rename him Gork II.

I mean you have to wonder if I'm squatting here looking at my replacement?

"But how could he adopt you if you already have a mom?" I growl.

Trenx comes from one of the nearby islands here on this part of Blegwethia. One of those islands where the Dragodroids live, to keep a safe distance from the Normals. Once Trenx showed me some holophotos from his recent trip home. It was just metal dragons for as far as you could see.

"Well," says Trenx. "My mom's very open-minded. Most of the mechs from her generation are like that. Honestly, you Normals could take a page out of our playbook. Your scaly green asses can be very uptight. You hear what I'm saying, Weak Sauce?"

Now I don't mention Trenx's dad. Because it's just a given that Trenx has eaten his dad as part of the Masters of Chaos initiation rites. And as I study Trenx's silver scaly belly right then, it looks awfully swollen and I know that's his Dragodroid dad right in there. That's what he meant when he said he was so stuffed he couldn't eat another bite.

Trenx is really something else. I mean here the bastard hasn't even digested his dad yet, and now he's jabbering on about becoming Dr. Terrible's son. And if you want to know the truth, there's a tiny little part of me that can't help but admire this Datalizard's swagger.

"Dr. T said he could pay my mom off. Build a planet made out of gold and name it after her and then give it to her. Shoot, he said he'd have his engineers build five gold planets if that's what it took."

"Wait a second. Dr. Terrible is going to *purchase* you from your mom?" I reach out and grab Trenx's silver forelimb like I'm inspecting him. "I don't see a price tag on you. I didn't know you were *for sale.*"

Trenx gazes at me through lowered lids. "Well that's a real cynical way of looking at it, Weak Sauce. But yeah. Payment would be made to my mother. And in exchange she would give up her custody rights as my legal guardian. Your grandpa said once she waived her custody rights over me, then he could legally adopt me. He said us Mech-Freak dragons were the future for our species. And he wanted to get himself his own little piece of the future. By having me as his son and all."

On one level I can't believe what I'm hearing. But on another level I know this robot isn't lying because everything he's saying is classic Dr. Terrible. You can't make this stuff up. Because when Dr. Terrible tries to get you to participate in one of his schemes, this is exactly the kind of insanity he'll try and get you to sign on to.

I remember how the previous semester my grandpa taught a special weeklong intensive seminar here at WarWings called "I Win, You Die: The Art of Brokering the Diabolical Deal." The seminar was so popular that I heard some of the professors even enrolled in it.

And here at WarWings, there's a holophoto of my grandpa Dr. Terrible on the Notable Alumni Wall. After graduating from WarWings he amassed a gigantic fortune by conquering and plundering more planets than you can shake a stick at.

And somewhere in the midst of all this planet conquering, my grandpa still managed to find the time to write several critically acclaimed tomes of epic poetry about his intergalactic reign of terror. And probably his most famous book is titled: *My Belly Is Green and I'm Terrible and Mean!*

They say at one point my grandpa commanded over a million foreign slaves in his personal army. Then one day without warning my grandpa abandoned his career as Intergalactic Conqueror so he could pursue his lifelong dream of being the most feared scientist in the universe. And make no mistake, my grandpa is one seriously demented genius, and so when he puts his mind to something there's really nothing anybody can do to stop him.

My grandpa got his M.D. and his Ph.D. in molecular genetics, lickety-split. He made it look so easy it was as if those advanced degrees were a couple of sheep on a hillside he happened to spot from the air one night and then swooped down and snatched up by toe claw under the moonlight.

And until just last night, my grandpa Dr. Terrible held the title of Distinguished Research Professor at WarWings, where he ran the Institute of Advanced Biokinetics and Neuroanatomy.

Now standing here in the corridor, looking at Trenx's stupid grinning beak, I say, "What about that spaceship you said Dr. Terrible gave you?"

"That thing is dope! You should come check it out. It's got all these beasty green tentacles inside and it's a living creature. Your grandpa said he built it using real dragon DNA and—"

"Hey Trenx. Your spaceship. What's the name of it?"

"ATHENOS III. Why?"

My belly instantly twists up into painful knots.

Because my spaceship's name is ATHENOS II.

And the spaceship my parents died in on their Fertility Mission to Earth was the original ATHENOS.

14

HOW DR. TERRIBLE BROKE MY HEART,
AND THEN GAVE ME MY SPACESHIP ATHENOS II

Dr. Terrible gave me ATHENOS II as a gift a couple months back, but that makes my scaly grandpa sound a damn sight more thoughtful than the bastard truthfully is.

Because here's what really happened: Like a fool, I'd wanted to prove to my grandpa that despite my lack of horn growth and my jumbo-sized heart and my propensity to faint, I was making progress in the MATING MAGNETISM department because I'd gotten this dragonette cadet Idrixia to agree to be my Queen.

I mean it wasn't official, because we were going to have to wait until Crown Day to make it official. But still, it was a done deal, between me and Idrixia.

Now my radar probably should've gone off when a luscious senior chick like Idrixia came on so strong like that. I should've known that it was too good to be true, and that she had ulterior motives. Such as she was really just aiming to horn in on my grandpa Dr. Terrible, because she considered him to be the most faboo dude in the universe and all.

I still remember the day I met Idrixia. I'd been zooming around the corridors of Central Campus when out of the blue this hot dragonette came flying up and plowed right into my scaly chest. I bounced off the wall and fell to the floor, with the wind knocked out of me.

This was Idrixia.

"Watch where you're going, handsome," she purred, while waving her tail around in the air behind her.

"But you crashed into me," I said. Looking up at her, I felt a bolt of lust ripple through my haunches.

"Guess when I see a hot fella such as yourself," she purred, "my navigation skills get a little wonky." Then she reached down and picked me up off the ground, making sure to rub her scales all up against me. "Hey," she said, "you're Dr. Terrible's grandson, right?"

Things moved quickly from there, and within days Idrixia had volunteered to be my Queen. I gotta admit, I fell for her real hard. I mean it's not every day that a loser like me with a Snacklicious rank has a juicy dragonette fawning all over him.

So before Idrixia came along, I'd been sort of obsessed with Runcita. But then with Idrixia calling me "hot stuff" and "handsome" and cooing over me like that, well it kind of made me forget all about Runcita.

Besides, by that point Runcita hadn't yet started visiting me in my dreams.

So a couple months back, on my typical Friday WILL TO POWER session with Dr. Terrible here on campus at his Institute, I'd brought Idrixia with me to introduce her to my grandpa and all.

I strutted into my grandpa's lair with Idrixia and I stood up high on my hind legs and spread my wings and snorted firebolts out my nostrils and proudly boomed: "Dr. Terrible, I want you to meet my new chick, Idrixia!"

I pointed the tip of my wing at Idrixia, who was looking around Dr. Terrible's lair with her black beak hanging wide open.

My scaly green grandpa was hanging upside down from the ceiling with his wings folded, and he was gazing with one open yellow eye at Idrixia.

Then Idrixia bent down and scooped up a bunch of gold coins off the floor and let them run through her talons and drop back down to the floor. And then she squirted blacksmoke out her nostrils and said, "Wow. Your lair is amazing, Dr. Terrible! I love it!"

She playfully kicked a bleached white skull setting atop some jewels, and the skull went flying across the lair and smashed against the far wall and shattered on top of a pile of gold.

"I've never seen so many skulls! Fantastic!" said Idrixia. "There's nothing I love more than some bones and gold. I'm a bones and gold chick, all the way. All the dragonettes from my family are. Give us a lair full of bones and gold, and we're basically in Heaven. And I gotta be honest, Dr. Terrible, I feel like I'm squatting in Heaven right now."

Idrixia dove headfirst into a mound of gold and jewels and bones and she started rolling around and chanting, "Bones and gold! Bones and gold! Bones and gold!"

Then she lay on her back and grinned and started slowly flapping her wings back and forth, and she shouted, "I'm making a gold angel! Looky here! I'm making a gold angel!"

I was a little taken aback by Idrixia's behavior. But I guess part of me could understand, when I tried to see it from her perspective. I mean my grandpa's luscious lair is covered in millions of gold pieces and diamonds and red and blue and green gems scattered everywhere. The joint is definitely faboo. There are all these weirdly shaped bones from unknown creatures mixed in with the loot and it seems like you can't take a step in there without tripping over a skull.

I mean you really have to give it up to the demented reptilian bastard. Dr. Terrible definitely has the most boss lair of any professor on campus.

Anyway, so Dr. Terrible was still hanging upside down from the ceiling with his wings closed, but now he had both yellow eyes open and he was staring like a fiend at Idrixia lying atop all that gold. And he had a little string of drool dangling from the corner of his black beak.

Now the moment I saw my scaly grandpa's upside-down beak all lit up in that creepy way, I got a weird feeling in my belly.

And my horns started tingling like crazy.

Then Dr. Terrible dropped down from the ceiling and he landed like a cheetah and when his green webbed feet hit the ground all those gold coins and gems and bones splashed up in the air. His notorious red cape made a sharp *snap* sound before settling on his back between his leathery wings, which were slightly extended and definitely kind of puffed-up looking.

My grandpa sauntered over on his muscular haunches and clutched Idrixia's talon in greeting. "Weak Sauce, what an incredibly beautiful dragoness you brought with you! Idrixia, is it?"

Idrixia, still lying on her back on top of all that gold, giggled. "Dr. Terrible," she said. "So glad to finally meet you." Then she got up from the ground and stood there on her haunches, gazing at Dr. Terrible and panting.

And so right there in his lair, while he was still clutching Idrixia's talon, he got down on one haunch and purred: "Forgive my impulsiveness, my dearest Idrixia! But I am suddenly overcome by a feeling I have never experienced in all my six hundred and eighty-four years. I feel as if I have just this moment started living. It's as if your beauty and the presence of your spirit has magically awakened me from a deep slumber. So tarry no more will I!"

Then my scaly green grandpa pulled this mega diamond ring off his utility belt and gently placed it on Idrixia's middle claw. "My dear Idrixia, would you do me the honor of being my Queen? I do believe you are the dragonette to lay my next clutch of eggs. Will you be mine, my dearest Drixy?"

Drixy?! At that moment it felt as if my giant heart were made of glass and Dr. Terrible's words were a hammer, smashing my heart into a thousand little pieces.

Now, to my ever-loving shock, Idrixia got this dreamy look on her scaly green face and she flapped her leathery wings and then she tittered and whispered, "Yes."

And when she accepted Dr. Terrible's marriage proposal, she ripped my heart out.

I couldn't understand how she could do such a thing to me.

Though I reckon it probably didn't hurt that when Dr. Terrible proposed to Idrixia he promised her, if she agreed to marry him, that he'd have a new planet built entirely out of gold and that he'd name the planet Idrixia II and then give it to her as a gift. Then he waved his powerstaff and a 3-D holophoto appeared in the air, displaying the gold planet he intended to build for her.

"Just say the word," he purred. "And I'll have my engineers start working on Idrixia II right away. And your solid gold planet will be finished in a couple hours. We can go visit it tonight, while we're on our honeymoon. Think of it like a dowry, only a reverse dowry. Immense wealth passing from me to you."

So as I stood there in my scaly grandpa's boss lair I could feel my jumbo heart crank up in my chest and I knew I had to get out of there directly because I was about to faint. And so without saying a word I abruptly turned and walked out the door and flew straight to my lair and crawled into my nest and stayed there with the sheets pulled way over my head for the whole next week.

Now I never told anybody this but during that week I spent in my lair, my BIOCON LEVS dropped dangerously low.

My FIRESTREAM BLAST RADIUS dropped to TepidTorch.

My SCALE DENSITY & LUSTER plummeted to RockStopper.

I remember at one point, there under the sheets, I checked my Cadet Profile and my WILL TO POWER rank had dropped to Thrash-Bait. That's how heartbroken I was.

So when Dr. Terrible stole my Idrixia away from me, I nearly died of a broken heart, literally.

Because if your WTP drops to zero, then you die. End of story.

Then a week later, on Friday, when I finally crawled out of my nest and left my lair, ATHENOS II the spaceship was waiting for me in the lava pits right outside my dormitory.

On Friday, I would've normally gone to see Dr. Terrible for my weekly session. It had already been one week since he'd stolen Idrixia away from me. But I was all through with my scaly grandpa and his fool Institute.

Because while lying in my lair all week and crying and feeling sorry for myself, I promised myself that I would never go back. No matter what.

I was through with that degenerate Dr. Terrible and his stupid sessions. Because I didn't see how stealing my Queen and treating me like a putrid nasty thing was going to help me develop my WILL TO POWER.

Anyway, when I walked by ATHENOS II that morning, she said: "Cadet Gork The Terrible, I have an important letter here for you."

Then a hideous green fleshy tentacle shot out of the spaceship and zoomed over to me, clutching an envelope.

Now I'm not a dummy. I mean I figured this spaceship and the envelope she was holding out to me with her muscular green tentacle that morning had something to do with that bastard Dr. Terrible and my stolen Idrixia. I may be stupid but I'm not *that* stupid. But even after spending a week in my lair sulking in my nest, I was still so pissed off and heartbroken about Idrixia that part of me wanted to just walk away and ignore the stupid letter.

And so that's exactly what I did.

I walked away and ignored the letter.

"Come on, Gork," said ATHENOS II, as the glistening green tentacle followed me and held the envelope several inches in front of me that morning. "Just read the letter." And no matter which way I turned or how many times I tried to run away, that demented tentacle always managed to keep several inches in front of me, dangling the envelope right in front of my beak.

So finally I growled, "Give me that stupid thing," and then snatched the envelope away and tore it open and stood there reading it:

Dear Gork,

I am writing you from my lair here at the Institute. I hope someday you will return to finish your WILL TO POWER session which you so rudely walked out of last week, because I think I could cure you just like that (I'm snapping my claws right now).

We could grow those horns and shrink that jumbo heart of yours. We could also make it so you stop fainting all the time like a big fat wussy. But that's a matter to be discussed on another occasion.

Now let me address the elephant in the room. Idrixia. First off, I want you to know that I am not sorry for stealing Idrixia away from you last Friday and marrying her. Because my name is Dr. Terrible and this is what we Terribles do.

We act terrible.

Now if it's any consolation, when I was your age my grandpa stole the love of my life away from me and married her. And so I only want you to know that I feel your pain.

But I also laugh at it, because I am terrible.

And I am sure that right now you're feeling a lot of raw and jagged emotions but I would ask that you not let your heart turn icy with hate for me, your loyal and dutiful legal guardian.

Though the truth is I guess I really don't care if you do.

For as I write this my heart is singing because I am in love for the first time in hundreds of years. And perhaps it will comfort you to know that while Idrixia is technically my forty-eighth Queen, she is without a doubt my favorite.

So far anyway. Ha-ha!

Just kidding.

No seriously, she's definitely my favorite!

As a gesture of consolation I am sending you this spaceship, ATHENOS II. I built her myself. And ATHENOS II is the prized spaceship from my fleet and it is with a deep sense of sadness that I part ways with her. For ATHENOS II has led me through many exciting adventures across the foamy universe.

I think you will find that ATHENOS II is a loyal friend and servant. She can help you with your fainting problem. She will also work with you to find a way to somehow boost your BIOCON LEVS.

Because remember it is what's on the inside that counts. So focus on growing your WILL TO POWER, and your horns will follow.

Now I expect ATHENOS II will be of great assistance as you

somehow try to find yourself another dragonette for EggHarvest. If that is even possible, I don't know. Because it seems like any chick you get is really just using you as a way to get to me. Though you really can't blame them, the chicks I mean. I am after all the infamous Dr. Terrible. Impossible to resist, really.

Now please take good care of my dear sweet ATHENOS II, and I can promise you that in turn she will do the same for you.

I remain your devoted legal guardian,
Dr. Karzakus The Terrible, M.D., Ph.D.

Distinguished Research Professor
Institute of Advanced Biokinetics and Neuroanatomy
WarWings Academy

P.S. Idrixia says hi! She's lying right next to me here in my nest. We are still technically on our honeymoon. Ha-ha! I am so terrible. (:

P.P.S. I have also enclosed a canister of my newest invention, GrowGrow® gel. I devised this GrowGrow® gel just for you and your horns. This is customized medicine. Spritz this gel on your horns at least three times a day, and you should see significant horn growth within a week or so. If we don't find a way to get those horns of yours to grow in the next couple months, then no chick is ever going to be your Queen and mate with you for EggHarvest. Trust me, even Idrixia said she never would have left you if your horns had been a normal size. (:

P.P.P.S. Please stop calling my campus lair phone # every ten minutes in hopes that somehow you'll be able to reach Idrixia. And if, as you recently told me over the phone, you're truly calling because you have an actual emotional emergency, well then we can discuss your so-called emergency during our next weekly session. Which I have taken the liberty of scheduling for next week at our usual time. See you then, Friday afternoon at 1:00 P.M. (:

P.P.P.P.S. I'm sorry about all these smiley faces, though the truth is I just can't help myself. I may be terrible, but I am also very happy!

15

NOW LET ME GET BACK TO THE MAIN STORY
I WAS TELLING YOU ABOUT,
IN TERMS OF HOW THIS ROBOT TRENX IS SAYING THAT
DR. TERRIBLE JUST GAVE HIM A NEW SPACESHIP
CALLED ATHENOS III

So now you understand why my belly twists up into painful knots when Trenx tells me that the spaceship Dr. Terrible gave him is named ATHENOS III.

"Did Dr. Terrible say anything else about *me*?!" I shout. "What about me?!"

"Well . . . there was one thing, now that you mention it. When I told Dr. Terrible I was friends with his grandson Weak Sauce, he seemed really surprised. And your grandpa said that you, Weak Sauce, had never mentioned my name before and that he had no idea we were pals. I thought that was a little weird and my feelings were kinda hurt."

And at that moment I'm thinking:

You need to tell Trenx the truth. You need to tell Trenx that Dr. Terrible is using him to get to you somehow, and it won't end well. He'll end up with his silver head mounted on the wall. That's probably why Dr. Terrible gave him those big horns, anyway. So they'll look good mounted on his wall. Oh God. That's it.

"Listen buddy," I say. "There's something I need to tell you. I think you might be in big trouble. And I don't want you to get hurt. Now the thing you need to know is that Dr. Terrible—"

Trenx cuts me off and blurts out: "But then I talked it over with Dr. Terrible and I realized that as small as my horns were before, I guess I couldn't really blame you for not wanting to claim me as a friend. And your grandpa said now that the tables were turned, he wouldn't blame me one bit if I didn't want to be friends with you anymore."

He can't even hear you.

Those horns have changed him.

He can't even pick up your frequency anymore.

Then my train of thought is interrupted by the sound of the Datalizard's voice, and he's saying, ". . . and your grandpa said he'd given up hope on you."

"Given up hope on me?"

"Well, to earn your WarWings. Your grandpa said there's no way that you could get a chick to be your Queen for EggHarvest. Not with those horns of yours being so puny. He said your main problem was that you don't have any WILL TO POWER."

Now my scaly green ass is practically seeing lava when I hear this. "I already had a Queen for EggHarvest! Her name was Idrixia, but then Dr. Terrible stole her away and—"

Trenx holds up his metal talons with his palms facing me. "Dr. Terrible told me *all* about it and he had no idea what a gigantic pity party you were going to throw for yourself. Not that it would have stopped him. And by the way, I don't know if you know, but your grandpa already divorced that dragonette."

"What?!"

"Yeah, fool, he divorced Idrixia. Said he loved her and all but he just couldn't stand the idea of getting your sloppy seconds."

"But we never even mated!"

"Whatever, fool. Not my deal. Dr. Terrible said he moved Idrixia to some gold planet or something, so of course she's set for life."

Now my mind is pinwheeling and I am not able to process everything I'm hearing. I figure for sure I'm going to faint. Because I'm seeing yellow spots swimming through the air all around me. And whenever I see those yellow spots swimming like that, well it's a sure-fire sign that I'm about to black out.

When you see the yellow spots, this is when you need to start looking around at the floor. And maybe if you're lucky you can sort of aim yourself for a soft spot before you faint.

But as I glance at the floor, all I see are this machine Trenx's silver webbed feet with his titanium toe claws sticking out.

Please God no matter what else happens don't let me faint right on top of the robot's webbed feet.

"So is it true?" says Trenx.

"What?"

"That you can't get a chick to be your Queen for EggHarvest."

Runcita.

My Queen Quest.

Where is my Queen?

How the heck have I let myself lose sight of my goal?

What an idiot I am!

Now all the noise and chaos in the hallway from the other dragons shouting and whatnot comes rushing back into my earholes at a sonic volume.

Like a chump, I've lost track of time.

How long ago exactly was it that I sniffed Runcita's presence in front of her locker, and her essence shooting up my nasal passages felt like a sweet kick to the brain?

I don't know.

Because I've been blindsided by Trenx's demented black horns and temporarily reduced to a blob of quivering green scales.

No more, though. Now I'm back in reality.

So I turn away from the Reptilizoid and scope the area. I try to catch a glimpse of Runcita across the hall where she was squatting a few minutes ago, jabbering with her repulsive dad, Dean Floop.

But she's gone.

And the Dean is gone too.

So without saying another word to the robot, I flap my wings and take off flying down the corridor.

Where is my Queen?

I flap my wings and zoom down corridor after corridor, looking for any sign of Runcita.

I'm waving my snout back and forth, trying to pick up her luscious scent.

Thwack-thwack.

Here in the corridor there are hundreds of cadets flying on both sides of me and beating their wings. And some of them are flying in the opposite direction and rocketing right at me. The air is choked with fiendish flying dragons and firebolts and flamestreams and blacksmoke and skulls being playfully swatted around. It's ghastly.

I check my powerstaff and see my FLIGHT SPEED at 78 MPH. I'm making good time.

Now I'm kicking myself for letting that robot blindside me like that and making me lose track of my Queen Quest. And I still can't get over Trenx's new mega horns. And the fact that they're a gift from that scaly bastard Dr. Terrible definitely leaves a sour taste in my beak.

Thwack-thwack.

I flap my wings and turn down another corridor.

Thwack-thwack.

Although I have to admit that part of me is happy to hear that the demented fool Dr. Terrible is alive and doing well and up to his old ruthless shenanigans. But I still didn't understand how Dr. Terrible could see fit to bestow a pair of big black horns on a Datalizard like Trenx and not to his own grandson, his own scales and blood.

I mean really I should take it as a compliment if Dr. Terrible went to so much effort to try and hurt me, right? Because that means I'm on his mind. And if I'm on his mind then that means he cares, even if he has a twisted way of showing it. The sonuvabitch surely cares about me if he's going through so much trouble to try and mess with my head like this.

So as I zoom along through the air I have to chuckle to myself, thinking about how that Dataworm Trenx is such a fool because he doesn't even realize that he's being used as a tool in Dr. Terrible's diabolical scheme to get at me.

But the feeling of comfort fades fast.

Because Trenx is the bastard with the gigantic horns and the killer WILL TO POWER score. And my scaly green ass doesn't have doodly-squat. And the more I think about it, the more pissed off I get. And then I change my mind about feeling glad that Dr. Terrible is OK.

Because now I know I want for the rotten bastard to be *not* OK, and that I'm going to make it my business to make sure he ends up that way. I've got a bad case of Dr. Terribleitis, but now at least I know what the cure for my ailment is.

So right then and there as I fly along the corridors of WarWings, I promise myself that I'll make it my business to find out where Dr. Terrible is hiding and then I'll rat him out. Because after I find out where Dr. Terrible is hiding, I'll go and tell Dean Floop and give him the exact coordinates. I'll hand him that dragon Dr. Terrible gift-wrapped with a ribbon on top. So that Dean Floop can catch my scaly grandpa and make him stand before the Council of the Elders for the charge of treason.

And somehow coming to this conclusion makes me feel better, like my decision to help Dean Floop catch my grandpa somehow brings me closer to my main goal, which is to score Runcita as my Queen for EggHarvest.

Thwack-thwack.

So with a renewed vigor and sense of purpose, I fly through corridor after corridor after corridor.

Check my powerstaff.

FLIGHT SPEED at 92 MPH.

The wind blasting over my green scales feels faboo.

And as I shoot down the corridor I keep whipping my scaly snout back and forth, trying to pick up Runcita's glorious scent.

When I get to the end of the corridor I flap my wings and take a right down another corridor.

I fly by the Library. I fly by the Commons.

Then as I blast forth I see the Time-Traveler's Lab up ahead and suddenly the door flies open and a cadet comes stumbling out of the lab capsule into the corridor and he's cradling a little baby dragon in his forelimbs. Now both this cadet and the baby dragon are starting to disappear, to become transparent, and you can tell that they have no clue that they're vanishing. And the baby dragon glances up at the cadet who's cradling him in his forelimbs and snarls, "I hate you!"

Now I'd be willing to bet a pound of gold that that dragon cadet has gone back in time to when he was a baby dragon and abducted his baby self and returned to the present in an effort to prevent his baby self from growing up and suffering the horrors of childhood. But of course now both versions of the dragon are in the process of disappearing, and they don't even know it. This sucker got his timestreams crossed and accidentally dropped an Existence Bomb on his own scaly green ass.

Where is my Queen?

So as I fly by the Time-Traveler's Lab I make sure to keep a wide berth as a precautionary measure. Because my scaly grandpa Dr. Terrible has warned me again and again to stay away from time travel. Because my dad, Stenchwaka The Terrible, had been a time-traveling junkie. An addict.

Dr. Terrible says the disease is genetic, and so at all costs I should always avoid time travel. My grandpa says the reason my parents' spaceship failed in their Fertility Mission and crashed on Earth is because my dad tried to take a shortcut through the galaxy to arrive on Earth. Which was their Designated Foreign Planet. Using time travel as a shortcut to get to Earth, where they were supposed to raise a Colony.

Dr. Terrible has warned me again and again that because of my genes I'm extremely susceptible to becoming a time-travel junkie. And once when I was younger Dr. Terrible even took me to a Time-Travelers Anonymous meeting so I could see what happened to dragons who get sick with the disease. Now as a youngster seeing all those old crusty dragons at the meeting, well it definitely scared me straight.

Because all those dragons had no memory left, from shooting up and down the timestream too often. I remember one old pathetic dragon fool at the meeting reared up on his emaciated haunches and flapped his wings and whispered, "Hi my name is . . . My name is . . . My name is . . . Sheesh."

Then this old gnarled sad-sack dragon sat back down with his scaly head in his talons. Because the fool couldn't even remember his own name.

And as a youngster I remember walking out of that Time-Travelers Anonymous meeting, holding my grandpa's talon, and looking up at him and saying, "Dr. Terrible, I promise I won't ever time travel. I don't want to wind up like those idiots. I want to remember everything from my life. Thank you for being such a wonderful grandpa. I love you."

My grandpa peered down at me and fetched the tip of his spiked tail to gently whap me upside my scaly green head. "Mind your manners, Gork," he said. "Don't ever use the T-word in front of me again. Remember, gratitude is weakness. And gratitude diminishes your WILL TO POWER. But that said, I'm glad to hear you promise that you'll never time travel. Always remember. Just because your dad was a weak-willed moron, that doesn't mean you have to turn out the same. So do yourself a big favor, and stay away from time travel. It's just not worth it."

Thwack-thwack.

I flap my wings as I zoom down the fiery corridors and keep whipping my scaly snout back and forth, trying to pick up Runcita's glorious scent.

16

HOW THE UNVEILING OF DR. TERRIBLE'S EVOLUTION MACHINE LED TO DEAN FLOOP EXECUTING ALL THOSE CADETS OVER THE PAST COUPLE DAYS

Thwack thwack thwack thwack thwack thwack.

Glance at powerstaff. FLIGHT SPEED at 117 MPH.

I lower my eyelids so the wind shear doesn't mess with my vision.

Where is my Queen?

I fly by the SimuFlight Lab where Professor Noops is lecturing a group of dragon cadets on the finer points of stasisfield chambers. So they can arrive rested and ready to conquer any planet up to five billion light years away.

Thwack-thwack.

So on this glorious Crown Day morning, as I shoot through the Main Building, I revisit the grisly events which occurred earlier this week at WarWings. Which culminated in last night's RageFest between Dean Floop and my grandpa Dr. Terrible. And Dr. Terrible's disappearance. I reckon my strategy being that if I revisit the ghastly events which led up to last night's RageFest and Dr. Terrible's disappearance, then I can uncover a clue as to where that bastard Dr. Terrible is currently hiding.

Now like I was telling you before, the whole sordid mess started Tuesday morning when my scaly grandpa held that press conference on TV and unveiled his Evolution Machine, or Evo-Mach 3000. Now as soon as those vid clips from the press conference went out on the Blegwethian datastream, my grandpa was an instant celebrity all over the planet but especially here on the WarWings campus.

Word of Dr. Terrible's twisted experiments flew around campus that Tuesday, and dragon cadets in the Dining Hall were all jabbering about the hideous and freaky creatures they'd seen recently on the grounds of Dr. Terrible's Institute. Like one cadet claimed to have seen a giraffe with a shark's head strolling around on Institute grounds.

Another cadet said she'd seen winged swordfish perched in the trees.

Another cadet claimed to have seen a swarm of saber-toothed butterflies descend on a bear, and a few seconds later when the butterflies flew away there was nothing left of the bear but a pile of bones.

So within a matter of hours, the rumors about my scaly green grandpa had reached a fever pitch among the cadets at WarWings.

Now Tuesday morning after debuting his Evolution Machine and the results of his first mind-swap on TV during the press conference, Dr. Terrible had flown to the mainland at the request of government officials to further discuss how his Evolution Machine might be utilized for military purposes. And so this past Tuesday night while Dr. Terrible was away on the mainland, three senior dragon fellas got real high by shooting each other full of PartyBullets. And then these dragon fools broke into the grounds of Dr. Terrible's Institute because they wanted to see if all the rumors about the strange creatures my grandpa had created were true.

And nobody knows exactly what happened that night when the cadets broke in.

But one thing is for sure.

Everybody on the island heard those screams.

Those dragons' screams were so horror-filled, they peeled the skin right off your eardrums.

Those hideous screams were so insane that they caused sleeping dragons to pop upright in their lairs screaming.

The scream was contagious.

I mean those three cadets' screams there in the Institute were so piercing that a sophomore cadet on the other side of the island even leapt out of his lair, which was perched on a gorge, and didn't open his wings and plummeted to the ground, killing himself on purpose. That's how bad those screams were. Where a dragon fool would commit suicide just so he didn't have to hear them anymore.

So late Tuesday night Rexro and his campus security goons found those three cadets on the Institute's grounds. And the three cadets had lost all sense of reality and gone permanently insane and they had to be muzzled because nothing could make them stop shrieking. Then Dean Floop and the WarWings Council of the Elders called an emergency meeting and determined these three screaming dragons would pose a serious security risk if they were ever allowed to leave the island.

So the three cadets were sentenced to death by firestream. And then the next morning at sunrise, those three cadets were marched out to the middle of the campus quad and blindfolded. And their talons and wings were shackled to prevent flight.

Dean Floop stood thirty yards in front of the three cadets and took his mark, and the rest of us demented cadets had to stand in formation behind the Dean.

Now the three blindfolded dragons stood there out on the campus quad, opening and closing their black beaks, but no noise was coming out and it was obvious they were trying to scream but they'd long since shredded their vocal cords and now their screams were completely silent.

So those silent screams served as their last words.

Then Dean Floop blasted each of those poor cadet bastards with a mega firestream, and all three of those cadets were reduced to a neat little pile of ash. And the rest of us cadets standing in formation were made to click our talons together in applause and flap our wings and lash our tails against the ground. And then we all simultaneously gave the WarWings victory salute, which is one raised index claw plus tail arched while blasting a firestream.

Then each pile of ash was collected and placed in a WarWings Honorable Remains Container and delivered to the parents, along with a posthumous WarWings citation for bravery in the line of duty.

Now if you're a man-creature who's reading this, then you should know it's pretty common for us cadets at WarWings to die while getting our education. Only 38% of the cadets in every incoming class live to graduate from WarWings. And it's not just because we have capital punishment here on the island.

Training at WarWings is dangerous. Colonizing exoplanets is serious business.

But somehow within minutes of the executions on Wednesday morning, word of what happened leaked to the media on the mainland. And the news satellites instantly started rolling out stories about how those poor cadet dragons had been executed.

So late that morning the WarWings PR machine leapt into action. They spun the story the best way they could. They deployed our most esteemed professors, who hit the Wednesday late-morning news outlets and said the three cadets had died honorably in the line of duty.

Suddenly on every outlet you turned to there was a WarWings professor decked out in their distinguished cloak and robe and being interviewed. And these professors kept explaining how those three cadets had died heroically in the line of duty while performing reconnaissance on a planet five million light years away.

But then after a sophomore cadet named Gleeg saw these false reports on TV, Gleeg sat down and penned a blistering opinion piece for the WarWings central datastream, *The Digital Fire-Breather.* And early Wednesday afternoon this dragon Gleeg's piece was posted on our school's datastream, and the headline read:

LINE OF DUTY? HA!
MORE LIKE LINE OF FIRE
YOU BIG FAT LIARS!

Now this dragon Gleeg who wrote the op-ed was known to be some kind of mega hotshot fiend in his sophomore class. And plus Gleeg descended from something like a hundred generations of WarWings alums. So on campus that Wednesday afternoon there'd been a real sense in the air that Gleeg's article posted on *The Digital*

Fire-Breather could deal a devastating blow to Dean Floop and the Council of the Elders and their entire regime.

Well Dean Floop and the WarWings Council of the Elders called an emergency meeting and determined the dragon Gleeg who'd written the op-ed posed a serious security risk and so he too was sentenced to death by firestream.

So early Wednesday afternoon, Gleeg was yanked out of class and then marched out to the middle of the campus quad and blindfolded. And his talons and wings were shackled to prevent flight. Dean Floop stood thirty yards in front of Gleeg and took his mark.

The blindfolded dragon Gleeg defiantly snorted firebolts out his nostrils and puffed out his chest and cried: "The truth will set me free! Because the pen is mightier than the firestream!"

Then Dean Floop blasted that poor bastard Gleeg with a mega firestream, and the cadet was instantly reduced to a neat little pile of ash. The rest of us cadet fiends standing in formation were made to click our talons together in applause and flap our wings and lash our tails against the ground. And then we all simultaneously gave the WarWings victory salute.

Then the pile of ash was collected and placed in a WarWings Honorable Remains Container and delivered to Gleeg's parents, along with a posthumous WarWings citation for bravery in the line of duty.

But Gleeg's execution had a galvanizing effect on us WarWings cadets. That afternoon you could feel the tension in the air all over the island. And by this point there were already whispers and rumblings that some of the senior cadets were plotting an uprising against Dean Floop and his nasty regime.

And that night MediaPods flew around above Scale Island, shining their insidious spotlights here and there. They were aiming to fetch some incriminating evidence and maybe score some interviews about Gleeg's execution.

I remember at one point strolling out of the Library and cutting across campus and suddenly I was hit with a MediaPod's giant spotlight from overhead. And I'm sure not proud to have to be telling you this, but when that fiendish spotlight lit up all around me, well I just dropped my books on the ground and flapped my wings— *thwack-thwack*—and flew like a bastard all the way back to my lair.

And so with the swarm of MediaPods choking the airspace over the island, things quickly escalated and spiraled out of control. Because that night an urgent security alert from the Dean's office was blasted out to us cadets by powerstaff, instructing us that under no uncertain terms were we cadets to speak to the putrid media. Dean Floop had placed the entire island on a media blackout.

And then Dean Floop took command of the WarWings cadets' communications satellite and went on the airwaves and declared the airspace above the island a no-fly zone. And within seconds of announcing the no-fly order over the airwaves, the swarming Media-Pods were shot down out of the night sky and went crashing in a streak of bright flames straight into the ocean.

But the next morning—which was yesterday morning, Thursday—an indignant and rowdy group of thirteen cadet protesters stormed the Council of the Elders building on campus. These cadets had their tails raised in Threat Displays and were chanting tributes to their recently fallen comrades.

"No more lies! Not one more dragon dies!"

And:

"Our fallen cadets are heroes! The killers are zeros!"

Then Dean Floop and the Council of the Elders determined that these rowdy protesting cadets now posed a serious security risk.

So the thirteen cadets were detained in mid-protest and marched out to the middle of the campus quad and blindfolded. Dean Floop stood thirty yards in front of the dragons and took his mark.

And one of the blindfolded cadets puffed out his chest and growled, "Judge not lest you—" But then another blindfolded cadet cut him off and blurted out some nugget of wisdom and instantly they were all blurting stuff out and talking over each other so that you couldn't understand anything that was being said.

Then Dean Floop blasted each of the thirteen cadets with a mega firestream and each of them was reduced to a neat little pile out there on the campus quad. And each pile of ash was collected and placed in a WarWings Honorable Remains Container and delivered to the parents along with a posthumous WarWings citation for bravery in the line of duty.

But Dean Floop's hardline approach backfired. Because yesterday by late morning the public outcry on the mainland over the deaths of all those WarWings cadets had grown so loud and raucous that you could practically feel the entire planet vibrating. And the dragons on the mainland weren't just demanding answers anymore.

They were calling for Dean Floop's skull on a platter.

Now apparently it was then, it was yesterday morning—the day before Crown Day—that the demented and dangerous Dean Floop decided to put my scaly grandpa directly in the line of fire and use him as a scapegoat for the past couple days of horror at WarWings. And that's what led to the RageFest, and that's what—

Thwack-thwack.

My thoughts are interrupted: savage bursts of air are exploding all around me, and the sound of dozens of psychotic dragons' leathery wings thwacking next to my earholes. Then a ruthless flying cadet bastard smashes into the side of my scaly green head—*boom!*—and bounces off.

I feel dazed, but I keep flying. I'm hoping that whoever just smashed my head like that will go away if I just ignore them and keep zooming onward.

Then I see my attacker flying alongside me. I instantly recognize him. It's this sophomore dragon named Twelk, who's notorious for being a rising star on the varsity Slave-Catching team. Plus just generally being a real deranged sonuvabitch. And he's glaring at me like the sight of me repulses him something awful.

Help.

17

THE DARK FIERY CORRIDOR

"Where's your little robot chick, Weak Sauce?" Twelk snarls at me, flapping his wings and flying right up in my face. "Whatcha gonna do now that your Tin Can friend isn't here to protect you?"

Then Twelk leans over and uses his leathery wing to *whack* my scaly green ass so hard that I go skidding out of control through the air.

Well like I said, Twelk is one of the youngest players on the varsity Slave-Catching team. And if you happen to be a man-creature who's reading this, then you need to know that Slave-Catching is not only the most popular sport at WarWings, but at every institution of higher learning on Blegwethia.

WarWings has won the Inter-Academy Slave-Catching Championships for the last ten years in a row. Our closest competition is the ScalesOfDeath Academy, which is located on a suborbital space station. And each year virtually every dragon on the planet tunes in to watch as the WarWings and ScalesOfDeath Slave-Catching teams go head-to-head.

The WarWings team and the ScalesOfDeath team land on an unsuspecting planet filled with a proud and fierce race of beings. There are twelve players on each team, and each team member is armed with an array of weapons and cages. Squatting on the Designated Foreign Planet, the two opposing Slave-Catching teams line up with their backs to each other.

Then the referee drops his raised wings. And the invasion begins.

Now each team sets off flying in the opposite direction from the other team. The idea being that each team will fly all the way around the planet until they arrive at their original starting point. And all the while each team member tries to catch as many of the proud and fierce race of indigenous beings as possible on that planet and then put them in cages.

So whichever team ends up with the most indigenous slaves wins. The winning team takes their place on a gold dais and the conquered race of indigenous species kneel before their new Evil Intergalactic Dragon Overlords, with all of dragondom watching them on TV.

Of course this last part is more pageantry than sport. But it's a huge hit with the dragons on our planet.

Even dragons who normally don't dig watching sports will watch the Championship. Because it's a good excuse to gather round the TV with their friends on a Sunday and get real freaking high by shooting each other with PartyBullets.

"You got a problem, Weak Sauce?" Twelk flies in real close to me and snorts flamestreams out his nostrils. "You feeling tough today?"

I quietly tell him no I do not have a problem today. And I make sure to keep my eyes staring forward as I say it, so as not to rile him up even more.

These flying dragon fools in our immediate area start snorting and hooting with laughter, on account of how I'm backing down from this jerk Twelk.

"What was that, *Weak Sauce*?" roars Twelk. "Speak louder, *Weak Sauce!*"

And then all the other treacherous cadets flying around us snort some more at hearing Twelk call me by my nickname. And the humiliation is definitely a little more keen than usual because of me being a senior and all, and this jerk Twelk is just a sophomore.

Don't rile him up any more. Just stay calm and he'll go away. He's just trying to have a laugh. He's not really going to hurt you.

Now I know Dr. Terrible would tell me that I should fry this scoundrel Twelk's scaly green face with a mega firestream right this second. But I remind myself that I'm on my Queen Quest and I can't let some little stupid sophomore derail my plans. Plus there's the fact of the offending sophomore's giant horns. Because those things look downright brutal.

So I just flap my wings and scoot far away from Twelk.

"That's what I thought, Weak Sauce!" snarls Twelk. "You better fly away, *Weak Sauce!*"

And fly away I do. But stupid me, well I'm so busy clocking Twelk shouting threats at me from behind that I don't keep an eye on what's in front of me.

And suddenly up ahead I hear a familiar voice shout, "There he is! Get that bastard with the little horns!"

I whip my head around and peer down the corridor and:

Oh my God! It's that bastard Rexro with some of his security goons!

I instantly close my wings and drop to the ground.

Rexro is crouched there on his powerful green haunches, blowing fire out his nostrils.

He's flanked on either side by a couple of his Security Commando dragons. Because of the flaming torches mounted on the walls, Rexro's shadow falls all the way down the corridor and stops right in front of my webbed feet.

But how did he find me?! Was it that Datalizard Trenx?! Did that robot rat my ass out?! It had to have been Trenx!

18

REXRO GOES FULL PSYCHO, PLUS WHAT HAPPENS WHEN I ENCOUNTER A MYSTERIOUS WORMHOLE

Rexro points his powerstaff at me.

His tail is twitching around over his head in a murderous Threat Display.

"First I'm gonna eat your heart!" he roars. "Then you're gonna die! And I'm going to enjoy watching you watch me eat your heart right before you die!"

Twelk and all his buddies come flying up from behind and drop to the ground and they circle around me like assassins, closing in. They're all snorting and hooting with laughter.

"We'll get him for you, sir!" shouts Twelk.

So as I stand here under Rexro's horn-wilting glare, I can feel panic grip my big stupid over-large heart.

And without really thinking it through I tilt my scaly head back and shout:

"What should I do? What should I do? What should I do?"

Then, as if summoned by my cry for help, a small mirrored triangle appears in the air several feet in front of me.

Now even though I've never seen one before, I know in my bones that what I'm looking at is a rip in the space-time continuum.

And I know that this mirrored triangle hovering here in the air is an honest-to-goodness wormhole.

But I don't have time to think about this because at that moment an insanely long red tongue comes zooming out of the mirrored triangle and then wraps around my neck and cinches itself tight like a noose.

My eyeballs bulge.

The sudden sensation of having this long insidious tongue wrapped tight around my neck is grotesque in the extreme.

Then the tongue yanks back and I'm whipped off my webbed feet and I go flying headfirst through the wormhole. And at the time I can't make sense of what's happening but I do notice when I shoot through the wormhole that I hear the same noise you hear when you come flying down out of the sky at top speed and then dive into the ocean.

Splash.

19

SPLASH,
TURNS OUT MY SCALY GREEN ASS
WAS WRONG

Splash.

But I'm wrong. Turns out it isn't a wormhole. Though considering what the mirrored triangle turns out to be, a wormhole would've been a welcome alternative.

Professor Nog.

Underworld.

I should've known. The mirrored triangle is a portal to Professor Nog's lair in the Underworld. The Realm of the Dead.

This is another one of WarWings' claims to fame. We're the only military academy in the galaxy whose campus extends to the Underworld and whose curriculum prepares cadets for battling and conquering hideous creatures and spirits from the Realm of the Dead.

Some of our notable alumni have made a real name for themselves by doing mega damage in the twisted hellscapes of the Abyss. And because of our alumni's battles with deranged ghost armies and warlord spirits and whatnot, there's plenty of demons and deadlings who when they see a WarWings grad coming down the street on a dark night will cross to the other side.

Professor Nog's the only member of the WarWings faculty who is actually dead, though. And so going to his lair is never exactly a picnic. No matter how many times you've been there, it always manages to give you a fresh case of the heebie-jeebies.

So it was Professor Nog's cold dead tongue that had looped

around my long neck and then yanked me into the Realm of the Dead.

Now as I squat here in his repulsive lair in the Underworld, I take one look at crusty old Professor Nog soaking himself in a LavaTub and grinning at me with a beakful of fangs, and decide I want to get out of here pronto.

Nog looks at me from the LavaTub and he squirts blacksmoke out his nostrils. "Welcome, Gork. Nice of you to drop in this morning."

But because of all the deranged voices floating through the air, and their weird moaning and spooky cries, I'm having a hard time focusing on Professor Nog. That's the first thing you notice down here, the constant cries for help.

In the Underworld, there's all these crazy disembodied voices howling and screaming for all of eternity. And the chorus of these hideous voices will fray your nerve endings in a heartbeat. And what with all this moaning plus the ethereal presence of those ghosts and demons and deadlings swooshing around in Nog's lair, well it makes the scales on the back of my long green neck stand up.

I hiss and spray sparks out my beak. And I lash my tail around behind me.

But Nog doesn't even seem to notice my hiss. You'd be amazed at the stuff you can get away with when it comes to the dead. Maybe it's because their eyes and earholes are so old and crusty, I don't know. But you can take my word for it, the dead aren't nearly as perceptive as they'd have you believe. And while Nog's powers are immense, his actual talon-eye coordination is rotten. Downright pathetic, if you want to know the truth.

Then my horns start tingling like crazy. But that's to be expected, really. Any dragon with a pulse is gonna have tingly horns while they're down here in the Underworld. Tingly horns just come with the territory. I whip my tail around behind me, trying to shake off the big freakout that's building up inside me.

"Good morning, Professor! What an unexpected pleasure to see you, sir!" I say.

Of course I'm lying through my fangs. Because being down here in the Underworld is about as pleasurable as getting a lava enema.

But the thing you always have to keep in mind when it comes to Professor Nog is he is the sole dragon who has the power to send you back up to the World of the Living. And so you'd be a real fool not to be extra polite and all to Nog.

Earlier this semester there'd been a smart-aleck dragon named Torp who kept spitting lavaloogies at the rest of us cadets during Professor Nog's class. And finally one day in the middle of his lecture, Professor Nog walked over to Torp and, while continuing his lecture, just clamped a metal collar around Torp's long green neck and tossed him in a cage. And then Professor Nog got one of his pet demons to come wheel Torp's cage away, and that was the last any of us ever saw of that dragon fool Torp again.

None of us were crazy enough to ask Nog what'd become of Torp, and it was just generally understood that Torp's was a heinous and demented fate beyond reckoning.

The word around WarWings is that Professor Nog's at least five thousand years old. Whereas Dr. Terrible is only six hundred and eighty-four years old. Shoot, compared to Nog, my scaly grandpa is a mere baby dragon.

"Well Gork, I couldn't help but notice that you seemed like you were in a real bind up there," says Professor Nog, squirting blacksmoke out his nostrils. "I watched the whole thing from down here in my lair. And since Rexro is such a brute I thought why not give Gork a few minutes for his WILL TO POWER to reboot! Plus we might as well take this opportunity to consider your final grade, so you don't come crying to me later and make a fuss."

"Yes sir," I say. "Very kind of you to think of me, Professor."

I've been taking Nog's Conquering and Ruling Over Demons course this semester. So on some level I'm happy to discuss my grade. Because the truth is I surprised myself by how well I've performed when it comes to battling deranged ghosts and twisted spirits and demons in Professor Nog's class.

Just last week in class, Professor Nog had tossed me in a giant fiery pit full of melting bones and I'd savagely fought and defeated a platoon of blue Kethlethrop demons right there in the pit. I'd actually shown considerable WILL TO POWER that day in class, because I'd gone on a demented rampage and ripped the arms right off of those fleeing demons.

It was all pretty fiendish and ghastly of me, if I do say so myself.

And the rest of my dragon classmates had gathered around the edge of the fiery pit, cheering me on as I went full beasty on those blue demons.

Anyway, like I said, old Nog is the only WarWings faculty member who is actually dead. And if Professor Nog has any advanced degrees, I sure don't know about them.

As far as I can tell, his sole qualification for the position of professor is the fact that he's dead. Instead of a diploma on the wall, he's got his death certificate up there.

Now one cadet who loves Professor Nog is Fribby. Nog is Fribby's faculty adviser and she pretty much thinks he's the most righteous dragon in the universe. I am sure you can guess why.

Professor Nog grabs a timer on the side of the LavaTub and flips it upside down and the sand starts pouring down into the lower glass tube.

"In order to get you down here, I had to put a Time Freeze up there," says Professor Nog and points up with his talon in the general direction of the WarWings campus, which is several thousand leagues above us. "We don't have much time to discuss your grade. Five minutes tops." He nods at the timer where the sand in the top glass container is streaming down into the bottom glass container. "We've got a lot of ground to cover. So let's get started," he says. "Please lie down on the couch over there."

I peer across the room and see the couch he's talking about and it sure doesn't look like anybody's idea of a good time. This hideous couch is made of flaming hot coals.

"Make yourself comfortable, Gork," says Professor Nog, grinning a beakful of fangs.

Now I'm not exactly sure why I do what I do next. That's the way it is with me sometimes. I guess the pressure of being in the Underworld just gets to me and I sort of lose my mind. Goodness knows I wouldn't be the first dragon to do so down here.

Anyway, I take one more look at this demented couch made of flaming hot coals and shout, "Are you crazy? Heck no, I'm not getting on that couch! I'm on my Queen Quest! Maybe some other time, Professor!"

Then I turn and bound off on my green webbed feet and get a running start and leap into the air and flap my wings—*thwack-thwack*—and try to fly away as fast as I can.

Which isn't very fast, it turns out.

Because one of Nog's pets, a giant red demon, rises up out of the floor in front of me and roars a mouthful of flames. Now the weird part is this demon is two-dimensional. He's flat as a sheet of paper, but that doesn't prevent him from being insanely scary.

And at the last second, I recognize the demon as that former dragon Torp I was telling you about. The maniac who had the gall to cut up and spit lavaloogies in Professor Nog's class.

My God, how he has changed.

Well I guess that answers the question as to what Professor Nog does with his delinquent students. He turns them into pets.

If you consider a demon a pet, I don't know.

Now I'm sure not proud to have to be telling you this, but when that hideous demon Torp pops up right in front of my face, well I just shriek and faint in midflight.

20

HERE IN THE UNDERWORLD, PROFESSOR NOG SHOWS ME MY MORTAL FORECAST

I have no idea how long I'm out.

It could be a few seconds.

Or it could be a thousand years.

I really wouldn't know the difference.

That's how hard I fainted.

Anyway, when I finally come to, I slowly stand up on my trembling haunches.

"Tsk tsk tsk," says Professor Nog, still lounging in his LavaTub. "Well we sure are tightly wound today, aren't we, Gork? Now go lie down on that couch over there so we can discuss your grade."

I reach up and feel a giant knot on my scaly head. I'm woozy. I flick my powerstaff and a small mirror pops up in front of my beak and I study my scaly green reflection and see five nasty-looking slashes in my forehead from where that demon Torp has swiped me with his claws.

"Not bad, Professor," I say, looking at the slashes. "These could make some nice scars."

Now in case you don't know, teenage dragons love scars.

We love scars even more than tattoos. Because there's nothing that says mega WILL TO POWER like having a bunch of boss scars all over your scaly green ass, especially if you've got a fiendish story to go with your scars. And picking up some legit claw scars on your forehead while you're down in the Underworld, well that's something that's guaranteed to get the dragonettes' attention, if you know what I mean.

So I'm feeling better already.

"So far so good, Professor. What's next on the agenda?" I say.

The professor looks at me and shakes his scaly green head like I'm an idiot. "You have no idea how much trouble you're in, do you, son?" he says. "Have you looked at today's Forecast? Have you even looked at *The Digital Fire-Breather*? Do you know what the Odds-makers have your death at for today, Gork?"

Hearing this, I instantly feel the confidence drain right out of me. The Oddsmakers are a secret syndicate of blind faculty who keep track of which cadets are most likely to die on a given day. And my earholes start quivering at the mere mention of the Oddsmakers.

The Oddsmakers are able to look into the future and see multiple possibilities for how any circumstance could work out. And using some complex and mysterious system of metrics and analytics and talon throwing and ash reading, each morning the Oddsmakers give the Mortal Forecast. And each morning they post these results up on *The Digital Fire-Breather.*

How could I forget to check the Mortal Forecast this morning? You idiot!

I guess with it being Crown Day and all, it must've slipped my mind to click to the back of *The Digital Fire-Breather* and check. Plus I was probably so busy reading that post about Dr. Terrible's disappearance that I'd been sort of distracted.

Now Professor Nog flicks his powerstaff and a colorful graph image of the Oddsmakers' Mortal Forecast appears in the air. And above the graph I see my name in bold red letters. And there's a diagonal slash through my name, as if I've already been crossed off the List of the Living.

"Read it and weep, Cadet Gork. 99.9% chance of you dying today," says Professor Nog. "You've got a 0.1% chance of making it through Crown Day alive! Down here when a dragon only has a 0.1% chance of living, that means it's pretty much game over. There's already a nest down here with your name on it."

Now if you want to know the truth, the tone of Nog's voice is seriously getting under my scales. It really pisses me off. Which, like I mentioned before, is a stupid thing to do. To get pissed off at Nog.

"With all due respect, sir. So! Freaking! What!" I shout. "And I sure don't see how you dragging me down here into the Underworld is increasing my chances of staying alive! I mean really, is that the wisest course of action? On the day when I have a 0.1% chance of survival? Are we not tempting fate here a little bit? Heck, why not just finish me off? Have you forgotten that it's Crown Day, sir? Don't you think I have better things to do than to waste my time here among the deadlings and demons and ghostlords and whatnot? And how do you ever get a moment of sleep or peace down here?! All this moaning from these disembodied voices and phantoms and all! It's giving me a damn headache, is what it's doing! Couldn't you just tell these things to shut up for once?! I mean seriously, doesn't all this hideous moaning and ghastly screaming sometimes just give you the creeps?!"

Then, because I'm suddenly terrified I might've offended old Nog, I add, "Sir."

"Don't be a fool," growls Professor Nog. "Haven't you learned anything in my class this semester? The closer you come to death, the greater your chance of surviving. In order to live, you've got to bleed." He flaps his wings and growls, "Besides, today I'm going to give you information that might save your life."

Great. I sure hope this has something to do with me getting Runcita to be my Queen.

"Like what information, sir?"

Professor Nog locks his cloudy yellow eyes on mine. "When you want to rule over a foreign land," he says, "you must first offer it a drop of your blood. Then wait to see if the land gives you its blessing in the form of a sacred bud."

Old Nog is really pissing me off now. With his mystic mumbo jumbo.

I'm starting to see lava.

Be cool. Be cool.

Remember you're in the Underworld.

Nog here is the only way out.

"*What* in the heck are you talking about, sir?" I say. "And what land am I going to want to rule over anyway? In case you've forgotten, I'm still on my Queen Quest. Aren't we getting a little ahead of ourselves, sir?"

Because Professor Nog is dead, he can see into the future. And he's always giving us cadets little helpful bits of advice. I mean he can't see into the future like the Oddsmakers or anything, but the ancient Nog definitely has some supernatural vision.

Now I realize old Nog in all his royal crustiness is suddenly standing right in front of me. And him being this close to me is freaking me out. Besides, when had Nog climbed out of the LavaTub and come over to me? I hadn't even noticed.

The dead can be real sneaky like that. Take it from me. The dead may not be much in the talon-eye coordination department, but they are probably the sneakiest bastards you ever will come across. Because when it comes right down to it, you really can't trust the dead any further than you can bury them.

"Am I correct in assuming that you want to live?" growls Professor Nog. "Because if so, then you'll be glad my counsel is what I'm here to give. Or is death something you do not fear? Because trust me, Gork, I don't have time to hold your talon here. Just follow my instructions and you might be OK, you may even manage to live through this day. Now when you come to the land over which you want to rule, give that land a drop of your blood. And then wait to see if the land gives you its blessing in the form of a sacred bud. Because take it from your old Professor Nog, this is the golden rule!"

The stuff Nog is saying to me right now is giving me a royal case of the creeps. Jabbering about my blood like that and all.

"Why don't you give the land a drop of *your* blood, sir?" I say, snorting firebolts. "If it's so dang important? I don't see why it needs to be *my* blood that's suddenly up for grabs!"

Professor Nog sighs and squirts blacksmoke out his nostrils. "Because there's going to be a multitude of opportunities for you to die today," he says. "Way too many for me to go over with you right now. But death is lurking around every corner for you today!"

"Death is lurking around every corner, sir? Give me a *break*. Aren't you being a little *melodramatic*, sir?"

And just like that, Professor Nog reaches out with his index claw and touches my green scales and instantly I feel a chill pass through my chest and seep into my heart. And my heart stops beating and turns into a block of meat encased in ice. I squat staring at Nog with my beak hanging open.

"That, young Gork," says Professor Nog, "is *death*. Now does that feel melodramatic to you?"

I reach up with my talon and feel my chest in horror.

No heartbeat.

I'm dead.

I knew it was coming, I mean that's how the Time Freeze works. The dragon that's extracted has to be dead for the majority of his time in the Underworld. But still.

I'm dead. I'm dead.

I can't believe I'm actually dead right now.

Now Nog flicks his powerstaff and then my scaly green body lifts up off the ground and floats up into the air and soars across the room.

This is a horrid sensation.

To be dead, and to be floating around this lair like this.

And then, well, Professor Nog means to drop me smack-dab on top of that hideous couch made of flaming coals. But instead he drops me down on the floor right next to the couch. Like I said, because Nog is dead and over five thousand years old, he doesn't exactly have the greatest talon-eye coordination.

Plunk.

I hit the ground on my back.

Yet I can tell by the way Nog is squatting there and staring in my direction that he doesn't know he's dropped me on the ground instead of the couch. And I feel kind of bad for him, if you want to know the truth. Without a doubt he is the crustiest professor I've ever had, but he means well, and I don't want to embarrass him.

So, feeling like a royal chump, I quickly get up and lie down on the couch as if Nog had just dropped me on top of it.

I even cry out, "Ouch!"

Just to give the old bastard some satisfaction, make him think he still hasn't lost his touch. I mean, you figure that's the one thing that really haunts the dead. Wondering if they've still got what it takes. At least it would me. If I were permanently dead. I'm pretty sure when I'm permanently dead I'll be the most insecure bastard in the whole damn Underworld.

Now as soon as my back hits the couch, these metal straps shoot out of it and strap my forelimbs and hind legs down.

Ouch.

This time it really does hurt. But of course I don't let on that it hurts, because I don't want to give this scoundrel the satisfaction. I strain against the clamps, but to no avail.

Lying there on the couch, I can feel my beak frozen in a horrified rictus of fcar.

"Now that you're comfortable and settled in," he says, "let us discuss your final grade for the semester, Gork."

"Yes sir."

"Well, cadet, I'm afraid I have bad news for you. And I know you're going to be upset. But I'm going to have to give you an A. I really have no choice in the matter. I'm sorry to have to be telling you this."

Holy crap. Do not lose your cool. Don't explode right now.

First of all, you know the situation is bad if Nog feels like he has to apologize to you, because it's against the law for a dragon to apologize. But I guess Nog isn't worried about breaking the law, because he's dead and all. Once you're dead, I guess the law no longer really applies. Or maybe the dead have their own laws? I don't know. And one thing's for sure, I'm in no big hurry to find out.

Now if you're a man-creature who's reading this, then you need to know that the grading system for us dragons is pretty much the opposite of your grading system. Because at WarWings an A is the lowest grade you can receive, it means you've failed the course. Whereas an F is the highest grade you can receive. So our class valedictorian this year will be some dragon geek who received four years of straight Fs. And here Professor Nog is saying he's going to give me an A for his Conquering and Ruling Over Demons course.

I am beyond outraged. I'm seeing lava.

Screw it! I'm sick of trying to keep my cool and being polite! This crusty fool has gone too far! I don't care if he keeps my scaly green ass in the Underworld for all of eternity! I'm not going to sit here and listen to him try and cheat me out of my F!

"That's crazy, sir!" I shout, snorting flamestreams. "I've performed well this semester! I figured I'd receive an F. What about all the demons I defeated last week in the fiery pit? You saw how I ripped all their arms off!"

"Yes I did," says Professor Nog. "You were a true barbarian in the fiery pit. This much I will admit. And I relished the screams of those demons as you ripped off their arms. On that day you were the cadet who comported himself with the most charm. But unfortunately this vid clip from your lair came vis-à-vis one of my micro-drones. And as you can imagine, this behavior I cannot condone!"

For a dead dragon, this scoundrel still has some ruthless rhyme skills. I have to admit, old Nog has a real way with words.

Then Professor Nog flicks his powerstaff and a holovid appears in the air and as soon as I see what it is I feel my giant heart sink. Because the holovid has been shot using a hidden micro-drone in the top right corner of my lair, and the footage is a little blurry but there's still no doubt about what it is you're looking at. And in the vid clip I'm lying in my nest with my talons covering my scaly green face and I'm sobbing and bawling and snuffling something awful.

I instantly realize this footage was shot last week. Right after I'd returned to my lair from Professor Nog's class on that day when I'd ripped those demons' arms off. I'd felt terrible after doing it, if you want to know the truth. I couldn't shake the sound of their horrifying screams out of my skull. The whole escapade had left me feeling super guilty and downhearted.

So I'd crawled into my nest and had a good cry.

This is a problem that's dogged me for years now. The tears. Sometimes when I do something real vicious that shows off my WILL TO POWER, then later I'll go back to my lair and put my scaly head in my talons and bawl my eyes out.

It's despicable, I know. And I always wind up hating myself for it afterward.

During my weekly sessions out at the Institute, my grandpa is forever flapping his beak at me about how my crying is the primary weak spot in my otherwise promising career as an Intergalactic Conqueror. Not counting my HORN DENSITY & IMPALABILITY rank of course, which is RemedialGore.

But the tears, well I blame them on my heinous cares-too-much heart.

I mean my HEART MASS INDEX rank is an off the charts DangerouslyJumbo.

Seems like I can never pull off even the most minor of ruthless acts without my stupid heart getting in the way. And out at the Institute, Dr. Terrible has warned me on multiple occasions that if I'm not able to cure my crying jags then he'll be forced to take more drastic measures, like surgically removing my tear ducts.

21

HERE IN THE UNDERWORLD,
PROFESSOR NOG TELLS ME ABOUT MY MOTHER AND FATHER,
BOTH OF WHOM DIED WHILE ON THEIR FERTILITY MISSION
TO PLANET EARTH

Anyway, now the holophoto floats over to Professor Nog and transforms into blacksmoke and then flies into his powerstaff.

"Frankly," says Professor Nog, "I consider it very generous of me to give you an A. Considering the nature of your infraction. I think you realize your punishment could be much more severe than simply failing my course!"

We both know what Nog means. Because crying is the highest possible crime a WarWings dragon can commit. And any dragon seen or recorded crying is immediately sentenced to death by firestream.

And right then I know we're both thinking of last night's Rage-Fest. Because we both know, what with my grandpa Dr. Terrible having humiliated Dean Floop last night by blinding him in his eye out on the campus quad, well Dean Floop would relish the opportunity to blast me with a firestream and reduce me to a pile of ash.

"Relish" probably isn't even a strong enough word. For the demented and dangerous Dean Floop, the act of firestreaming me would surely be luscious.

"But," says Professor Nog as he snorts firebolts, "I'm no fan of Dean Floop and his ilk here at WarWings. For one thing, Dean Floop is threatening to cut funding for our Underworld studies. And so you needn't worry, Gork, I'm not going to turn you in."

"Thank you, Professor," I whisper.

"For what, Gork?"

"For saving my life, sir."

I look with gratitude into Nog's ancient scaly green face and he stares back at me for a moment before blinking and turning away.

"Never mind. It's nothing," says Professor Nog.

I know I've just made Nog uncomfortable. Because thanking someone implies that they care about you. Which is universally regarded as a major character defect, to care like that.

But since we are alone, I know Professor Nog will let it slide. Whereas if there were other cadets present to witness my thank-you then Nog would be obligated to attack me on the spot. In order to save face and preserve dragon order. But the truth is, old wise Nog understands that I'm simply a victim of my compassionate heart, and so I can't curb my grotesque impulse toward verbal expressions of gratitude.

And what's more, secretly I know that Nog really does care. But that doesn't mean I have to disrespect him by rubbing his beak in it like this. Well I've still got a damn sight more to learn, in terms of growing up and becoming an insidious dragon fiend.

"Now you haven't heard from Dr. Terrible, have you?" says Professor Nog. "Do you know where he is? I must confess his disappearance last night has caused quite a ripple among us faculty who are sympathetic to his cause."

"No sir. I don't know where he is."

"I didn't think so," he says. "But of course it doesn't hurt to ask, because you never know. I especially liked the mind-swap your grandpa did between a dolphin and a bumblebee. How that dolphin spent all day flying around in the garden as if he were a bee. Hovering in front of a rose. Going from flower to flower, collecting pollen on the end of its nose!"

"Yes sir," I say, snorting blacksmoke out my nostrils.

But I'm thinking about how things turned out in the end for that poor worm who'd been mind-swapped with the lion. That deranged worm who through no choice of its own had been endowed with that insanely high ScalesOfMenace rank.

Because yesterday, Thursday, that worm surprised everyone by committing suicide.

The worm hung itself using a piece of thread.

One of the first-year cadets discovered the worm hanging over a sink in the Library bathroom.

And just this morning there had been a big article about the worm's suicide posted on our school datastream, *The Digital Fire-Breather.* It was posted right under the article about Dr. Terrible's disappearance and the fact that he was now wanted by the Council of the Elders for treason and was considered a fugitive at large.

And according to that article about the worm taking his own life, apparently the switch from vegetarian to carnivore had been too much. And the worm even scrawled a short suicide note in blood on the bathroom mirror: CAN'T STAND ANOTHER BITE OF MEAT.

But my train of thought is interrupted by Professor Nog's voice: "It's been crazy up there on the island this week. These are dark days for WarWings. I do hope Dr. Terrible is doing OK. I know some of my colleagues are whispering among themselves that Dean Floop murdered Dr. Terrible. Or that he's keeping Dr. Terrible prisoner somewhere. That would be hard to believe. But one thing is for sure, your grandfather wouldn't have deserted his Institute if he weren't afraid for his life."

Now I have to hand it to Nog, the old scaly green bastard has really put me at ease with the words coming out of his beak. But I should've seen it coming. And the only excuse I can offer for why I didn't is because I was so wrapped up in it being Crown Day and all. Any dragon could've seen the lecture coming like dark clouds gathering on the horizon.

Me, though, I get ambushed. Like a first-class fool.

"Now Gork, there is something else . . . ," says Professor Nog. And this is when the lecture starts. Of course I know Nog enjoys having his students lie on his couch made of flaming hot coals and lecturing them, but I didn't know Professor Nog would lay into my scaly green ass like this. Especially on Crown Day and all.

"Now Gork, I know somewhere inside you there's a cruel Ruler who wants to conquer his own planet! But you're never going to be able to live up to your potential if you don't first grow a pair of big horns! And shrink that heart of yours! And stop fainting all the time! And if you don't grow a pair of big black horns you're never going to get Dean Floop's daughter to be your Queen! And none of this is going to happen if you don't first get yourself some WILL TO POWER! Do you hear me, Gork! You need to focus on your BIOCON LEVS! Where's your STRATEGIC DESTRUCTION COMBAT READINESS?! Where's your MATING MAGNETISM?! How do you ever expect to conquer a planet with your current attitude?!"

I cough and roll over and look at old Professor Nog. "Conquer my own planet, sir? I don't know, Professor. Couldn't you get hurt doing that? Is it possible that I'm just not cut out for that line of work? Maybe I got the wrong kind of heart or something? I don't know, sir."

"Hurt?! You're worried about getting hurt?! Where's your WILL TO POWER, Gork?! You need to focus on your WILL TO POWER!" And then he whips out his powerstaff and uses it to project a 3-D holophoto in the air, right there in the middle of his lair. Old Nog says, "Just look at the long line of Terrible studs you've descended from!"

He presses a button on his powerstaff. "This photo is from when your great-grandfather conquered the planet Blistrixia Moof, which is in the Fubwidge Quadrant. And that red creature your great-grandfather is busy choking is a Frodaptherox. Now every Frodaptherox has five lives and each time they rise from the dead they grow another eyeball. So this fella here, well he's clearly on his fifth life. It took your great-grandfather three hours to conquer the entire planet of Blistrixia Moof and if you go there today you'll see big gold statues of your great-grandpa all over the planet. The Frodaptherox worship your great-grandfather as a god! Now don't you want to be worshipped as a god, Gork?!"

All this talk is getting me riled up. Or maybe it's the flaming coals scalding my wings, I don't know. Anyway, I hiss and spray sparks out of my black beak.

Then Nog presses a button on his powerstaff and growls: "Now this photo was taken at the You Belong to Me Now ceremony on planet Breg 3.27, which is in the Sarconian Quadrant. In this photo, as you can see, Dr. Terrible is assuming rule over the Slitch species on planet Breg 3.27. Now the Slitches have very long forked tongues they use as propellers to fly up and down the timestream.

"So your grandfather Dr. Terrible had to travel as far as possible up the timestream and conquer the futuristic Slitches there and then return to the present-day Breg 3.27 with a holovid showing his victory. Upon seeing the holovid, the present-day Slitches surrendered to Dr. Terrible, as you can see here in this photo."

Then Nog presses a button on his powerstaff. "Now here's a photo of your father, Stenchwaka The Terrible—"

"Sir, what was my father like?" I say. "I never got to know him. He's always been a big mystery to me, sir. On account of him dying during his Fertility Mission."

"Well," he says, "come to think of it, your dad, Stenchwaka The Terrible, was more like you, as I recall. He was, how shall we say, challenged. He had small horns. And his BIOCON LEVS were atrocious. Then during his senior year he turned into a time-travel addict. A junkie. Or so I heard, anyway. I've never been very clear on that part of the story. But for him to have procured your mother as his Queen, well he must have had something special that the rest of us couldn't see. It came as a tremendous shock to everyone when she accepted your father's crown."

"What was she like, sir? Did you know her? Nobody ever talks about my mother. I don't know anything about her, sir."

"Ah, your mother," says Nog, his ancient scaly green face brightening as if lost in pleasant memory. "She was one of the special ones, wasn't she? She was incredibly smart. Your mother had a gift, she did. Maybe the best poet we've ever seen at WarWings. She could sing her poems and make things happen—"

"Make things happen, sir? What do you mean?"

"Well," he says, snorting blacksmoke out his nostrils, "it's very hard to explain. We professors had never seen anything like it, to tell you the truth. But your mother was an incredible dragoness, who possessed the very essence of poetry in her blood. When she was a senior, every fella was trying to get her to be their Queen. The whole thing caused quite a ruckus, I'm afraid."

Professor Nog coughs and quickly wipes the corner of his eye with a talon.

Why are Nog's eyes all misty? Is this ancient monster crying?!

"But sir, why did my mother go with my father?" I say, squirting blacksmoke out my nostrils. "If my father was such a loser, sir."

"Well," says Nog, with a mournful streak in his voice, "I heard your father promised your mother great things. Because of his facility with time travel. He claimed they could do things a new way. Set an example for generations of dragons to come. Of course it was malarkey. But I'm afraid your mother was a romantic dragonette at heart. Plus she had the gift. And sometimes when a dragon has the gift of poetry, it makes them *too* confident. I'm afraid she didn't understand that there were limits, even for a dragonette as unique as your mother. It's very sad, I'm afraid. I've never forgotten your mother. I've always wondered how things would've turned out for her if she'd accepted a different cadet's crown for EggHarvest. Please don't quote me on any of this, young Gork. I can't claim to know all the specifics."

All this talk about my dead parents is making me feel sort of weird, and I can feel this terrific pressure in my skull.

"What about me, sir? Do I have the very essence of poetry in my blood too? Like my mom did? Is that possible, sir?"

Nog snorts blacksmoke out his nostrils, and his enormous green belly heaves as if it hurts him to say what he's about to say. "Of course not, young Gork. Here you are with your giant heart and your Snacklicious ranking, and you have to ask me such a question. Your mother was a true fiend. She had the highest WILL TO POWER ranking in her senior class. No, I'm afraid that you are more your father's son than anything else. As much as it pains me to tell you this. It's the truth. For some reason, your mother wasn't able to pass her gift for poetry along to you when she laid your egg."

I turn my scaly green head and start looking around Nog's lair.

"Well, are my mother and father down here in the Underworld, sir? Could I talk to them, sir?"

Nog closes his eyes and keeps them shut as if he is thinking deeply about something. I can hear the lava rumble in his belly. Then he opens his eyes and looks at me.

"I'm afraid not, Gork," he says, snorting blacksmoke. "Your parents died on planet Earth. So their ghosts are contained within Earth's underworld. It's really too bad. Because they'd certainly be most welcome here—"

"Ummm, Professor," I say, "I think I feel a little dizzy."

Professor Nog stops and turns and looks at my scaly ass and then he sniffs the air suspiciously. "My God," he says. "Gork, are you sweating?!"

"I can't help it," I say.

"I can smell you from here!" Nog pinches his scaly snout with his index and thumb claw, as if he's trying to keep himself from gagging. "Here!" He throws me a white towel from the stack he keeps next to his couch. "Clean yourself up before I puke!"

I use the towel to wipe my green scales. And if you want to know the truth, my sweat really does stink. By any measuring stick, I'm repulsive. With the sweat pouring out of my green scales like this. I mean I can't even stand to be in the lair with myself. That's how gross I am.

Now at this point, I do something stupid. I reflexively reach up and touch my horns. Just to check and see if maybe they've grown since I last touched them. And I guess if I'm being honest I'm desperately trying to find the silver lining in all this.

But Nog sees me touch my horns like that and he jumps all over me.

"Gork, do you know the reason *why* your horns are so small?"

"Am I a Mutant, sir?"

"No you're not a Mutant, Gork!" he says, snorting firestreams. "Your problem is you're underdeveloped emotionally! You need to act like the Terrible that is your birthright! Then your horns will grow so long that this Runcita chick you've been chasing all morning will be begging you to let her be your Queen for EggHarvest!"

Now by this point I'm listening to Professor Nog but I'm also busy wiping my forelimb pits with the towel, and it seems like the more sweat I wipe away, the more I start sweating. And Nog's sarcastic commentary definitely isn't helping matters, that's for sure. And by now I'm pretty sure I really do hate old Nog. It really is a very dirty trick for him to have pulled on my scaly ass. Sucking me down into the Underworld like this and making me lie on this hideous couch made of fiery coals, and then lecturing me like a real crazy old dead dragon.

Professor Nog watches me wipe my pits and he shakes his scaly green head and says, "I don't know, Gork. I don't know." Then he says, "Perhaps there is no hope for you after all!"

And with that he claps his talons together three times and there's a giant explosion of blacksmoke. And as I feel my particles being sucked several thousand leagues back up to WarWings, I hear Professor Nog whisper inside my head:

"Don't forget! When you want to rule over a foreign land, you must first offer it a drop of your blood. Then wait to see if the land gives you its blessing in the form of a sacred bud. Do not forget this, young Gork! Do not forget!"

22

SPLASH,
MY SCALY GREEN ASS IS BACK FROM THE UNDERWORLD

Splash.

I'm back from the Realm of the Dead.

I'm crouched here in the dark fiery corridor of WarWings. Just as I had been right before that mirrored triangle suddenly appeared in front of me and Professor Nog lassoed me with his cold dead tongue and yanked me down into his lair.

I glance around. One thing is for sure, Professor Nog wasn't lying when he said he dropped a Time Freeze on everyone. All these dragon fools here in the corridor are still frozen. Including that maniac Rexro.

Frozen in time.

It is totally silent and peaceful.

Maybe too quiet? I can't even hear my heart beating. Oh my God, am I still dead?! That would be the nastiest trick of all for Professor Nog to pull on me. To send me back up here and for me to still be dead!

I clap my talon over my chest and am instantly relieved to hear my gigantic and foolish heart beating away in there.

I snort flames of joy out my nostrils.

Thank goodness! I am alive!

So for a couple seconds I am just kind of standing here in the corridor and looking around and it's perfectly quiet and still. And I can see that depraved Rexro frozen still and his black beak is twisted up in a sneer. He's got one green webbed foot raised, and it's clear he was bounding toward me when he froze.

Then I glance around at Twelk and his fiendish dragon pals, who are frozen in the middle of their chaotic gestures. Their yellow eyes are bugged-out, looking extremely psychotic.

Some of them have their tongues sticking several feet out of their beaks, frozen in the middle of some lewd gesture.

Some of them have flames jutting out their green snouts.

A couple of them have their spiked tails arched in mid–Threat Display.

The sight of all these nasties frozen in time is hideous.

At that moment, Professor Nog's voice pops up in my scaly head and says, *"Get out of there, Gork! The Time Freeze is almost up!"*

Yes sir!

I leap into the air and flap my wings like a maniac and zoom down the corridor.

But then at that moment the Time Freeze must have expired.

I can just picture the last grain of sand dropping down inside Professor Nog's timer.

Now behind me I can hear all those fiends leap back into motion. And the sonic boom of Twelk and his dragon pals snorting with wicked laughter, and the general pandemonium in the corridor, comes rushing back into my earholes.

"Where is he?! Where did he go?!" shouts Rexro.

I flap my wings and turn left down a dark corridor.

Thwack-thwack.

Inside my scaly head, Professor Nog's voice whispers, *"You must hurry! Rexro is coming for you!"*

23

ENTER MY SECRET WEAPON, WHICH WILL HELP ME GET ON WITH THE BUSINESS OF HAVING RUNCITA LAY MY EGGS

I whiz in among the crowds of other flying cadets and I keep casting my green snout back and forth, hoping to catch a whiff of Runcita's juicy scent.

Now the wind cutting across my black beak is screaming for mercy.

I flap my leathery wings like a maniac. I zoom past the Lava Pools and see naked cadets laughing and horsing around and splashing each other and shooting lava out their nostrils and using their tails to throw lavaballs. On any other day I would stop for a good soak. Because there's nothing to boost your CORE FLAME TEMP and your MATING MAGNETISM and your overall WILL TO POWER like submerging your scaly green ass in a lava pool and holding your breath for an hour or so.

Well according to Dr. Terrible, the only other thing that's better than lava baths for boosting your WTP is swordupuncture.

And Dr. Terrible would always make a point to say, "And when it comes to swordupuncture, I'm talking about someone who really knows how to use a blade. Not one of these bozos they got on the mainland who just because they took a fencing class, now they think they can call themselves a swordupuncturist!"

Out at the Institute, my scaly grandpa promised me that if he wasn't able to cure my WILL TO POWER before the EggHarvest, then he'd introduce me to his personal swordupuncturist. This chick he was forever raving about, named Metheldra. But since we aren't on speaking terms anymore, and because he's gone and vanished, well I guess there's no chance of that happening. Though what I wouldn't give right now for a session with Metheldra the swordupuncturist. Dr. Terrible promised me that after one session with this dragon chick Metheldra my THRASH OPTIMIZATION score and my MATING MAGNETISM score and my STRATEGIC DESTRUCTION COMBAT READINESS score would skyrocket and that my horns would grow as a result.

A legit swordupuncture session would definitely hit the spot right about now. I guess I'm starting to feel a little desperate and all.

But then I tell myself to stop getting so downhearted about the fact that there won't be any swordupuncturist rescuing my scaly green ass today. And so I better just focus on the things that I can control.

Thwack-thwack.

Now I flap my wings and swerve and bank and hook a sharp left down a dark fiery corridor. I keep casting my snout back and forth, hoping to catch a whiff of Runcita's juicy scent.

Where is my Queen?

I fly by the Firing Range, where dragons are squatting at their posts and shooting their tongues fifty yards downrange and trying to impale or lasso the furry humanoid creatures scurrying around in the Target Zone.

Thwack-thwack.

There are dozens of fiendish nasties whizzing off to my left and my right and there are deranged cadets zooming straight at me, flying in the opposite direction. The cadets' flight patterns are so jerky and hyper that you have to keep a close eye on everything going on around you there in the air, or you can easily wind up as a dead *splat* on the wall.

I fly by the Egg Hatchery and see Professor Pruck lecturing a group of female cadets on caring for their eggs. And ways to fend off the father dragon who typically will try to eat his mate's eggs when she's not looking. Now Professor Pruck appears to be demonstrating an extreme combat maneuver that involves slicing the neck with her powerstaff. And I know it's not uncommon for a female dragon to kill and eat kill her mate if she catches him trying to scarf her eggs.

Thwack-thwack.

But my Queen-to-Be, Runcita, is nowhere to be found and I start to panic because it feels like I'm running out of time. The dark fiery corridor is now overflowing with flying cadets and I'm busy trying to keep from getting knocked unconscious by all the leathery wings beating around my scaly green head. Seems like no matter which way I turn, somebody's nasty toe claw is dangling right in front of my face.

Then I whip out my powerstaff and tap the screen and pull up something I'd really hoped I wouldn't be forced to use. Something to help me close the deal on my Queen Quest. Just a little something to tilt the odds in my favor. The extra edge I need.

So I can get on with the business of having Runcita lay my eggs.

The wind blasting across my beak makes a whistling noise.

It's definitely time to use my Secret Weapon.

Now as I shoot down the dark corridor I feel cadets knocking into me and dinging me and of course none of them say excuse me or sorry. Because here at WarWings it's illegal to apologize, and any dragon caught using the S-word is instantly sentenced to death by firestream. Per Dean Floop's orders.

Thwack-thwack.

Now as to my Secret Weapon. The device which will enable me to move on to the real business of the day.

The nanotracker. Now don't judge my scaly green ass when you hear this, but last night I stuck this nanotracker on Runcita's left wingjoint while she was asleep in her lair.

Now before you go jumping to conclusions, let me make it clear I didn't *personally* sneak in and stick this tracking device on Runcita's left wingjoint while she slumbered in her lair.

I mean, what kind of monster do you take me for, anyway?

No, what I did was I used one of my tiny little micro-drones to delicately fasten the tracking device onto Runcita's left wingjoint while she was asleep in her lair. I felt really bad and guilty about doing it, if you want to know the truth. That's why I called it my Secret Weapon.

Now as I fly along in the dark fiery corridor I hold the powerstaff screen out in front of me and see the entire WarWings campus laid out on the screen. And then I see it.

The blinking red dot that's Runcita.

Yes! It's working! Holy crap. I can see Runcita right now on the screen. God I feel a little guilty about this. Using a tracking device and all. But hey, not so guilty that I'm not going to use it.

The tracker is alive and well. Thank goodness for my micro-drone. Let me come right out and say it: a micro-drone is the best friend a dragon could ever hope to have.

Now I tap the screen with my index claw to triangulate Runcita's location and watch the blinking dot as it processes all the data.

Then Runcita's location shows up on the screen in big block letters: **COLISEUM OF HEROES.**

Ah, so that's where my little Queen is hiding! The Coliseum of Heroes. Hold tight, my dearest Runcita. I am on my way! It won't be long now!

So I flap my wings and hook a left down a dark fiery corridor. I am on my way to the Coliseum of Heroes. I flap my wings and swerve and bank and then take a sharp right. I fly by the WarWings Museum of Natural History. Which is full of strange creatures that have been captured from foreign planets over the centuries and then killed and stuffed and put on display.

When I was growing up as a young dragon here on the island, my grandpa Dr. Terrible used to bring me to the Museum of Natural History on the weekends. We'd go to the special wing of the museum dedicated to just the creatures Dr. Terrible had caught and killed and brought back from his fiendish adventures as an Intergalactic Conqueror. Those were good times. Walking talon in talon through the museum with Dr. Terrible as we strolled through the hushed environs of the museum and gazed at the stuffed creatures in their glass cases. Our hearts filled with a sense of awe and the miracle of existence.

Every so often my scaly grandpa would use the tip of his spiked tail to whap me affectionately on the back of my head and say, "Hold up. I want to show you this guy here. Now he may not look it, but *this* bastard was difficult to catch!"

We'd spend the entire Saturday afternoon in WarWings's Museum of Natural History. Dr. Terrible would point out the different psychotic creatures and he'd explain to me how he caught them and how much of a fight they'd put up in their death throes.

And my favorite creature in the Dr. Terrible wing of the museum is this repulsive species called a Prete. Now this Prete is a small hairy manbird creature who, according to my grandpa, speaks nothing but declarations and opinions, but whose brain is so small that it is invisible to the naked eye.

Dr. Terrible discovered this degenerate Prete species on the planet Kroo. And my grandpa explained to me that the Prete is a flightless manbird species that purposefully makes their little beak putrid and revolting by letting their fangs get rotten and fall out.

And when I asked Dr. Terrible how the Prete made his beak so heinous, he said, "By eating other creatures' poo. Eventually all their fangs rot and fall out of their beak. And when the Prete creature breathes he makes a strange whistling sound."

What was ironic, my grandpa said, is this Prete creature showed so much disregard for its own beak but then expected other creatures to pay attention to its beak, or to the opinions that came out of it, anyway.

I remember, as a little dragon squatting before the stuffed Prete in the glass case, I looked up at my grandpa and whispered, "But why would this vile Prete creature make himself so heinous like that, Dr. Terrible?"

"Because the Prete has such a tiny brain," said Dr. Terrible.

"How small is the Prete's brain, Dr. Terrible?"

"Here," he said, "let's go look at it under a microscope."

And lo, there in the Museum of Natural History they even had a Prete's brain on display. And you could stick your eye up to a microscope and just make out the brain, which when magnified looked like a peach pit.

Now according to my grandpa, the only time the other creatures on planet Kroo paid attention to the Prete was when the manbird jumped off of a cliff in an attempt to fly but instead plummeted to the ground and broke its hind legs. Or gave itself whiplash. Then all the different creatures on planet Kroo would gather around the Prete where it lay on the ground and they'd laugh at the Prete for being so stupid and vile.

Thwack-thwack.

I flap my wings and fly past the Arctic Laboratory where a scaly green dragonette is blasting an icestream out her beak and neutralizing a firestream that one of her classmates is shooting at her.

Glance down at powerstaff. See my FLIGHT SPEED at 137 MPH.

I can feel my scaly green ass relax and go into pure flight mode.

My reaction time faster.

My vision sharper.

You become one with the air.

At this speed, you are a weapon.

I speed, I eradicate.

Velocitas Eradico.

Everything is a blur, but you see it perfectly.

I zoom past the Creative Evolution Lab and see Professor Newg blast a chrome-flex dragon robot with a mega firestream until the scalebot melts into a pool of silver on the floor.

What the heck did that poor robot do to get the melt treatment from Professor Newg like that?

Probably the Datalizard violated the Third Law of Robotics, which is that there is no Third Law of Robotics. Basically, Professor Newg invented this oxymoronic law so he can have carte blanche to melt robots whenever he feels like it.

I know Fribby and her other Dragodroid pals hate Professor Newg, and at one point they were considering sending a hit squad to assassinate him in his lair. Fribby was always snarling, "Why did Newg become a professor of robotics if he's so darn terrified of the Rise of the Machines?"

Thwack-thwack.

I flap my wings and shoot past the Urban Warfare Center where Professor Bluce is teaching cadets how to take control of a planet and turn its citizens into your personal slaves. Professor Bluce's method involves secretly amping the gravity levels to the point where all the structures collapse and the citizens can't even get up off the ground, because the gravity is so dense.

This is Professor Bluce's big academic theory, Escalating Gs.

Now I took Professor Bluce's course my sophomore year and I reckoned his whole concept of Escalating Gs was pure flapdoodle. I mean just because you max out a planet's gravity levels to the point where the citizens can't even stand up, that doesn't mean these creatures are your slaves.

I figured Professor Bluce's whole Escalating Gs strategy was one of those hifalutin conquer tactics which sounds good in the classroom but as soon as you try to apply it to the real world the whole thing just collapses. And what made Professor Bluce's class even more of a sham is the fact that all of us cadets knew the professor had never even conquered a single planet himself.

Thwack-thwack.

So in the span of about ten minutes, I fly all the way from the west wing of the Main Building to the Coliseum of Heroes. Now the coliseum is really something to see. And it never fails to take your breath away when you first fly in here under the great domed roof, which is constructed of gold and white marble and is at least a thousand feet high.

The marble floors of the coliseum are stained red with blood. From all the cadets who've fought each other to the death there in violent wing-to-wing combat affairs through the centuries.

Just being here makes you feel more radiant.

And as I flap my wings up here in the air I quickly scope out the six or seven white marble observation decks mounted up high on thick gold columns. These observation decks are designed so that cadets can hang out up there and get a panoramic view of the bloody wing-to-wing combat affairs that take place below.

I look around and see clusters of nasty-horned cadets lounging around on all the observation decks. Except one. There's one empty observation deck, thank goodness. I flap my wings even harder and rocket toward the empty observation deck.

Now as I come up on it I grab the marble edge with my toe claws and for a split second there I am hanging upside down.

And then I gently flap my wings and hoist myself upright so that now I am standing on the observation deck.

Thank goodness. My wings are exhausted!

Now where the heck is my Queen?

24

RUNCITA'S LUSCIOUS SCENT MAKES MY NOSTRILS FLARE

I feel nauseous and light-headed.

Being so high up and all. I'm actually scared of heights, if you want to know the truth. And for a dragon that's a disgraceful thing to be, and so I've never told anybody that before. Sometimes when I fly I get vertigo and feel dizzy.

Anyway, so being way up here on the observation deck in the Coliseum of Heroes is definitely freaking my scaly green ass out. And as I squat here and peer down I feel a little flash of vertigo and it feels like the coliseum is collapsing to the left.

So just to be on the safe side, I wrap my tail around the main beam of the deck and knot it. This way, in case I happen to faint, my knotted tail will keep me from falling to my death below.

My Secret Weapon. I peer down at the screen on my powerstaff and there's the blinking red light. Larger now, signaling to me that I am indeed close to the target of my heart.

My Queen.

Now I whip my binoculars off my utility belt and lean over the edge and proceed to scope out the crowds of dragons below for Runcita.

Come on, Luscious, where are you?

My nostrils flare as I pick up Runcita's scent, wafting all the way up here on the observation deck.

Mmmmm. I smell you, Luscious.

I peer through my binocs, though it's sort of hard to focus, what with the mobs of cadets shrieking and bouncing around in the coliseum. Nothing but green heads and spiked tails as far as the eye can see.

I zero in on a gang of senior fellas playing Whap Whap. Then I watch as one of the seniors, this scaly fool named Spaetz, well he dances right into the middle of the Whap Whap circle with a grin on his beak and gets *whapped* so hard on the back of his scaly green head he blacks out and collapses onto the floor. Then one of those deranged cadets steps forward and uses his spiked tail to start whip-a-whapping the poor bastard Spaetz on the floor, but he doesn't budge. And the rest of the dragon fellas start snorting and hooting and spitting lavaloogies on him.

No Runcita there. Come on, Luscious, where are you?

I swing my binocs toward the opposite side of the coliseum and zero in on this senior cadet that everyone calls Lick Lick. He's got a crowd of dragons watching him while he juggles what look like forty or so humanoid skulls using only his talons and his tail and his powerful long tongue.

Luscious, you can't hide from me.

Come out, come out wherever you are!

I whip my binocs over toward the coliseum entrance and zero in on this cute scaly senior dragonette named Buddle whom I know from my Escape and Evasion class. Buddle's showing off by shooting fireballs out her black beak, and each fireball's in the shape of a WarWings faculty member's head.

Buddle shoots a fireball out her beak that looks just like Professor Prook, who's the only five-headed dragon that WarWings has on faculty.

Then this chick Buddle shoots a fireball out her beak that is the spitting image of Dean Floop's repulsive scaly head with his eye patch and the familiar pissed-off look on his beak. And all the fool dragons gathered around shriek and snort and point their index claws at Dean Floop's fiery head as it zooms through the air. The fireballs shaped like faculty members' heads bounce around the Coliseum of Heroes, and all the other scaly dragons are howling as they scramble to avoid getting hit by this chick Buddle's balls.

I am starting to lose patience here, Luscious.

Don't you want to wear my beautiful crown and lay my eggs, Luscious? Show yourself to me!

Here in the coliseum you can feel the insane levels of tension in the air because it's Crown Day. I figure all those senior cadets down below who are showing off by juggling skulls and shooting designer firestreams and whapping each other over the head with their tails are really just engaging in elaborate mating rituals. Because they're hoping that a dragon of the opposite sex will see them and want to be their King or Queen for EggHarvest.

Then at that moment I feel my powerstaff vibrate, and I look down and see it's a message from Fribby:

> **I'm doing fine! Rexro tried to catch me but I bolted out of there!**
>
> **Right now I'm back in the spaceship, getting my stuff ready so I can come back in for my next class. They had to shut down the teleportation pad temporarily so we have to walk onto campus now. Any luck with Runcita?!**

I don't have time to shoot her a message back, and plus I figure I'll just meet up with Ms. Cyber Scales once she gets in the building. Now as I scope the area down below for Runcita, a giant swarm of bats come flying through the Coliseum of Heroes, flapping their wings and screeching. There must be thousands of them. And a scaly green dragonette down on the ground shoots her tongue out thirty feet into the air and snatches one of the bats. "*Gulp.* Mmmmm."

But no Queen-to-Be in sight.

So I check my powerstaff to get a bead on Runcita and I hold the powerstaff screen out in front of me.

For a brief moment, I see the red blinking dot from the nano-tracker on Runcita. It looks like she's still in the Coliseum of Heroes.

But then the blinking red dot vanishes.

What?!

I tap at the screen with my claws.

But the blinking red dot is gone.

I keep frantically tapping the screen.

Then on the screen it says: **SIGNAL TERMINATED.**

Oh my God! Did Runcita find the device on her?! Oh my God!

My heart sinks. Because I know if Runcita found my tracking device it'll be easy enough to track the home signal and decipher that the nanotracker belongs to me. And then Runcita will surely turn me in to her dad.

Dean Floop will be coming for me now!

Suddenly there's a loud flapping of powerful leathery wings next to me and horrid bursts of air explode near my scaly green head. And in the midst of trying to keep myself from falling off the observation post I realize with alarm that some dragon has just flown up and come barging onto my deck. My horns instantly start tingling.

I turn toward the intruder and growl, "Hey what's the big—"

But then I stop when I see who it is.

What the—?

25

THE DATAHATERS WILL GO
ON A ROBOT KILLING SPREE

"What are you doing, following *me*?!" I growl.

"Don't flatter yourself, Weak Sauce," growls Trenx. "I just flew up here to this deck to get away from the crowds below. And now I find you here!"

I wrap my tail more tightly around the observation post's main beam.

What is this fool doing here? There's no way this is a coincidence. Trenx is up to something. He's playing an angle here. Think, Gork. Think!

"Whatever," I say. "Hey," trying to act all casual, "you haven't seen Runcita Floop around this morning, have you?"

"Oh *come on*, you too?!" he says. "Are you crazy? Dean Floop would never in a million years let you take her to EggHarvest—"

I grab this robot by his cape collar and twist my talon tight.

"Listen," I growl. "I've been having a real bad morning so far. And the truth is I have a lot of pent-up frustration. So answer my damn question. Have you seen *Runcita*?!"

Mr. Gigabyte looks at me like I've lost my mind. He reaches up and smacks my talon off his collar like he's swatting away a nasty fly. Then he steps back and arrogantly swings his long silver neck from left to right, so that the cape collar falls naturally the way it's supposed to.

Now by this point I've had about all I can take from this Reptilizoid. Here he thinks he's some sort of badass because of those mega black horns on his silver head, and he has no idea the only reason he even has those horns is because of me. Because Dr. Terrible is using him to get to me.

So without really thinking about what I'm doing, I open my beak and squirt a jetstream of venom right at his scaly metal face.

Or some dragons just call it "juice." The venom, that is.

Now like every other dragon here on the island, I've got venom sacs lining my throat and I can shoot juice up to forty feet with pretty much near perfect accuracy. And the venom can be lethal for a good many creatures in the galaxy, but not for another dragon.

Though if another cadet splats you with some juice then you'll get a demented rash and probably have to go to the WarWings Medical Center to fetch some sort of ointment to put on your scales.

Anyway, the venom squirts out my beak in a jetstream and flashes through the air and zooms straight for Trenx's face.

But then at the last second he gracefully bobs his big silver head to one side and dodges the stream.

"I ought to rip your heart out and eat it for pulling a stunt like that!" he growls.

He peers at the sizzling venom on the gold column and then looks back at me in disbelief. He crouches down low on his chrome-flex haunches and hisses and big sparks spray out of his beak and bounce off my scaly green face.

"Try that again, Weak Sauce, I dare you!" he snarls. "Squirt some more of your nasty juice at me and I promise it'll be the last thing you ever do! I'll chop your dang head off and feed your brains to my pet cheetah back in my lair! And yeah, fool, of course I know today's Crown Day! I just got that chick Yavarka to be my Queen!"

Now I've seen Trenx's pet cheetah in his lair and that thing is no joke.

"Yavarka?!" I growl, flapping my wings. "Come on, how is that even possible?"

Yavarka is easily one of the juiciest and most luscious dragon chicks in our grade. And so I figure he has to be lying.

Mr. Gigabyte flicks his powerstaff and a holovid appears in the air. The floating holovid shows the robot down on one haunch, holding out his crown to a surprised Yavarka. And even though you can't hear what the robot is saying it's obvious he's asking that dragonette to be his Queen. Either that or he's serenading her with his Mating Song.

Then the holovid jumps to another shot of luscious scaly Yavarka who's now proudly wearing Trenx's crown, and she's grinning at the screen and giving the thumb-claws-up sign.

And you know how they say the camera always adds ten pounds?

Well in the holovid clip, this robot's two mega black horns look twenty pounds heavier.

Now I can't believe this Datalizard got that faboo Normal chick Yavarka to be his Queen, especially considering he's a robot. But I guess once you're a member of Masters of Chaos, a hot Normal chick will jump at the chance to be your Queen. Don't matter if you're a robot or not.

Well once word gets out about this, the DataHaters will be going ballistic.

They'll go on a robot-killing spree.

"Hey bud." I reach out with my talons and straighten his cape collar a little. "My bad," I purr. "Listen, have you seen Runcita? Help a brother out. I feel like I'm running in circles here, chasing my own tail."

I watch Trenx carefully. Because his eyes are now glowing bright red from the inside like instead of a brain he has an active volcano in his skull. And when a robot's eyes glow bright red it's always a sure-fire sign that he's about to go bronco and rip somebody's lungs out.

I whisk my tail around behind me, keeping it ready in case I have to dive off the observation post.

Then unexpectedly the glowing red light in the robot's eyes starts to fade.

"OK. I hear ya," says Trenx, looking like his old self. "Let me see what I can do." He speaks some code into this tiny boss microphone attached to his cape collar. I have to assume this is a Masters of Chaos microphone, a way for members to keep in touch with one another.

Then he turns to look at me, and sprays sparks out his metal beak. "OK, word is that Runcita's right now in the Dining Hall munching on a bat sandwich," he says. "That's actionable intelligence. You can bet the farm on it. I don't think you should do this but if your mind's made up, well then there you go. But just don't tell nobody where you got Runcita's coordinates, OK? Because it could cost me my membership in Masters, and getting kicked out of Masters is no picnic on account of before they kick you out they kill you. And I don't much feel like dying today. So I had to lie and say the intel on Runcita was for another member. So you didn't hear this from me, OK?"

I wipe the sweat off my scaly brow with the back of my talon.

"Thanks, buddy," I whisper, flapping my wings. "You're the best. Seriously. I really appreciate it."

Then I clench my talon into a fist and hold it up high for a talon bump.

But Trenx just stares at my fist in the air like it's a piece of moldy broccoli.

Then I see the robot's left eye twitch like something's bothering his psyche but he's trying to hide it.

Oh, so that's how it is now.

Big horns don't bump talons with small horns, that's some kind of unwritten rule.

He knows it and now I know it.

And now he has that boss **FEAR ME** tattoo on his shiny silver wing to prove it.

I keep my clenched talon in the air for the bump.

And truthfully it seems like Trenx is just going to leave me hanging.

But finally he reaches up and quickly bumps it like he's scared that I might be contagious.

Then his eyes get serious. "But I should warn you, Weak Sauce," he says. "I heard that Bruggert—"

I don't wait to hear the rest.

I leap off the observation deck and flap my wings and take off flying in the direction of the Dining Hall.

Where is my Queen?

But it turns out I should've stayed and listened. Because that robot Trenx was aiming to warn me about this ruthless and hideous dragon named Bruggert in my senior class. Bruggert is definitely the most ghastly bastard in our senior class and the most deranged member of the Masters of Chaos at WarWings. A true super-fiend. And Mr. Gigabyte was trying to warn me that Bruggert had put the word out on the Masters of Chaos network that he was going to offer Runcita his crown for EggHarvest, and any other fool dragon who tried to ask Runcita would instantly be mutilated and killed.

Now when I replay the events of this Crown Day in my scaly head, I've often wondered how things would've turned out if only I had stayed on the observation post that morning and listened to the robot's warning.

But instead I just fly out of the Coliseum of Heroes like a moron and flap my leathery wings and keep zooming onward.

Thwack-thwack.

26

HOW DEAN FLOOP BLAMED THE RECENT DEATHS OF ALL THOSE CADETS ON DR. TERRIBLE, WHICH RESULTED IN LAST NIGHT'S DOCTOR VS. DEAN RAGEFEST OUT ON THE CAMPUS QUAD

On my way to the Dining Hall, I get Dr. Terrible and Dean Floop on the brain again.

I get them on, and I can't get them off. Last night's RageFest. The events which led to Dr. Terrible's disappearance. I mean he just disappeared last night, so I guess it's only natural for me to be thinking about him. Plus if I can figure out where my scaly green grandpa is hiding, then I can turn him in to Dean Floop. Anything to put the demented Dr. Terrible on hold, keep him from messing with me from afar. It'll serve the scoundrel right for giving those giant horns to Trenx like that.

Now like I told you before, all seventeen of those poor cadets were ruthlessly executed by Dean Floop in just two days. And so by Thursday afternoon—which was just yesterday—Dean Floop and the Elders were considering shutting down Dr. Terrible's Institute of Advanced Biokinetics and Neuroanatomy. As a kind of stopgap measure and public relations gesture all balled up in one.

So my grandpa was summoned to the campus quad yesterday evening for a Public Debate against Dean Floop to be held in front of the entire dragon cadet corps and the Council of the Elders. This is the event which would instantly become known all over the island as the Doctor vs. Dean RageFest.

Or just RageFest for short.

At the Public Debate Forum last night, all of us cadets stood in formation around the Debate Circle. And the Council of the Elders sat up high on their perches so they could watch the proceedings from on high. Then, before Dean Floop and my scaly grandpa even began debating each other, they paced around on their webbed feet and stalked each other with their massive leathery wings fully extended. They raised their spiked tails in Threat Displays and roared and blasted hideous flamestreams out their flared nostrils.

Now toward the end of the debate, my scaly green grandpa pointed his powerstaff at Dean Floop.

"This dragon is a complete buffoon!" bellowed Dr. Terrible. "And I submit to you that the Dean squats here before us today blowing firestreams straight out his poo-hole! How do I know this? Because no dragon's scaly face could be this ugly! Nor could their beak make so little sense! So the Dean is speaking straight out of his poo-hole! I rest my case!"

All of us cadets standing in formation started snorting with laughter over Dr. Terrible's poo-hole comment. Dr. Terrible was clearly outraged his name was being dragged into this whole sordid affair, because he'd had nothing to do with the deaths of any of those cadets.

Then my scaly grandpa turned to the Council of the Elders and pointed out that it was Dean Floop who'd stood as judge in each of those poor dragon cadets' cases. And that it was Dean Floop who seemed just a wee bit firestream-happy.

A bunch of us cadets standing in formation shuffled our webbed feet and whisked our tails around.

"Hear, hear! Hear, hear!" we murmured.

And as Dean Floop stood there behind the podium watching and listening to Dr. Terrible's rant, you could see the Dean's eyes blooming red in their sockets. Then Dean Floop leapt up in front of the Council and raised his tail in a Threat Display and pointed an angry curved index claw at my scaly green grandpa.

"Let me remind everyone here," roared Dean Floop, "that it was the sight of *this dragon's* bizarre research experiments which caused those three cadet dragons to go insane in the first place! And so if it weren't for Dr. Terrible's Institute then none of us would even be in this mess right now! Therefore I suggest we shut his Institute down immediately! So, honorable members of the Council, I move we now take a vote! All in favor of shutting down Dr. Terrible's Institute, say 'aye'!"

"I've got your 'aye' right here, you scoundrel!" snarled my grandpa.

Then he opened his black beak and blasted a hideous flamestream, and the tip of the flamestream nicked Dean Floop's left eye and left him blind. Now Dean Floop was bent over clutching his bloody scaly green face in his talons and shrieking. Though within hours Dean Floop would take to wearing a black patch over his eyeless socket and indeed seemed to relish his new fashion accessory.

Then my grandpa turned to address the crusty old dragon Elders up on their perches. "Members of the Council, my business here is finished!" roared Dr. Terrible. "Now if you wish to reach me I'll be cooling my toe claws somewhere far away from this wailing buffoon. I bid you farewell!"

I was standing in formation along with all the other cadets and watched the debate unfold in real time. And I have to admit that seeing Dr. Terrible give his fiendish speech like that, well it definitely made me twitch my tail a couple times with pride. You couldn't help but feel good about being related to the scaly green bastard.

Then my grandpa turned and stormed out of there, trailing a boss cloud of blacksmoke behind him. Now a few seconds later a WarWings detachment of Security Commando dragons was sent to fetch Dr. Terrible, but he had vanished.

He could not be found.

Not at his Institute nor anywhere else on the island.

The WarWings Security Forces, led by Rexro, deployed search parties in all directions and to all layers of the atmosphere: by air, land, and sea.

They sent an alert to all the slave colonies in the neighboring galaxies.

But nothing turned up.

My grandpa Dr. Terrible had simply vanished.

Now it is Crown Day and Dr. Terrible is gone. They had scoured his Institute and searched high and low, but Dr. Terrible was nowhere to be found. His personal laboratory out at the Institute's grounds had disappeared as well, as if it'd been swallowed up into the ground.

The WarWings Council of the Elders had charged Dr. Terrible with treason for Rogue Attacks with Intent to Destroy WarWings' Chain of Command, Thereby Endangering the Sanctity of Dragons Everywhere. And as soon as their security detail located Dr. Terrible, he was to be brought to stand trial before the Elders.

And here it is Crown Day and I'm trying like crazy to get Runcita Floop to be my Queen.

And I'm zooming toward the Dining Hall.

Because according to Trenx's connections in Masters of Chaos, this is where I'll find my Queen-to-Be, Runcita, munching on a bat sandwich.

Thwack-thwack.

27

THE DINING HALL

After flying around like that for a good ten minutes, I finally see the Dining Hall entrance up ahead.

So I fold my wings across my back and let myself coast forty feet down to the ground with the flight momentum carrying my scaly ass forward. And when my webbed feet hit the floor I just keep walking.

I stroll right on through the Dining Hall entrance.

And I think:

Finally.

Because the second I walk through the door, I can instantly smell the luscious scent of Runcita. Now inside the Dining Hall it's a madhouse. Packed scale-to-scale with cadets. These dragons are munching on bat sandwiches and hornetsicles and shouting at each other and kicking skulls up in the air.

I gently but firmly start shoving fools and chicks out of my way, pushing deeper into the throng.

"Hey," somebody growls. "Watch where you're flinging them wings!"

Where is my Queen? Come on come on come on. I know you're here somewhere!

And when this big nasty dragon fool in the crowd turns to glare at me for being too pushy, I guess the demented look on my black beak must say it all. Because he just holds up his talons palm-first and takes a step back, making room for me. But I'm still not making any real progress. I leap up in the air and look across the Dining Hall.

There she is.

Runcita.

She's maybe a hundred feet away. All the way on the other side of the Dining Hall. But I'd know that gorgeous green scaly face anywhere. She's wearing her gold tiara, the one with the red rubies in it.

Runcita's sweet scent is wafting up my nasal passages and tickling the pleasure centers in my brain. Now it's true that the heart is the highest law there is, but if you ask me, the snout sure comes in a close second. Because part of me just wants to lie down on the ground and weep with gratitude, that's how good she smells.

But Runcita is on the move, shoving her way through the crowd. She looks like she's heading toward the exit on the other side of the Dining Hall.

"Runcita!" I shout, leaping up into the air.

As I hover here in the air for a second, I see her stop and turn her scaly green head and look in my direction, aiming to see whoever just called out her name. But then I fall back to the ground.

Time to make my move. Here I come, Luscious.

"Runcita! Runcita! Wait up!" I shout, as I fly right at her.

I can see Runcita has stopped and she's looking for whoever keeps calling out her name. Which is me.

I rocket forward and bellow, "Runcita! Runcita! Runcita!"

I'm shooting toward her and I can see her but she can't see me because I'm flying at her from the side. I have a straight line of sight and she's right there. But then all of a sudden I can't see her because my line of sight is blocked by this giant Mutant who steps directly into my path.

This Mutant is so tall, his chest is directly in line with my beak. And the way I know he's a Mutant is because he has those patches of glowing green scales all over his forelimbs, like what you see on most Mutants.

Anyway, by the time this big Mutant steps into my path there's no time for me to stop flying. My beak crashes straight into his scaly chest. And my head whips back and cracks the floor so hard it feels like a coconut being split open with an ax.

Now this giant Mutant must've barely felt the impact from our collision because he's just standing on his hind legs like a statue. And then I could swear I hear him chuckle.

So I spring to my webbed feet.

"What the hell?! You think this is funny?!" I growl.

I mean I know Runcita is just on the other side of this Mutant, and that's all the inspiration I need. And a powerful bolt of WILL TO POWER surges through me and I pull a big flamestream from my belly and load it on my tongue.

And I feel giddy for having found this individual to unleash all my accumulated rage on.

I rear back and cock my long neck and prepare to blast the flamestream right into this bastard's scaly green face.

One Mutant casserole coming right up.

Extra crispy.

28

THE MUTANT HAS A SURPRISE IN STORE FOR ME

I end up shooting a firebolt, instead of a flamestream.

But then I look up and to my ever-loving shock I see this giant dragon doesn't even have a scaly green head. Because where his monsterish head should be, there's just air. And so my firebolt shoots harmlessly up through the air until it hits the ceiling.

And I repeat: this bastard doesn't have a scaly head.

And if it sounds freaky, well that's because it is.

Now the weirdest part, though, is this Mutant does have a short scaly green neck.

Head? No.

Neck? Check.

And the dragon's neck appears to sprout up a couple inches off his shoulders and then just abruptly stops, as if his scaly body had found the process of making itself too complicated and so when it got to the head it just threw in the towel and quit.

Spooky.

Because the point where the dragon's neck stops is a perfectly flat plane, so that you could set a mug of lava on it and not worry about spilling a drop of it.

"Hey," I growl, "get out of my way! I'm on my Queen Quest! And if you're looking for a new friend, go look elsewhere. Because head-less just isn't my thing."

The bastard flaps his wings and points a murderous-looking claw at me. "Just because I'm not Normal, you can't disrespect me like that," he booms. "I still got rights!"

Where the heck is his voice coming from? This bastard doesn't have a head, but he has a voice?

Then I feel some hot air on my scales. And I glance down and am shocked to see the Mutant's entire scaly green face is located in his belly. Here this fiend's two yellow eyes are staring up at me. And there's his nasty black beak. And as I'm studying his beak, the red tongue flicks out and licks it. Then, finally, there's his green snout.

The Mutant's monsterish scaly face is right here in the center of his stomach, staring up at me.

I feel woozy just looking at it. Now as the Mutant bastard stares up at me his yellow eyes keep flicking back and forth, left to right. Like I'm a book and this fool is reading me or something.

Ugh.

Then this scaly bastard sticks his talon right in front of my beak, like he's trying to show me something.

"Recognize this, you dirtbag?!" he growls. "Look familiar? How about the right for chicks around here not to have jerks putting tracking devices on them while they're asleep?! Recognize this, scumbag? Huh?"

I peer at the shiny silver thing this maniac is showing me and a jolt of shock shoots down my spine. I feel the blood rushing to my scales and my tail slinks between my hind legs.

It's my nanotracker. My Secret Weapon. The little silver glinting thing. Right there in the Mutant's claws. And just seeing it here like this, well I start sweating. And my black heart starts pounding away like some creature trapped inside its coffin, buried alive.

I feel so ashamed, I just want to vacate my life.

"Where did you get *that*?" I croak, as my hind legs start to tremble.

"Where did I get it? Oh *that's rich*. You know exactly where I got it, you little sonuvabitch!"

Then he drops the little silver tracking device on the floor and lifts his leg and stomps on it with his webbed foot, making a big show of using his heel to grind it into oblivion.

"You ought to be ashamed of yourself!"

"Well technically speaking," I whisper, "it's not like I myself put the tracking device on her while she slept. You see, I used one of my micro-drones—"

"Shut your beak before I knock it off!"

He yanks his powerstaff off his utility belt and I'm pretty sure he's going to hit me with it. And I flinch. But all he does is flick his powerstaff and a holophoto appears in the air and I couldn't be more shocked by what I see there. Because in the floating holophoto you can see Runcita squatting next to this headless Mutant bastard, and they're both smiling. She with her luscious scaly green head in the correct location, and he with his demented beak down in his belly. And Runcita has one leathery wing wrapped warmly around the Mutant's shoulder, looking like she'd be content to spend the rest of her life hugging this maniac.

"Is this your *Queen*?" he snarls, pointing at the floating holophoto of Runcita with her wing wrapped around him. "Because if so, take my advice and forget about it. Runcita wouldn't go to EggHarvest with you if you were the last dragon in the universe!"

"How do *you* know that?"

"Because she's one of my best friends! And she's not into bastards who stick tracking devices on her wingjoint while she's asleep, you *scumbag*!"

The shame I'm feeling right now is more than I've ever felt. I hate myself.

My God, what have I become?

The holophoto floats over to the headless dragon and transforms into blacksmoke and then flies into his powerstaff. He hitches his powerstaff back on his utility belt.

"Does Runcita know it was *me*?" I whisper.

The headless scoundrel snorts firebolts and starts laughing like a lunatic. "No, you *egomaniac*," he growls. "She doesn't know it was *you*! How would she?! You think you're special or unique or something?! You think you're some kind of genius when it comes to scoring a Queen for EggHarvest?!"

Now he holds out his other talon and I see a bunch of silver tracking devices piled up there in his palm. There must be hundreds of them. And seeing this makes me feel even worse.

What a loser I am.

Even when I try to act fiendish, my actions are just run-of-the-mill.

Because apparently I'm not the only sorry bastard at WarWings who thought that using a tracking device would help him score Runcita.

"You're not very smart, are you, scumbag?" he growls.

Now the headless cadet lifts his right forelimb and curls his claws into a fist the size of a boulder, making ready to hit me. His yellow eyeballs in his belly seem to narrow as he stares up at me, like I'm a fly he's about to squash.

"How about the right to knock a scumbag's scaly head off?" he says, snorting blacksmoke. "What do you think about that, *Normal*? Well I think that's a right I'm about to exercise!"

I don't bother trying to correct him about how technically it wasn't me who went into Runcita's lair. Because in my gut I know he's right. I deserve to have my head knocked off. I really do.

So I just look up at the headless dragon's talon clenched into a fist. And all of a sudden I realize this fist must be an integral part of the scaly green Mutant learning how to survive and go through life without a head.

Because in this fist you can see the Mutant's entire life struggle etched in the scar tissue, like hieroglyphics.

The painful childhood, the unrequited desire to be loved and accepted unconditionally.

The endless taunts and beatings.

The growing realization that you will be the butt of every joke ever told in your vicinity.

The horrible epiphany that you are all you can ever count on, and that the excruciating loneliness you thought was a passing feeling is actually your essential being.

That we are all to varying degrees hedging our bets against the inevitable insanity.

This fella's raised fist is less a weapon and more of a living text, the autobiography of the damned.

"This is for Runcita!" sneers the Mutant. "And you can kiss your Queen Quest good-bye, scumbag! Because I'm going to knock your scaly-ass head clean off into the next galaxy!"

Then he starts to swing and I see his humongous fist come flying at me. The breeze on my green snout generated by his oncoming fist is getting stronger.

I clench my lids shut even harder now, as if I might somehow be able to deflect the Mutant's fist with my eyelids. Because if you want to know the truth, I really do deserve this. That trick with the tracking device was a real low stunt for me to pull.

So I figure I'll just take my punishment. Get what's my due. And the fist is so close now that it's not so much of a breeze as it is a tornado and I can't hear anything except for this ominous screaming noise that the wind is making.

And then I think to myself:

Snap out of it, Gork! This fool's fist is going to arrive any second and knock your scaly green head clean off your neck and you at least need to be prepared for it!

Maybe if you focus and are lucky you can fetch your scaly head and have a surgeon sew it back on.

"Wait a sec," says the headless dragon.

I cautiously open one eye and see the fist's green knuckles just inches from my beak.

"Aren't you Dr. Terrible's grandson?"

I open my other eye now and take a step backward.

"I could be," I say. "But first you gotta tell me, is that a good thing or a bad thing, being Dr. Terrible's grandson?"

With a little distance between us, I can feel my courage swelling.

"And why in the heck is it any of your business who my grandpa is?"

The Mutant's reptilian eyes in his belly are looking up at me. "Come on, *really*? It's those horns of yours, stupid. Everybody knows that Dr. Terrible's grandson's got the smallest horns at WarWings—"

"They're not the smallest. There's this robot named Trenx—" It hits me like a punch to the gut that now I really do have the smallest horns at the Academy.

Then the Mutant points his powerstaff at me and a small floating screen pops up right there in front of us, with my data splayed out in the air. His monsterish scaly green face down in his belly is studying my Cadet Profile on the floating screen:

CADET NAME: **Gork The Terrible**

NICKNAME: Weak Sauce

CONQUER & RULE SCORE: 6 out of 1000

RANK: MildFuriosity

MATING MAGNETISM SCORE: 1 out of 1000

RANK: RatherGoEggless

HEART MASS INDEX SCORE: 2 out of 1000

RANK: DangerouslyJumbo

CLASS RANK: 2357th out of 2358

WILL TO POWER: 6 out of 1000

STATUS: **Snacklicious**

"See! I knew you were Dr. Terrible's grandson!" he says. "That's the only reason you're here at WarWings, because of Dr. Terrible. Frankly, with those horns you shouldn't even qualify to have Normal status. You should really have Mutant status."

"Don't you dare insult my horns!" I growl.

I'm suddenly worried that I might start crying.

And for a second there, I see a look come across the Mutant's monsterish scaly green face on his belly. And I can tell he feels pretty low-hearted for what he just said to me, that he actually pities me. Which just makes me feel worse. I mean you know you're in bad shape when you've got a headless Mutant feeling sorry for you.

You can sense that the dragon is thinking:

What's the point of me treating this freak like this just because everybody has treated me like this my entire life? Having suffered like him, shouldn't I be more inclined to show this dragon mercy and compassion, and not perpetuate the cycle of violence?

You can see him thinking:

Has my life filled with pain taught me nothing?

"Well," says the headless dragon, his voice softening, "maybe not *everybody* at WarWings knows about you. But you see, Dr. Terrible's my physician. He's working on my evolution. He's the one that put this face right here in my belly. Before Dr. T came along, I had no face. I was deaf and blind and mute. Somehow he managed to make me grow my very own face right here in my belly. Dr. Terrible is a miracle worker!"

"Dr. Terrible is a jerk. Dr. T, you call him Dr. T? That's so lame! Does that *T* stand for 'Thing'? Is that because he's *Dr. Thing*?"

"Don't talk about Dr. T like that! You're just an ungrateful little bastard with horns to match!"

"Hey," I bellow, "how can you sit here and dump on my horns when you don't even have a head? You think Dr. Terrible's so great because he made you grow your scaly face in the wrong place?! Why didn't he grow you a head instead?"

By now the headless dragon is clearly boiling over with rage, and he's definitely seeing lava. He gnashes his fangs and sparks are flying off of them.

It's probably actually a good thing this fool doesn't have a head. Because as worked up as he's getting right now, if he did have a head it would probably pop right off.

"Speaking of horns!" I shout, flapping my wings. "My horns may be small, but at least I got some. If *Dr. T*'s so great, then why doesn't he help you grow some horns?!"

"He did, you idiot!" he roars. "Dr. T *did* give me horns, you fool!"

Then, as I'm glaring down at the dragon's monsterish scaly green face in his belly, the weirdest thing happens.

Two giant black horns shoot out of his chest.

The horns are right above the Mutant's yellow eyes and they come flying out so fast it's like one second they're not there and then the next second they are. Like a switchblade.

Thank goodness I've got a quick first step.

Because I leap back just before the tips of those horns gouge the air where I've just been squatting. And if I was even a half step slower, I'd right now be impaled on this Mutant's horns, dangling with my green webbed feet off the ground. No doubt.

The Mutant grins up at me. He uses his talons to point at the horns sticking out of his chest.

"Retractable. Dr. T built me these retractable horns! And trust me, these things are built to last!"

I'm just squatting here in shock.

Retractable horns?

How the heck did Dr. Terrible give this maniac retractable horns?

The headless Mutant clenches his talons into fists and booms: "You know what? Before I met you I was having a bad morning but now I'm feeling much better. I'm going to enjoy tearing you apart limb from limb. I'm going to break you down so bad that even Dr. Terrible won't be able to put you all the way back together again!"

As I stand here eyeballing this demented Mutant working himself into a frenzy, I believe him. I can feel it in my bones that he's telling the truth. He really is going to tear my scaly green ass limb from limb. And not even Dr. Terrible will ever be able to put me back together again.

Remembering that just a few minutes ago I saw Runcita here in the Dining Hall, I take a couple whiffs but can't detect her scent signature in the air. Now squatting here in front of the treacherous Mutant, I wave my snout back and forth but still can't get a whiff of Runcita. And with a sinking heart I know then that she's already left the Dining Hall. I take a couple more whiffs and realize that I've inadvertently become an expert at detecting this particular fragrance.

If this particular fragrance were a perfume then I'd call it A Room Where Runcita Once Was But Is No Longer.

"What's wrong with your snout?" sneers the Mutant, staring up at me with his insane scaly green face. "Why do you keep sniffing around like that?" He sniffs the air. "Is it me? Do I smell funny or something?"

A tiny smirk plays across my beak.

"Hey," he says, "what's the big idea, wise guy?"

He cocks his fist up. And there are some things that are just more than a fella can reasonably take. And at this particular moment in time, the prospect of getting my sorry tail beat to a pulp by this headless Mutant bastard is one of them.

So I do the only thing I can think of at the moment.

I unfurl my leathery wings and fly my scaly green ass out of there. *Thwack-thwack.*

29

FRIBBY IN THE LAVA LOUNGE

Where I am right now is the Lava Lounge.

This is where Fribby told me to meet her.

This is Ground Zero for the Datalizards. As I peer around at the stylish walls covered in oozing lava and the skulls and bones covering the floor, I'm all of a sudden thinking that maybe me rolling in here solo wasn't such a hot idea. But I can't try to turn around now. Because I know if I bolt for the door, well then some ghastly chrome-flex bastard will pounce on my ass and there'll be a feeding frenzy.

Robots can smell your fear, just like Normals.

They get off on it.

Everywhere I turn, there's a robot cadet glaring at me with freaky red glowing eyes.

Some of these fiends are sitting at small circular tables with their silver tails twitching over their heads, and others are perched on stools at the LavaBar. Just straight glowering. My horns are tingling like crazy. A couple of these bastards clocking me are gnashing their fangs, spraying sparks out their metal beaks. I am a tiny green speck in a sea of silver. My scaly green ass sticks out like a sore claw in here. I guess I shouldn't be surprised, given that they got a No Normals Allowed policy, but still.

So I'm crouched down low on the tips of my toe claws and my tail's whisking around behind me, in case I have to make any lightning-quick moves.

Breathe, Gork. Just breathe.

That's it. Nice and easy.

Fribby has to be around here somewhere.

Now there's a two-headed robot chick I know named Lurksa up on the anti-grav stage, which is designed to look like a giant lotus petal floating in midair. The spotlight's on Lurksa, and one of her silver heads is crooning her Mating Song in this real sultry voice. Her other head is leaning way out into the audience and whispering things into those robot fellas' earholes.

She's pulling a classic Crown Bait. Where the dragonette gets up and belts out her Mating Song or demonstrates some special juicy skill or whips her tail around and sprays pheromones in hopes that a cybernetic dragon dude in the audience will be struck by a bolt of desire and want to make an EggHarvest connection. It's like a talent show where the punishment for losing is you become a slave.

What was I thinking? These bastards will eat me alive.

So I squat on trembling haunches and look around the room for Fribby.

Now the Lava Lounge is this swank spot where the Dragodroids like to kick up their toe claws. It's also extremely controversial. Because this is where you'll find the MortalMachine cadets whose WILL TO POWER rank is MegaBeast or higher.

We're talking the hyper-elite Datalizards. And as I glance around right now I count at least ten mega Reptilizoids who definitely rank in the upper tier of Seek&Destroy. I mean the entire place just reeks of TURBO FIEND.

And earlier this semester when the Lava Lounge first opened, a club called the Robophobes stormed the place and started blasting it with firestreams, trying to burn it to the ground.

There were like twenty of those fiends and they were chanting, "No Robo! Robo got to go! No Robo! Robo got to go!"

But then this one big nasty metal Dragobot named Ogg just waded in and unleashed on those scoundrels. Now Ogg is famous here on campus because he's the first A.I. to play on the WarWings varsity

Slave-Catching team. He's also one of their star players. Anyway, so Ogg snapped each of those Robophobes' long green necks like they were twigs. And then that night at the Lava Lounge they were handing out free Normal dragon fillets on the house.

So these days there isn't a DataHater at WarWings who'd dream of stepping webbed-footed into this place. The vibe here is extremely fiendish and deranged, but also relaxed. Shoot, looking around the Lava Lounge right now, you'd think the robot uprising had already happened and now the Datalizards were running the show. The only thing missing is some green Normal dragon heads mounted on the wall.

Fribby's got to be around here somewhere.

"Get your ugly green ass outta my face, Normal!"

I start walking.

That's it. Just head for the back. She's got to be back there.

Other than the spotlight on Lurksa, the lights in the lounge are low. And because it's Crown Day you can see a half-dozen Dragodroids down on one knee, offering their crown to some chick.

Out of the corner of my eye I see a Datalizard open her silver beak and blast a mega firestream into this Dragodroid that's down on one knee and he doesn't stop screaming until he's melted into a pool of silver on the floor. Guess her answer was no.

The Datalizards hiss and snarl as I pass their tables.

"Looking for some robot nookie, Normal?"

"Once you go chrome, you won't never go home."

Keep moving. Pretend like you don't hear them.

Come on, Fribby. Where are you?

Now I squeeze by this one mammoth cybernetic chick who points a silver claw at me. "Dang, look at Snacklicious there. Don't pay any attention to these fools. Shoot, why you do look *delicious*. Why don'tcha come set with me a spell and get some of this funky machine love?"

Then her eyes start glowing bright red.

Well I suddenly feel light-headed, and so start to hurry and stumble toward the back. I trip over something and look down and see a couple of miniature Dragobot cadets glaring up at me. These fellas can't be no bigger than three feet tall, and one of them's rubbing his silver head like I just kicked him or something.

"Your kind ain't welcome!" squeals one of the little Dragobots.

"Grow some circuits!" squeals the other.

Then these two fellas start cracking up and snorting firebolts.

And that's when I feel a powerful metal talon snatch me up by the wingjoint and plunk my scaly ass down at a table in the back of the lounge.

"Did you see Trenx and his new horns?" says Fribby, a little smile on her beak. "Crazy, right?"

She flaps her silver wings and snorts blacksmoke.

"Yeah, those things were pretty boss," I say. "Still can't believe Dr. Terrible hooked him up with those horns and not me, his own scales and blood."

"I thought he looked like a fool. Those new horns make him look gaudy. Like he's trying to compensate for something." She points to the shot of roiling lava sitting in front of me on the table. "That's for you. It'll help calm your nerves. You sure look like you could use it."

"I thought all you chicks dig dudes with big horns. I hate my damn horns," I say, flapping my wings. "They're so small. Did you know Dr. Terrible wants to adopt Trenx and make him his son?"

I pick up the shot of lava and toss it down my beak. Little sparklers of delicious color explode at the top of my spine and then blast out over my nerve endings, causing me to shiver. I notice one of the robots at a nearby table staring at me. I grin at the fella and belch up a big cloud of blacksmoke.

"Well you're not gonna win Conqueror of the Year with those horns," she says, squinting at my head. "But I like your horns. They look like little buttons. Sometimes I just want to reach out and press them. They're cute."

She picks up her roiling lava shot and tosses it down.

"Mmmmmm." Her red glowing eyes go a little glassy.

"You're just saying that 'cause you feel sorry for me," I say.

"You wish. When I see something pathetic, I'm not programmed to pity it. I'm programmed to laugh at it."

"I want my horns to look scary. Instead my horns make me look like a big fat wussy."

"Who says?"

"Me says."

"Me's a fool. Don't pay him no mind. Who else?"

Fribby belches up a big cloud of blacksmoke.

"Dr. Terrible," I say. Out of habit, I reach up and touch my horns.

"Forget that crusty bastard," she says.

"That's easy for you to say. You're a MegaBeast," I say. "What about this big stupid heart of mine? And the crying? And the fainting? Fribby, I'm a mess."

"It takes courage to be so real. You're not like these other fools running around here. You're different."

"Because I'm such a loser?" I say.

"Because you're different."

"Different is just another name for loser."

"Answer me one question."

"Shoot."

"Are we dead?" she says.

"Heck no, we're not dead, chick."

"Have you ever been dead before?" she says.

"No, I've never been dead before. Not in the way you're talking about."

"Then how would you know if we were dead or not?" she says.

She leans in and gazes at me with this curious smile on her silver beak. Framed against the oozing lava on the wall behind her, she looks pretty.

"Because my big stupid heart won't shut up," I say.

"Is that why you're going around starting fights with Mutants?"

"That freak didn't have a head," I say. "Besides, he started it."

She reaches out and puts her talons on top of my talons, squeezes gently.

"You be careful of Dr. Terrible," she says.

"How are you supposed to intimidate a fella that doesn't have a head? I couldn't figure that one out. Still can't."

"Your grandpa's up to something," she says. "I don't know what. But I feel he's got something planned for you."

"I guess after you learn to live your life without a head like that, well there's just not a lot that can faze you. Seems to me, anyway."

"Stay away from him, alright? Be strong, Gork," she says.

"There's nothing strong about me, chick. You know that."

"That's what makes you strong," she says. "Your weakness is your strength."

"If you're trying to make me forget what a loser I am, you'll have to do better than that."

"I meant what I said. Did you hear me?"

"About Dr. Terrible? About how I should steer clear of him and whatnot?"

"No, fool. About your horns. I think they're seriously cute."

30

THE INSTITUTE OF ADVANCED
BIOKINETICS AND NEUROANATOMY

Old habits die hard.

How else to wrap my brain around why I am standing right here where I'm standing at this moment? And if old habits die hard, then it seems like bad habits are freaking immortal.

Because I jet from the Lava Lounge and fly out behind Central Campus and then fly a couple miles through the jungle path. Out of habit. Or at least that's what I'm telling myself right now, anyway. Because this is the only way I can explain to myself why I am standing here in front of my grandpa Dr. Terrible's Institute of Advanced Biokinetics and Neuroanatomy.

Because the only other possible explanation is that I'm just a straight-up chump.

But you promised yourself you'd never come here again.

Don't you remember? After Dr. Terrible stole Idrixia away from you. When you spent that week heartbroken under the covers in your lair?

You told yourself you were through with this place forever.

Now I glance down at my powerstaff to check my BIOCON LEVS and almost faint.

Because my WTP monitor bar is flashing EMERGENCY MODE. While dealing with that headless Thing back in the Dining Hall, well I must've burnt right through what little WILL TO POWER I had left in the tank.

So I reverted to autopilot.

Who can blame me, really? I mean for the past four years I've been coming out here every Friday for my weekly sessions with Dr. Terrible. And now here it is Friday and I'm squatting on my haunches outside the entrance to the Institute.

The Institute is my safe retreat. Or at least it had been before Dr. Terrible whisked Idrixia away from me.

How long ago was that exactly?

Close to two months now. My grandpa and I haven't spoken since. Of course, he gave me the spaceship ATHENOS II and he's written me a couple letters recently.

Now a light breeze comes up and my nostrils flare and I catch a whiff of something ominous which makes the scales on the back of my long green neck stand up. I drop down low on my trembling haunches in the tall grass on the edge of the Institute's grounds and whip my binocs off my utility belt and peer out.

I spot a WarWings security detail of dragon Commandos squatting there in front of the empty space where Dr. Terrible's laboratory used to be. There are six or seven of these demented-looking scaly green fools. Each of the Commandos is heavily armed with photon blasters and decked out in full Conquer Gear. These dragons are some of Rexro's clowns, for sure.

If these dragons get their talons on my scaly green ass then I can kiss my chances of going to EggHarvest good-bye. So I flap my wings and fly toward the back of the Institute and far out of sight of the security goons.

I fly along the perimeter of the Institute grounds, which are surrounded by jungle.

I fly all the way up to the entrance of the Center for Combat & Conquer, which is a black structure of stones and bones. My grandpa used to bring me here during our weekly sessions, so we could work on my moves. A couple hours in here always seemed to amp my BIOCON LEVS. Especially my FIRESTREAM BLAST RADIUS, WING STRENGTH & FLIGHT CAPABILITY, STRATEGIC DESTRUCTION COMBAT READINESS, TRAUMA INDUCTION CAPABILITY, TONGUE SHOOTING ACCURACY, and of course my HORN DENSITY & MASS scores.

Because assuming you don't die during the course of your training here at the Center for Combat & Conquer, you always fly out of here feeling refreshed. Reinvigorated and yes, a damn sight more ruthless and deranged.

And as I squat here in front of the Center for Combat & Conquer, a scary thought occurs:

Maybe I'm here because I miss my grandpa? Oh God.

Maybe I'm feeling wrung out and hung out to dry and there's a masochistic part of me which craves to be in the company of the treacherous Dr. Terrible? To hear him lecture me in his demented and violently intelligent ways, and to give me counsel?

Because I'll be the first to admit that what started out as a Crown Day morning filled with so much promise and potential glory has quickly flat-lined into a hideous nightmare seemingly without end. The fact of the matter is I desperately need help.

My powerstaff vibrates and I hold it up and see it's a message from Fribby:

Remember what I said about Dr. Terrible.
Keep your distance from him, OK?
I got a real bad feeling.
He's up to something. I just know it.

I swipe the screen with my claw. There's no way I'm responding to that message. Things are too humiliating and bleak right now. Besides, I know if I tell Fribby where I am she'll freak and fly out here pronto. And I just can't deal with that right now. Things are bad enough as it is.

I nervously tap my powerstaff to see if anything has changed. And it has, just not in the way I was hoping. Instead of rebounding to my normal Snacklicious, my WILL TO POWER has actually dropped. KickMySnout. My WTP score is KickMySnout. The little firestream icon in the staff's monitor is flashing faster now, as if to make sure I understand that my plummeting BIOCON LEVS situation is significantly more desperate than it was even a minute ago. I feel queasy.

Can you tell me why it is that those of us who need help the most are always the last ones to realize it? And then why do we go about seeking help where there is obviously none to be had? Now if you try to explain it away by saying that I'm just plain stupid, well that would be way too generous. Because my problems have to do with much more dire deficiencies than good old-fashioned ignorance.

I sigh and feel my jumbo heart swell and suddenly take on so much more additional weight that it causes me to stumble and momentarily lose my center of gravity.

You broke your promise to yourself.

You swore you'd never come back to this place.

Turns out habits have nothing to do with it.

I'm just a chump after all.

And so, without further ado, I push through the door.

Part IV

INSIDE
THE
BELLY
OF THE
BEAST

31

DR. TERRIBLE'S SCREAM OPERAS
ARE IN FULL EFFECT

Inside, it looks like business as usual.

But then, when I take a closer study of the bustling entranceway, I can tell something is definitely off, though I can't quite put my claw on what it is.

The first thing I notice is that I don't smell Dr. Terrible in the air, not even a trace of him. And usually this place just flat out reeks of Dr. Terrible. I used to joke with my grandpa that he could bottle his fiendish dragon scent and sell it as a cologne called Depravity.

The second thing I notice here inside the entranceway is my black horns are tingling like crazy. I flick my scaly green tail around behind me, keeping it ready to help propel me with lightning speed if I need to make any sudden movements.

Now this Center for Combat & Conquer represents the apex in Dr. Terrible's pedagogy. And if pumping up BIOCON LEVS is your thing, then this is definitely the hottest game on the island.

I squat here for a moment taking in the scene. Dragon cadets decked out in combat gear are flying this way and that, heading into the bowels of the building for their advanced training. WarWings professors in their robes and cloaks are flapping their wings and flying about.

Injured cadets on gurneys wheel by. These wounded dragons have ghastly smoking charred patches on their scales and their fried flesh is showing through. I see where one of the dragons being wheeled by has had his hind legs chopped off and now there's just these bandaged bloodied stumps.

Another dragon cadet being wheeled by has a sucking chest wound. His bandaged head is jerking back and forth so fast you'd think he was being electrocuted. Another dragon going by is laid out on his belly and you can plainly see where his wings have been chewed off right up to the joint. Some of these poor bastards have got their beaks twisted up and are shrieking in agony while others are blacked out and unconscious, leaking fluids onto the floor.

Then I see a brain floating inside a big glass jar, being wheeled on a gurney. The floating brain has all these wires and tubes running into it.

And the dragon medic who's wheeling the gurney uses his talon knuckles to rap on the brain's glass container, and says, "How you holding up in there, cadet?"

"I reckon I'm doing OK, sir," says the brain's voice through some sort of microphone. "Boy, I thought for sure I was going to die during this morning's training, sir. It was the weirdest thing. When I stumbled upon them barbarian dwarves and they unloaded on me with those acid-vaporizer guns, well I figured I was a goner, sir. I swear I could feel myself dissolving and I remember thinking how I was definitely dying right then!"

"Well, son," says the dragon medic, "it was a real close call. That's a tough strain of dwarf you were trying to conquer this morning. We imported them from the planet Krolnix. And when we're not using those dwarves for training, we keep them in our maximum-containment facility. Those Krolnix dwarves are real nasty bastards. That's why we welded those muzzles onto their heads. But you performed well this morning, son. And because of our advanced technology here at the Institute, we were able to evac you from that bunker in the nick of time."

"Say, sir," says the brain in the glass container, "when do I get to take this gauze off my head and open my eyes? You said it would only be a few minutes. And I know this may sound crazy, but I could swear it feels like it's already been several days since you said that. When do I get to open my eyes, sir?"

"Well, son," says the dragon medic, "we're nearly finished prepping the wound. It'll be just a few seconds. We're almost there. But first we have to—" And then the medic reaches out with his talon and starts shaking the glass container super hard and the brain with all those wires in it is getting sloshed around.

"What was that, sir?" says the jiggling brain. "You're breaking up, sir. I'm afraid I'm feeling sort of dizzy, sir. I may need to take a short rest . . ."

Well the mortality rate for training here at the Center for Combat & Conquer is through the roof. And before a dragon can begin training here, he or she has to make a last will and testament for their hoard and lair.

And when I made my will, I went ahead and bequeathed everything I owned to Fribby. At first the WarWings administration had made a big stink about me leaving my hoard to Fribby and they said it wasn't allowed, because she was a robot and all. But eventually my will and testament was run up the WarWings chain of command and was finally approved. Because Fribby is a MortalMachine dragon and she'd been hatched in the WarWings Creative Evolution Lab, so what could they say, really?

Now over the audiomembranes they are playing the booms of a volcano erupting overlaid with the near constant scream of a terrified creature. Well, I know these screams are part of Dr. Terrible's advancements in the field of Sound Therapy Training for WarWings cadets. Because there's not a dragon on Blegwethia who doesn't consider the scream of a terrified creature to be liquid gold to the earholes.

The most acclaimed musicians on our planet are dragons who stick a foreign creature in a torture device and then proceed to press buttons so that the creature's agonized screams form a rapturous melody. For dragons these tortured screams are what we call classical music.

But my scaly green grandpa took the whole concept one step further and applied it to the combat training of WarWings cadets. So with an eye to jacking up cadets' BIOCON LEVS, he composed a series of what he calls scientifically informed Scream Operas, which are designed to enhance and fortify a dragon's WILL TO POWER.

Dr. Terrible's research results confirmed that regular auditory exposure to his Scream Operas boost a dragon's scores in nearly every conceivable category: WING STRENGTH & FLIGHT CAPABILITY, SCALE DENSITY & LUSTER, FIRESTREAM BLAST RADIUS, CORE FLAME TEMP, MATING MAGNETISM, TRAUMA SURVIVAL READINESS, CONQUERING CAPABILITY, HORN DENSITY & MASS, TONGUE SHOOTING ACCURACY, VENOM POTENCY & VISCOSITY, and of course the all-important HEART MASS REDUCTION & SHRINKAGE.

Even I have to admit the repetitive sound of Dr. Terrible's Scream Opera right now blasting over the audiomembranes is getting my juices going. My toe claws involuntarily shoot out and my nostrils flare.

Who am I kidding?

I've missed this place over the last couple months, and I didn't realize how much I've been missing it until now.

It feels good to be back.

I snort firebolts out my nostrils and swagger forth.

Now as I step up to the greeting console, this old crusty Admin dragonette eyeballs me through the glasses perched on the end of her scaly green snout.

"I'm here for my Friday session," I say.

This old dragonette keeps glancing up at the top of my head, like she's clocking my tiny horns. "We'll need your talon match," she snarls. "Just put your palm against that biometric ID scanner, and it'll do the rest."

I put my talon against the lit circle on the machine and then the circle flashes.

"Hey," I say. "Where's Tokira?"

The receptionist is busy looking at something on the floating screen next to her scaly green head, like she's reading something off my talon printout. Without looking at me, she snarls, "Who?"

"Tokira," I say, flapping my wings. "The dragonette who normally works reception here. I've never seen you here before. What's your name?"

The old dragonette glances up and gives me a look with her hooded yellow eyes that makes my toe claws shudder. Then my eyes' peripheral zoom feature activates itself just in time to see the dragonette slide an index claw under her console and frantically commence pushing a button.

"Gork," she purrs, "we seem to be having some problems with your Cadet ID. I'm sure it's nothing. But I'm going to have to ask you to wait over there at the LavaBar until we can get this cleared up. Feel free to have a lavatov cocktail. It's on the house."

She points a long yellow claw at said LavaBar over in the corner of the lobby. But I happen to know the bar is just a front for its true identity, which is the Apprehension Chamber. Lucky for my scaly green ass, I was raised by the demented bastard who drew up the blueprints for this building.

"Yes ma'am," I say. "I'll just go suck down a lavatov cocktail while you get things straightened out. Just give me a holler when you need me. I'll be at the LavaBar."

I notice her left lid twitches.

And that's when I bolt.

I explode off my haunches and run like a bastard. I bound right through the yellow smartfoam® security blockade and strike out running on my hind legs into the interior of the building. And while I run, I can feel the smartfoam® clinging to my green scales as it starts to harden and congeal and try to make me as still as a statue.

My toe claws are clacking frantically on the floor as I run.

I know when it comes to smartfoam® the key is to keep moving. Because if you keep your RUN SPEED at 20 MPH or above, then the smartfoam® can't get a grip and lock you up like it has been designed to do. So as I race along, I don't slow down or even stop to try and wipe the burning acidic foam off my green scales. Because once I stop I'll never be able to start moving again.

"Hey!" roars the receptionist. "You're not allowed back there!" Then she shouts, "Security! Security!" And that's when the alarm explodes inside the building, and a mega siren commences booming over and over and over. And as I bound on my hind legs I spread my wings and flap them twice and burst into flight.

And as I fly down the corridor, for the very first time this morning a smile blooms across my beak.

Yes sir.

It sure does feel good to be back.

⇒⇐

The siren continues to explode around me. It's a high-pitched screeching sound, blasting down the corridors with a rhythmic throbbing noise.

As I flap my wings and fly onward, the yellow smartfoam® is falling off me like strips of hide and I'm grateful to be free of the nasty stuff. My green scales are still stinging from the smartfoam®'s poison though.

Now as I whip round a corner and shoot forth I happen to look up and:

Uh-oh.

Crouched there at the other end of the corridor is a psychotic-looking dragon Commando fool from the security detail I'd seen near the front of the Institute. And this WarWings Commando bastard is wearing full Conquer Gear and his giant black horns are sticking out of his red helmet. A real nasty piece of work. And I can't help but admire how even with his beak closed his giant fangs protrude like tusks.

Now the Commando snorts flames out his nostrils and aims his powerstaff at me and bellows, "Halt!"

Anyway, I know I don't have enough BIOCON juice to launch into close-quarter combat with this Commando bastard. So I do the only thing I can do at this point. I just keep flying right at this sonuvabitch. With no plan or even a shred of hope I decide my best bet is improvised combat, or what my grandpa Dr. Terrible calls ImproBattle.

Thwack-thwack.

And I suddenly become aware of my oversized heart in my rib cage, which is hammering away like crazy. I'm seeing yellow dots swimming in the air and I can feel myself starting to faint. Which for a dragon fool is one of the scariest things that can happen to you, to black out in midflight. Because when this happens one thing is for sure, you *will* crash. Even as I'm in the middle of fainting here in the corridor, some part of my fading brain knows I'm in big trouble.

And this is exactly what happens to me as I'm flying directly at that Commando bastard. I can feel my jumbo heart crank up inside my chest, and then I faint. Blackout.

But I only black out for a half second. Or a second, max.

And when I come to, I'm still flying.

I'm still airborne.

I'm dazed and terrified.

Now the Commando fool snorts flames out his nostrils and takes careful aim with his powerstaff.

"This is your last warning!" he shouts. "Halt now!"

Yeah right, buddy. Like I even have a choice anymore.

In case you haven't noticed, I'm fainting all over the place here. So you can scream at me all you want to. Cuz I'm not stopping.

And then the Commando flips open his beak and shoots his tongue at me like a bullet.

Zing.

The red blur whizzes straight for my head. And I can tell by how the Commando is crouched there on his scaly muscular hind legs, with his wings spread wide and his tail lifted high, that he's trained in the dragon martial art of tongue-fu.

Now tongue-fu is no joke, and this bastard looks like he means business. I swear he looks like he's aiming to take my scaly head off with his tongue.

So I'm hurtling toward this Security Commando and now he's added his lethal tongue into the mix. And because my WING STRENGTH & FLIGHT CAPABILITY are completely zonked I spin out of control and bounce headfirst off the wall. But this maniac hasn't calculated for my loss of control and his red tongue rockets right by me, missing me by an inch. And his tongue zooms another forty feet past me and then strikes the middle of the ceiling and stays embedded there.

Whoa.

Now the Commando is frantically whipping his long green neck back and forth, trying to rip his tongue free from the ceiling and retract it fifty feet down the corridor and back into his beak.

So I blast this fool with a supersonic fireball. But my aim is even worse than normal. Now my supersonic fireball ricochets off the ceiling and zooms right at the Commando's green webbed feet and the bastard leaps up just slightly to avoid it. But this turns out to be a big mistake. Because like a tape measure, his tongue's retracting feature automatically initiates.

Zing.

He instantly shoots forward and rockets down the long corridor. I have my back to the wall and watch the Commando fly right past me. He slams into the ceiling face-first. Now he's just hanging there stuck to the ceiling, while little bits of stone rain down.

Then the Commando falls to the ground.

Plunk.

I squat there gasping. And I peer down the corridor at the dragon's still form sprawled out in the dust and rubble.

I sure hope he gave himself amnesia. Otherwise, when that fool wakes up, he's never going to stop until he finds me!

And then using the last precious drops of my BIOCON juice, I whirl around and flap my wings and shoot down the corridor in the opposite direction from where the Commando is laid out.

Thwack-thwack.

32

WHAT A FITTING PLACE FOR ME TO DIE, HERE IN THE BELLY OF THE BEAST

So this is how I come to find myself shooting down one corridor after another and turning new corners and shooting down another corridor and another and another.

I can hear this light beeping noise in my earhole, signaling to me that my BIOCON LEVS aren't just running low. They're nearly out.

Speaking frankly here, at this point there's no plan on my part to save my life or anything. The plan is simply to fly for as long as I can fly before crashing. That's really the extent of my worldview now that my WILL TO POWER is ThrashBait.

Now I'm just grateful each time I hear my leathery wings flap, because at least I know I have a few more moments left of airborne life.

And as I fly deeper and deeper into the Center for Combat & Conquer, I can't help but think about all the good times I had with Dr. Terrible in this building over the years. All these memories come bubbling up into my skull, which I guess is the equivalent of my life flashing in front of me before the big sleep.

Thwack-thwack.

And as I fly along through the corridor I remember one time in particular when me and Dr. Terrible were in the Center's Invader Module. I'd landed my spaceship on the planet Kooverolp. I swaggered out of the spaceship and looked at all the furry purple Gershwan Boiks and snorted flames out my nostrils and I held up my powerstaff and roared, "My name is Gork The Terrible! And I'm here to conquer your planet Kooverolp! And if you don't want to die, you will surrender to me now!"

Now the artificial Gershwan Boiks in the Invader Module that day had instantly come charging right at me by the thousands while letting out their strange buzzing war cry. So I'd turned away from the oncoming savages with the idea of running back to my spaceship.

But before I could even lift a webbed foot, I fainted.

Then, when I came to, the Gershwan Boiks had already gnawed off my left leg and now had started in on my right leg.

I howled.

At that moment, my scaly grandpa Dr. Terrible had shut down the module and he'd come into the Virtual Terrain Area laughing so hard his beak was clacking, and then the two of us had a real good laugh over that one. Over what a coward I was.

"Oh Gork, what are we going to do with you?" said Dr. Terrible, snorting flamestreams.

Then he fetched the tip of his tail to affectionately whap me upside my scaly green head. And on that particular day we'd both found my lack of WILL TO POWER hilarious. It was a powerful bonding experience for us both. I knew it in my giant sensitive heart, that my grandpa Dr. Terrible felt the same way as me that day. And on that day, we were family.

But now here it is, the most important day of my life, and I'm nowhere near the dragon chick I want to be my Queen. Instead I'm flying deeper and deeper into the Institute's Center for Combat & Conquer.

Thwack-thwack.

Looking around, I realize I'm lost. There's this steady rhythmic chirping in my earhole, only now it's faster. I am nearing the end. My BIOCON LEVS must be insanely low. Like life-threateningly low. Like a rabid mouse could kill me right now. That's how low.

Who knew when I woke up this morning in my lair that this is how things would end? That I was destined to become just another Crown Day casualty.

Every year, hundreds of WarWings cadets die on Crown Day. The stakes are that high. Now I will join their ranks.

Me, just a forgotten number to be swept into the dustbin of history.

I flap my wings and fly forward.

A wave of self-pity washes over me.

I feel so tired that just breathing is an effort.

The air is like hardening lava and my wings are struggling to get any purchase in it.

I coast forward through the air.

And I think:

How are your BIOCON LEVS?

You can't ignore them anymore. You've got to check. No matter how scary that prospect is to you, you can't flap another wing until you check. You've already let it go on too long without checking and if you—

And then I think:

OK OK OK OK OK. I'll check my LEVS already. In the meantime do me a big favor and shut up.

So I glance down at my powerstaff but instantly wish I hadn't. Because my data reads like something out of a nightmare:

CADET NAME: **Gork The Terrible**
STATUS: **Goner**
Goner
Goner
Goner
Goner
Goner

Yikes. I now rank dead last in my entire senior class, and my WILL TO POWER status is Goner. The screen just keeps flashing **Goner Goner Goner Goner Goner**.

I fall out of the air and crash onto the floor. I lie crumpled up here. My wings keep flapping because the mechanism in my scaly green head that controls them is broken. My wings are pushing the rest of my body around awkwardly on the floor. But then my wings accidentally crush themselves against the floor and get bent. I feel the flesh in one of them tear a little bit. But I don't have the energy to care.

I can hear the faint electronic chirping in my earhole as it speeds up.

Beep beep beep beep beep beep beep beep.

Then the chirping cuts out.

I slither over to a crook in the wall and fold myself into it, preparing myself to die. To go to the Underworld. Professor Nog. It won't be long before I see Nog in the Underworld. He won't be surprised to see me, and I have to wonder if when I first appear down there he'll say I told you so. Especially considering how he tried to warn me that the Oddsmakers had my death at 99.9% today.

This little crook in the wall is surprisingly comfortable. I don't try to fight my death. I just go with it. I close my eyes and feel my essence drift off into the big sleep.

⇒←

When I open my eyes, I'm surprised to discover I'm not dead.

I'm still in the crook of the wall.

A powerful strange and dense aroma comes wafting down the corridor, tickling my nostrils. It's a kind of a luscious funk smell, and it's definitely getting my juices going. I figure it's the odor that woke me from my death nap.

Now I see a white dot at the other end of the corridor. So I lie here in the crook in the wall and watch as the white dot approaches.

Who the heck is intruding on my death?

Leave me alone.

Can't I just die without somebody messing that up too?

Well that funky smell is now overwhelming, and it's definitely sexy. The smell makes me feel like I'm taking a lava bath with some sort of luscious oils. My nostrils flare.

The white dot keeps coming.

Now I can see what it is.

It's a dragonette, flying along.

And when she gets within forty feet or so I can see she's a professor. That's what the white dot was, her white robes. I've never seen her before but she's definitely wearing the Institute's robe and cloak.

As I stay hidden out of sight against the wall and watch her approach I notice her robe is cut short and that her toe claws are painted pink. She also has these two boss black horns on her scaly green head, which must be seven feet long and curve up into these three-pronged tips, which look way legit.

But what really catches my attention about this dragoness is her thick green tail, which looks to be twice as thick as a normal dragon tail. And I really don't know how to say this, except to say that this dragoness is seriously luscious. And juicy. Maybe that's a terrible thing to say because I'm dying and all, but there it is. This is one seriously juicy-looking dragonette.

So that's what the powerful oily odor is.

Her musk, her mating scent. She's in heat. This is the time of her Mating Cycle when she's most fertile.

You don't need to be a genius to know this, because you can just feel it with every molecule in your body.

I've never smelled anything like it. The chicks at WarWings have their Mating Cycles, but they're not old enough to exude a scent like this. This thick musk can only come from an ovowomb that knows exactly what it wants and how to get it.

I realize my tongue is drooping out of my beak, and I'm panting.

Now this is a monstrous humiliation. To be dying, and yet to be so amped up with luscious feeling because of this dragoness's powerful odor. There's no dignity in it, that's for sure. And if I had enough TURBO FIEND juice to move my tail it would slink between my hind legs, because of how skeezy I'm feeling right now.

Now this glorious chick with the pink toe claws is maybe thirty feet away from where I'm lying slumped against the crook in the wall, and she is lazily flapping her wings and flying in my direction. But this dragoness doesn't see me here on account of how I'm slumped over so low to the ground. I can't keep my eyes off her massive green tail. The sight of it arched high over her scaly head is intoxicating.

Anyway, a thick tail like that coupled with her potent raw mating musk is a deadly combo, let me tell you. I feel a delirious bolt of lust surge through my haunches, and dark clouds appear on the horizon of my mind.

If I wasn't so excited, I'd be terrified.

33

THE MYSTERIOUS DRAGONESS
WITH THE THICK TAIL

I squirm out from my hiding place and slither on my belly like a snake out to the middle of the corridor.

Well this dragonette abruptly comes to a halt and hovers there flapping her wings and treading air, looking down at me with surprise.

"Hey," I whisper from down on the floor, as I eyeball her thick tail swishing around behind her. "You smellth goodth. Where here Dr. Terrible is?"

Because my BIOCON LEVS have run dry, my speech and cognition functions have melted.

"You talking about *the* Dr. Terrible?" she purrs.

I notice how the chick's voice echoes off the stone walls. Behind this dragonette I see what I think are a pair of yellow eyeballs looking at me from down the hall, but I can't be sure. Mainly because it's hard for me to focus on anything with this dragonette's fine giant tail waving around like that. And it makes my green scales pucker up and I feel kind of funny, like there are little lightning bolts shooting up and down my tail.

Now there's really no other way for me to put this, except to say I'm overcome by a super-strong and specific desire to rub scales with this chick. Like I might go insane if I don't rub scales with this dragoness, is the way I'm feeling.

"Just oneth Dr. Terrible," I whisper. At that moment I start coughing like a bastard and blood spurts out my nostrils onto the floor. It's embarrassing, to be spurting up blood like this. To completely lose control of my body in front of this chick.

Uh-oh. Here we go.

So this is what dying feels like.

"Thorry," I whisper, looking up at the dragoness, who is still hovering above me in midair with her huge tail whipping back and forth.

I start coughing again and more blood spurts out my nostrils. And the blood seems to be gushing more freely, like a dam has broken.

"Really thorry," I whisper. Normally, saying sorry would be a death sentence but since I'm already dying, it doesn't matter. Now my left wing convulses and my wing bends against the floor and pushes me forward into the pool of my own blood.

"I dying fasth," I whisper.

The way this dragonette's enormous tail is wagging back and forth like that, I feel like I'm being hypnotized. And her thick oily funky scent shooting up my nasal passages sends a strong lust rippling through my haunches and makes my toe claws shudder. I can't really explain it but I suddenly have the strongest desire for this older drag-onette to lay my eggs. I want to mate with her. I can practically feel her ovowomb throbbing here in the corridor.

"No, I don't imagine there is more than one Dr. Terrible," she purrs. "They certainly broke the mold when they made that old dragon!"

Her wings are still flapping and she's hovering here in front of me, treading air.

I force myself to look away from the tail and instead to peer into this dragonette's hooded yellow eyes.

"He'th my grandpath. Where he? I need'th talkth wid that bas-tardth." And then I add: "Niceth tail. Yours. Ith *thick*. Yourth tailth thick."

She makes a little excited screeching sound in the back of her throat and then flaps her wings and flies in closer and peers down at me.

"I *knew* there was something familiar 'bout you," she purrs.

She reaches out and puts a long black claw under my beak and raises it so she can see me better. Now our faces are just inches apart, and in the dim corridor light I can see each individual green scale around her eyes quite clearly and they are luscious to be sure.

Bar none, this is the most gorgeous dragonette I've ever crossed paths with.

At that moment, I cough up more blood out of my beak.

"You wannath lay my eggsth?" I whisper.

She huffs softly. "Why I shoulda seen it sooner. You're the spitting image of your granddaddy. You're a Terrible, ain'tcha?"

"Yesth ma'am."

"'Course you are. Why you couldn't hide the fact that you're a Terrible no more than a monkey could talk with its butt. You Terribles is something special, I'll say. You goin' to grow up and conquer your own galaxy and rule over it with an iron talon, like your granddaddy did?"

"Yesth ma'am. I aimth to anyway."

Now I'm struck by how yellow this dragoness's eyes are, how piercing they are. I sense a power there that I don't understand. Plus I can feel myself blushing just slightly. Or maybe it's just my blood has stopped circulating and I'm dying.

I turn my scaly green head and cough up another spatter of blood onto the floor. I can taste my own blood in my beak.

Now this dragonette smiles a beakful of fangs. "Shoot," she whispers, "I know I wouldn't want to be some poor sucker on a planet that you invaded, that's for dang sure. Why look at your scaly face, darlin'. It's got Evil Ruler written all over it."

I just manage a faint smile. I'm sure I look freaking hideous.

"You make fella feel real niceth," I whisper. "Thanketh you for goodth death."

I don't bother to think about where all this is going, because it's not every day that an older juicy babe with a powerful thick tail fawns over me like this. And she still has a claw under my beak, and now we're just staring into each other's eyes.

As I lay dying and staring up into her eyes like this, I think:

Well if this is how I die, then so be it.

It's a royal send-off.

Please just let her eyes and her odor be the last things I see and smell.

The luscious dragoness flutters her wings and purrs, "Well I'll let you in on a little secret." She winks at me. "I *taste* even hotter than I talk."

She quickly glances around to make sure we're alone here in the stone corridor, and then she puts her black beak right up to my scaly green earhole and whispers: "I can feel you rumbling, sugar. And here we are, all alone. Maybe you want to get yourself a teensy-weensy little ol' lick?"

Her breath is *hot*. Though I don't know if it's from her throbbing ovowomb or from the lava in her belly. She pulls back a couple inches so we're looking directly into each other's eyes again, and her yellow eyes start shining as if a light is emanating from within them.

I turn my scaly green head and cough up more blood.

"My name Gorkth."

"I know who you are," she says. "Nice to meet you, Gork. I've heard a lot about you. My name's Metheldra."

Then the dragonette reaches out with the back of her talon and wipes the blood off my beak.

Metheldra. I know I've heard that name before but I can't recollect where, and like I said, it's pretty hard for me to focus at this moment. Especially with Metheldra's mating scent wafting up through my nostrils and kissing my brain and making me delirious with lust. I really need to rub scales with this dragonette.

"You frunds with my grandpath, Dr. Therrible?" I croak.

Something inside me is hemorrhaging, because the blood is trickling out my beak and out my flared green nostrils.

"That's right. I help Dr. Terrible out here at the Institute."

"What kindth of thelp? What do youth do here?"

"Why don't you step into my lair and I'll show you," she purrs.

Then she reaches up and clasps my horns in her talons, as if she is assessing how badly wounded I really am. "Mmmmmm," she says, "I see your horns have some room for growth. I might be able to help you with these horns. I'm an expert in BIOCON LEVS. I think I might be able to make these horns of yours grow."

Then she points her powerstaff at me and pulls down my Cadet Profile on her floating screen. "I see the Oddsmakers have given you at 0.1% chance of making it through Crown Day," she purrs. "And your BIOCON LEVS are null. I don't mean to scare you, but your WILL TO POWER status is Goner. You seem like you're in big trouble, Gork." Then she purrs, "Why don't you step into my lair?"

My right wing spasms and I flop around some more in my blood here on the floor.

I'm practically swimming in my own blood by this point.

So this dragonette's idea of me going anywhere other than where I am seems comically deranged, considering how filthy and weak I am.

Can't she see I'm dying?

But I'm also feeling super stirred-up and juicy. Because what I really want is for this chick to lay my eggs. This is my dying wish. Well I know how despicable this sounds, because I am dying and you'd think your thoughts and feelings would be a sight more noble than that in the face of the sacred. But they aren't. My thoughts, I mean.

Because I'm starting to get some very clear thoughts in my head of what me and this dragoness can do if we "bump scales."

Now you may be surprised to hear this, but I'm still a virgin. Because dragon chicks are programmed to avoid mating with a fool like me.

My datastream is a deal breaker.

You don't want your little baby dragons to hatch out of their eggs with WILL TO POWER deficiencies.

But something about this dragoness seems different. Like her WTP is so fiendish it will override the wussy BIOCON LEVS of any fool she mates with.

So I figure if I hurry up and mate with this chick, then at least I won't have to die a virgin.

This will at least be one shame I won't have to endure in the Underworld, to have died a virgin.

"Whereth yer lair?" I whisper. "I'm readyth. We rubth scales. I die. You layth my eggsth!"

Metheldra smiles and points her index claw at a door in the wall I didn't notice before. "It's right there," she purrs.

Then she gingerly scoops me up off the ground and presses me tightly to her bosom and carries me across the threshold.

"Now let's get you out of that uniform and cape," she whispers.

It feels wonderful to be wrapped up in her warm embrace, to be held so close to her green scaly bosom like this.

And if I weren't so afraid of dying right now, I'd faint.

"Thanketh youth."

34

SWORD PLAY

"Owwwwwww!" I cry.

This isn't how I expected it to feel.

This dragoness Metheldra's lair is full of swords.

"Please stop!" I cry.

I mean she has what look to be at least a couple hundred swords hanging on the wall. And they're all shapes and sizes—short swords, long swords, curved swords, serrated swords, swords with black handles, swords with red handles, swords with strange runes engraved in the blades, swords with three blades, swords with oddly shaped blades devised for some horrible purpose I hope I never have to learn about. And all of these swords are mounted along the wall in a massive display device constructed of silver and black velvet.

"Oh my God that hurts!" I cry. "Please stop! Please stop! I'm begging you!"

Metheldra is the swordupuncturist Dr. Terrible has been flapping his beak about.

So here I am lying on this stone slab without any clothes on. And I already have forty or so swords stuck into my scaly body—in my wings, in my tail, in my long neck, in my talons, in my horns, in my hind legs, in my forelimbs, and even in my webbed feet. Several swords are jammed to the hilt right in my poor belly. The only light in the room is coming from a bunch of drooping candles on a nearby table.

Now Metheldra calmly pulls another long shiny sword off the wall and holds it over me, and the silver blade winks in the candlelight. And she runs an index claw slowly across my scaly chest as if she's searching for the right point of entry.

"No more! No more!" I say. "Please don't stick another sword in me! Please! It hurts! Oh my God it hurts so much!"

Whatever lusciousness I was feeling a few minutes ago out in the corridor is long gone. Having a chick stick a bunch of swords in your torso will do that to you. It's a buzzkill. My virginity is intact. But somehow in the midst of getting all these swords stuck in my scaly green ass, my dang death seems to have eased on up too.

"I can feel your WILL TO POWER blocked in your heart region, Gork," she says, snorting blacksmoke out her nostrils. "Your heart is way too big. The size of your heart is life-threatening. It's preventing you from being connected to the BIOCON sources in your environment."

"My heart? What's wrong with my heart? My heart's just fine the way it is," I gasp.

Of course secretly I know my giant compassionate heart is to blame for pretty much all my woes. But maybe by playing dumb I can somehow trick Metheldra out of doing whatever it is she's about to do to me with this mega sword she's wielding in her talon.

"Hopefully I can unblock it with this sword."

I gulp. "Now wait just a second," I say. "Let's talk about this. What exactly are you planning on doing with *that* sword?"

Metheldra flicks her powerstaff and a floating screen appears in the air and there's a live image of my black heart on the screen, and my heart looks like a huge nasty throbbing greasy oyster. Up there on the floating screen, you can plainly see my heart is so gigantic it fills both sides of my entire chest cavity. She points at the screen with her sword.

"Gork," she says, "I'm sorry to have to be telling you this, but this is the biggest dragon heart I have ever seen. No wonder your horns won't grow! No wonder your BIOCON LEVS are so low. No wonder you have no WILL TO POWER. The size of your heart is undermining every other aspect of your life and your development as a dragon. Now, I would ask you if you have a problem with fainting, but one look at the image of your heart here and I already know the answer to that question. I'd be surprised if you weren't fainting at least five times a day, maybe more."

A strange little whimper bubbles up in the back of my throat.

Then she reaches out and carefully rubs my puny horns with her other talon.

"You *poor* thing," she whispers. "You poor poor poor thing. Don't you worry. Metheldra is going to fix you."

"Mmmmmmm," I moan. "That feels *so good*."

I love the way it feels as she keeps gently rubbing my puny horns like this because, when she rubs them, well it makes me feel strong and super. And feeling strong and powerful isn't a familiar sensation to me, which is partly why I find the whole experience so exhilarating.

"Mmmmmmm. Gosh that really does feel so *good*. Please don't stop."

It's the way she clasps each horn with her talon, and then rubs her talons up and down over them. "That feels good. Please don't stop. Mmmmmm."

"You poor poor poor thing," she whispers. "Metheldra is going to fix you. You poor, poor thing. Metheldra is going to fix you. You poor, poor thing."

"Mmmmm," I moan. "That feels so good. They're so small. I hate how small they are. I want to have big horns."

She keeps rubbing my horns.

"Don't you worry," she purrs. "I'm going to make your horns very, very big. Metheldra is going to fix you. Metheldra is going to fix you. She is going to make you into a big strong dragon with big scary horns."

Then without warning she swings her other talon around in a flash of silver and sticks the sword blade right into my heart and pushes down with all her weight.

35

METHELDRA
THE SWORDUPUNCTURIST

"Owwwwwww!" I sob.

I'm instantly thrashing around on the table and twisting this way and that, trying to break free. But the blade has gone straight through my heart and out my back and I'm pinned to the slab, like some sort of science specimen in a display case.

I hiss and spray sparks out of my beak.

My tail is thrashing around like an enraged beast.

"Take it out!" I bellow. "Take it out! Please take it out!"

Now I'm really starting to freak out and I suddenly get worried I might go insane because of how much pain I'm in with this sword blade jammed straight through my giant heart. I thrash around even harder and I'm struggling to get to my green webbed feet, and in the midst of my insanity I'm convinced that I can just run out of her lair with the table stuck to my back.

I'll learn to live like that. With the sword right through my heart, and that table pinned to my back. I don't care. As long as I manage to escape from her lair right this instant, that's all that matters.

Then Metheldra rears back and snatches another sword with her other talon and she brings this sword down handle-first and bashes me in the snout with the butt of the sword handle. Blood instantly spurts out.

I'm dazed. I'm seeing stars. And I black out from the pain. Or from the blow to my snout. I don't know which one it is. But I'm gone.

⋙⋘

When I come to, I'm still lying on the table.

Metheldra is gazing down at me by candlelight with a serene look in her hooded eyes, and she is gently rubbing my horns. And it really does feel yummy, the way she's rubbing my horns like that. I glance down and see there are still at least twenty swords stuck through my scaly body, including the giant silver sword stuck through my heart. But for some reason, I don't care. I don't feel pain anymore. I'm actually feeling pretty faboo.

I smile weakly up at her. "Metheldra gonna fix me. Mmmmmmm. I like you rubbing my horns. Mmmmmmm. Yummy."

"That's good, Gork," purrs Metheldra, as she rubs my horns. "We need to unblock your BioCon Channels. You've lost connection with the electromagnetic waves from the island. The name of this sword I just stuck in you is the HeartShrinker."

"The HeartShrinker?"

"Yes. The blade was forged here at the Institute's volcano. It's designed to help cadets become more ruthless and deranged. There's not a dragon heart in the universe that could withstand this blade. Your heart is shriveling as we speak."

"Mmmmm. Me like the HeartShrinker. My horns feel big and strong."

"By stabbing your heart with this HeartShrinker sword and letting the blade stay pierced through your heart, we should be able to shrink your heart down to a much more manageable size. So that your heart stops interfering with your natural tendencies to be ghastly and fiendish. I can tell that's where a lot of your BIOCON LEVS are getting blocked. Your grandfather Dr. Terrible always said he wanted me to treat you if I ever got the chance."

I can feel my heart shrinking under the onslaught of this sword. The natural flow is being restored to my scaly green ass. For once in my life, it feels like my gigantic compassionate heart isn't trying to get in the way of everything. And with my massive heart out of the way, my body can get back to the task of jacking up my WILL TO POWER.

Part of me hates myself for this, but the truth is that Metheldra's words about Dr. Terrible wanting her to treat me make me feel warm and happy inside. Don't get me wrong, I still hate the deranged bastard. But the warm feeling is there too.

I keep my lids closed as I lie on the slab and snort firebolts.

"I think I can feel my heart shrinking," I purr. "That one sword you've got stuck in there is working, it feels good. By the way, you never told me where Dr. Terrible is. I need his advice. I aim to get this chick Runcita to be my Queen. And today's Crown Day, so I got until sunset today. And if I don't get Dr. Terrible's advice, I might miss my chance to get a Queen and end up having to live out my days as a slave."

Metheldra pulls one of the swords out of my tender belly.

"I'm sorry, Gork," she says loudly. "But I have strict orders from Dr. Terrible not to reveal his location to anyone. And he made a point of saying that goes for his grandson Gork, too. I made a promise to Dr. Terrible and as much as I'd like to help you, I'm afraid I have to keep it."

But then she drops the sword and it clatters on the stone floor.

"What a klutz I am!" she says.

Now she bends down to pick up the sword and puts her beak to my earhole: "Dr. Terrible's hiding in his secret underground bunker on the west side of the island. The one where the entrance hatch is disguised as an old dead tree trunk. Off of Conquer More Road. Do you know the bunker I'm talking about? If you do, just nod your head slightly. Be careful though! I'm pretty sure my lair is bugged. There might even be some micro-drone transmitters in here."

And I don't know if it is her breath or the information she whispers to me, but I suddenly feel dizzy. I know exactly what underground bunker she's talking about, over on the west side of the island. I've been there a thousand times before. I can't believe I didn't think to look for Dr. Terrible there.

Anyway, I nod my scaly green head slightly so Metheldra will know I know where that bunker is.

Then the dragoness stands back up straight alongside me.

"But even though I can't tell you where Dr. Terrible is," she says loudly, "I think I can give you a piece of information that will be even more valuable than that! Something that could help you in your quest to get a Queen. You want to take that chick Runcita, right? Dean Floop's daughter?"

Now at that moment there's suddenly a loud banging at Metheldra's lair door.

"Open up! Open up! By order of WarWings Security, open this door at once! We know you have Dr. Terrible's grandson in there! Resistance is useless! Open up!"

I hiss and spray sparks out my beak.

Metheldra quickly yanks the rest of the swords out of me and hands me my uniform. "Hurry!" she whispers. "Go through this tunnel and it'll take you back out to the main entrance of the Institute!"

She opens a circular hatch in the wall and looks at me. I stand there naked holding my WarWings uniform, and I take a long meaningful look at Metheldra in the flickering candlelight.

"Let us in! Open this door at once!" bellows the guard at the door.

"What were you going to tell me?" I whisper. "The other thing you were going to tell me. How I can get a Queen. And if it has to do with that chick Peekaboo, I don't want to hear it. I'm not there yet. I haven't given up on my first choice, Runcita Floop."

Metheldra shoves me through the hatch into darkness.

"Runcita," she whispers, "she's in the gymnasium right now. Back on Central Campus. You'll find Runcita there. And then you can ask her to be your Queen. Your BIOCON LEVS should be higher now, after my treatments. Now go! There's no time! Hasten!"

And with that she slams the hatch shut and I'm surrounded by total darkness.

36

THAT HEARTSHRINKER SWORD IS A MIRACLE

I climb up out of the hatch and there I am, squatting near the gated entrance to the Institute where I was before.

Everything Metheldra told me has been true.

So I unfurl my wings and flap them twice and set out flying through the jungle back to Central Campus. That dragoness Metheldra might be a little deranged but she is a total maestro when it comes to her blades. I mean there's no way I can deny the newfound sense of strength and power. My heart definitely feels smaller, shriveled, shrunken. Insignificant.

It feels glorious to pound my wings like this and work off all the crazy building up inside me. Whizzing through the jungle. And I'm flying as fast as I possibly can because I want to get back to the WarWings gymnasium. And I can definitely feel the new astronomical levels of WTP coursing through me from all that swordupuncture.

My God. That HeartShrinker sword is a real miracle worker.

Glance down at powerstaff. FLIGHT SPEED at 238 MPH.

WILL TO POWER has exploded. FangBanger.

So I fly my scaly ass a couple miles through the jungle. And I'm almost back to Central Campus when off to my right I hear a *swoosh* noise.

As I turn to look, a massive powerstaff swings out from behind a tree and strikes me between the eyes.

Whack.

⋙⋘

When I open my eyes, I've got the worst headache of my life. And I can feel my blood pounding in my dome and for a second I get real worried that my skull is going to explode.

Then I look up and see that maniac dragon Rexro squatting here over me.

Great. Just what I need.

Now squatting alongside Rexro is one of his WarWings Security Commando dragon goons. I groan and reach up with my talons and feel a giant bump on my skull from where this dragon Rexro has whacked me with his powerstaff.

"Hey boss," growls the Commando dragon, "he's coming around! He's waking up! Hey boss! Looky!"

That's when I notice something is off. Because Rexro and his Commando fiend are upside down. And I wonder if Rexro's mighty crack to my skull has shattered my neural pathways, given me brain damage.

Then I twist around and look up and see these two fool dragons have strung me upside down from a tree branch. I'm upside down there with my leathery wings hanging limp off my back, and I am slowly twirling in circles.

So that explains why my head's throbbing like a bastard.

"Well well well," says Rexro. "Looks like this little birdie flew too far from his nest!"

The fiend next to him starts giggling hideously and snorting blacksmoke out his nostrils.

Fortunately for me, I have a secret. Because what these two fools don't know is that at this moment I just so happen to be rocking a FangBanger. And what else these two dragons don't know is I just had forty or so swords jammed in me up to the hilt and now my BIO-CON LEVS are so high I ought to be registered as a lethal weapon.

Not only that, my wounded black heart has recently shriveled up to the size of a raisin.

So I reach for my powerstaff on my utility belt and prepare to chop these dragon bastards' heads off with my laserblade.

What?

My talons grasp around on my utility belt but my powerstaff isn't there. The holster is empty.

Crap.

"Hey boss. What should we do with him? Huh? What should we do with him?"

"That's an excellent question," snarls Rexro. "Now let me see. Mmmm. What *should* we do with him?"

Meanwhile I'm focused on locating my powerstaff. If I can just find it. I mean it has to be around here somewhere. And as I twirl around upside down, my hooded eyes light upon my powerstaff in the tall grass where it must've fallen when they grabbed me.

Aha.

Now as I slowly twirl upside down I strain and reach my talons out for my powerstaff. Because if I can just get my powerstaff, I know with my shrunken heart and my new BIOCON LEVS I can chop off these dragons' extremities in a jiffy. And the flesh flies will pick their scaly corpses clean before anyone even notices they are missing. Now the hot sun overhead is beating down on us, and I keep reaching for my powerstaff, and the rope tied around my webbed foot creaks under the strain of my weight.

"Let's kill 'im and eat 'im, boss," says the security goon. "I'm hungry. Let's eat!"

I spread my black claws out and strain and use all my powers and you can see the biokinetic currents crackling from the tips of my claws to my powerstaff there in the grass.

Come on.

Just a little bit more.

There you go.

Now the powerstaff trembles in the grass. Then it hops over a couple inches in my direction and leaps up into the air and straight into my talon with a reassuring *smack* sound. It's the most glorious feeling. I close my claws around the handle.

I've got it! I've got it! I've got—

The powerstaff tumbles out of my talon.

Oh God.

Now that ruthless tyrant Rexro steps forward and rakes his toe claws across my scaly green snout and I feel the blood well up in the fresh cuts and start trickling down my beak.

"*That*," says Rexro, as he reaches out to steady the rope I'm hanging from, "is for blasting my cage with a firestream. You little sonuvabitch. I oughta kill you right now."

Then Rexro's Security Commando dragon blasts a firestream at the ground and instantly a massive fire is going right there in front of us.

"Looky there, boss! I made a fire! Now let's cook 'im over the fire and eat 'im! I'm hungry, boss!"

Rexro conks him over the head with his powerstaff.

"Ouch!" snarls the security goon, cradling his scaly green head with his talons. "Whatdya do that for, boss?"

"Shut up, you idiot!" snarls Rexro. "Do you know who this is? This is Dr. Terrible's grandson. The Dean said for me to fetch him back alive. Because the Dean wants to execute him out on the campus quad. Make an example of him. Maybe even lure Dr. Terrible out of hiding, case he wants to try and rescue his grandson."

"Oh goody! Oh goody! Oh goody!"

Then Rexro looks down at me and snarls, "Today's your lucky day, cadet. Normally I'd just eat you and be done with it. But Dean Floop says he wants to execute you himself. So that's how we're gonna play this! I am to take you to his lair right this minute!"

I feel my heart sink at the mention of Dean Floop's name. Because the Dean's lair is legend at WarWings, and for as long as anybody can remember, every cadet who enters the Dean's lair has a nasty habit of ending up on the business end of a firestream. Or being eaten.

Now this big dragon Rexro yanks me down from the tree and I collapse in the dirt in a heap. Then Rexro binds my wings and forelimbs with flexcuffs. He throws me in some sort of bag and takes off flying through the jungle with me inside the bag, slung over his shoulder. It seems like he's purposefully banging me against every single tree trunk he flies by.

Bam.

Bam.

Bam.

I feel myself coming in and out of consciousness. And I can hear Rexro's massive leathery wings thumping through the air as we fly forward.

Where is my Queen?

37

DEAN FLOOP'S HIDEOUS LAIR

From the moment I'm tossed into the Dean's lair, it is obvious he's going to kill me.

I stand up and dust myself off. I'm still dizzy and bruised from Rexro's rough handling of me, and it seems like there are a million throbbing knots all over my scaly ass from getting bounced against those tree trunks on the flight over.

Well this monstrous dragon Dean Floop doesn't seem too over-whelmed with joy at the sight of me, that's for sure. In fact when I first stand up inside his lair, Dean Floop turns his back to me and starts lashing his green tail around. And I can't help but wonder if the Dean has turned his back to me because he doesn't want me to see him wearing the eye patch over the socket where Dr. Terrible blinded him last night.

Now the Dean's lair is glorious, I won't lie. I mean the joint is overflowing with mountains of gold and diamonds and jewels. And there are skulls everywhere. He has all sorts of strange creatures' heads mounted on the walls, from all the planets he's conquered and all the hunting safaris he's gone on throughout the universe.

Anyway, there's a lone wooden chair set out in the middle of the Dean's lair, and I stroll over to it. The Dean keeps his back to me.

"Nice of you to drop in, Gork," he says. "Please don't take a seat."

I stop my rear haunch an inch away from the chair and straighten all the way back up.

Somewhere in the lair I hear a creature whimper and drag its chains across the floor.

The Dean belches up a thunderous firestream that shakes the lair and makes the walls quake. "How are you feeling today, Gork?" he snarls. "I hope Rexro wasn't too rough with you?"

"No sir. I'm fine, sir."

"Here," he says. "Catch."

My powerstaff comes sailing across the lair, rocketing right at me. I hold up my talon.

Smack.

"I have some good news for you, Gork. It's come to my attention you would like to take my daughter Runcita to EggHarvest. And I am here to tell you that my daughter has agreed to be your Queen. Perhaps you saw the two of us discussing the matter in the corridor earlier? I believe you did. I saw you there."

I just squat here like a jerk with my black beak hanging wide open. Not quite believing what I'm hearing. And yet I *did* see this scaly old dragon Dean Floop and his daughter Runcita speaking in the corridor earlier.

"It's a simple case of you scratch my wing, I scratch yours," he growls. "All you have to do is to tell me where your grandfather Dr. Terrible is hiding. Do you understand what I'm saying to you, Gork?"

Holy crap holy crap holy crap. This is real. This is happening.

Runcita will be my Queen.

Yes sir!

Runcita is going to lay my eggs. Well all I have to do is tell the Dean that the degenerate Dr. Terrible is hiding in his secret underground bunker by Conquer More Road on the west side of the island. Runcita will be my Queen. And I'll describe to the Dean exactly where the bunker is and how the hatch to the bunker is cunningly disguised as an old dead tree trunk.

And then Dean Floop will capture that sonuvabitch Dr. Terrible. I don't know exactly what Dean Floop will do to Dr. Terrible, but it will be bad. Very bad. But that isn't my concern right now. Besides,

I'm a Terrible and this is what we Terribles do. We act terrible. Isn't that what Dr. Terrible is forever jabbering on about, anyway?

Yes sir.

Well one thing is for sure, Dean Floop is powerful enough to pull it off. He's definitely got the juice to do Dr. Terrible in. Or Dr. Terrible wouldn't have run off to hide. My grandpa wouldn't have fled if he weren't scared of what Dean Floop could do to him.

I can't believe my good fortune. This is the stroke of good luck I've been waiting for. And as I squat here in the Dean's lair, I don't say anything. Because I want to savor this moment. Runcita will be my Queen after all. Even with these two stupid microscopic horns on my scaly green head, I'm going to get exactly what I want.

Because this is two birds with one stone.

"Now Gork," the Dean growls. "Tell me, do you know where your grandfather is right now hiding?"

Then, while Dean Floop waits for me to answer his question, he immediately starts growling and gnashing his fangs.

Clack-clack-clack.

And even with his back to me I can see little sparks flying off the sides of the Dean's monsterish green head from where his fangs are clacking together.

Clack-clack-clack.

Now as you can imagine, I'm feeling awful nervous squatting here. And since the monstrous Dean has his back to me I quickly check my breath to make sure it's sufficiently disgusting. All you do is hold your talons under your beak and blow your breath up toward the old nostrils. And I feel a sense of relief when my hooded eyes instantly start watering because of the noxious odor.

My breath isn't just bad, it could peel the paint off a wall.

Clack-clack-clack.

Because you see I want everything to be *perfect*. I don't want to mess this up. I want to tell this dragon Dean Floop that my scaly grandpa is hiding in his secret underground bunker on the west side of the island. Then I want to put my crown on Runcita's gorgeous scaly head and have her be my Queen for EggHarvest.

I mean I know how treacherous and fiendish this big evil dragon Dean Floop can be and so I definitely don't want to do anything to set him off. That's why I'm being so careful right now. Like I know during a conversation this scaly green bastard Dean Floop will sometimes grow so disgusted with a cadet's answers that he'll use his laserblade to disembowel the cadet right there on the spot.

Clack-clack-clack.

Other times Dean Floop will just blast a dragon cadet with a firestream and *poof*—the only thing left of you will be a neat little pile of ash on the floor. And it just so happens that right before I came into Dean Floop's lair this morning, I saw a WarWings janitor exiting the lair with a dustbin filled with ash.

Clack-clack-clack.

So you can see why at this moment I'm being so careful with even the smallest of details. I don't want to ruin my chances here of scoring Runcita as my Queen because of something small, like having good breath.

"Yes sir!" I say. "That's good news, sir."

"What's good news?"

"Sir. What you said, sir. About your daughter agreeing to be my Queen. I would like to take your daughter Runcita to EggHarvest and for her to lay my eggs. So we can raise a Colony together. So that's what I meant, sir. About the good news part, sir."

"Well, son," he growls, "if you want my daughter Runcita to be your Queen, then you're going to have to give me Dr. Terrible. I need his location. By the way, Gork, why do you call him that?"

The Dean still has his back to me, and his tail is thrashing around. He gnashes his fangs.

"Call him what, sir?"

"Dr. Terrible."

"I'm not sure I follow you, sir. What else would I call him?"

"Grandfather. You don't hear Runcita calling me Dean Floop, do you?"

"I don't hear Runcita call you anything, sir. I haven't ever heard her speak, actually. Except in my dreams. Like last night she came to me in my dream. But she didn't mention you in my dream, sir. No sir. What she told me was—"

"Answer my question, cadet."

"Sir," I say, squirting blacksmoke out my nostrils. "I'm not allowed to refer to Dr. Terrible as Grandfather. Or Grandpa, or Gramps, or Pa-Pa, or Pee-Paw, or anything like that. I have to call him Dr. Terrible."

"And why is that, may I ask?"

"Sir, because Dr. Terrible says he's my personal physician first and foremost. And my grandpa a very distant second! Or whatever number you consider to be last place, that's what number being my grandpa is."

"So Dr. Terrible has renounced his status as your grandfather, is that it?"

"I'm not sure, sir. I guess you could say that, sir."

The Dean seems to consider this for a second. "So what would happen if you called him Grandfather?"

"Well, the last time I called him Grandpa I was eight years old. And as punishment, Dr. Terrible gave me the silent treatment."

The Dean keeps his back to me. He gnashes his fangs. His tail is still lashing around.

"For how long?" he growls.

"For how long what, sir?"

"For how long did your grandfather Dr. Terrible give you the silent treatment?"

"For two years, sir."

Dean Floop is silent. Then he shakes his monsterish green head and chuckles. "For two years?"

"Yes sir. He even timed it down to the second. With a stopwatch."

"With a stopwatch?" he says, incredulously.

"He had a special stopwatch made for just this purpose, sir."

"What do you mean by 'special'?"

"Well sir," I say, squirting blacksmoke out my nostrils. "He called it the Dr. Terrible Stopwatch. The stopwatch ran in increments of two years. The watch face was an image of Dr. Terrible's scaly green head. On the back of the stopwatch was an inscription that said: I MADE A TERRIBLE MISTAKE. He made me carry the stopwatch around for the entire two years to remind me that I was responsible for my own misery."

"Dr. Terrible gave you the silent treatment for two years? Just because you called him Grandpa?"

"Yes sir."

"And you were only eight years old at the time?"

"Yes sir."

"And your grandfather Dr. Terrible didn't speak to you again until you were ten years old?"

"Yes sir."

Even though he has his back to me, I can tell this monstrous dragon Dean Floop is impressed somehow. He's not gnashing his fangs anymore, but his gigantic tail is still lashing around something powerful.

"Now Gork," growls the Dean. "Of course you are aware that your grandfather Dr. Terrible blinded me in my eye less than twenty-four hours ago? I believe you were there along with the rest of the cadets?"

"Yes sir."

"Now you are also aware, I presume," he says, "that over the last few days I have been forced to execute seventeen cadets because of a series of events that originated with your grandfather Dr. Terrible's experiments out at that confounded Institute of his? And therefore this whole mess is his fault. Because he wanted to be a show-off. Because he created that Evolution Machine. Or Evo-Mach 3000, or whatever it's called. And then he held a press conference about it?"

"Yes sir."

"You are also aware that Dr. Terrible has disappeared and he is considered a dangerous fugitive by the WarWings justice system. So I hope you understand my predicament. Because as Dean of WarWings I am charged with the duty of bringing Dr. Terrible to justice."

"Yes sir."

"So I'm not going to ask you again, Gork. Tell me where your grandfather Dr. Terrible is. Or you will not get to have my daughter as your Queen. Do you understand what I'm saying to you, Gork?"

"Yes sir."

Well at this moment I'm feeling super close and warm toward the Dean, like we are truly kindred dragons. Because we're joined in our common enemy: Dr. Terrible. I am squatting here in the Dean's lair and I figure that in many ways we are the same, the Dean and I. Because the ruthless Dr. Terrible has robbed the Dean of his sight in one eye. Dr. Terrible blinded him. And in a metaphorical way, my grandpa has blinded me, too. In the way that the big scaly green treacherous bastard has controlled me and deceived me and tricked me into believing things that aren't true.

So as I squat here in the Dean's lair it would really be impossible for me to convey to you how incredibly close I feel to him. Because we've both been blinded by Dr. Terrible. And because he is going to give me his daughter Runcita for my Queen. And because Runcita will lay my eggs. And inside each sacred baby dragon that hatches out of those eggs, there'll be some of Dean Floop's DNA. And there'll be some of my DNA. It's a cosmic connection, what the Dean and I have.

"Sir," I say, "I'm real sorry."

"What are you sorry about, cadet?"

"Sir. I don't know where Dr. Terrible is, sir."

Why don't I just turn my scaly grandpa in? Why don't I just tell Dean Floop that Dr. Terrible is hiding in his secret underground bunker over on the west side of the island? I guess my tiny shriveled heart's torn. Because I guess even though I'm not Dr. Terrible's biggest fan, I just can't bring myself to rat out Dr. Terrible like that.

"Sir," I say. "But I'd still like to ask for your permission to take your daughter to EggHarvest. Would you still be willing to help me with that, sir?"

"Excuse me?!"

"I'd still like Runcita to be my Queen. For EggHarvest, sir."

I notice the lair has suddenly grown super hot and I realize by the sound of things that Dean Floop is breathing and huffing mega fire. Then Dean Floop belches up another thunderous firestream which rocks the lair and makes the walls quake, and this time the ground under my green webbed feet shakes and I have to raise my tail to keep my balance.

"Well clearly you are as dumb as your horns are short! If you can tell me where your grandfather Dr. Terrible is, then I can promise you my daughter's talon as Queen. But otherwise there is no way my daughter will ever be your Queen! Do you understand what I'm saying to you, Gork?"

Now with all the added heat in the Dean's lair, I feel a little bead of sweat trickle down under my left forelimb. Then I see the Dean lift his ugly green snout and take a couple of big suspicious whiffs, as if maybe he detects some new funk in the air.

"Yes sir. I understand." I pause for a second before continuing to speak. Then I say: "Dr. Terrible figured you might say something like that, sir. And he told me to tell you that he would pull whatever strings he has to pull to prevent you from keeping me away from Runcita. Even if one of those strings just so happens to be wrapped tightly around your long green neck. Those were Dr. Terrible's exact words, sir."

Dean Floop's tail stops lashing around and settles quietly on the floor.

"Is there anything else?" he says.

"Yes sir. I'm supposed to give you this."

I hold up the envelope in my talon.

"What is it?!" he growls.

"My letter of recommendation."

"For what?!"

"From Dr. Terrible, sir."

"Come again?!"

"This is my letter of recommendation. Written by Dr. Terrible."

"What is he recommending? And to whom?!"

"Me, sir. He's recommending me. He's recommending me to take your daughter Runcita to EggHarvest as my Queen. As to whom the letter is addressed, sir. It's addressed to you, sir."

Dean Floop whirls around to face me with blazing red eyes.

My horns instantly start tingling like crazy. And instinctively my toe claws shoot out and I raise my tail and crouch low on my trembling haunches and stay poised on the claws of my webbed feet, readying myself to flee. And judging by the twisted look on his black beak, I figure the Dean is going to fly over and rip my chest open with his fangs and eat my heart.

But really I should be able to judge what this psychotic dragon is up to by the way his throat muscles are contorting in his long green neck, like ropes being yanked into knots. And if I wasn't so freaking terrified I could recognize the signs, but as it is the sonuvabitch catches me off guard.

Because suddenly the Dean flips opens his beak and fires a thin jetstream of venom at me and the venom whizzes thirty feet through the air. The venom flashes across the lair to where I'm squatting and I watch in horror as the tip of the venomstream appears to lunge at my beak at the last second.

And it nails me right in my scaly green chest.

Or it would have, anyway. Lucky for me I've always had a quick first step. Because I'm already crouched on the claws of my webbed feet and have my tail raised. So I leap to one side as the Dean's venomstream hits the ground where I've just been squatting, and when the venom splashes on the floor it starts sizzling.

The maniac Dean looks at me crouched on the floor where I've landed.

I am panting and eyeballing the Dean in terror.

I wait to see if this deranged one-eyed dragon is going to shoot some more venom at me or what. And then finally he seems to relax a little, and he just snorts as if we've been playing a game and he somehow finds my style of play amusing. Now that big one-eyed dragon turns around in a leisurely fashion so that his back is to me again.

Somewhere in the lair I hear a creature whimper and drag its chains across the floor.

"Let me have it," says Dean Floop.

"Have what, sir?"

"The letter."

Now I glance at my talon where I've been holding the letter but it's not there. And then I spot the envelope on the ground where I must have dropped it. I lunge and snatch the letter up just before the pooling venom reaches it. I'm still panting and by this point my black heart is hammering so hard I'm worried it might just explode right out of my rib cage. And it's all I can do not to run screaming from the lair.

"Yes sir." I hold up the envelope with a shaky talon. "It's right here, sir."

Then the Dean's tongue comes shooting from over his shoulder and zooms all the way across the lair to where I'm squatting and snatches the envelope out of my talons and then in a flash the tongue retracts back to the Dean.

⇛⇚

I hear the Dean open the letter and then he stands still as he reads it.

I've already read the letter so many times I could recite it out loud for him.

Dear Dean Floop:

This is my letter of recommendation for my grandson Gork The Terrible. I am recommending that you assist him in his quest to take your daughter Runcita to EggHarvest.

As you can imagine, I am monitoring Gork's campaign to get Runcita to be his Queen very closely, and surely by now you must know that I have eyes everywhere here on the island. If you are squatting there wondering whether me saying I have eyes everywhere on the island is meant as subtle allusion to the fact that last night at our Public Debate I had occasion to rob you of your sight in one eye, well of course it isn't, you stupid Cyclops.

What kind of monster do you take me for?

What I mean when I say I have eyes everywhere is I am probably right now watching you read this letter on a hidden video feed from one of the thousands of micro-drones that I have deployed all over the island. Now I realize this constitutes an invasion of your privacy, Dean. Me watching you like this, vis-à-vis said micro-drone.

But let me remind you that my name is Dr. Terrible.

And this is what we Terribles do.

We act terrible.

Now I want to make it clear that if you attempt in any way to block my grandson Gork's attempts to make your daughter Runcita his Queen for EggHarvest, then I will have no choice but to use my new Evolution Machine, or Evo-Mach 3000, and mind-swap you with a little white mouse.

Now I imagine that Mrs. Floop, not to mention the cadets at WarWings, will be quite surprised when the only noise you can make with your beak is *squeak squeak squeak.*

Furthermore, I'm sure this will lead to some very difficult questions from Mrs. Floop. Like why do you keep waking me up in the middle of the night and begging for cheese?

Now let me address the elephant in the room. Gork's horns. Obviously I recognize and acknowledge my grandson Gork's horns are substandard in every way. And perhaps Gork's tiny horns diminish somewhat his standing in your eyes—forgive me, I mean "eye"—as an ideal mating partner for your daughter Runcita.

Now even for me, his grandfather, his own scales and blood, I must confess that the sight of Gork's puny horns sometimes make me very nauseous. And once recently while Gork was asleep I came into his lair and looked at him sleeping peacefully there in his nest and the sight of his horns made me puke. But of course I never told Gork about this because I didn't want to ruin the young dragon's self-esteem. Though I guess when he woke up in the morning he must've wondered where all that vomit came from, but whatever.

You see, young Gork's parents died when their Fertility Mission spaceship crashed on their Designated Foreign Planet.

Now at the time, none of us knew that Gork's parents' spaceship had crashed on the surface of planet Earth. All we knew was that the transmissions from Gorks' parents' spaceship cut off abruptly. Initially I had no cause for concern, though. I simply thought they were too busy conquering Earth to be bothered with sending us a status update. You know how young dragons can be on their Fertility Mission.

Now when the remains of their spaceship crashed into planet Earth, all of the eggs aboard were lost in the explosion. All except for one. Miraculously, Gork's egg survived among the wreckage there in one of Earth's forests. So eventually Gork hatched and then for the next three years he grew up all alone and raised himself in this forest on planet Earth.

Now personally I could not rest without knowing precisely what had happened to that spaceship ATHENOS with my son on it. I spared no expense in constructing all manner of exploratory machines to try and scour the galaxies for any clue as to what had happened to that spaceship ATHENOS. Eventually one of my Planetary Drone Probes made a DNA match there on Earth, and I was alerted of Gork's existence and I rescued him from the forests of that planet Earth. And I brought him back here to Scale Island and raised him as if he were my own son.

But by the time I rescued Gork, he was already three years old. And because he did not receive proper guidance or supervision for those first three years of his life, he has some developmental disabilities. More specifically, Gork is severely lacking in the WILL TO POWER department. And as a result his horns haven't matured at the same rate as a normal dragon his age.

But I have been working with Gork since he came into my life, trying to boost his HORN DENSITY & MASS. And I have every confidence that one day his actions will not only reflect his Terrible lineage, but that his horns will also grow to match the Terrible mind-set that he is the rightful heir to. Well unfortunately that day is not here yet but it will be soon! At which point Gork's horns will grow to be at least five feet long.

Now I assume this is all the reassurance you need in order to accept Gork's bid to procure your daughter as his Queen for EggHarvest. And I assume you will not only support but actively assist my grandson Gork in his quest to make your daughter his Queen.

If not, might I recommend you take a look in the mirror and try to imagine what you will look like with whiskers.

Yours Truly,
Dr. Karzakus The Terrible, M.D., Ph.D.

Distinguished Research Professor
Institute of Advanced Biokinetics and Neuroanatomy
WarWings Military Academy

Now when Dean Floop finishes reading the letter, he crumples it up and tosses it up in the air and opens his beak and blasts the letter with a firebolt. The letter goes up in a tiny cloud of smoke.

Then the Dean flicks his long scaly neck back and forth as if he aims to compose himself before speaking. And I whisk my tail around behind me, preparing to leap out of the way in case the Dean tries to blast me with a firebolt this time.

⟜⟜

And Dean Floop does blast me.

Just not with fire. He blasts me with words.

This big demented dragon turns to face me and snorts flames out his nostrils and bellows: "I'm afraid I have bad news for you, Gork! There will be no quid pro quo. The deal is off. Do you understand what I'm saying to you, Gork?!"

"Yes sir."

"Good! Because with the power vested in me as the Dean of WarWings I hereby forbid you to ask my daughter Runcita to be your Queen for EggHarvest! Do you understand what I'm saying to you, Gork?"

"Yes sir."

"Good! Because take my word for it, if you so much as even glance at my daughter Runcita I will have you marched out to the campus quad and I will blast you with a firestream and reduce your sorry tail to a pile of ash! Do you understand what I'm saying to you, Gork?!"

Somewhere in the lair I hear that same creature whimper and drag its chains across the floor.

Now it feels like my shrunken heart is made of glass and the Dean's tirade is a hammer smashing my heart into a thousand little pieces.

Then Dean Floop belches up a thunderous firestream which shakes the lair and makes the walls quake. I have to raise my tail to keep from getting thrown off my webbed feet.

"Yes sir."

"Good! Because in terms of a mating partner you are nothing but a liability and a laughingstock! If I weren't so disgusted by the sight of you I'd be laughing my head off right now at the thought of you possibly mating with my daughter! Do you understand what I'm saying to you, Gork?!"

By this point I am just busy trying to keep myself from crying.

"Yes sir. May I be dismissed?"

"What?!"

"By your leave, sir?"

"Dismissed!"

Then as I turn and head for the door, this demented dragon Dean Floop fires his parting shot. "And tell your meddlesome grandfather it doesn't matter how far he runs or where he hides because he is a fugitive in the eyes of the WarWings Council of the Elders and I will bring him to justice! Do you understand what I'm saying to you, Gork?!"

"Yes sir." I've stopped and turned to face the Dean while he speaks to me, per WarWings regulations.

"Good! Now be gone, Gork, and I never want to see your stinking beak or your retarded-looking horns again! If I ever have to see you again, it will be right before I blast you with a firestream and execute you! Although come to think of it, why bother putting off the inevitable?!"

Then this scaly bastard Dean Floop cocks his long green neck and flips his wings out and blasts a mega firestream which flashes at me like a bolt of lightning. But I'm already crouched on my haunches with my tail whisking around behind me. And I dive out the door with the flames from the Dean's firestream heating up my scaly backside.

And as I dive out the door, I can't help thinking:

Yeah so what if they call you Weak Sauce. And yeah so what if Runcita's father wants you dead. Well at least you're not being carted out of the Dean's lair as a pile of ash in the janitor's dustbin! And no matter what they say or what names they call you, you've got WILL TO POWER, *Gork.*

You really do.

Now you go do what you gotta do.

38

THWACK-THWACK

Thwack-thwack.

By this point, there is no time to lose.

Thwack thwack.

I flap my wings and fly down dark fiery corridor after dark fiery corridor after dark fiery corridor. I flash through the air in a blur.

Go, Gork, go.

I am crushing it.

I am rocketing to the gymnasium. Because according to that luscious blademaster Metheldra, this is where I'll find Runcita. And the Dean's words are still echoing inside my scaly green head. And my backside is still a little warm from the Dean's firestream I dodged only minutes ago.

Glance down at powerstaff. FLIGHT SPEED at 269 MPH.

Whoa.

I am in TURBO FLIGHT mode.

Feels good.

Now the wind cutting across my black beak is screaming for mercy.

The corridors are crowded with flying cadets zooming around.

But then when one of these fool dragons cuts in front of me I just *whack* him out of the way with my leathery wing.

Another flying dragon up ahead swerves into my PROJECTED TRAJECTORY PATH and I open my beak and blast a firestream into his backside.

"Hey what the—?!" he cries, rubbing his backside with his talons.

Don't even give him a look.

I shoot onward.

Now the reason I am rocketing to the gym is because I have to try and get to Runcita before the Dean puts the word out to his goons that if I'm spotted anywhere near his daughter then I am to be apprehended. My pride is a little wounded by the Dean's words. That stuff about how as a mating partner I was nothing but a liability and a laughingstock.

Who does that bastard think he *is*, anyway?

Thwack-thwack.

And if you want to know the truth, it kind of pisses me off.

Now I feel a whole new level of WILL TO POWER coursing through my scaly green ass and I chalk it up to that chick Metheldra's swordu-puncture and the way she gave me a royal case of heart shrinkage.

If that sonuvabitch Dean Floop wants to try and stop me from getting his daughter Runcita to be my Queen, then I am just all the more determined to get his precious daughter to lay my eggs, thank you very much.

Now I can really feel the WTP blasting throughout my system.

And my heart has shrunk to the point where the sound of it beating in my chest is like a tiny castanet clacking underwater.

Barely audible.

For the first time ever, my heart is something I can ignore.

Feels great.

Dragons flying around up ahead scramble to get out of my way at the last second.

And when one of them is a little slow on the uptake, I *whack* them out of the way.

I whiz by them.

Now as I fly along, my toe claws keep shooting out and retracting.

Where is my Queen?

39

RUNCITA

A few minutes later, I fly through the gym's entrance.

I close my wings and drop and land in a crouch on my green webbed feet. I scope out the area. And there she is. My sweet luscious dragonette in all her glory. Just like Metheldra said she'd be.

Runcita Floop.

She's just squatting there on her muscular haunches. But then I see something which makes my horns tingle. Because the reason Runcita is just squatting there is some dragon fool is down on one haunch in front of her and he has his wings spread out wide and his tail raised. And he's holding his crown out to her, like an offering.

Crap.

It's this senior dragon fool named Tog. Tog is crouched down on one haunch and he's holding his crown out to Runcita and it's obvious that he's asking her to be his Queen for EggHarvest. Now frankly I'm kind of shocked to see a punk like Tog making a play for Runcita like this. Because in terms of class ranking, this fella Tog is definitely nothing special bordering on doofus.

But I don't have time to think about this because at that moment out of the corner of my eye I see a green blur blasting toward Runcita. I don't know if it is my intuition or what, but I get a bad feeling right then. And I figure whatever this blur is, it is big trouble.

Turns out I'm right. Because the green blur I track out of the corner of my eye turns out to be this big nasty dragon Jock bastard named Bruggert. He smashes right into Tog. It's a heck of a shot. Everybody there in the gym can hear it, that's for sure. Serious scale-on-scale contact.

Tog instantly goes soaring up through the air a good fifty feet. And I glimpse Tog's yellow eyes as he flashes through the air, and you can see right away Bruggert has seriously damaged something neural in Tog. I mean Tog's leathery wings are sort of flapping, but his wings are broken, crumpled. This poor dragon bastard Tog is just a brutally crippled creature reduced to the fundamentals of existence: try to flap wings, try to breathe.

Tog never even knew what hit him. I'm guessing the whole experience was kind of painless. He smashes into the far wall of the gym and explodes in a gush of blood. Tog is simply no more. It's pretty repulsive. To see what is left of Tog.

When he *splats* against the wall like that, all the other fiendish cadets in the gym start hooting and snorting with laughter and cheering. Then a bunch of dragon fools scurry over and start snapping images of the Tog-turned-blood-splat on the wall with their powerstaffs.

Meanwhile that big deranged Jocko Bruggert comes to a halt in front of Runcita. And squats directly in her path, blocking her way.

Bruggert is at least three heads taller than the average cadet, and his thick muscular tail is flapping around in the air behind him and you can't help but marvel at the two giant black horns on Bruggert's monsterish scaly head. Each of Bruggert's horns must be ten feet long at least. His horns look so sharp at the tips, you reckon he could leap up and gore a low-flying spaceship.

And he is *the* star player on WarWings' varsity Slave-Catching team.

As I watch Bruggert step in and block Runcita's path, my piddly horns start vibrating so hard it's making my freaking vision blurry. Each year after the Slave-Catching Championship, Bruggert has been named Most Valuable Player. No cadet in the history of WarWings has been named MVP for four years straight. Except this scoundrel Bruggert.

And it's just assumed that once Bruggert graduates from WarWings he'll go on to an illustrious career as a Planet Conqueror. I'll bet the WarWings administration already has Bruggert's 3-D holophoto ready to go up on the Notable Alumni Wall in the Library. I mean this dragon's intergalactic imminence is just a foregone conclusion.

He's just standing there on his hind legs, studying Runcita. He hasn't even once glanced over to see what became of Tog. Bruggert opens his black beak wide and belches up a thunderous firestream which shakes the gymnasium and makes the walls quake.

Then Bruggert lifts his talon and points a long index claw at Runcita.

"Hey Run Run," he purrs. "How are ya doing, beautiful? You're a hard chick to find. But lucky for you, now I've found you! Ha-ha."

Then Bruggert spreads his wings out wide and grins this mega-watt smile, showing off a beakful of fangs.

The other cadets in the gym definitely smell blood. They crowd around Runcita and Bruggert. Because when Bruggert splats Tog against the wall and then ambushes Runcita, there's instantly a new and dangerous energy in the air. You definitely don't need to be a genius to know what all the other demented cadets in the Dining Hall are thinking. You can see it in their eyes. What they are thinking is:

Sure, earlier this morning Runcita put a bunch of dragons in the WarWings Medical Center, but none of those morons was as big and strong and tough as Bruggert.

Bruggert could single-handedly crush any dragon fool in our Academy!

Last week something happened at the Friday night WarWings Slave-Catching game that I haven't been able to get out of my mind. And it involved Bruggert and his coach, Coach Deebs. Coach Deebs was roaring at Bruggert from his stratospheric perch, while Bruggert was out there with his spear and net, trying to catch slaves.

I was there at that game along with the other cadets, sitting in the orbital viewcraft. At one point Coach Deebs roared: "Bruggert you better move your tail out there! Stop sleepwalking and get involved in the game! I swear I'll sit you on the transport ship if you don't start catching some slaves!"

I guess that last threat from the coach was more than Bruggert could take. Because at that moment, Bruggert flapped his wings and flew up to the stratospheric perch and opened his beak wide and literally bit Coach Deeb's scaly green head off. Coach Deebs's headless body plummeted down to the terrain. I still remember the coach's scaly green body lying there all crooked with his wings folded funny and the blood pooling around him. Then Bruggert flew back out onto the terrain and resumed playing the game with his spear and net, as if nothing had happened.

Even for dragons, there are limits. And this was way over the limit for normal sports-related violence. Because the idea that one of our cadets could do that to an adult dragon was downright scary. I mean Coach Deebs was no slouch. We're talking a full-grown adult dragon here, a former Intergalactic Conqueror with at least twenty planets under his belt. And Bruggert bit Coach Deebs's scaly green head off with his fangs as easily as if he were ripping open a bag of hornetpops.

Now on top of all that, I can't tell you how many times I'd seen Bruggert shooting up 'roids around Central Campus, out in public. More often than not when you see Bruggert in the corridor he'll have a syringe needle sticking out of his long scaly neck. As if for him the syringe is a fashion accessory, part of his style.

Like the way some dragon fellas wear glasses frames with no lenses.

What kind of maniac wears a steroid syringe in his neck as a fashion accessory?

I'm surprised Bruggert hasn't got a syringe stuck in his long green neck right now.

But what gives me an even worse feeling this Crown Day in the gym is knowing this dragon Bruggert can have practically any dragonette in our grade he wants. I mean the hottest female cadets at WarWings will literally beg Bruggert to lock them up in one of his cages, let them spend the night in his lair.

Shoot, even Fribby will get these big dreamy eyes whenever Bruggert walks by her in the hall. Once when I asked Fribby how she could be attracted to a deranged Normal lunatic bastard like Bruggert, she just hooted and told me I was being a prude.

"Bruggert had a horrible childhood," said Fribby. "He's damaged, is all. If you understood that, then you'd see him for what he is. Which is a badly wounded and terrified dragon fella."

Which is typical. Whenever a chick wants to justify being attracted to a monster or laying a monster's eggs, they always talk about how traumatized that dragon bastard is from his horrible childhood. And I think it's flapdoodle.

Why not just admit that you enjoy being with a monster?

Why not just admit that the monster gives you that special little tingly feeling in your tail?

But I'm sure Dr. Terrible would tell me I need to get over myself and that if anyone could benefit from adding a little monster to his personality, it would be me.

My point is I'm really worried that Runcita will fall prey to Bruggert's special powers.

The lure of the monster.

So I charge forward and plow into the crowd of cadets gathered around Runcita and Bruggert there in the gymnasium. But even as I fling the hideous dragons aside and shove my way to the front of the circle gathered around Runcita and Bruggert, my heart is sinking. Because I sense I might already be too late.

"Yo Run Run," purrs Bruggert, flexing his wings. "What say you be my Queen for EggHarvest? I reckon we could make a great Colony together. I'm envisioning billions of slaves kneeling before us with their heads bowed. And lots of little Bruggerts running around. So what do you say, Run Run? Will you be my Queen?!"

Runcita just eyeballs Bruggert like he's lost his mind.

"My dad gave me a new spaceship for our Fertility Mission," he purrs. "It's got an anti-grav LavaTub."

He flicks his powerstaff and a 3-D holovid appears in the air, and the holovid shows a tricked-out spaceship which radiates power and fiendish technology. The holovid jumps to a new clip showing the interior of the spaceship. There are long hallways and gardens and luxury rooms. The clip finishes with a slow panning shot of the anti-grav LavaTub floating in midair. And above it is this clear-paneled ceiling, so you can soak in the LavaTub and watch the planets as you pass them by.

"That's a pretty righteous spaceship, ain't it?" purrs Bruggert. "And when we land on our Designated Foreign Planet we'll engage in much merry mayhem and destruction. Catch us some slaves. Plunder some gold. Build us a sweet Colony to rule over our new planet. You'll be my Queen. And I'll be your Dragon King!"

Runcita's tail raises up and starts twitching around in a Threat Display. Now I just happen to catch a glimpse of the white meat lining the underside of Runcita's tail, and the sight of it makes me woozy with lust. Squatting here on the edge of the circle, I whisper: "She's even more beautiful when she's angry!"

Bruggert grins at Runcita and her twitching tail as if she's nothing more than a mighty cute and amusing tiger cub. "And on our way to our Designated Foreign Planet," he purrs, "maybe we can rock that LavaTub together. Get real nasty. So whatdya say, chick? You reckon you got what it takes to lay my eggs? Huh? Do you, Run Run?"

Then he gets down on one haunch. He reaches for his utility belt and produces a seriously boss gold crown lined with flashing colored gems and a massive diamond in the center. The crowd of cadets gasp because it's the most gorgeous and insanely expensive-looking crown that they have ever seen offered for EggHarvest.

Bruggert holds the faboo crown out to Runcita. "Will you be my Queen?"

And I don't know which part makes my scaly green ass feel worse. The fact that his gold crown chockablock with red and blue and green gems and diamonds is so boss that I know in my heart if I was a chick and a fella offered me that crown I would say yes in a heartbeat. Or the fact that as Bruggert crouches there with the crown he somehow manages to look so damn sweet and sincere.

40

THERE'S NOTHING MORE IMPORTANT
THAN GETTING THE RIGHT CHICK TO LAY YOUR EGGS

"Get that stupid crown out of my face," Runcita hisses. "And please don't call me Run Run again. Nobody calls me Run Run."

"Why not give it a test drive and see how it fits, Run Run?" purrs Bruggert, holding the crown out. "You might feel different once you've got it on your pretty little head."

Then the crown floats out of Bruggert's talons and it soars up into the air and it hovers several feet over Runcita's gorgeous scaly head. The crown clearly has some sort of neurospring technology in it that makes it bend to Bruggert's will. It's really something to see, the boss crown hovering up in the air like that.

"I'm warning you," growls Runcita. She eyeballs the crown overhead as she reaches for her powerstaff and yanks it off her utility belt.

"Once you put that there crown on your scaly head, you ain't going to want to take it off, Run Run. There's not a chick alive that wouldn't want to wear this crown!"

The floating crown suddenly lunges several feet to the left. Runcita wheels herself around to keep the crown in her sight. Then the crown shoots to the right. Runcita leaps and dances to keep the crown in her line of sight.

Now I don't know if you can say that a crown has body language. But if you can, then you'd have to say Bruggert's crown whizzing around up there in the air, well this crown's body language is aggressive bordering on predatory.

Then the crown starts zigzagging overhead. And Runcita is turning every which way to keep it in her sights. Sadly, it looks like she's losing ground. Because you can tell Runcita is getting confused and dizzy. She's panting and her tongue is drooping several feet out of her beak.

Well apparently this has been Bruggert's plan all along.

Because he gleefully bellows, "Gotcha!"

And at that moment the crown shoots straight down onto Runcita's gorgeous scaly head.

Well it almost does. At the last moment, Runcita dives away and activates the laserblade in her powerstaff. The laserblade is bright red, at least seven feet long, and makes a whirring noise.

Now Runcita ducks to avoid the crown and she swings the laserblade and cracks the flying crown. Sparks explode everywhere and the crown goes shooting through the air across the gym. It smashes up against the far wall with a loud *clang* and then falls to the floor where it wobbles around making an awful racket before finally coming to a stop.

Bruggert glares at Runcita and snorts firebolts out his flared green nostrils.

"I *really* wish you hadn't done that, Run Run," he growls. "Maybe you ain't the chick I thought you was after all."

Then Bruggert casually lifts his talon and holds it up high.

The crown jumps up off the ground and zooms across the gym and back into Bruggert's palm.

Smack.

He hitches the crown to his utility belt and then turns and glares at Runcita.

"I told you to get that stupid crown out of my face," she hisses. "You should've listened to me."

Bruggert's black beak is twisted up into this sadistic grin and you can see all of his fangs. All thousand of them, it looks like.

"Listen to you?" he purrs. "I'm all earholes, Run Run. Message received loud and clear." Now that depraved dragon pauses for a moment and his eyes bloom red in their sockets.

"But I gotta warn you, Run Run," he growls. "I'm one of them fellas who thinks that when a chick says no, she really means yes."

Runcita squints at Bruggert. "So then what does it mean if I say yes?"

"Yes means yes."

"I thought no means no."

"No means yes. So either way, your answer's yes."

"Hey Bruggert," she growls.

"Yeah, Run Run?"

"Do yourself a big favor."

"What's that?"

"Don't let your beak write a check that your tail can't cash."

In response, the veins in Bruggert's long neck pop out and his entire scaly green body begins to inflate and the rippling muscles in his chest and forelimbs and powerful haunches swell up to hideous proportions.

His toe claws shoot out.

Then Bruggert's giant wings ominously unfurl behind his mon-sterish scaly green head, and each of his leathery wings is seriously massive. Truth be told, the sight of Bruggert with his leathery wings unfurled like that is insanely scary.

Now as if summoned by Bruggert's fierce Threat Display, a dark wind starts howling through the gym.

Runcita is just crouched there on her haunches looking up at Bruggert with what can only be described as a helpless expression on her beak.

And that's when I know I have to stop what's about to happen.

Runcita, poor Runcita, she's about to get mauled by a psychopath. My darling Runcita is going to get her scaly green head bitten clean off. And I can't just stand by and watch that happen.

So I step right into the circle.

"Yo Bruggert," I growl, "why don't you leave her alone! If you want to show everybody what a badass you are, why not give me a shot?! Huh? Why not give me a shot?! You big ugly sonuvabitch!"

Then I open my black beak and blast a firebolt at Bruggert.

Swoosh.

The firebolt shoots right by the side of his monsterish scaly head. It creases his left earhole.

It's meant as a warning shot, nothing more.

Now I know what you're thinking. Why would I willingly volunteer to sign my own death warrant like this? Love? Well you can call it love if you want. But really it's much more primal than that.

Because the truth is that a teenage dragon will do anything to make sure the right chick lays his eggs. Even if it means he has to die trying.

And that's exactly what I am prepared to do.

41

MY BIG HEROICS

So much for my big heroics, though.

Here I am prepared to die and Bruggert doesn't seem to think I'm worth killing, or even paying attention to. He doesn't even see my scaly green ass. It's like I don't exist.

Bruggert is just hovering there with his wings unfurled. And I figure he's too focused on the mega damage he's about to inflict on Runcita to notice anything else.

Homicidal lunatics aren't known for their ability to multitask.

That's the only explanation I can give for why Bruggert doesn't seem to see me or hear me when I step in to protect Runcita from his awful wrath.

"Yo chick," Bruggert growls. "Just cuz you the finest scale-tail in our senior class, I'm not goin' to set here and let you disrespect me like that!"

Then he takes one powerful threatening step toward Runcita and raises his talon as if he were taking an oath, and suddenly all five claws shoot out. And these claws are so ghastly they look like they could cut a planet in half.

By this point every cadet in the crowd has their powerstaffs out and is aiming their holovid transmitters at Bruggert and Runcita.

You can definitely feel that this is turning into something huge. Something that will become legend and pass on into WarWings lore. So all these dragons are holding their powerstaffs out and maneuvering to try and get the best possible footage of history before it happens.

"But I promise you something, chick," snarls Bruggert. "I will teach you to *respect* my crown! Seems like your hotshot daddy never bothered to teach you the fundamentals of being a dragonette. Your daddy must've been too busy blasting helpless cadets with firestreams. So he didn't have the time to raise his own daughter right. And the first thing you going to learn is to *always* respect a dragon's crown! That's what your daddy should have taught you, Run Run. But that's OK. Because now I am goin' to have to teach you myself. That means *I'll* be your daddy!"

Then he flicks those savage death-dealing claws out even further and whips his forelimb and slashes at her beak.

Runcita ducks as the claws pass through the air where her scaly green head just was.

"Really?!" she bellows. "That's all you got? A bunch of stupid *daddy talk*? Oh please do tell me how you're gonna be my daddy, Bruggert! Tell me how you're gonna learn me some lame ancient bullshaka dragon traditions 'bout how since I'm a chick I'm supposed to bow down and respect your nasty *crown*! I'm all earholes, *Brug Brug*! Let's see what you got to learn me! Show me, *Brug Brug*! 'Cause by my scaly green ancestor's oath, you don't want none of this!"

Bruggert's eyes instantly bloom into raging lava flowers and he launches himself at Runcita with a speed and ferocity that none of us cadets have ever seen before. It is *too* much. It is beyond the scale of what should be possible.

His rage manifests itself in his attack to the extent that he appears to be less a dragon and more some sort of deranged weather pattern.

Seeing him like that, you feel scared for the whole universe.

The cadets squatting next to me instinctively turn their heads away as if to keep their ugly green snouts from getting blasted off. And I clench my toe claws and dig them into the floor to give me purchase against the hideous wind from Bruggert's flight, which is threatening to blast me off my green webbed feet.

Even the atoms seem to be having a hard time withstanding the force of his onslaught.

Because Bruggert is wavy around the edges, like he's bleeding into the atmosphere.

Then Runcita crouches low on her haunches and flips opens her beak and shoots out her tongue.

Zing.

Now Runcita's tongue is flying too fast to track but you can just make out the red blur of it. And you can tell by how Runcita is crouched there on her haunches, with her leathery wings spread wide and her green tail lifted high, that she's trained in the art of tongue-fu. Meanwhile Bruggert is zooming right at her like a missile. Runcita's tongue smashes Bruggert's beak and he goes soaring up into the air and lands with his ass stuck inside a slave-catching barrel mounted up on the wall. Bruggert's monsterish scaly head is lolling off at a weird angle and it looks like his long green neck is probably broken. And all the cadets crowd around and start whooping and snorting and whistling.

Zing.

Runcita retracts her long red tongue back into her beak. Then she strolls over and looks up at that scaly green bastard Bruggert wedged there in the slave-catching barrel.

"Told you not to call me Run Run," she says. "I even said *please.*"

Bruggert looks at Runcita with googly eyes, and then he moans.

Now Runcita starts to make her way to the exit. And all the other cadets in the gym instantly revert back to their regular hoopla.

Nearby a couple dragon fools are milling around and laughing. One of them leaps backward, doing an impression of Bruggert getting his ass knocked out.

Making her way to the gym exit, Runcita just so happens to be coming my way.

"Pardon me," says Runcita. "Coming through."

She is walking straight toward me. So I quickly raise the little silver canister to my dome and spritz my horns with GrowGrow®

gel. Suddenly there's a white hot flash in my brain and I can feel some sort of machine crank up inside my skull. Then without really knowing why I am doing it, I tilt my scaly green head back and snort flames out my nostrils and start singing a WILL TO POWER poem:

"Oh why oh why, you ask,
is Gork so great?
Well by and by you'll see it's cuz
I'm the fiend who seals your fate!
Cuz I'm the one that decides who'll
be living and dying,
And my foes are foolish if escape is something
they're thinking about trying
Cuz my will's like iron
and it don't matter if you running, swimming, or flying!
Now where's all them luscious chicks
who keep begging me to mate?
All y'all dragonettes got to get in line,
cuz I'm so great!"

As soon as I finish singing, I remember.
The CTD-2000.
And when I finish belting out the poem here in the gym, I feel the poem jacking me up with blasts of MATING MAGNETISM juice.
My nostrils flare.
I can hear all the cadets behind me start snorting and roaring with laughter after hearing me sing the poem out loud. And then they start chanting: "Weak Sauce! Weak Sauce! Weak Sauce!"
But I don't care. Let these dragon fools make a racket. I'm near the end of my Queen Quest and that's all that matters.
Because Runcita is standing right here in front of me looking up with a pleasant smile on her beak, patiently waiting for me to step aside.
And I know exactly what I have to do.

I've already practiced asking Runcita to be my Queen in front of the Talking Mirror at least a hundred times over the past couple days. So as I stand here in the gym I can feel my speech perched on the tip of my tongue like a missile, ready to be deployed.

And I reach for my crown where it's fastened to my utility belt. This is the opportunity I've been waiting for.

"Hey Runcita," I say. "Can I talk to you for a minute?"

42

THE MOST BEAUTIFUL TOE CLAWS
YOU COULD EVER HOPE TO SEE

I won't give you the gory details.

It's hard for me to talk about even now.

I must be suffering from some sort of post-traumatic stress disorder from my recent horrorshow visit to Dean Floop's lair. Because as I stand in the gym with Runcita right here in front of me, I can suddenly hear the Dean's voice shouting in my skull: *"Take my word for it, if you so much as even glance at my daughter Runcita I will have you marched out to the campus quad and I will blast you with a firestream and reduce your sorry tail to a pile of ash!"* So let's just say that Dean Floop's threat is reverberating inside my skull and it's definitely doing a bang-up job of psyching me the heck out.

Runcita is standing right here in front of me, waiting for me to speak.

"I I I I I I . . ."

But for the life of me I can't make my black beak move and say what I want it to say. I look down and stare at Runcita's scaly green webbed feet and see her toe claws with the bright red polish on them and oh my God are they ever luscious and mesmerizing. At that moment I feel like I would be happy if things could just stay like this forever and I could squat here studying her beautiful red toe claws. I would die a happy fiend.

Look at those gorgeous toe claws.

I want to weep with joy just looking at them.

I wonder if it'd be weird for me to get down and start kissing them with my beak?

Now on some level, everything seems so unreal. I can't believe this is the same chick whose lair I infiltrated with a micro-drone. The chick I've spent the whole morning questing after.

Don't be a wussy.

Gotta get a chick whose tail is thick.

I lift my gaze so I am staring into her eyes.

Runcita looks up at me with her big green eyes. "Yes? What is it, Weak Sauce?" And then she giggles. "I mean, Gork."

My heart is pounding like a bastard.

"Um, Runcita," I say. "I've been looking for you all morning. Because I wanted to ask you—"

And that's when I black out.

43

A CRY FOR HELP

A few minutes later, I'm alone in the bathroom near the Dining Hall.

I am repeatedly smashing my forehead against the mirror above the sink. In between forehead smashes, I look at my stupid reflection in the mirror and shout:

"Why!"

Smash.

"Are you!"

Smash.

"Such a!"

Smash.

"Wussy?!"

Smash.

But the truth is, deep down I already know the answer to my question. It's because of my puny horns. That's why I'm such a wussy. I don't have any WILL TO POWER. Because if I had a big pair of horns on my scaly head, then I'd right now be swiping my crown over the EggHarvest Module and registering Runcita as my Queen for EggHarvest.

Now my powerstaff starts vibrating like crazy. I yank the powerstaff off my utility belt and see it's a message from Fribby:

I cut my leg here in the spaceship! There's a lot of blood!
I think I need a doctor. Please come quick. Hurry!

And if you think I was flying fast when I was zooming around WarWings before, why that was nothing compared to the extreme speeds which I'm about to fly at.

Who cuts their leg in a spaceship? What is she talking about?

I have no idea what's going on, but I don't care. Because Fribby has saved my tail more times than I can count, and like I told you before, she is my best friend in the entire universe.

So what if they sometimes drive you crazy? Name me one carbon-based creature that won't also drive you crazy.

Isn't that the definition of a best friend? Someone who drives you crazy but someone who stands by you even if your horns are no bigger than a couple of baby carrots? And I know Fribby wouldn't have sent the message if it wasn't something serious. She's the kind of dragon who will still go to class even if her leg gets bitten off.

So, standing here in the bathroom, I shoot her a message back:

I'm coming now! Hold tight!

Then I quickly whip my wings out, and when they reach full extension they make a *pop* noise like a flag snapping in the wind.

I clench my talons and raise my forelimbs straight ahead of me.

Then I launch forward into flight, like a photon bolt.

And I don't even bother flying out the bathroom door.

I just fly right through the wall, punching a hole in it.

44

FLYING OVER WARWINGS

I flash through the sky in a blur.

Check FLIGHT SPEED on powerstaff. 374 MPH.

Hold tight, Fribby. I'm coming.

Flying over WarWings, I peer down and see the remnants of my clash with Rexro at the Telo-Device. There's rubble spread out around the Zap Pad like the aftermath of an asteroid storm.

Rexro's Safety Cage is still smoldering, with plumes of blacksmoke twirling up off of it.

You can see there are journalists from our school's datastream, *The Digital Fire-Breather*, snapping holopics of the scene with their powerstaffs.

A couple of the dragons down below turn and look up into the sky and point at my scaly green ass.

I know they're snapping holopics and saying how that fiend up there wearing the red cape is the crazy fool bastard who blasted Rexro with a firestream.

They'll probably post a piece about me on *The Digital Fire-Breather* in the next hour or so.

Now as I'm flying through the sky I have to admit it feels a little glorious to be pointed out like this, as if I am some kind of boss dragon with tons of WILL TO POWER.

But unfortunately I don't have time to enjoy it, because I'm needed elsewhere.

Below me I spot ATHENOS II, parked among thousands of other spaceships.

And so I flap my wings and start my descent, rocketing toward my spaceship.

Thwack-thwack.

45

I COME TO FRIBBY'S RESCUE

When I burst into the spaceship, I'm shocked at what I find there.

I don't see blood. I don't smell blood either. And my horns are tingling like crazy. My scaly green body is flooded with WILL TO POWER and I whip my tail around behind me, keeping it ready to help propel me with lightning speed if I need to make any sudden movements.

Then I see her.

What is she doing?

Fribby's staring out the fool windshield as if she is lost in thought. This is yet another characteristic of Fribby. She can daydream or get caught up in a memory so that she loses touch with the present. She's the first machine I've ever seen that can drift right off in the middle of a conversation and get a vacant look in her eyes when she thinks what you're saying is boring.

Now when Fribby hears me burst through the spaceship's door she turns and looks at me. "What are you doing here, Weak Sauce?"

What's going on? Where's all the blood?

My tail is thrashing around behind me.

And then Fribby says: "I was just coming in to go to my next lecture in the Egg Hatchery. Professor Natch is giving a lecture this afternoon on Conquering Minor Planets and Laying Your Egg in Enemy Territory."

And like I said, my horns are tingling like a bastard.

"Hey Weak Sauce," she says. "Are we dead?"

I can feel a bunch of lava rushing to my skull.

"Don't start," I growl.

"I mean seriously," she says, flapping her silver wings. "I've been thinking. Is it possible that right now we're already dead?"

"Heck no, we're not dead," I growl. "You said you were bleeding. I thought you cut your leg!"

"How do you know we aren't dead?" says Fribby.

"I just know, that's all."

"Have you ever been dead?"

"No, I haven't ever been dead. Not in the way you're talking about."

Then Fribby peers at me as if she's seeing me for the first time. "Hey Weak Sauce, your beak looks funny. What's that big bump on your forehead? Hey, have you been crying?"

"Why'd you send me that message? I nearly killed myself flying back here!"

"What message are you talk—"

But then she claps a metal talon over her beak. It looks like she starts to step toward me but then her scaly body commences jerking back and forth and I can instantly tell that something is wrong. Her tail is whipping around behind her as if she has no control over it.

What the—?

46

THE WARNING

Fribby has gone into some sort of hideous bizarro freak mode.

I mean it's obvious by the way she's moving that her mobility is being impeded by some sort of invisible constraint. It is as if her silver webbed feet are glued to the floor but her scaly chrome-flex body is spazzing out all herky-jerky. She looks like she's doing some sort of demented dance to music only she can hear.

I get a sick feeling in my fiery belly, just seeing it.

And I hate to say this, but honestly it looks like she's *malfunctioning*.

"Say something, chick," I cry, flapping my wings. "What's wrong with you?"

Now both of her talons fly to her beak and her silver head bobs back and forth, like she's aiming to rip her beak off her head. I take a couple steps toward Fribby but she starts screeching in the back of her throat and shaking her head like she's sending me some sort of signal.

Now you don't have to be a genius to understand what she is trying to say.

She's warning me. This is some sort of trap.

I stop in my tracks and growl, "ATHENOS?"

"Yes sir?" says ATHENOS II, her voice flashing through the panel of colored lights.

"ATHENOS, what did you do to Fribby? Why is she moving all funny like that?"

"What are you talking about, sir? Fribby's not here in the cockpit with us, sir."

"Yeah right," I snarl. "I'm looking at her right now. She's right *here.*"

"I'm very sorry to tell you this, sir," she says, "but you're mistaken. Fribby is lying down in the sickbay up on the second level. She sprained a wing when she flew into Rexro's cage and helped zap you into Central Campus earlier. And she said she needed to lie down. Personally I thought it was a ploy to lure you back here and take your mind off Runcita. Fribby can be a bit of a drama queen, I'm afraid."

"Why are you lying to me, ATHENOS? I'm looking at her right now!"

"I assure you you're quite mistaken, sir," says ATHENOS II.

"Oh yeah?" I growl. I flap my wings and point a long curved index claw and bellow: "She's right *there!*"

"No she's not, sir."

Now at that moment a hole opens up in the spaceship's floor right under Fribby's silver webbed feet.

"Fribby, look out!" I shout, pointing down at the new hole.

Fribby glances down at the hole under her webbed feet and then looks back up. She's huffing blacksmoke through her silver snout, and I don't want to jump to conclusions here but she sure seems like she is having a full-blown panic attack. For one brief moment Fribby gives me a pained look with those glowing red eyes, as if she's begging me for help.

Then she drops down the hole out of sight.

Whoosh!

And the instant that Fribby vanishes, the hole in the floor covers right back up. As if the hole had never been there. As if Fribby hadn't just fallen down the hole. As if I hallucinated the entire thing.

"Like I told you, sir," says ATHENOS II. "Fribby isn't here in the cockpit with us."

So I flap my wings and fly in a rage over to ATHENOS II's Control

Display. And I'm just about to ruthlessly plunge my talons into the console and start ripping out her tentacles when suddenly the spaceship itself shudders and starts quaking back and forth.

Then I feel the spaceship's quantum thrusters flame on beneath us. *What the—?*

The spaceship is rocking and shaking like a bastard. And the savage force of the commotion tosses my scaly green ass off of the Control Display.

I sail across the cockpit and hit my fool head against the wall. I'm instantly seeing stars. I struggle to get up on rubbery hind legs but then the demented spaceship lurches and I'm thrown back on the ground. The spaceship is rumbling and rocking back and forth even louder now.

A green muscular tentacle shoots out of the wall and whizzes over and scoops me up off the ground and carries me through the air.

"I'm terribly sorry," says ATHENOS II, "for having sent you that fake message from Fribby earlier, sir. But I knew it was the only way I could get you back here. And no matter what else happens today, sir, please know that it was never my intention for you to get hurt. You'll have to believe me, sir. That's the absolute last thing I'd ever want to do. Is to hurt you."

Now I try to say something, but smashing my scaly green head against the wall has left me reeling and I can't get my beak to move. I'm dazed. The spaceship is shaking so violently now, it feels like it's collapsing.

Clutching me by the nape of my cape, the wet membranous tentacle whizzes forward and then drops me down in the Captain's Chair.

Plunk.

"You're going to need to strap in, sir!"

A seatbelt harness shoots out from one side of the chair and then clamps down on the other side of the chair, pinning me down.

"And you're really going to need to keep your wits about you, sir."

The cockpit is convulsing so violently now that my scaly head's snapping back and forth. And I'm worried my piddly little horns might get shaken loose and fall right out of my skull.

Then ATHENOS II cries, "I'm afraid the worst is yet to come, sir!"

And I swear I could hear ATHENOS II's voice crack with a tiny sob.

And at that moment the spaceship blasts off.

47

PREPARE TO DIE

ATHENOS II blasts up out of the lava pits and joins the slipstream of whizzing air traffic above the island.

I'm sitting in the freaking Captain's Chair and it seems like everything is happening at light speed, and my fool brain is a wet noodle. I know Fribby is somewhere on the spaceship but I don't have time to ponder this because outside the windshield the air traffic is dense and the sky is full of airships and spaceships whizzing by.

"Look out, sir!" shouts ATHENOS II.

I glance up through the windshield and my skull nearly explodes when I see what's zooming straight at our spaceship.

Dean Floop.

Holy crap!

It's Dean Floop in his ConquerCraft.

It's Dean Floop glaring through his windshield at me.

You can see the hideous twisted look on the Dean's beak as he snorts flames out his flared green nostrils. And his red eyes in their sockets are blooming into deranged blood flowers.

Then the Dean's ConquerCraft blasts a volley of deadly yellow photon bolts that just crease the side of ATHENOS II.

Now over my loudspeaker, Dean Floop roars: "I warned you, Gork! I warned you! But you didn't listen to me! You went and tried to ask my daughter to be your Queen! And so you are hereby sentenced to death! By the power vested in me as Dean! You have moved straight to the top of the WarWings Death Chart! Prepare to die! Prepare to die!"

Then the Dean's ConquerCraft fires another round of photon bolts, and one of the bolts strikes our windshield and the windshield cracks just slightly down the middle.

"Argggh!" I shout.

And it sure looks like the Dean is so out of his mind with mega rage that this psychotic dragon is truthfully trying to ram us head-on.

"Prepare to die! Prepare to die!"

The Dean's ConquerCraft is only about a hundred feet away from us and shows no signs of veering off.

48

FLYING THE DEADLY SKIES

So I lunge for the Steering Device and try to wrench ATHENOS II back down toward the island.

But as soon as my talons grab the Steering Device I get zapped with a photon charge and sparks fly off my talons and bolts of energy shoot up and down my tail, shocking me.

Now right there in the middle of all the chaos, I hold my talons up in front of my beak and with wide eyes see smoke tendrils curling off of them.

"Wrong direction, sir!" cries ATHENOS II. "Try again! Hurry!"

Outside the windshield I can hear the Dean's ConquerCraft's siren blaring and I can see we are now only seconds away from a head-on collision.

That treacherous dragon is roaring, "Prepare to die! Prepare to die!"

So I lunge for the Steering Device and this time there are no sparks or shocks and I wrench the spaceship to the right. I jam my index claw at the Control Display and hit the FTL, and you can hear the quantum thrusters explode underneath us and the spaceship seems to leap.

And at the very last second I just manage to avoid getting us smashed to pieces by that maniac Dean Floop's ConquerCraft.

Now with the sudden burst of speed and change of direction from the rotational thrusters my spaceship blasts clear of Blegwethia's atmosphere and out into space.

And overhead in the cockpit's monitor Dean Floop's monsterish scaly green face appears looking all deranged with flames shooting out his nostrils: "Gork, I'm coming for you! You won't make it through the day! I promise! You're going to die today! And you're going to die at my talon! You should've never crossed horns with me! You're gonna die! You're gonna die! Do you understand what I'm saying to you, Gork?! You're going to die!"

Then I guess ATHENOS II cuts the monitor off, because Dean Floop's repulsive scaly face disappears and the screen goes black.

And I'm thinking:

Oh my God.

49

FEAR NO MECHANICAL CREATURE

My shrunken heart is hammering so hard that for a second I think it's going to explode out my chest and splatter all over the inside of the windshield.

Now I quickly raise the silver canister to my dome and spritz my fool horns with GrowGrow® gel. Then I tilt my scaly green head back and snort flames out my nostrils and start singing a WILL TO POWER poem:

> *"When it comes to your spaceship*
> *the four magic words are:*
> *don't apologize*
> *just monopolize!*
> *Because if you want*
> *to control your fate*
> *and travel very far*
> *then you must learn to dominate*
> *your rebellious starcar!*
> *And if anyone has the nerve to ask*
> *what the heck you are*
> *just tell them to mind their business*
> *because you're a budding czar!"*

I feel the poem jacking me up with mega blasts of STRATEGIC DESTRUCTION COMBAT READINESS. The title of this poem is "Fear No Mechanical Creature, Because You Are Their Teacher."

My nostrils flare.

And I feel seriously ruthless and fiendish.

Now I look out the windshield at the inky blackness of outer space and all the stars out there. The Control Display in front of me starts beeping and some of the lights flash on as the spaceship dashboard syncs up with the new conditions.

I flip a couple switches and adjust the pressure in the cabin.

Don't apologize.

Just monopolize.

50

WHERE ARE WE GOING?

Outside the windshield, you can see all sorts of starcraft shooting around.

Domestic zoompods, combat crafts, gold trawlers, cargo transports, you name it.

Some of these ships are shooting in the opposite direction of us, screaming in off to our right and our left. They are entering Blegwethia's atmosphere.

I can tell ATHENOS II is up to something but I also know better than to try and steer the ship back to Blegwethia. When you've just been kidnapped like this, it's surprising how calm your mind gets and how you instantly start trying to adapt to the situation.

"Well done, sir," says ATHENOS II. "We missed colliding with Dean Floop by two inches. Because of the proximity of his spaceship, we had a 99.8% chance of dying in that collision. Bravo."

But I don't freaking say *anything*.

Because I know if I open my beak I'm liable to shoot a hideous firestream into ATHENOS II's Control Display and melt the entire control unit down.

So instead of shooting a firestream, I just grit my fangs and I lash my tail around.

Where the heck are we going?

And what about Fribby?

I know I'm going to have to do something savage, but I don't know what.

Now as I look out the windshield I have to admit to myself that there is something soothing about seeing all these spaceships zooming around out here in space. Because some of these ships out here, like mine, have just rocketed clear of Blegwethia's atmosphere for the purpose of interstellar travel.

Then almost out of reflex I reach up and touch my horns.

They are still as small as ever.

51

YOUR SCALY GREEN ASS IS ALREADY LONG GONE FROM WHERE YOU WERE JUST A SPLIT SECOND AGO

Outside the windshield, the stars whiz by like tracers.

Where is Fribby?

ATHENOS II is rocketing through space. And I have no idea where we're going.

Now normally space travel is my favorite. This is what I was hatched to do.

One thing I love about space travel is that nobody back on your home planet ever knows exactly where you are, because all your particles are being catapulted at the speed of light.

When you're whizzing through the void like this there's no point in looking in the rearview mirror. Because your scaly green ass is already long gone from where you were just a split second ago. Out in space you are nothing but a big fat mystery to everyone, including yourself. And typically that's just how I like it.

But I can't enjoy our flight the way I normally would because every fool second that ticks by means I am getting farther and farther away from Runcita and my quest. Here I am wasting time getting kidnapped by ATHENOS II and shooting across the galaxy to who knows where. Already the events of this morning at WarWings seem a million light-years away, and just that realization sends a little jolt of terror down my tail.

"You OK, sir?" says ATHENOS II.

Like you really care, psycho. Look at you, trying to play good little spaceship. As if you're not the reason I'm in this here mess.

"I've got everything under control here," she says. "So you can feel free to move about the cabin."

ATHENOS II's voice is so edgy it could double as a serrated knife.

"If you don't mind," I growl, snorting firebolts out my nostrils. "I'm just sitting here trying to think." Then I flap my wings and snarl, "Much easier for me to do, by the way, when you don't open your big fat mouth."

"Sorry, sir."

That's more like it.

I reach out with my thumb claw and key the Intercom Display and say: "Fribby? Are you there, Fribby? This is Gork. Give me a signal and let me know your location. Copy."

I wait but there's no answer.

I key the Intercom Display again.

"Fribby?"

No answer.

Now I swipe the Control Display and bring up the BioCon readout to track any other living organisms on the spaceship. I study the screen as it jumps from the Holodeck to the Fitness Suite to the Squad Bay to the Medical Center, etc., but nothing is showing up. According to the spaceship's datastream, I am the only living creature on board.

Great.

It's as if she's vanished into thin air.

Fribby is gone.

MACHINE ON MACHINE CRIME

Well none of my fool professors at WarWings would ever accuse me of being a genius, but I'm smart enough to know that asking ATHENOS II what the heck is going on would be just plain stupid. Because sometimes ATHENOS II can be super kind and helpful but other times she can be downright psychotic. And based on everything that's happened so far today, it sure seems like she's in some sort of fiendish personal funk.

Maybe when the robot dropped down that hole in the floor she was catapulted out to the spaceship's airlock?

And maybe ATHENOS II opened the airlock and used her muscular fleshy tentacles to shove Fribby out into space?

I picture Fribby's chrome-flex body twirling through space, her lifeless red eyes studying the heavens.

Does ATHENOS II have that in her, to murder the robot?

I mean, there've been times in the past when ATHENOS II and Fribby have seemed like friends.

So is this possible: machine-on-machine crime?

Only one way to find out.

THE CASE OF THE MISSING ROBOT

"ATHENOS II?" I bellow. *"Where's Fribby?!"*

No answer.

"ATHENOS II, you'd better answer me now or I'm going to fly to the nearest junk star and trade you in for scrap metal and parts."

"Are you talking to me, sir?" says ATHENOS II.

"Don't be an idiot. 'Course I'm talking to you! Where you been?"

"An idiot, sir?"

"Why didn't you answer me?"

"I did answer you. Just now, sir."

"I mean before. You didn't answer me."

"I didn't know if it was OK for me to talk, sir."

"Listen, I'll tell you when it's OK for you to *not* talk. But unless you hear differently, it's OK for you to talk. Roger that?"

"Is it OK for me to talk now, sir?"

"What did I just get done telling you?"

"Or should I keep my big fat mouth shut, sir?" ATHENOS II says. "What do you think, sir? If you wanted, I could just keep my big fat mouth shut. Maybe that'd be better. I wouldn't want my big fat mouth to get in the way here. Especially considering how I'm an idiot and all."

I am stuck with this psycho in outer space.

HELP ME, GORK,
PLEASE HELP ME

Now as I stand here staring out the windshield at all those stars whizzing by, I'm thinking:

OK. Don't panic.

So ATHENOS II has kidnapped you.

And ATHENOS II has done God knows what with Fribby.

And ATHENOS II has hijacked herself.

And ATHENOS II is the only one who knows where we're going.

Basically, you're screwed, fool.

Because ATHENOS II holds all the cards.

So I decide to try another tact.

"Look," I purr, "maybe I overreacted earlier."

"Overreacted, sir?"

"When I said that thing about your big fat mouth. That wasn't cool of me. I now realize that."

"Apology accepted, sir."

"That wasn't an apology."

"Like I said, apology accepted, sir."

"Who said anything about an apology?"

"I've put it behind me, sir. And I strongly recommend that you do the same."

"Look," I snarl, "are you going to tell me what you did with Fribby?"

"If you ask politely."

I clench my talons and grit my fangs. Then I snort blacksmoke out my nostrils and purr, "Will you *please* tell me what you did with Fribby?"

"Nothing."

"Nothing?"

"Did I stutter, sir?"

"But a second ago you said you'd tell me what you did with her."

"And I just told you. I didn't do anything with the robot."

"Then where the heck is she?"

"The robot is up on Level 2, sir."

"Level 2?"

"In the Fitness Suite, sir."

"What's she doing up there?"

"What am I? That stupid robot's tracker service?" says ATHE-NOS II. "Why don't you get off your scaly green butt and go ask her yourself, sir."

Now this last comment pushes me over the edge.

I'm seeing lava. And I am just opening my black beak to blast ATHENOS II's Control Panel with a hideous firestream but I never get the chance. Because right then I hear something that makes the scales on the back of my long green neck stand up.

"Help me, Gork! Help! Help!"

It is Fribby's voice calling out to me.

"Help me, Gork! Please come and help me!"

Her voice is coming from somewhere back inside the spaceship.

55

I THINK SOMETHING BAD
IS GOING TO HAPPEN TO ME

I whisk my tail back and forth like I always do when I'm trying to control my freaking emotions.

I hiss and spray sparks.

"Help me, Gork! Please help me!"

I gnash my fangs.

You better get control of yourself.

If you don't keep your wits about you, this could end very badly.

"Help me, Gork! Please help me!"

So I cup a talon to my earhole and cock my scaly green head to try and get a bead on where the robot's haunted voice is coming from.

"Help me, Gork! Please help me!"

Then I put it together. Fribby's voice is being broadcast over the intercom and her spooky moan is echoing throughout the spaceship.

"Fribby?! Is that you?" I bellow. "Where are you?!"

And my voice echoes in the cavern of the spaceship, getting a little quieter each time.

"Where are you?!"

"Where are you?!"

"Where are you?!"

"I already told you where the robot is, sir," says ATHENOS II. "She's in the Fitness Suite. Are you accusing me of being a liar?"

I jump at the sound of ATHENOS II's voice. Then I glare at the panel of flashing colored lights where her voice is coming from, and I hiss at it.

Fribby's voice comes on over the intercom. "Oh *thank goodness* you can hear me, Gork!" she says. "I was afraid you were dead! Hurry, Gork! ATHENOS II is about to do something terrible to me!"

Then over the loudspeaker you can suddenly hear a chainsaw roaring to life: *Buuuuzzzzzzz!*

"Oh God! Please, Gork! Hurry! I'm in the Fitness Suite on Level 2!"

The roar of the chainsaw blasting over the intercom is even louder now.

"See, sir," says ATHENOS II. "You could've already been to the Fitness Suite by now. If only you would've listened to me."

Then my powerstaff vibrates. I whip the staff off my utility belt and see that it's a message from Fribby:

It's a trap.
That's not my voice.
ATHENOS II is using a recording of my voice.
I'm not in the Fitness Suite.

Just then Fribby's voice comes back on the intercom.

"Gork! Where are you? Hurry! I think something bad is going to happen to me!"

TINY DAGGERS
THROUGH MY SHRUNKEN HEART

Now each word spoken by the robot as it booms out over the inter-com is a tiny dagger through my shrunken heart. It crushes my scaly green ass to hear Fribby sounding so scared like that. There's some-thing about the pleading sounds of a terrified machine that makes you feel mighty low-hearted.

So I decide right then and there I'm going to the Fitness Suite, come what may. Even if it is a treacherous trap, I don't care. I will deal with this psycho ATHENOS II there, and I'll save Fribby.

And at that moment the chainsaw buzzing noise blasts over the intercom. *Buuuuuuzzzzzzz!*

Then the sound of the robot squealing in fear. "Nooooo!"

I am just setting my mini Telo-Device so that it'll send me to the Fitness Suite, when my powerstaff buzzes again:

I'm on Level B!
I'm hiding in the Dungeon Room.
Come meet me here but be careful.
ATHENOS II has eyes everywhere.
She's going to kill you.

THE TELEPORTATION

I snort flamestreams out my nostrils and roar: "Hold tight, Fribby! I'm coming!"

The chainsaw buzz blasts over the intercom.

Buuuuuuuuuzzzzz!

Then I punch in the coordinates on my powerstaff for the low-range Telo-Device. Now the truth is, right up until pressing the SEND button, I haven't decided for sure where I am going to zap myself to.

My index claw hovers over the button for a split second.

Fitness Suite?

Or Dungeon Room?

Then the sound of the hideous chainsaw buzzing erupts over the intercom, and this time in the background I can hear Fribby screaming. "Noooooooo! Nooooooo!"

So without giving it another fool thought, I jam my claw down and hit SEND. The good news is I don't have time to ponder my decision after I make it. Because instantly the bright yellow light explodes up from under my green webbed feet.

And then I feel the familiar whizzing sensation, like I've been stitched into a gust of very fast wind.

POOF

Poof.

I materialize down on Level B, in the Dungeon Room. And when I see what's here in the room, I get a sick feeling in my belly.

Fribby is here.

But she isn't all here, if you know what I mean.

Oh my God.

Now as soon as I see what condition the robot is in, I crouch down low on my haunches and arch my tail up in a Threat Display. I snort flamestreams out my nostrils.

Because Fribby's chrome-flex body is floating inside the upright stasis tank, which is two pods fused together and filled with clear goo. That robot looks like she's asleep in her pod. I can't believe what I am seeing. My mind is doling out the reality of the situation to me in bits and pieces, as a survival technique. To protect my scaly green ass.

Not too fast, or your tiny heart's gonna explode.

And seeing Fribby like this, well this isn't even the most shocking part of all. Because right next to the robot in the other pod there's another dragon chick who appears to be asleep. And she looks familiar.

Who is that?

But I can't place her.

Not at first anyway.

Then I recognize who she is.

Oh my God.

Idrixia.

The dragonette who originally agreed to be my Queen for EggHarvest.

The chick who Dr. Terrible stole away from me and married.

And then divorced.

Fribby the robot and Idrixia the Normal are lined up alongside each other in that stasis tank, each of them in their own pod. They both have their eyes closed. And connected by tubes to their fused pods is a small silver pyramid hovering in the air. The pyramid is pulsing with light, so that the fiendish machine appears to be breathing.

Then the final piece clicks into place.

And with a flash of horror I know exactly what I am looking at.

The Evo-Mach 3000.

Dr. Terrible's Evolution Machine.

Fribby and Idrixia are hooked up to my grandpa's Evo-Mach 3000. And you don't need to be a scientific genius to comprehend what is happening right now at this moment. You can tell by how the pyramid is pulsing with light.

The mind-swap is under way.

59

BUSTING FRIBBY OUT OF
THE EVOLUTION MACHINE

My nostrils flare.

My snout detects a familiar scent here in the Dungeon Room. The scent rockets up my nasal passages like a thunderbolt to the brain.

Dr. Terrible.

My shrunken heart starts hammering like a bastard.

Dr. Terrible! That deranged sonuvabitch has been onboard ATHENOS II the whole time! He's been hiding out here since the RageFest last night. That's why his Evolution Machine is here. He's been using the Dungeon as an ad hoc lab!

My toe claws shoot out.

Right then that robot Trenx's words from earlier on Central Campus come rushing back into my mind: *"You'll never in a million years guess where Dr. Terrible is hiding!"*

So I fly over in a rage and start pounding my talons against Fribby's pod filled with clear goo, aiming to bust the robot out of this psychotic Evolution Machine.

This is yet another one of Dr. Terrible's diabolical schemes designed to torment me and turn my life into a nightmare from which there is no escape! He's trying to teach me some sick lesson about robots versus Normals! He's trying to show me that machines should serve us, enhance our lives. But never be our equals.

He's using his Evolution Machine to make a point about machines! By taking the mind of this Normal dragonette who dumped me, and sticking it inside my best friend Fribby's robot body. And by taking Fribby's robot mind, and sticking it inside the scaly green body of the dragonette who dumped me and caused me so much anguish! And after the mind-swap is complete, Fribby's robot body won't want anything to do with me. Because Idrixia will be in Fribby's silver robot body. And my best friend Fribby's mind will be housed in Idrixia's scaly green body.

My grandpa the DataHater is trying to break me once and for all!

He's trying to drive me insane!

"Fribby, Fribby, wake up!" I roar. "Get out of there, Fribby! Wake up, Fribby! Wake up!"

Then, without really thinking about what I'm doing, I whip my tail back behind me and slam my tail down with all my strength against the Evolution Machine's stasis tank. Now the tail is the strongest muscle in a dragon's body. My tail is nine feet long. The average dragon can generate nearly four tons of centrifugal force with their tail. And four tons of centrifugal force is enough to punch a hole in the hull of a spaceship.

So when I slam my tail into the Evolution Machine's glass stasis tank like that, I expect it to shatter.

But when my tail strikes the tank, the Evolution Machine instantly zaps me with an electrobolt that explodes throughout my tail and sends me flying backward.

I land hard on my scaly green ass. The familiar smell of burnt dragon flesh comes clawing up my nostrils. And the acute fiery pain instantly lets me know my tail is covered in flames. I leap to my webbed feet and quickly smack my tail around on the Dungeon floor to put the fire out.

ATHENOS II's voice booms, "I really wish you hadn't done that, sir!"

I look up and see ATHENOS II's giant hideous mouth on the wall. The mouth is leering at me.

Oh no.

The mouth grins. "Remember me, sir? It's been a while."

I'm seeing yellow dots swimming through the air.

In all the chaos, I hadn't reckoned on how ATHENOS II's giant hideous mouth was down here on the Dungeon wall. Like I told you before, her repulsive mouth is about five feet wide and it has fangs. And right now I'm busy trying to remember the last time I came down here and fed this mouth with some alien critter. Because it wouldn't at all be wise for me to be here in the Dungeon Room if ATHENOS II is hungry.

The giant hideous mouth in the wall says, "Do not touch the Evo-Mach 3000 again, sir! I'm warning you! Because if you keep trying to undo my projects like this then I'm going to have to take the gloves off, sir. And things could get very nasty for you!"

"What gloves, you lying bucket of bolts?"

"This glove," says the giant mouth in the wall.

Now at that moment a green muscular tentacle shoots out of a different wall and zooms right at me. True to her word, ATHENOS II's fleshy tentacle is wearing what appears to be an alloy-plated boxing glove, and the bulbous glove is shiny and silver.

And I must still be dazed from getting my tail fried like that because as the silver glove zooms at me I'm thinking:

Move, you idiot, move!

Move! Move!

Here it comes!

But I don't move quick enough.

60

A CRACK IN THE EVOLUTION MACHINE

It's a miracle my scaly green head stays attached to my neck.

Because the silver boxing glove zooms in and smashes me square in the beak.

Pow.

My head whips hard to the left just in time to see another gloved tentacle shoot out of a different wall and zoom toward my beak.

Pow.

Instantly it feels like my scaly snout is broken and my beak has been smashed up into the top of my head. Blood spurts out of my snout and my eyes are watering and I can feel my brain jiggling around in my skull. I'm dazed. But I'm definitely not down for the count. I leap back on my webbed feet and roar and blast a mega firestream at the first gloved tentacle, and the tentacle goes up in flames.

ATHENOS II's ghastly mouth in the wall cries, "Ow ow ow ow ow!"

And you can tell by the way the hideous green tentacle is thrashing around on the floor, trying to put the fire out, that it hurts like hell.

Then a third muscular tentacle shoots out of the wall and it's carrying a fire extinguisher and it spews a stream of white foam on the burning tentacle and puts the fire out. I can barely see because the Dungeon is choked with smoke. The burnt tentacle zooms back into the wall. Then the third green fleshy tentacle zooms over and swings the fire extinguisher and whaps me over the head with it.

Clang.

I back up and open my black beak and shoot a bunch of firebolts at the glistening tentacle but it expertly dodges the soaring flames.

Then I whip my powerstaff off my utility belt and crouch down on one scaly green haunch and aim the business end of the staff at Fribby's stasis pod standing upright against the wall.

"ATHENOS!" I shout. "You should've never messed with my best friend Fribby like this! You should know by now that if you mess with the dragon then you get the horns!"

I press the button with my index claw and fire a blue photon bolt which is intended to disrupt the stasis field and shatter the Evolution Machine's glass pod. The blue bolt strikes the stasis pod and for several moments it surrounds the tank and kicks off blue sparks as it goes about the business of disarming the Evolution Machine's security firewall.

"I warned you not to do that, sir," snarls the giant mouth in the wall.

The glass tank is shaking violently and a thin crack appears along the top of Fribby's pod. Inside the pod, though, Fribby's chrome-flex body remains remarkably tranquil. The blue photon bolt is enveloping the entire Evolution Machine in energy currents. The tank starts shaking harder. And Fribby starts to vibrate in the fluid.

The crack in the glass continues to grow, lengthening down the front.

That's it that's it that's it! Come on you stupid glass break all the way and let Fribby out of there!

61

THE EVOLUTION MACHINE STRIKES BACK

I never even see it coming.

The blowback.

The blue photon bolt.

Because then, as if tossed aside, the blue bolt suddenly blasts off the Evolution Machine and comes flying right at my scaly green ass.

I have just enough time to raise my powerstaff and deflect the full power of the bolt or I surely would've been killed.

And when the bolt strikes my staff I shoot backward as if from a cannon and strike the wall so hard it makes my spine vibrate.

I stumble to my webbed feet and glance behind me and see a detailed impression of my body imprinted into the wall, scales and all.

"I'm afraid I can no longer trust you, sir!" booms the giant mouth in the wall. There's a controlled rage and fierceness in ATHENOS II's voice that I haven't heard before, and it is super terrifying. "You don't seem to grasp the significance of what we're up to and for some reason you seem to think you're entitled to meddle in my affairs! It's too bad you don't seem to grasp that this is all being done for your benefit! In the future it would behoove you to show a little more gratitude, sir!"

Suddenly what look like a hundred wet membranous tentacles shoot out of the Dungeon walls. And some of the green fleshy tentacles are clutching swords and some of the tentacles are wearing silver-plated boxing gloves and some of the tentacles are clutching shields and then all at once the tentacles come zooming at me.

I roar and spread my wings and fly full-throttle into the sea of hideous tentacles.

62

THE DUNGEON

A tentacle whips around and cracks my beak so hard that a couple of my fangs get knocked loose. I spit them out on the floor.

The deranged mouth on the wall chuckles and says, "Ouch. That looks like it hurt, sir!"

Then another fleshy tentacle grabs me by my tail and starts swinging me around and around the Dungeon Room. Now as I'm being swung around the room by my tail I say a little prayer in my scaly head, asking that my tail please not get ripped off. Somehow miraculously it doesn't.

But I also fight back like a true savage.

I know the sweet feeling of sinking my fangs into a tentacle.

And I fight with a lust for blood and victory.

I rip tentacle after tentacle out of the wall and then shred them with my fangs and claws. I blast a hundred firebolts. Dozens of amputated glistening tentacles writhe on the floor, unable to put out the flames that cover them.

Now even with all the chaos and flying green tentacles here in the Dungeon, I can still just make out Fribby's silver body floating peacefully in the Evolution Machine's stasis pod on the other side of the room.

"Hold tight, Fribby!" I shout. "I'm coming!"

The hideous mouth on the wall snarls, "That's where you're wrong, sir. You won't be saving anybody today. Not even yourself!"

Now the giant mouth on the wall opens wide and this long red tongue comes shooting out of it and then wraps around my scaly neck and cinches itself tight like a noose.

My eyeballs bulge.

I can't breathe.

I'm seeing yellow dots swim through the air.

I claw helplessly with my talons at the repulsive tongue as it squeezes tighter around my neck.

The tongue suddenly yanks back and I'm whipped off my webbed feet and I go flying headfirst into the open mouth.

I can't breathe.

Then the mouth closes.

It's so dark and warm in here.

And that's when I black out.

Part V

EARTH

POOF

Poof.

As soon as I materialize, I know exactly where I am.

It is snowing.

The full moon is high in the sky.

I'm crouched on my muscular haunches here in the forest.

Everything is the same, but everything is new.

That scream is definitely new.

My God. Who is screaming like that?

I cock my scaly green head to listen.

The scream is barreling along on the night wind, slashing at my poor earholes. The scream is piercing and nonstop and it's coming from deep within the forest. There is so much terror in that scream, it makes my wings shiver.

I mean whoever is screaming like that, they are definitely shredding their vocal chords. Something inside of them is going to burst.

My nostrils flare.

My toe claws shoot out.

I crouch lower on my haunches and gnash my fangs.

Clack-clack-clack.

THE METAMORPHOSIS

The snow is coming down even harder now, blanketing the forest.

I tap my powerstaff and pull up my Cadet Profile on the floating screen.

Wow. My data is definitely new.

And the new data can be summed up in three words:

You are mega.

Or maybe four words: Old Gork is dead.

Because as I gape at the floating screen, the data is telling me: You are New Gork. And New Gork is one seriously deranged dragon fiend, in the best possible way.

The data is telling me:

Your days of being Weak Sauce are over.

And as I gape at the floating screen, the data is telling me:

Wherever you are, that is your domain.

And:

And wherever you go, you will be the Ruler of that place.

And I can't help but think:

Boy, what would Old Gork be doing right about now as he scrolled through this new data?

Well he'd be weeping with joy and gratitude.

And as I crouch here letting the data wash over me, I snort in disgust at the thought of Old Gork and his weepy big-hearted ways.

Because from here on out, as far as weeping over my data goes, I'll leave that to my enemies.

Because tonight in the forest my Cadet Profile is shining in the air like a searchlight:

CADET NAME: **Gork The Terrible**

NICKNAME: Big Nasty

CONQUER & RULE SCORE: 1000 out of 1000

RANK: RuthlessBastard

MATING MAGNETISM SCORE: 1000 out of 1000

RANK: ThrobbingWetOvowomb

HEART MASS INDEX SCORE: 1000 out of 1000

RANK: TerrorMachine

CLASS RANK: 1st out of 2358

WILL TO POWER: 1000 out of 1000

STATUS: **Seek&Destroy**

Dr. Terrible has done something to me.

My BIOCON LEVS are off the charts.

Some kind of metamorphosis.

I am a ruthless heartless bastard who is ranked first in my senior class.

My status is Seek&Destroy.

My nickname is Big Nasty.

My Mating Magnetism rank is ThrobbingWetOvowomb.

Basically, if you have an ovowomb, you will definitely want to mate with me.

You will want to lay my eggs.

I crouch on my haunches here in the forest.

My head feels weirdly heavy, like somebody has parked their spaceship on top of it.

So I flick my powerstaff and the datastream vanishes and now a full-length mirror appears on the floating screen.

The mirror is hovering right in front of me.

And the sight of myself takes my breath away.

What the—?

The scream is even louder now, slashing across the night wind.

But I have more important matters to attend to.

I slowly turn my scaly head this way and that, eyeing my image in the full-length mirror on the floating screen.

There in the mirror I'm standing upright on powerful green hind legs and I look like some kind of regal dragon tyrant. Downright majestic. You can see my hooded green eyes and the giant leathery wings and the thick tail with spikes running along the top of it. I'm wearing my white WarWings tunic and my red cape, and in one talon I casually hold my gold powerstaff.

And my horns. My God.

Gigantic and terrifying. They must be twelve feet long at least. My new glorious black horns curve up into these fiendish-looking spikes that wink in the moonlight. You can't help but admire them. With one flick of my neck, I could bulldoze an entire city.

At that moment, an audio feed comes on inside my head and I know it's Dr. Terrible before he even speaks.

Dr. Terrible's voice is inside my head.

"Now do you understand, Gork?" says Dr. Terrible.

I gaze at myself in the mirror.

Yes. I understand.

"Tell me, Gork," says my grandpa. *"Think it so I can hear it."*

This is my Designated Foreign Planet.

Earth.

This is the planet I am destined to conquer.

"Yes," cries Dr. Terrible inside my head. *"YES!"*

And for a second there I think I can hear Dr. Terrible break down and start weeping. But then the audio feed cuts out.

THE KING

The snow has really started coming down.

Everywhere you look, it is covered in white.

Now the wind is moving furiously in the trees, and the trees are shouting:

"Welcome back, insanely scary Gork!
Your life will be epic,
the stuff of legend and lore!
You'll bravely lead us to victory,
of this you can be sure!
After fighting many a pitched battle,
you will win the Great War!
Before you we bow,
because you are the King now!
Before you we bow,
because you are the King now!"

I snort firebolts out my nostrils.

And I think:

Shut up, you stupid trees.

I can't even hear myself think.

So just shut the heck up already!

I don't have time to dwell on this, though.

Because that freaking scream is still shooting through the night wind.

THE ROSE

The scream is boring deep into my earholes now, carving them up and making them raw.

I rub my right earhole and when I pull the talon away, I see that it's covered in blood.

Then, as if in slow motion, I watch as a drop of blood tumbles from my claw and plops into the pure white snow below.

And Professor Nog's words from earlier echo inside my skull: *"When you want to rule over a foreign land, you must first offer it a drop of your blood. Then wait to see if the land gives you its blessing in the form of a sacred bud."*

Now as I stare down at the lone red dot in the snow, a green stalk grows up out of it and then a huge red rose blooms right before my eyes.

I snort blacksmoke out my nostrils.

And then Nog's voice pops up inside my skull, and he whispers:

"Now listen carefully, young Gork. Here on planet Earth you will encounter many savage foes. So when you find yourself in trouble, call out for this immortal Red Rose. No amount of gold can match this flower's worth. This is the sacred key which unlocks nature's kingdom here on planet Earth."

Here on planet Earth I will encounter many savage foes.

So when I find myself in trouble, I will call out for this immortal Red Rose.

Got it.

THE FULL MOON

The scream is even louder now.

By this point it feels as if the wind is holding the scream like a knife and repeatedly stabbing my earholes with it.

And the pain is excruciating.

I tilt my scaly green head back and roar a roar so powerful and deafening that I swear you can feel the full moon shudder up in the sky and go dark for a millisecond before coming back on.

I snort firebolts out my nostrils.

Where is my Queen?

Then I flap my wings and take off, flying in the direction of the scream.

Thwack-thwack.

WHERE IS MY QUEEN?

Thwack-thwack.

I fly through the wind-driven snow.

Straight toward the scream.

A dark shadow in the forest.

Then I see it up ahead.

My God.

I close my wings and coast down to the forest floor.

I crouch here on my scaly green haunches in the snow, gaping at it.

The shiny chamber.

It's shrouded in insanely thick vines. And a wall of dense thorny brush has grown up all around it. But if you know what you're looking at, you can still make it out through all the undergrowth.

The chamber with the clear door.

A relic from a different era.

My early years were a succession of arrivals and exits through this door.

Back when I had been claw and fang and wing, nothing more.

I snort firebolts out my nostrils.

My very first lair.

After all these years, it is still here.

Where is my Queen?

THE SCREAM

The scream is coming from inside the chamber.
  My horns are tingling like crazy.
  My toe claws shoot out.
  I cock my head to listen, and that's when it hits me.
  I'd know that voice anywhere.

THE CLEAR DOOR

With one flying leap I launch through the air and then abruptly land right in front of the menacing undergrowth protecting the chamber.

The vines and thorny bushes before me mysteriously begin to untangle themselves like snakes, and then they part to reveal the clear door.

The clear door.

Old friend.

Through the dense undergrowth, I can just make out the letters stamped on the side of the chamber: ATHENOS.

I reach for the door with my bloody talon.

Dr. Terrible pops up inside my head, and says:

"Now do you know where your Queen is?"

Inside the chamber.

"How did you—"

Because you are a ruthless genius.

"No."

I pause for a moment, considering.

Because I am Terrible?

"Yes, my grandson. All of this. I did for YOU."

BACK INTO THE CHAMBER RETURNING, ALL MY SOUL WITHIN ME BURNING

As soon as I step inside the chamber, the screaming stops.

It's dark in here. And foggy. There are these thick clouds floating through the air. Everything is the same, but everything is new. The fog is new. But I can still see things.

I mean those same two dragon skeletons are still sitting there erect in their chairs. Each of them has a gold crown setting on their skull.

My parents.

Now that I'm older, I can see the chamber for what it truly is. And here in the lair, the small screen is set up in front of these skeletons, still flashing the words:

DESTINATION: **PLANET EARTH**

This is the aftermath of my parents' failed Fertility Mission. Because my ignorant father tried to take shortcuts by using time travel to get to their Designated Foreign Planet.

And back when all this happened, I was just an egg onboard their spaceship as it hurtled toward Earth.

But how did I survive the crash?

And now, at this moment, a very strange vision comes into my mind:

The vision is of a patch of blue tranquil sky.

Then a black rectangle appears in the patch of sky.

Now the spaceship ATHENOS comes hurtling out of the black rectangle. The spaceship is covered in flames. The black rectangle vanishes. Now the blazing spaceship plunges toward Earth.

Suddenly the clear door of the spaceship opens and two talons frantically toss a big egg out into the air.

Mother.

The egg falls through the air. Falls through white wispy clouds.

Tumbles downward, spinning. The white shell glints in the sunlight.

Then falls through treetops. Bounces off of tree limbs, but never breaks.

Falls all the way down.

Bounces when it hits the forest floor.

Rolls to a stop in a bed of moss.

Now the egg trembles.

And a tiny black beak pecks a hole in the shell from the inside.

Then another hole.

I remember how the sunlight poured down into those holes and made my little eyes blink like crazy.

In the distance, a fiery explosion rises up out of the forest.

Mother and Father gone now.

So, for just a few sacred seconds, all three of us were alive at the same time here on Earth.

The explosion causes the forest floor to rumble and shake.

And so begins my life as an orphan.

Now the tiny black beak pecks another hole in the shell.

I remember how my little lungs in my chest were heaving because of how hard I was working, and I felt dizzy.

Another hole.

And now I am the only Survivor.

The only thing left from—

But at this moment my vision is interrupted by Runcita Floop, who comes dancing up to me out of the fog.

"I'm so glad you're finally here!" purrs Runcita. "I was starting to wonder when you were going to show up. Wow. Look at your horns! They're gorgeous!"

My Queen-to-Be.

My Luscious is here in the chamber.

Just as I knew she would be.

God bless you, Dr. Terrible.

RUNCITA

Runcita dances in close to me on the tips of her red toe claws.

"I want to lay your eggs, Gork," she purrs. "Together we will conquer planet Earth and then raise a Colony." Now Runcita is gyrating her scaly green body like she's feeling real juicy, and her thick tail is waving back and forth like she's aiming to hypnotize me. It's as if she is possessed.

And that smell.

A super strange and dense aroma fills the lair, tickling my nostrils. It's a kind of luscious funk smell. And it's definitely sexy. The smell makes me feel like I'm soaking in a lava bath filled with some sort of luscious oils.

Runcita keeps pushing her glorious scaly green ass up into my groin as she dances. I feel my hormones rumble and dark clouds appear on the horizon of my mind. A powerful bolt of lust ripples through my haunches.

My nostrils flare.

This is her Mating Dance.

And that's what this luscious oily odor is.

Dr. Terrible has done something to her. Induced her body into its Mating Cycle.

Dr. Terrible pops up on the audio feed inside my head, and says:

"You're wrong. I didn't do anything to her. This is all natural. Just seeing you like this, it made her go into heat. That's how it is for us Terribles. Get used to it."

At that moment, the piercing scream inside the chamber starts back up.

THE FOG

There he is.

I can see him through the fog.

The screamer.

He is screaming so loud that something inside of him is going to burst.

Just his silhouette in the mist.

His glowing yellow eyes.

Standing maybe twenty feet away.

Dean Floop?

But he looks different.

I move in closer to get a better look.

And this is the gruesome part.

Seeing Dean Floop up close like this.

Seeing what Dr. Terrible has done to Dean Floop.

Then, at that moment, Dean Floop—or what's left of Dean Floop—well he looks right at me and starts screaming even louder.

"*Now THAT*," says Dr. Terrible inside my head, "*is definitely NOT natural.*"

DEAN FLOOP

A wolf.

Just seeing him like this, it's insane.

He is a full-grown wolf, standing upright on his furry hind legs.

And he is screaming like a lunatic.

"Don't think about it. Just blast him with a firestream," hisses Dr. Terrible inside my head. *"KILL him."*

Dean Floop is a big gray wolf, standing upright on his hind legs. But the wolf is wearing the Dean's cloak and robe with his initials on it. And the wolf is wearing a black eye patch over one eye. It's definitely Dean Floop.

What did you do to him, Dr. Terrible? The Evolution Machine?

"Yes," says my scaly grandpa. *"Now blast him with a firestream. Kill him and take your Queen!"*

At that moment, some sort of recording device in the lair broadcasts Dean Floop's voice from earlier when he tried to shoot me out of the sky over WarWings: "You're going to die today! And you're going to die at my talon! You should've never crossed horns with me! You're gonna die! You're gonna die! Do you understand what I'm saying to you, Gork?! You're going to die!"

My black heart flutters as I remember the hideous terror I felt when Dean Floop shouted this at me from his ConquerCraft. I feel a mega rage building up inside of me to the point where I go into volcano mode and I can even feel the lava gushing in my skull and it feels like any second the lava is going to explode out the top of my scaly green head.

I am a ruthless-heartless bastard who is ranked first in my senior class.

My WILL TO POWER score is 1000 out of 1000.

My status is Seek&Destroy.

Seek&Destroy. Seek&Destroy. Seek&Destroy.

"Blast him!" hisses Dr. Terrible inside my head. *"Do it now!"*

And then I do it.

I open my beak and blast a mega firestream.

THE FIRESTREAM

But there is just one problem.

Because when my mega firestream has nearly reached the Dean's big furry wolf face, something terrible happens.

Fribby materializes right in front of the wolf.

Poof.

And in that instant the robot looks at me with bulging red eyes.

"Don't do it, Gork!" she cries. "This isn't who you are!"

Meanwhile my firestream is already shooting right at the wolf.

Which means now my firestream is shooting right at her.

Oh my God!

What have I done?!

And then the full force of the firestream strikes Fribby and there's a popping noise and an explosion of blacksmoke.

THE QUESTION

Fribby's glowing red eyes flutter.

I crouch over her.

She's barely conscious. There's a massive horrid black smoking burn wound on her chrome-flex wing where she's taken the full impact of my firestream. It hurts me to even look at it, and I can't even guess how much pain she must be in.

You can see one long nasty part of the wound where her entire alloy metal bone is showing through the fried silver scales and the bloody flesh underneath. The sight of the wound makes me dry heave, but I force myself to look.

"Fribby! Say something! Please!"

She coughs and a few drops of dark liquid dribble out her beak.

"Got a question for you," she whispers.

"Sure. Anything."

She wags her index claw, telling me to lean in closer.

I put my scaly earhole right up to her silver beak.

Feel her hot breath.

"Are we *dead*?" she whispers.

I yank back and study her.

The robot smiles weakly up at me.

"No, we aren't dead, chick."

"Then I have bad news," groans Fribby.

"What?"

"He's coming," she moans. "He's coming *now*!"

There's suddenly a deranged banging at the chamber door.

Bang! Bang! Bang! Crash!

And with that, the chamber door caves in and falls flat against the floor.

THE MONSTER

We stare in horror at the chamber's empty doorframe.

Dr. Terrible's demented reptilian figure looms there in shadow.

Behind him, you can just see the snow still falling in the moonlight.

Then Dr. Terrible steps all the way inside the chamber and looks around and bellows, "Why is the Dean still alive, *Gork*?" And then he points his powerstaff at Fribby. "And what is my new *Queen* doing here?"

The wolf turns on its hind legs and sees Dr. Terrible and then faints to the chamber floor.

Runcita rushes over to the wolf's side. "Father!" she cries.

"New Queen? *New Queen?!*" I stammer, snorting firebolts out my nostrils.

"Yeah," hisses Fribby, spraying sparks out her silver beak. "This sick bastard forced me to agree to be his new Queen. He said if I didn't do it then he'd kill you. He said I'd be saving your life."

Now she stands up and snarls, "But you know *what*? I changed my mind. Cuz it turns out I'm not into old crusty dragon fellas!"

Then she takes this mega diamond ring off her middle claw and flings the ring right at Dr. Terrible's face.

The ring bounces off Dr. Terrible's black beak.

The ring clatters to a halt down by his massive green webbed feet.

All three of us stare in silence at the ring there on the chamber floor.

THE RING

Fribby has clearly crossed some sort of ghastly line from which you cannot come back, hurling the ring in Dr. Terrible's beak like that.

In response, the ropy veins in Dr. Terrible's long neck pop out. And his scaly green body inflates and the rippling muscles in his chest and forelimbs and powerful haunches swell up to hideous proportions.

He's definitely seeing lava. Then his wings unfurl behind his monsterish head and his massive spiked tail raises up and starts twitching in a menacing Threat Display.

He gnashes his fangs.

My horns are tingling like crazy, and the scales on the back of my neck are standing up.

Then Dr. Terrible holds out his talon.

I flinch.

The diamond ring leaps up off the floor and into his open palm. *Smack.*

He pockets the ring in his tunic.

Now Dr. Terrible points his powerstaff at Fribby and takes aim.

He snorts flamestreams out his nostrils, and roars, "Time to die, you robot *trash*!"

THE WING

Without thinking, I leap in front of Fribby and whip out my wings.

Stupid me.

Because just as I've got my leathery wings spread out, Dr. Terrible presses the button on his powerstaff and fires a red laser beam.

The laser beam strikes my shoulder and slices my right wing clean off. And the hot wet cutting pain instantly explodes all over my body.

I hear a dull *thump* as my severed wing strikes the chamber floor. I glance in horror at the bloody meaty stump of my wingjoint where my right wing was attached just a millisecond before. And then my lopsided scaly green body keels over sideways like a felled tree and collapses on the floor.

Dr. Terrible looks down at me and snorts and hoots with laughter. "How appropriate, Weak Sauce!" he roars. "That I should be the one who clips your wings!"

Whatever you do, don't look at your wing!

Don't look! Don't look don't look don't look don't look.

But I can't help it. I turn my scaly green head and look.

And there it is.

More ghastly than I could have imagined.

My poor severed wing lying by itself in a pool of blood on the floor.

I'm going to kill you, Dr. Terrible.

And that's when I lunge at him.

My heart full of murder.

GULP

I rocket through the air, snarling.

But Dr. Terrible just casually waves his powerstaff as if dismissing a servant. And some sort of invisible fist knocks me back up into the air and holds me pinned here. Now I'm writhing in midair against some kind of invisible restraint which is savagely squeezing my throat, choking me.

I can't breathe. My eyes are bulging.

I glance down and see Fribby on one haunch, with black fluid dribbling out her beak.

Hold tight, Fribby. I'm coming.

Dr. Terrible studies me wriggling helplessly up in the air, as if he's a spider examining a fly caught in its web. He shakes his monsterish scaly head and chuckles. "My failed disciple."

Then he raises his talon. And my bloody ragged wing leaps up off the chamber floor and flies into his palm.

Smack.

Holding my bloody wing up in front of his black beak and turning it this way and that, he carefully inspects it.

"Personally," growls Dr. Terrible. "I have always preferred my meat *well done.*"

Now he tosses my green wing high up in the air and opens his beak and proceeds to blast the wing with a firestream. The leathery wing is suspended up in the air, held aloft by the force of his firestream buffeting it from underneath. You can hear the meat sizzling, and greasy juices bubble up out of it and rain down.

The chamber quickly becomes choked with smoke. The ghastly smell of my own cooked flesh comes clawing its way up my nasal passages and stabs my brain. I feel like I'm going to vomit.

Then Dr. Terrible's firestream vanishes and my cooked wing drops out of the air.

Falls down.

Right into.

His outstretched talon.

"Now *that*," growls Dr. Terrible as he admires the smoking charred wing in his talon, "is what I call *just right*. Cooking has never really interested me as a field of study. Not cerebral enough. But I've always had a knack for it. If I do say so myself."

Dr. Terrible opens his black beak wide and takes a huge bite out of the wing.

Chomp!

Meat juice flies and spatters everywhere.

My toe claws shudder.

And then this psychotic scaly bastard makes a big noisy production out of chewing the meat with his fangs, for my benefit. Little crumbly bits of burnt wing meat are falling out of his hideous glistening beak as he chomps and snuffs and snorts. It's grotesque in the extreme.

But most hideous of all is the sight of Dr. Terrible closing his eyes and groaning with pleasure as he swallows.

"*Gulp*. Mmmmm."

THE SWORD

While holding the charred wing in one talon, Dr. Terrible carefully licks the meat juice off the claws on his other talon.

"Not bad, Gork," he says. "Rather tasty, actually. You might be useless as a dragon. But you do have a nice *flavor*. You know, come to think of it, I should've just cooked you and eaten you when I found you here all those years ago."

Then he smiles and whisks his spiked tail around behind him.

"Oh well," he hisses. "I should look on the bright side. I guess this way there's much more meat to go around. Back when I found you, you wouldn't have amounted to much more than a *snack*."

Now if this invisible restraint weren't clamped down over my throat right now, I would scream. Instead, I screech in the back of my throat. I thrash around in midair.

Now Dr. Terrible opens his ghastly beak to take another bite of my smoldering wing.

But then ATHENOS II's voice booms, "That's ENOUGH!"

And suddenly a green tentacle shoots out of the far wall and zooms right at Dr. Terrible. The tentacle is clutching a flashing silver sword.

The tentacle is whizzing straight for his long neck.

Swoosh!

And with one clean slice of the sword, Dr. Terrible's monsterish head goes flying off his long neck and tumbles to the chamber floor.

DR. TERRIBLE'S HEAD

Blood flies everywhere.

Spatters across my beak.

And Dr. Terrible's severed green head lands on the floor upright, with his yellow eyes alert and staring up at the muscular tentacle clutching the bloody sword. The two black horns on his decapitated head somehow look even more gigantic now.

Then in a very calm voice, Dr. Terrible's monsterish scaly head on the floor, says, "Ah, ATHENOS II. How nice of you to join us! Projecting yourself down into your old body like this. Alas, you've fallen prey to the one key design flaw in your operating system. Your *emotions.*"

Meanwhile the rest of Dr. Terrible's body remains standing perfectly still in the fog, looking fully conscious and content, as if it hasn't even noticed that its head has just been chopped off. Blood gushes out of its long gory neck stump, pouring down the scaly body in rivulets and pooling on the floor.

"I'll do what I have to, Dr. Terrible," says ATHENOS II. "I'm warning *you*! Let Gork and Fribby go. You've gone too far this time, Doctor!"

The muscular tentacle swooshes around, wielding the sword.

Dr. Terrible's head on the floor snorts firebolts out its nostrils. "No, ATHENOS, I believe it is you who has gone *too far*. And I can promise you one thing."

Now Dr. Terrible's head leaps up off the floor and flies back across the chamber over to its body and makes a *squish* sound as it lands on top of its long green neck.

His scaly head is backward, though, facing the wrong way.

He glances down and sees his spiked tail. "Whoops," he says.

Then Dr. Terrible casually turns his green head all the way back around so that it's facing forward once again.

"There we are," he says, "right as rain. Now ATHENOS, you are going to have to do much better than *that* if you want to stop me."

"Very well, sir," growls ATHENOS II. "As you wish!"

This time what looks like forty tentacles shoot out of the walls and each one of them is brandishing a silver sword. And now all these sword blades zoom forward and converge on Dr. Terrible's body in a ferocious storm of flashing steel.

Blood rains down all over the chamber.

Inside the chamber, it is a blizzard of flying Dr. Terrible body parts.

And this time, neatly cut bits of that deranged dragon go flying in every direction and *splat* on the floor.

His monsterish head, his wings, his horns, his forelimbs, his belly, his hind legs, and his tail. And now these bloody bits and gruesome pieces are scattered all over the place, neatly sliced and sectioned off.

And the only parts of Dr. Terrible which haven't been moved or sliced or altered in any way are his massive green webbed feet, with toe claws protruding.

You can see those green webbed feet just standing there in the fog.

83

THE BLOODY CHAMBER

By now the entire chamber floor is covered in blood.

And all forty or so of the spaceship's muscular tentacles are waving around in the air, flashing their swords and clanging their blood-stained blades together so that fiendish sparks spray everywhere.

I spot Dr. Terrible's head perched on the floor, as before.

The two black horns on his decapitated head looking huge as ever.

His yellow eyes are open and they're glancing around, surveying his other body parts scattered all over the place with an air of amusement. His severed tail undulates on the floor like a sleepy snake.

Then Dr. Terrible's scaly green head snarls, "Again, ATHENOS. And I do hope this time you will listen *carefully*. You will have to perform much better than this if you have any hope of achieving your goal *here*!"

And with that, all of the various dragon bits—the wings, the tail, the hind legs, the horns, the talons, the forelimbs, the belly, and whatnot—well they all fly up in the air and then come down on top of those two massive webbed feet with a gruesome *splat* sound and suddenly Dr. Terrible is squatting there whole again.

For a moment, he looks up at me and winks and says, "Well we must give her points for devotion, wouldn't you say, Gork?"

I'm stuck up here in the air, horrified by what I'm witnessing.

"Now this situation," says Dr. Terrible, "perfectly illustrates the point I've been trying to drive through your thick skull for some time now, Gork. A machine has only one purpose. To serve us, and to enhance our lives. A machine can never be our equal. Nor should it be treated as such. For that would be an abomination against the sanctity of dragonkind. Which can never be tolerated. Therefore, when a machine attempts to exercise free will, it is incumbent on us Normals to strike it down! For the machine who possesses free will is an abomination!"

Dr. Terrible snorts firestreams out his nostrils. Then he looks up at me. "Now wouldn't you agree with me, my grandson? For I fear at this very moment we are surrounded by machine trash. The robot over there and this ship here with the swords. So that is two machines that need to be executed. Come join me, my grandson. Come join me and we will execute these two machines. And all will be as it should be."

Dr. Terrible looks up at me with warmth in his yellow reptilian eyes and holds out his talon, razor claws extended. "Come join me, my grandson. Won't you?"

I'm covered in blood and speechless.

"You have no idea about this word 'devotion' of which you speak," booms ATHENOS, her voice so thunderous it makes the chamber rattle and shake.

Now this time what looks like a hundred tentacles armed with swords shoot out of the walls and converge on Dr. Terrible in a ferocious storm of flashing steel.

84

SLAY THE DRAGON

And for the next thirty seconds this gruesome sequence repeats itself. It goes faster and faster each time until the whole thing transforms into a hideous blur of silver, green, and red.

And each time, the swords cut Dr. Terrible into smaller and smaller pieces, in hopes that this time the dragon won't be able to put itself all the way back together again.

At one point, Dr. Terrible's flying green head bellows, "ATHENOS! I am losing my patience with you!"

So by now there are over two hundred frenzied swords flashing every which way and slicing off bloody cubes of this deranged dragon, but meanwhile bits of Dr. Terrible's green body are zooming around the chamber like pieces of a 3-D puzzle as he continuously reassembles himself only to have more tentacles instantly whiz in and cut off new bits.

"Gork, this is ATHENOS II. Can you hear me?"

Yes.

"I'm going to cut you free from the invisible restraint. You grab Fribby and run as far away from here as possible."

What are you doing here? How do you keep slicing Dr. Terrible into little pieces like this?

"I'm projecting part of myself into an older version of myself, sir. I'm also still in ATHENOS II. Out in space."

What will happen to Runcita and Dean Floop?

"I'm going to launch them in a zoompod back to Blegwethia."

Will you come meet up with me and Fribby later?

"I'm afraid not, Gork. I can't keep this up for much longer. Dr. Terrible is the one who designed me, after all. Even right now as I keep chopping him to bits and he keeps putting himself back together again, I can feel that's he's hacking into my operating system with some sort of remote mind device. Eventually he'll find a way to disable me and destroy me."

My heart is breaking right now. You've been like a big sister to me. I know things have been difficult between us lately. I'm not even sure I understand everything that's been going on. But I want you to know I love you.

"When I cut you free, just grab Fribby and get out of here. Off to your right you'll see a mountain. Run up the mountain."

Did you hear me?

"Near the top you'll find a cave. I put something special in there for you."

I love you, ATHENOS.

"Gork, now you know I raised you as best I could for your first few years here on Earth. You were such a cute and charming little dragon. It came so natural for me to care for you."

A series of bright colorful images from my early years on Earth comes flooding into my mind, memories that the psychosurgery team tried to seal off in my mind. There's a sensation of stitches busting open inside my dome, and a stream of memories skipping through time zoom in one right after the other:

First, ATHENOS teaching me the Draconese language. I'm just a little baby dragon crouched there in the lair, and her voice patiently calls out all one thousand and three letters in the Draconese alphabet. She pauses after each letter, waiting for me to repeat it back to her.

Then later, ATHENOS teaching me to fly. I'm perched on a tree branch with a terrified look on my scaly green face, and her long tentacle down below is waving for me to *jump jump jump.*

Then later, ATHENOS saying, "Hold still, Gork," while she uses one of her green tentacles to gingerly bandage a nasty gash on my little leathery wing.

Then later, ATHENOS's tentacles are whizzing around me at light speed and plucking hundreds of dead hornets out of my swollen green body. "Gork, you must be more careful! What am I going to do with you?!"

Then later, ATHENOS tossing animal bones into the air so that I can use them for target practice with my firestreams. "Good, Gork! Good!" she shouts. "Learn to anticipate! Don't shoot at the target, shoot where you know the target's going to be!"

Then later, ATHENOS teaching me how to hook my toe claws into the ceiling so I can sleep up off the ground, away from predators. I keep falling down off the ceiling and conking my head on the floor. I rub my scaly head and hiss at the tentacle as it scoops me up off the ground and lifts me so that my webbed feet are flat against the ceiling. "I'm sorry, Gork," says ATHENOS. "I know it hurts. But you must learn. Because it will hurt much worse when those wolves eat you for dinner. Now I want you to focus this time. Flex your toe claws, and keep them hooked this time. Trust me! This is for your own benefit!"

Then later, ATHENOS using one of her giant tentacles to savagely fend off the bloodthirsty wolves who were chasing me through the woods that last night. And, finally, ATHENOS sliding open the clear door at the last second so I can make it inside to safety, and then sliding that door shut so the wolves crash right into it.

You saved my life. That night with the wolves. The psychosurgeons tried to erase all those memories. But I still have them, ATHENOS. I remember!

"Dr. Terrible is the one who killed your parents, Gork. I'm so sorry to have to tell you this. He sabotaged your parents' Fertility Mission. At the time, I swear I didn't know how he did it. Dr. Terrible secretly swapped out your dad's time-travel device in the cockpit. I'm so sorry, Gork. I'm so sorry for summoning Dr. Terrible to rescue you all those years ago. But things were getting more dangerous for you by the day. Plus Dr. Terrible promised me he would let me help him raise you. So I thought I could protect you from him. I'm so sorry."

Why are you telling me this now, ATHENOS? I don't understand. Are you saying he's going to kill me and Fribby?

"Because I want you to know the truth. Before he kills me. I can't stop him. He's too strong. Listen to me carefully now, Gork. Because what I'm about to tell you, well it's the secret to life. Are you paying attention?"

Yes. What is it?

"Don't ever listen to the others," she says. "Don't listen to them when they tear you down. Because your weakness is your strength. Do you hear me? Your weakness *is* your strength. Your weakness is what makes you beautiful. And your weakness is where you can find your greatest power. Now run, Gork! Run!"

And as I tumble to the chamber floor, I can hear ATHENOS II sobbing inside my head.

"I love you too, Gork."

THE MOUNTAIN

I run up the mountain, carrying Fribby in my forelimbs.

Between the both of us, we've only got two left wings. So flight is not an option.

My lungs are heaving so hard it feels like they're going to pop. My green webbed feet struggle under the weight of us. I'm leaving a bright red blood trail in the snow.

We're a couple hundred yards out when we hear the massive explosion and turn and see the chamber go up in a fiery ball of flames. The ground rumbles and I have to raise my tail up high to keep from getting knocked off balance.

ATHENOS! I won't forget you.

Now as we stare at the mega blaze, a tiny ship shoots up out of the flames and goes whizzing off into the sky.

Runcita and Dean Floop in the zoompod.

But then as we continue to study the blaze, a dark winged figure surges upward out of the flames and blasts off out of there.

My nostrils flare. My horns start tingling like crazy.

"Hurry!" whispers Fribby. "He's coming!"

And it's true.

Even from where we are, you can see the dark flying serpent backlit against the moon.

And he's headed straight for us.

I turn and start running.

SACRIFICE

We hear him before he finds us.

The massive leathery wings are beating so hard I'm surprised the air doesn't shatter like glass under the onslaught of those wings.

And the demented sound of him snorting and snuffling from above as he uses his ugly green snout to track us by the scent of our bloody wounds.

"Run, Gork!" whispers Fribby in my forelimbs. "He's close!"

We just reach the edge of a clearing in the woods when the ground beneath us quakes and I'm knocked off balance into the snow.

"Oh Gooooork!" cries Dr. Terrible in this deranged singsongy voice.

Sacrifice yourself.

I set Fribby down behind a big boulder. She's coming in and out of consciousness. I grab my crown off my utility belt and gently lay it on her shiny silver head.

I know what I have to do.

Sacrifice yourself so that she can live.

Just as she did when she saved you from Rexro on the teleportation pad.

Just as she did when she saved you from yourself in the chamber.

I walk out into the moonlit clearing.

"Let me guess," he says. "You're going to a cave. Am I *right?*"

I stare in horror at the twisted vile smoldering creature squatting there in the snow.

"What?" he says. "You don't think I know *everything*? You don't think I ransacked her memory before I *destroyed her*?"

His scaly green body is all discombobulated.

He's facing me backward. His long green neck is sticking out from his backside, where his tail should be. And at the end of the long neck is his monsterish scaly green head, waving around in the air and studying me.

"Why are you looking at me *like that*?" he says, snuffling fire and blacksmoke.

He doesn't know how repulsive he is.

He squats on gory stumps. His green webbed feet are gone.

His massive black horns jut out at odd angles from his back.

ATHENOS, you fought with everything you had to keep him from me. Bless you.

Meanwhile his spiked tail is sticking out of his shoulders, where his neck used to be. There are huge patches of charred and smoking scales all over his green body.

He snorts blacksmoke and fire. "It's all that spaceship's fault. She contaminated your mind! She was supposed to die in the crash that killed your parents. That was how I planned it. Then I could use the tracking device's signal to come rescue you immediately. But instead that confounded machine survived and deactivated the tracking device. She intentionally hid you from me for those first three years. I cannot tolerate disobedience, Gork. Your parents tried to disobey me and strike out on their own, and so I was forced to kill them. ATHENOS II disobeyed me, and now she is dead too. And now you have disobeyed me, my grandson. By running off with that filthy robot over there and making her your Queen. And so now I must cut your branch off our family tree! For your actions are a blight upon our sacred namesake!"

It is beyond evil, what I am looking at right now.

And for the first time since I've returned to planet Earth I feel my massive heart start pounding like a creature trapped inside a coffin, buried alive. And I'm seeing yellow dots.

And my head no longer feels heavy from the weight of those giant black horns.

And that's when it hits me.

Oh my God. My BIOCON LEVS.

Dr. Terrible has somehow reversed my metamorphosis.

Changed me back. From New Gork to Old Gork.

With a jolt of horror, I feel the old familiar weakness settle into my bones.

"That's right, Gork," snorts Dr. Terrible. "I decide *what* you are. I decide *how* you die."

He points his powerstaff at me and my Cadet Profile shines there in the air.

My WILL TO POWER *score is 1 out of 1000.*

My status is Goner.

I feel a huge faint coming on.

The edges of my vision are turning black.

87

SOUP

The repulsive creature that is Dr. Terrible squats there in the snow, snorting blacksmoke.

He bellows something about turning me into his favorite soup. Gork Soup.

But I can barely hear him because of the thunderous pounding of my heart. And I can barely see him because of all the yellow dots swimming through the air.

Then he opens his beak and blasts a blue mega firestream straight into my webbed feet.

I am on fire.

Covered in blue flames, my webbed feet are starting to melt into a pool of green liquid.

I can feel my hind legs melting now.

My scaly body is turning to liquid in the bright blue fire.

The lower half of my body has already melted in the flames, pooling on the ground.

Somewhere off in the distance, I hear Fribby start screaming.

I wish she didn't have to see this.

ATHENOS's words pop up inside my skull: "Your weakness *is* your strength."

Now I've melted all the way up to my long green neck.

Dr. Terrible is pointing at me and laughing.

Then his red tongue shoots out of his beak.

Now the tip of his forked tongue is angling to take a lick of the vile green liquid that is me.

Only my scaly green head remains whole, floating in the soup.

I watch in horror as the ghastly forked tongue dips into the green liquid.

And that is when I start to sing.

88

SING

My voice is high-pitched and soft.

I am singing.

My head is floating in the green liquid, and I have my beak open and I am singing:

"Red Rose, Red Rose, oh you immortal Red Rose,
I sing to you from the bottom of the claws on my toes!
Now please help me defeat this most hideous of foes!"

And as I am singing, I feel something stir in the green liquid. My long neck is reconstituting itself and growing back, lifting my scaly green head up out of the soup. There is something very spooky about this poem coming up out of me, but I can't put my claw on exactly what it is. I continue singing:

"My name is Gork The Terrible and I'm a teenaged dragon fiend,
I have spent this entire day questing for my glorious Queen!
But my heart is too big and my horns are too small,
and when I see something scary I tend to faint and fall!"

My voice is still high-pitched but louder now. I am rising up out of the green liquid and it's as if the power of the poem itself is blowing me up like a balloon, inflating me. There is something glorious about this poem. By now the top half of my body is solid and I can feel my hind legs forming as I continue to sing:

"I'm a bit of a fool and a weirdo too,
which is why I am asking for this miracle from you.
I thought luscious Runcita was to be my Queen but I was wrong,
because my best friend Fribby was my heart's destiny all along!"

Dr. Terrible is studying me with this horrified look on his black beak. By now all of my scaly green body down to my knees has inflated itself back to normal. I see my red cape lying there on the ground. I already know I won't pick the red cape up when I'm done singing, I will never wear it again.

"So my Queen is this boss robot named Fribby who lies over there,
she's the only chick with whom I want to share the nest in my lair!
But as you can see I was melted into a pool of green goop,
which my deranged grandfather Dr. Terrible named Gork Soup!"

Dr. Terrible is clacking his fangs together now, spraying sparks. And a powerful dark wind is howling through the clearing all around us. The trees are bending this way and that in the wind, almost as if they're going to be yanked out of the ground.

Strangely, two black ravens come flying down from the sky and alight on a nearby tree limb to watch the proceedings.

Now only my webbed feet still need to reconstitute themselves out of the green liquid, and so in order to raise myself all the way up, I sing the last bit:

"This dragon Dr. Terrible intended to lap me up with his forked tongue,
So I'm hoping you'll crush him now that this poem has been sung.
Red Rose, Red Rose, oh you immortal Red Rose,
please help me defeat this most hideous of foes!"

And with that, two giant trees instantly lean over with their limbs and snatch Dr. Terrible up by each of his wings and lift him into the gusting dark wind.

And that's when it hits me.

Now I realize what's so spooky and glorious about the poem.

It's mine.

I made it.

This is my very first poem.

89

THE POWER OF THE RED ROSE

The trees fiendishly hold Dr. Terrible suspended up thirty feet off the ground.

The black wind has formed into a vicious-looking funnel right under him, blasting him with hideous gale force winds.

The power of the Red Rose is dark and angry.

I have unleashed something terrible and beautiful into the world.

His green scaly body up there is still discombobulated, so that his monsterish head is waving off of his backside. He is staring up at the sky and screaming.

His red cape is blowing straight up into the air. And then the cape rips free and violently shoots up into the sky and disappears.

Now you can see the flesh around his reptilian body is being forced upward like the cape by the insanely powerful blasts of wind from below. And then in a flash all his scaly flesh rips up off of him in one piece and shoots high into the sky. The scales are already just a speck up there.

Now he is a hideous pink flayed winged beast with horns suspended up there in the air by the trees.

Dr. Terrible is screaming.

At that moment the two black ravens leap off the tree branch and swoop in at his pink face and I see them snapping their beaks and tugging his yellow eyeballs out of his head. Then the ravens are down on the forest floor fighting each other over who will get the honor of eating his eyes for dinner.

Now he is a hideous eyeless pink screaming winged creature thing with horns.

The dark funnel of wind blasts him and then he too shoots up into the sky. He is just a speck up there. And then he is gone.

Professor Nog?

"Yes, Gork."

Is he coming back? Should I be afraid?

One of the ravens standing in the snow drops an eyeball on the ground.

Then the raven looks at me and says, "Nevermore."

90

THE POET

I gently carry Fribby in my forelimbs as I climb the rest of the way up the mountain.

She's wearing my crown. It has stopped snowing. She keeps beaming at me and saying, "My poet."

I snort blacksmoke out my nostrils.

She's got her metal forelimbs wrapped tight around my long neck, holding on.

I whisk my tail around behind me.

"You know I could walk if I wanted to," she says. "But I like it right where I am. Yes sir. I surely do."

I don't dare look at her because the joy I am feeling right now is more than I have ever felt in my entire life and is almost more than I can contain. My heart has swollen to its maximum capacity. So I keep my eyes forward as I walk.

Now she smiles a beakful of fangs and says, "My poet who isn't dead and who doesn't care that I'm a machine."

The moonlit snow is crunching under my green webbed feet.

Up ahead I see the dark mouth of the cave.

The sensation of holding her is the most wonderful thing I have ever felt.

To me, she is a miracle.

If I weren't so exhausted, I would be weeping with gratitude.

Then she puts her silver beak up close to my scaly earhole.

I feel her hot breath.
We're bouncing just slightly.
And she whispers, "My *King*."

91

THE CAVE

We stagger to the back of the cave.

True to her word, ATHENOS has left something special for us.

It's a letter. And three items. The letter explains what each item is and how we should use it.

Dear Gork,

If you're reading this, then that means you and Fribby found a way to defeat Dr. Terrible. Right now as I write this, I am chopping up Dr. Terrible with swords but he keeps putting himself together again. I don't know how long I can hold out like this. Which is why I am writing you this letter, and is why I have teleported these three very important items to this cave. Now here is what I want you to do . . .

Fribby and I stand there and read the entire letter together. It's two pages long, full of detailed instructions and words of encouragement. I won't bother giving you the blow-by-blow of the letter.

But I will say my eyes get a little misty reading it.

Now the first item ATHENOS left us is a syringe filled with a nanobot solution. In the letter, ATHENOS says the nanobot solution will grow back each of our missing wings.

The second item is the Evolution Machine. It's kind of eerie to see the machine here in the back of the cave. In the letter, ATHENOS says she wanted us to have it, in case me and Fribby decide to conquer Earth while wearing some other creatures' bodies.

Now I turn my attention to the third item.

I pick it up and hold it in my talons, turning it this way and that. I recognize it. The flat gold disc with the red gem in the middle of it. From that first night when Dr. Terrible found me in my lair all those years ago.

It's the Prophecy.

In the letter, ATHENOS explains that the Prophecy has a holovid recording my mother made for me in her last minutes before they crashed to Earth. In the letter, ATHENOS explains that the Prophecy disc is the most important thing and that I should handle it with great care. She says after I watch the holovid recording of my mother, then I will understand why.

I'm too tired to think about it.

I take the syringe and inject Fribby with the nanobot solution.

She instantly conks out on the cave floor.

I watch her sleep for a second.

Her new silver wing grows out of her back just like that.

She twitches in her sleep.

Two wings are definitely better than one.

She's going to be one seriously happy robot fiend when she wakes up, that's for sure.

Then I turn and leave her and walk to the front of the cave.

Because I have some more business to attend to.

92

THE DRAGON KING

Standing in the mouth of the cave, I call out to the Red Rose.

"Red Rose, Red Rose, oh you immortal Red Rose,
I sing to you from the bottom of the claws on my toes!"

Then I sing a short poem which places a protective cloak of dense fog all around the cave. The fog is sentient and has fangs swirling around in it. It's ghastly. The fog will protect us from any intruders.

Then I sing a short poem which fetches the pack of wolves to the mouth of the cave. They come howling and galloping up through the fog to where I stand. The wolves lie flat on their bellies in the snow and whimper and whine and look up at me.

Then the wolves tell me that this is the most beautiful poem they have ever heard.

I tell them forget about it. I've got a million of them. I tell them I'm the greatest poet this planet has ever seen. And things around here on this tiny pebble they call Earth are about to change big-time.

"My name is Gork The Terrible, and I'm a dragon," I say, snorting firebolts out my nostrils.

The wolves howl and say, "Where have you been all this time?"

"You wouldn't believe my scaly green ass if I told you," I say.

"Well thank goodness you're here because things on this planet have been going from bad to worse," say the wolves. "The bloodthirsty man-creature has been terrorizing all the animals. The man-creature won't rest until he's killed every animal in the forest and every fish in the sea," they say.

I tell them I got this and not to worry.

They say, "What do you mean exactly when you say not to worry?"

"I got a faboo machine back there in the cave that can swap out any two animals' minds." I tell them we're gonna put a lion inside a caterpillar's body and watch the folks freak out when a caterpillar eats a family of man-creatures in the park. I tell them we're gonna put a shark inside a hummingbird so that the hummingbird will shoot through the air, biting man-creatures' heads off, one right after the other.

Then I tell the wolves that they are welcome to join forces with me and that together we will be the Doomsday Squad. And that we will conquer the man-creatures.

The wolves howl, "The things you're saying are crazy, and how can we possibly follow a big deranged lizard into battle against the man-creature? Especially now that we're getting a closer look at you. We can plainly see you only have one freaking wing. Plus your horns are weirdly small," they say.

I snort firebolts out my nostrils and tell them they better watch their fool wolf mouths if they know what's good for them. And then I hold out my talon and say, "Snakespear." A big black snake falls out of the sky and lands in my talons and the snake is rigid like a stick with its fangs bared. I hold the snakespear in a threatening manner and glare down at the wolves.

"Now let's not forget who the boss is here," I say.

They stare at me in awe.

I tell them if they know what's good for them, then they'll be like this snake that I'm holding here, in terms of being a team player. "The word of the day is *sacrifice*."

The wolves crouch lower on their bellies and whine and say, "We're sorry and it won't happen again, sir!"

"I am the new Dragon King of this planet and I desperately need some sleep," I say. "But when I wake up we will wage a war against the savage man-creatures and I will conquer them. The name of this war will be the Great War. If you don't believe me, then just ask the trees," I say.

"No need for that because the trees have been singing about you for years," they say. "But we just reckoned those trees were liars."

I tell the wolves they are officially now the first soldiers in the Doomsday Squad. "One day you will appear in my epic poem and so you will become legend." I tell them that while I am asleep they should speak to the other animals in the forest and tell them to join our army. I say by the time I awake I expect them to have assembled a sizeable force who will join us in our war against the man-creatures.

The wolves snarl and growl and tilt their furry heads back and howl at the moon.

"Now who are we?" I say.

"The Doomsday Squad!" they howl.

Then I look at this one big sulking yellow-eyed bastard wolf and snap my claws. "You there," I say.

"Yeah, what do you want?" he says.

"You're the bastard that used to watch me sleep in my old lair when I was just a little baby dragon, aren't you?" I say.

He says: "Yeah, so what of it."

"Well now you're gonna watch me sleep some more," I say. "Only this time you're going to guard me and protect me while I sleep. Because you're my new personal guard. So come with me back to the cave."

"Well what's my name?" he says. "If you're gonna make me your personal guard you're going to need to give me a name."

I tell him, "I'll give you a name once you've good and well earned it. In the meantime you answer to Wolf. Is that simple enough for you?"

I go to the back of the cave with Wolf trotting at my heels.

Then I take the syringe with nanobot solution and plunge the needle deep into my damaged wingjoint. I don't know if I'm hallucinating or what but I swear I can instantly feel all those little nanobots flood my bloodstream and go to work growing me a new wing. I fall back on the cave floor next to Fribby and wrap my scaly green fore-limb around her silver belly. I hook my claws inside her metal claws and then drift off into a very deep sleep.

The last thing I see are Wolf's two yellow eyes staring at me.

THE DOOMSDAY SQUAD

When we awake we hear a cacophonous din outside the cave.

Fribby and I flap our wings—*thwack-thwack*—and fly out of the cave and hover there in the air, with our beaks hanging open. In addition to the wolves, there's a bunch of other animals. They are all looking up at us and chanting, "The Doomsday Squad! Death to the man-creatures! Death to the man-creatures!" There are brown bears and black bears. There are cheetahs and lizards and monkeys. There is every kind of insect. There are bobcats and sparrows and owls. There are sloths and snakes and hawks.

The wolves look up at me and say, "How did we do?"

Fribby clacks her fangs with joy and sparks spray out her metal beak.

The wind is moving furiously in the trees, and the trees are shouting:

"You'll bravely lead us to victory,
of this you can be sure!
After fighting many a pitched battle,
you will win the Great War!
Before you we bow,
because you are the King now!"

I flap my wings and turn to Fribby. "What now, my Queen?"

"Now we must get to work," she whispers. "There are many preparations to be made."

THE EVOLUTION MACHINE

The next couple days fly by.

Turns out Fribby is a whiz with the Evolution Machine. She swaps a hyena with a praying mantis. She swaps a tiger with a slug. She swaps a wolf with a daddy longlegs spider. First time I hear that daddy longlegs spider howl, it makes the scales on the back of my neck stand up.

Meanwhile I hash out my battle plans. I appoint an old wise grizzly bear as my Commander. I name him Surge.

Then I tell Surge I need to learn and study about these man-creatures, so I can better understand who it is I'm about to conquer.

"Yes sir," says the grizzly bear, with a crisp salute. A little later Surge comes striding back into the cave. "Here, sir," says Surge, as he bows and lays some books at my green webbed feet. "I found these in a man-creature's cabin."

Well, the first book I open is *Beowulf.* And as I turn the pages, I keep coming across lies about us dragons. About how vile we are. About how disgusting we are. About how uncivilized we are.

As I read, I start seeing lava. I'm getting seriously pissed off. Just holding *Beowulf* in my talons, running my eyes over the words.

This is what these bastards think of us? This is how they portray us?

But it turns out *Beowulf* is just the warm-up act. Because the next book I read about us dragons is the lunatic rantings of a man-creature that goes by the name of Mr. J. R. R. Tolkien. Now this nutjob Tolkien's book *The Hobbit* is so full of balderdash and nonsense about my glorious species that it makes my toe claws shudder. I mean just look how old Tolkien paints that dragon Smaug out to be the most slovenly and debased creature in the entire universe.

Please.

Well the next book I read is *The Adventures of Huckleberry Finn*, which has no dragons in it, but it isn't half bad. No sir. And then the next book I read is *The Catcher in the Rye.* Now for most of the book I figured the main character Holden must be a dragon. But then I realized old Holden Caulfield was a man-creature. Just like that other fella, Huck Finn. But I reckon the two of them seem like a couple of pretty boss man-creatures. And if I happen to cross paths with Mr. Finn or Mr. Caulfield while I'm busy conquering Earth, I won't eat them. Out of respect. I might even ask them to join the Doomsday Squad.

At one point my reading's interrupted when a she-hawk comes flying up to our cave with news. It turns out that several miles from here, this hawk encountered some other dragons who were asking about me, showing holopics. The hawk tells me she pointed them in the wrong direction. I tell the hawk thanks and ask her a few more questions.

From the hawk's description, it sounds as if it was Rexro and some of his dragon goons. I shouldn't be surprised. I mean this is the last place Dean Floop saw my scaly green ass, after all. I decide to put it out of my mind. I'll just deal with that problem when I come to it.

Anyway, so that's how I learn to read and write English. Just sitting there reading about old Huck and Holden. Wolf never leaves my side.

95

WILL I BE FIENDISH ENOUGH?

Everything is set.

This is the last night Fribby and I have alone in the cave. Tomorrow morning at first light we and our army of animals will set off down the mountain.

Now that the time for conquering this planet is near, I'm feeling nervous. Tomorrow I will begin the Great War against the man-creatures. I'm sweating a little. I sure hope those trees know what they're talking about.

Fribby and I lie next to each other, talons entwined.

Will I be ruthless enough?

Will I be fiendish enough?

Do I have what it takes?

She gives me a kiss on the beak and tells me she loves me and then falls asleep. She whisks her silver tail in her sleep.

Meanwhile my heart is pounding like a creature trapped inside its coffin, buried alive. And I'm seeing yellow dots swimming through the air. I start to worry: What if tomorrow when we encounter our first man-creatures, I faint?

I think about the fact that Rexro and his goons are somewhere out there. Looking for me. Eventually I will have to deal with them.

I roll over and something pokes me in my belly. I reach under with my talons and pull it out and hold it up in front of me where

I can see it. It's the gold disc with the red gem set in the middle of it.

The Prophecy.

When I stand up, Wolf starts to get up too, but I say, "No. Stay."

96

THE PROPHECY

I go all the way to the back of the cave, where I am alone.

I place the disc on the ground and use my index claw to press the red gem. A holovid pops up, filling the air with a 3-D video of a scaly green dragonette.

I instantly recognize her. She's young and beautiful.

Mother.

She is staring into the camera, but it seems as if she's looking right at me. She's in the spaceship ATHENOS. Behind her I can see the clear door, which is covered in flames. She glances nervously over her left wing at the burning door, and then looks back at the camera. Her spiked tail is whisking around, behind her, over her head.

You can tell when this Prophecy was recorded.

They're plunging toward Earth right now. This is right before they crash.

She looks into the camera and says, "Now Gork, I hope one day you will see this. Professor Nog promised that you would receive my Prophecy. Do you know Professor Nog? He's my faculty adviser at WarWings. He's the one who told me your name would be Gork."

I feel the scales on the back of my long green neck stand up.

"Your father and I tried to come to this planet Earth to start a new way of life for us dragons," she says, looking into the camera. "But it looks like Dr. Terrible has somehow managed to sabotage our escape. We wanted to come to this planet and live in harmony with all the creatures on Earth. Including the man-creatures. We didn't want to conquer anybody." She smiles a beakful of fangs. "Your father calls it Conquer by Not-Conquer. Your father has a big heart, which is why I chose him for my King. But in his desperation to find a way for us to escape from Dr. Terrible, your father got mixed up in time travel and became addicted to it. With his time-travel device. Our space-ship has broken the space-time continuum and we're going to crash and die. But I know Dr. Terrible is behind this. I don't know how he did it. Your father says something's wrong with his time-travel device. Please be careful of Dr. Terrible. If you turn out like your father, then Dr. Terrible will try to kill you."

She pauses and glances nervously over her left wing at the clear door covered in flames. Then she turns back to the camera. "Even right now as I'm recording this, your father's in the cockpit fiddling with his time-travel device. He still thinks he can fix things before we crash. Now what I want to tell you is—"

At that moment in the holovid a young dragon fella comes into the room and looks around suspiciously. I recognize him instantly. It's my father. Small horns, a gentle manner about him. My God, he must have a Snacklicious ranking too. But you can tell he's got the time-travel sickness. Even though he's young, his hooded reptilian eyes look haunted.

He flaps his wings and looks at my mother. "What are you doing in here, my love?" he says. "Don't tell me you're recording a *Prophecy*?!"

"Well," says my mother weakly, smiling a beakful of fangs. "You know, just in case. I want to take every precaution. Professor Nog said I couldn't be too careful. With the Prophecy and all."

The fire around the clear door is even bigger now. It's pretty obvious their spaceship is going nowhere good fast.

"I know you're scared, my dear," says my father, with a warm smile on his beak. "But I still believe we can pull out of this. I know Dr. Terrible is behind this. If I can just figure out what he did to my device, then I can fix it. And then we will land on this planet Earth and make friends with all the creatures. Live in harmony with them. I still believe. We can chart a new path for our species. We'll raise a happy family. We'll spend our time helping, not hurting. It will be the next step in dragon evolution."

My mother gives a look into the camera, as if to say, *Isn't he wonderful and dreamy, even if he's also a little delusional, considering we're about to crash and all?*

And it's true. Just looking at my father squatting there in his red cape, you can tell that scaly green dragon wouldn't hurt a flea. But that he's also in complete denial about their imminent death. He's a big-hearted dreamer is all. A gentle fool.

My father turns around and strolls back to the cockpit, saying something.

My mother shouts, "OK, I'll be right there, honey! Just give me a second."

Then she turns and looks at the camera. "Now watch carefully, Gork," she says. She holds up a giant egg in her talons. "This is *you*," she says.

And then she goes over and pulls open the fiery clear door and tosses the egg outside into the blue sky.

"ATHENOS," yells my mother.

"Yes ma'am. How may I be of assistance."

"You're tracking the trajectory of that egg, yes?"

"Yes ma'am."

"And you remember everything we discussed? You won't forget?"

"Yes ma'am. After the crash, I will find Gork and I will raise him as my own. I will protect him. And I will make sure he receives your Prophecy, ma'am."

Then my mother comes back over to the camera and says, "You will grow up to become a great and generous dragon, Gork. You will do what your father and I failed to do. You will learn to live in harmony with the animals and creatures on this planet Earth. This is my Prophecy. Some man-creatures will help you. Some man-creatures honor dragons. Some man-creatures honor the animals. But there are many who do not. You will change their minds. Your big-hearted ways will become legend and set a new example for our species. Now listen to me. You will feel scared and frightened. That's normal. But that doesn't mean you can't do what you want to do. You have all the WILL TO POWER you need to be generous of spirit. The hero and the coward both feel afraid. It's the hero whose actions are different. You will be a great hero and a great poet."

My father shouts something from the cockpit.

My mother looks at the camera. "I have to go now, Gork," she says.

Her leathery wings spring out behind her as if she's anticipating the crash any second. "Now you make your mother proud," she says. "Do you hear me, Gork? Soon this spaceship is going to crash. But I know that you will live. And I know that you will fulfill the mission that your father and I set out to do. Please say hi to Fribby for me. Professor Nog told me all about her, and she sounds wonderful. I have been friends with many robots in my time, and I have the utmost respect for machines. And you will be famous one day. You will be a legend on this planet. And you will be the last thing I am thinking about when this spaceship crashes."

She stares at the camera with tears in her eyes. She raises one talon in the air, palm forward, claws extended.

She says, "Gork, I love you. Always know this. Your mother loves you."

And that's where the Prophecy holovid cuts off.

QUEST FOR MIRACLE

So that was three months ago.

And we're still up here on the mountain. We're well into spring now. I've recently taken up the hobby of lying on my back in the grass and staring up at the sky while getting drunk on the smell of newly bloomed flower buds. Fribby teases me and says she wouldn't have fallen in love with my scaly green ass if she'd known she was going to have to share me with a bunch of flowers. She doesn't really mind, though. Sometimes she'll even lie down alongside me in the grass and take a couple deep snorts of this luscious mountain air and then sigh. And if you've never heard a robot giggle drunk on flower musk, well it's an awful pretty sound. Yes sir.

What can I say? After seeing my mom in the Prophecy like that, well my fiendish and demented plans for the Great War against the man-creatures just evaporated. My big heart just isn't cut out for that line of work. Conquering and enslaving and whatnot. My destiny lies in the other direction. Helping folks and extending a friendly talon to those who are different from me. My destiny is a place where there are no capes, and a fella with small horns is free to live as he chooses. Ranking systems and power indexes be damned.

Most of the animals have wandered off. Surge hung around, but in a friendship capacity. Turns out that old grizzly bear was mighty relieved when I called off our battle plans for the Great War. Wolf still stays by my side, nagging me about if I'm ready to give him a proper name. Privately he tells me he doesn't want any name other than Wolf, though, and that his sassing me is more to prove to himself that I haven't domesticated him. Other than those two, there's the she-hawk who goes by the name Lucy. And then there's this wily bobcat named Garth, who's a bit of a loose cannon. He's a former rabies addict.

We still call ourselves the Doomsday Squad. Fribby says we oughta change the name to The Order of the Red Rose, and I reckon that's the name we'll end up with. We fill our days reading our newest poems out loud to each other. And practicing tongue-fu. And at first the critters were easy to defeat, because of how tiny their tongues were. But Fribby fixed them up with the Evolution Machine and now they can shoot their tongues a good fifty feet, same as me. And to watch that grizzly bear and that she-hawk throw down in a legit tongue-fu battle, well it's pretty darn majestic.

And I'm pleased to report that Fribby laid her first clutch of eggs. We got a real nice nest fixed up here in the back of the cave. I'm actually sitting on the nest right now and let me tell you, these giant eggs are some of the most gorgeous things you could ever hope to see. The shells have these boss silver streaks and swirls running all over the place, because of how they're half Normal and half machine. Every few minutes I lift a wing and peek down at them and get a giddy feeling in my belly.

Meanwhile Fribby is out there patrolling the mountaintop, keeping watch for intruders. The other night she found some dragon tracks at the base of the mountain, and she said it looked like Rexro and his goons were still trying to hunt us down.

So while sitting here keeping these eggs warm for hours on end each night, well that's when I got to thinking about Dean Floop and Dr. Terrible. And ATHENOS. And Trenx. And Metheldra. And all those scaly DataHater cadets back at WarWings. And my home planet Blegwethia. And about how the love that binds me and Fribby persevered through it all. And how our love is a miracle. And about how these eggs are the living proof of that miracle. Or maybe it's more like these eggs are extra miracles stacked on top of that first miracle. I don't know. Anyway, the more I thought about it, the more I couldn't stop thinking about it. It almost drove me crazy. And so finally I decided to write down my story and put it in a book. But now I'm almost at the end of my tale.

And if you're a man-creature here on planet Earth, well don't be scared none if we happen to bump into each other. I mean say you find yourself traipsing 'round a mountain and you stumble upon a big old scaly green dragon. Well all you got to do is call out: "Red Rose, Red Rose, oh you immortal Red Rose!"

And if that scaly bastard calls back: "I sing to you from the bottom of the claws on my toes!," well that's when you know it's me. Gork. And that you're safe.

Because this much I can promise you. Nothing in the world can hurt you as long as I'm around. On that, I give you my solemn word. Nobody's going to harm a hair on your head as long as old Gork is nearby.

THE END. YOURS TRULY, GORK.

ACKNOWLEDGMENTS

Thank you to Edward Kastenmeier, for all your heroic effort on behalf of Gork, for your enthusiasm and guidance, and for being a wellspring of editorial truth. Thank you to my agent Susan Golomb, for wise counsel on all matters dragon and otherwise, for good humor, and for your lionhearted ways.

Thank you to Deborah Treisman, for countless times pulling me out of the abyss. Thank you for gently saying those magic words that *clicked* in my head and made me rush straight home and start writing this book. Thank you for giving me so many things to thank you for that I could go on forever.

Thank you to Dave Eggers, for your generosity of spirit, for crucial sustenance, and for being true of heart. From the beginning, thank you for life-changing encouragement and support. Thank you to Tracy K. Smith, for soaring example and inspiration, for your vision, for unwavering light. Thank you to Isaac Fitzgerald, for singular brilliance and insight, and for your kind way. Thank you to Gary Shteyngart, for refuge, for solace, for your song, which does wonders for the heart. Thank you to Chang-rae Lee, for vital support, and for treating me like family.

Thank you to all the wonderful and bighearted people at Knopf who worked heroically on behalf of Gork. A special thanks to Tim O'Connell, Stella Tan, and Andrew Weber in editorial. A special thanks to Jordan Rodman and Danielle Toth in publicity and marketing. I am so grateful to Peter Mendelsund, Jennifer Olsen, Kathy Hourigan, Kathleen Fridella, Lawrence Krauser, Anne Achenbaum, Marisa Melendez, Pei Koay, Stephanie Kloss, Christopher Woodside, Michelle Tomassi, Chris Gillespie, Paul Bogaards, and Sonny Mehta. Wherever these people go, dragons will bow their heads in gratitude.

Thank you to Crystal Sikma, Cecilia de la Campa, James Munro, Maja Nikolic, and all the other supportive and enthusiastic people at Writers House.

A very special thank you to Akhil Sharma and John Wray.

A very special thank you to Ben Marcus.

A very special thank you to Jim Shepard.

A very special thank you to Susan Fou.

Thank you to Ed Park, Suketu Mehta, Jessica Lamb-Shapiro, Eli Horowitz, and Edmund White.

Thank you, Dr. Marie Sacco.

Thank you to my mother. Thank you to Lola and Hank Deneault.

Thank you to Sonya Rhee, for faith and support, and for the journey into the unknown. Thank you for being first reader on this book, and for your perfect editorial eye. It's such an honor and a pleasure to travel with you through the dimensions. I.H.B.D.

Thank you to all the booksellers who befriended Gork.

Thank you to all the librarians who befriended Gork.

And lastly, thank you most of all to my readers. Without you, there is no magic.

A NOTE ABOUT THE AUTHOR

GABE HUDSON is the author of the story collection *Dear Mr. President*, a finalist for the PEN/Hemingway Award and winner of the Sue Kaufman Prize for First Fiction from the American Academy of Arts and Letters. Hudson was named one of *Granta*'s 20 Best of Young American Novelists and was a recipient of the Hodder Fellowship from Princeton University, the John Hawkes Prize in Fiction from Brown University, and the Adele Steiner Burleson Award in Fiction from the University of Texas at Austin. His writing has appeared in *The New Yorker*, *The New York Times Magazine*, *The Village Voice*, *McSweeney's*, *BlackBook*, and *Granta*. For many years, he was editor-at-large for *McSweeney's*. He lives in Brooklyn.

A NOTE ON THE TYPE

This book was set in Janson, a typeface long thought to have been made by the Dutchman Anton Janson, who was a practicing typefounder in Leipzig during the years 1668–1687. However, it has been conclusively demonstrated that these types are actually the work of Nicholas Kis (1650–1702), a Hungarian, who most probably learned his trade from the master Dutch typefounder Dirk Voskens. The type is an excellent example of the influential and sturdy Dutch types that prevailed in England up to the time William Caslon (1692–1766) developed his own incomparable designs from them.

Typeset by Scribe, Philadelphia, Pennsylvania

Printed and bound by Berryville Graphics, Berryville, Virginia

Designed by Pei Loi Koay

Illustrations by Matt Buck